Meet NOA

THE BRICKLAYER

and hang on for the ride of your life!

"Noah Boyd brings his FBI experience to this dazzling thriller. The pace is frenetic, the action is unique, and the drama intense. We have a new American hero in Steve Vail."

Patricia Cornwell

"Thrilling . . . Depending on who's judging, Vail is a cool maverick with his own moral compass or a dangerously loose cannon. Fans of Sam Spade and Jack Reacher will feel right at home with this new tough guy."

Boston Globe

"Even mediocre thrillers provide entertainment and escapism. But the best come with a healthy dose of authenticity that draws readers quickly and inexorably into the story. Such is Noah Boyd's novel *The Bricklayer*. . . . If you think you can resist, just read the opening sentence. . . . Boyd, a former FBI agent with twenty-plus years of experience, invests *The Bricklayer* with an insider's knowledge of his subject. . . . With a fine combination of cynicism and heroism, *The Bricklayer* is taut and twisty—and powerfully addictive."

Richmond Times-Dispatch

"A standout procedural thriller."

Pittsburgh Tribune-Review

"If the rest of the series is as sensational as *The Bricklayer*, Vail should have a long, happy life and readers should enjoy every installment of it."

San Francisco Chronicle

“Vail is in the mold of Lee Child’s Jack Reacher and Robert Crais’s Joe Pike, though more playful than either one. . . . The reader is treated to some of the snazziest, smartest, and often surprising dialogue likely to show this or any season. . . . Vail is fun to watch as he outthinks everyone else in the room, no matter the room. . . . That there will be more Bricklayer tales is unquestioned. This guy has movie written all over him.”

Chicago Sun-Times

“It’s a good, fast-paced story. . . . Great action. Great writing. Great story.”

San Jose Mercury News

“This is an impressive and suspenseful debut whodunit by a rebellious former FBI agent about a rebellious former FBI agent. In other words, Noah Boyd knows whereof he writes. . . . *The Bricklayer* is action-packed and never slows down. . . . A refreshingly unpredictable mystery destined to become a bestseller with many sequels.”

Winnipeg Free Press

A compelling page-turner . . . The adrenaline-charged action never slows and the abundance of plot twists will satisfy even the most jaded mystery lover.”

Lansing State Journal

“A blistering debut . . . [The] cat-and-mouse game between Vail and the Pentad’s chief [has] enough jolts to create a legion of fans. . . . Irresistible red meat for connoisseurs of action thrillers.”

Kirkus Reviews

"It's the stuff of fiction: FBI agent with a heart of gold goes rogue, turning the agency on its head, exposing an underbelly of ambitious bosses putting career ahead of justice. In the end, our anti-hero emerges from the wreckage wiser and usually better off than when he started. It's a page-turner, especially for Noah Boyd, for whom it's not just fiction, but his life."

Manchester Union Leader

"A top-shelf thriller. The book begins with a bang. . . . The story employs numerous plots and twists. . . . Moreover, just when you think the investigation is winding down, bang, another bad guy emerges with yet another puzzle to ponder. . . . A mouth-watering story."

New York Journal of Books

"The person behind the Pentad is one of the more clever villains I've seen in a long time. He's not really all that brilliant, but he is just smart enough to anticipate what the FBI will do next, and foil its efforts. . . . Boyd's writing is solidly paced with few, if any, inconsistencies. Probably his greatest strength is in conveying the action and tension of a Jason Bourne movie or *Casino Royale.* Taut, rapid-fire, and relentless."

January Magazine

"Get in on the crack debut of a compelling new character. . . . This fictional detective thinks as intricately as a modern Sherlock Holmes. . . . Boyd, the author who might have lived some of Vail's adventures, creates consistent tension and dialogue. . . . Don't miss it, nor the purported sequels to come. Grade: A."

Cleveland Plain Dealer

"There are plot twists and turns enough for the most devious mind, the pace is unrelenting, and Vail is believable. . . . For readers who enjoy the Prey books of John Sandford, Vail will probably be another addition to your list of go-to guys. Vail is a man of principle, a man with standards. . . . It's a pleasure to read about guys like that, especially when the writer is as good as Boyd is. Not all writers of thrillers can do that well. Boyd can. And does."

Reviewing the Evidence (online)

"Readers will root for the tough, intelligent Vail, while savoring the sexual tension between him and his FBI handler. . . . This fast-paced thriller includes many authentic-seeming details about the Bureau's bureaucracy."

Booklist

"In an age when every male protagonist in a thriller novel is being compared to Lee Child's Jack Reacher, here finally is one that actually comes pretty close. But Steve Vail is different enough to avoid any claims of copyright infringement. He can use both his brawn and his mind to creatively problem solve. He leads a solitary life and enjoys it. . . . The story [is] very entertaining and suspenseful. . . . Steve Vail and his creator Noah Boyd (a pen name for a former FBI agent) have a very bright future."

Deadly Pleasures Magazine

"Lots of fun, plenty smart, and great escapist reading. And Steve Vail is a magical FBI agent. If I had my way, I'd read stuff like this every minute I'm not on deadline."

Seymour Hersh

"The intricate and detailed plot continually picks up speed toward a thrilling (and surprising) resolution. Steve Vail's irreverent outlook on life lends itself to witty repartee between him and the other characters, which is further supported with very clever, intriguing narrative. Noah Boyd has a sure-fire winner in this exemplary start to a new series."

FreshFiction.com

"*The Bricklayer* is full of twists and turns and ingenious scenes of murder and mayhem. The fast-paced novel never lets up and . . . reader[s] must remind themselves to breathe occasionally. *The Bricklayer* sizzles. . . . Steve Vail's my new hero."

Examiner.com

"Noah Boyd develops the characters of Vail and Bannon in ways that make you want to see more of them—much more of them. A five-star suspense that is fast-paced and well-written."

Armchair Interviews

"Non-stop action and non-stop authenticity make this a real winner."

Lee Child

"There's a new hero on the bookshelf. Imagine Lee Child's Jack Reacher as a disgruntled ex-FBI agent who makes ends meet by laying bricks. . . . But what really sells *The Bricklayer* is Boyd's inside perspective. The bureaucratic posturing, the under-appreciated heroes, and the mind-set of evil are razor sharp in Boyd's unflinching prose."

The Clarion-Ledger (Jackson, MS)

By Noah Boyd

THE BRICKLAYER

Coming Soon in Hardcover

AGENT X

NOAH BOYD

THE BRICKLAYER

An Imprint of HarperCollinsPublishers

Hardcover and premium editions of this book were published February 2010 and September 2010 by William Morrow and Harper, respectively, both Imprints of HarperCollins Publishers.

This is a work of fiction. References to real people, events, establishments, organizations, or locales are intended only to provide a sense of authenticity, and are used fictitiously. All other characters, and all incidents and dialogue, are drawn from the author's imagination and are not to be construed as real.

HARPER

An Imprint of HarperCollins*Publishers*
10 East 53rd Street
New York, New York 10022-5299

ISBN 978-0-06-206857-6

First Harper digest printing: January 2011
First Harper premium printing: September 2010
First William Morrow hardcover printing: February 2010

Printed in the United States of America

Visit Harper paperbacks on the World Wide Web at www.harpercollins.com

10 9 8 7 6 5 4 3 2 1

For Esther Newberg

THE BRICKLAYER

BEFORE

AS MICKEY STILLSON STARED AT THE GUN IN HIS HAND, HE ABSENT- mindedly reached up and adjusted the fake ear that was his entire disguise and wondered how a born-again Christian like himself had wound up in the middle of a bank robbery.

A year earlier, he had been so certain of his religious conversion that when he went before the Illinois parole board, he let his inner peace sell itself. He asked its members to address him as Michael—a name that he felt emitted a soft, evangelical glow—because like Saul giving way to Paul, prison had been his personal road to Damascus. Confinement, he explained to the stony faces in front of him, had actually been his salvation. Without it, he would never have found God, the void that had sent his previous life tumbling end over end, resulting in a three-year-long incarceration for forgery.

He couldn't help but wonder now if finding God hadn't in fact been strictly a means of survival. After all, his ear had been cut off by an inmate they called "Nam" the first week Mickey had been released into the prison's general population, leaving little argument that surviving on his own would be difficult. Although Nam had never been in the military, Stillson's was the third ear he had collected in as many years. No matter how thoroughly Nam's cell was searched after each incident, the appendages were never found, giving rise, due largely to inmates' need of fiction, to the rumor that he had devoured them in some sort of ritual he had become addicted to in Vietnam.

Within a month, Stillson had found God. As his wounds healed, he found the gnarled stump did have some benefit. While some men displayed tattoos or scars as warning to others, Stillson was missing an ear—an entire ear—which was something that even heavyweight champions couldn't claim.

He pulled his hand away from the fake ear in disgust. Maybe he *was* just a jailhouse Christian, but none of that seemed to matter at the moment. He would have liked to believe that just committing an armed felony demanded that his faith be reevaluated, but he had to admit that the police officers who had surrounded the bank probably had something to do with it. He cursed himself for thinking he could ever be a real bank robber. Hell, he wasn't even much of a forger.

He peeked outside, around the frame of one of the bank's full-length front windows, to see if the police had moved any closer, but they were still the same distance away, lying with weapons at the ready across the trunks and hoods of their cars, apparently waiting only for the slightest provocation. At a safe distance behind them were satellite dishes on top of the television news vans, ensuring this was going to play out to the end.

Greedy—that's what he and his partner, John Ronson,

had become. They hadn't been satisfied with just robbing the tellers. Instead, they decided the take could be doubled, or even tripled, by "getting the vault." It was Ronson's idea; actually he had insisted on it. Stillson had deferred to him, since he was the expert, if a previous conviction and prison stretch for bank robbery could be considered know-how.

Nervously, Stillson reached up again and touched the artificial ear. Ronson had made him wear it. "Don't you watch TV? The cops are lousy with technology since we went inside. All they got to do is check their computers for convicted felons with one ear and they got you. And once they got you—no offense, Mickey—they got me." So they went to a costume shop and bought a half-dozen fake ears, trying, with minimal success, to match the color of Stillson's skin. He also had to let his hair grow a little longer so when they tied the ear in place with clear fishing line, he could comb his hair over the almost invisible filament. Ronson thought the disguise looked good; Stillson was fairly certain he looked ridiculous.

Stillson stood on his tiptoes to look over the counter and into the vault, where Ronson was stuffing bundles of cash into an optimistically large hockey bag. Tall and extremely thin, Ronson had been released six months earlier from the state prison at Joliet, where he had been paroled after serving one-third of his twenty-year sentence for attempted murder and the armed robbery of a bank. The deadly assault charge stemmed from shooting it out with the arresting detectives. He had surrendered only after running out of ammunition.

Stillson's job during the robberies was to keep all the customers and employees covered while Ronson vaulted the counter and cleaned out the tellers' drawers. This time, as Ronson was taking the time to force the manager to open the vault's day gate, the first police car showed up in response to a silent alarm. At the moment, everyone was aware of the increasing potential for violence and was lying facedown obediently, trying not to be noticed.

"How are we going to get out of here?" Stillson yelled over the counter.

"One thing at a time," Ronson shot back, and continued stuffing the bag with money.

"How can you think about the money?"

"Because if we get out of here, we're going to need every dime of it." After zipping up the bag, Ronson threw it ahead of him and vaulted back over the counter. He yanked an elderly woman to her feet.

"No, no, please don't!"

"Shut up, you old broad. You've already lived long enough." He pushed her toward the front door, and as they disappeared around a wall that separated the door's alcove from the rest of the bank, he yelled back to Stillson, "Just keep everybody covered."

Stillson couldn't deny that he liked the control he had over everyone during the robberies. And for some reason, with the cops outside, that feeling was even more intense. To demonstrate his willingness to fully execute his partner's orders, he backed up a couple of steps and slowly swung his gun from side to side. That was when he noticed a man lying next to a watercooler. His gold-colored Carhartt work pants as well as his boots were covered with concrete dust. His faded black T-shirt clung to his thick shoulders and arms.

He was the only one with his head raised, and he seemed to be watching the gunman with a mixture of curiosity and insolence.

The one-eared bank robber didn't know it, but the man had been tracking and analyzing his movements, measuring his agility, the length of his stride, his reaction time. He judged Stillson as a man who had not built a career on physical prowess or intimidation. His only authority seemed to be the gun in his hand, which he was holding too tightly.

As the man continued to stare at Stillson, he admonished himself: *You don't carry a gun anymore, stupid. Next time, you use the drive-through.*

"What're you looking at?" Stillson demanded.

The man's mouth went crooked with a sneer as he silently mouthed words, causing Stillson to think he was having trouble hearing. He reached up and checked the rubber ear to make sure it wasn't blocking the auditory canal. When he found it in place, he realized that the man had figured out it was fake and was taunting him. "Think that's funny?"

The man spoke a little too loudly now. "I *said*, I'm watching you so I'll get it right at the lineup."

Stillson took two quick steps toward him, thrusting the black automatic forward, being careful not to get too close. "Are you nuts? You some sort of tough-guy construction worker? Is that it?"

"Bricklayer."

"What?"

"I'm a brick mason," the man said.

Stillson took another half step, raising the gun to eye

level. "Well, meat, you're about to undergo a career change. You can be either a floor kisser or a brain donor. Your call."

The bricklayer slowly lowered his head.

Next time, meat, definitely the drive-through.

Shielded by the woman hostage, Ronson opened the front door enough to expose her and yelled a demand for the cops to leave and, even though he couldn't see any, to clear out the snipers. Almost before he finished speaking, a loudspeaker ordered him to surrender. Ronson cocked his gun and pressed it against the side of the woman's head. "You've got five minutes, and then I'm going to begin shooting people, starting with this old goat. Understand?"

Stillson couldn't hear exactly what was being said and took a couple of steps back, trying to get a more advantageous angle to see and hear. Then he heard something he couldn't immediately identify—a couple of deep liquid *glugs.*

The watercooler!

He swung his gun back toward the bricklayer, who was up off the floor and coming at him, just a couple of steps away. In front of him, he held the almost-full five-gallon water bottle sideways, pressed tightly between his hands to keep the water from escaping.

Stillson fired.

The bottle exploded, absorbing the impact of the bullet. It was all the time the man needed to close the distance between himself and the robber. In a blur, he stepped sideways, minimizing himself as a target, and grabbed the barrel of the gun, twisting it outward in a move that seemed practiced. With Stillson's wrist bent back to its limit and his finger being dislocated inside the trigger guard, the gun was easily ripped out of his hand. As the robber started flailing, the man used the weapon to strike him once in the temple cleanly, dazing him.

Then the bricklayer grabbed him and with relative ease hurled him through one of the bank's full-length windows. Amid a shower of glass, Stillson skidded across the concrete and lay unconscious. Fluttering in the air and then landing on top of him was the rubber ear.

The bricklayer ran to the wall that separated the front door from the rest of the bank's interior and flattened himself against it. The woman hostage was pushed around the corner of the alcove, followed by Ronson, who was screaming at Stillson, demanding to know what he was shooting at. The mason's hand flashed forward, and the muzzle of the gun he had taken from Stillson was pressed against Ronson's throat.

Ronson hesitated, and the man said, "Do me a favor—try it. . . . Do everyone a favor." Ronson recognized the seething tone; he had heard it many times in prison; this man was willing to kill him. Ronson dropped his gun. As the man bent down to pick it up, the bank robber started to run toward the opening left by the shattered window, but the bricklayer caught him. Ronson swung and caught him full on the jaw, but it didn't seem to have any effect. The mason countered with a straight right to the middle of the robber's face, snapping his head back violently and buckling his knees. The bricklayer grabbed him, turned, and launched him through the adjoining window, shattering it as well.

Outside, one of the reporters yelled to his cameraman, "Did you get it? Both of them?"

"Oh, yeah. Every beautiful bounce."

Suddenly the front door flew open and the hostages came streaming out, running past the police line and into the safety of the crowd. While one group of officers ran up to search and handcuff the two gunmen, a SWAT team rushed into the bank, leapfrogging tactically to secure the building and ensure there were no more robbers. It was empty.

With the aid of a couple of bullhorns, the police rounded up the hostages and herded them back inside. Each told the same story: that the man in the gold-colored Carhartts and black shirt was the one who had disarmed both robbers. When the detectives asked the witnesses to point him out, they were astonished to find that the bricklayer had vanished.

ONE

AS CONNIE LYSANDER TOOK THE TOWEL FROM AROUND HER, SHE looked at her body's reflection in the full-length mirror and ordered herself to be objective, *really objective*. She held herself erect and, turning a few degrees in each direction, tightened her stomach muscles. It was no use, she decided; her once-taut figure had lost its sleekness. Fifteen years earlier she had been a reporter on *Beneath Hollywood*, a local television show that scraped together questionable bits and pieces of the "real" story behind the bountiful missteps of the crowned princes and princesses of the movie industry. The three years the show aired, it had better-than-average ratings. She knew her popularity had been due largely to her figure and the way she dressed. She had worked little since the show was canceled. When her auditions for more mainstream news shows would fail, her manager blamed it on her being "typecast" as a tabloid reporter. In the interim years, she floated in and out of various jobs, eventually marrying. When that ended two years earlier, she vowed to get back into media any way she could.

She stepped over and opened the door leading out onto the lanai. One of the things she loved about Los Angeles was the weather—maybe it was the thing she loved most of all. Its warm, arid consistency was reassuring for her, something she could count on, unlike while she was growing up in the damp, aching loneliness of Seattle's Puget Sound. It was a daily reminder that life was just better here. Even the Southern California architecture reflected the climate. Family rooms, kitchens, even bathrooms, featured doors that opened directly to the outside, bringing the outdoors in.

A light breeze brought in the floral sweetness of her small garden. But then she thought she smelled the aroma of coffee. She had not had any caffeine in three months, part of her new regimen, and her neighbors were out of town. Probably just some sort of latent craving. Maybe she would get dressed and go have a cup; decaf wouldn't hurt anything.

She went back to the mirror for a few more moments trying to decide whether an even more extreme exercise program would return any part of her physical appeal, and then, in a flash of honesty, she decided that it wouldn't. She took a step closer to the mirror and started examining her face. Plastic surgery was not as easy a fix as it seemed, at least not in Hollywood. It fooled no one but instead marked her as someone who was moving onto the cusp of has-been-hood, joining a long and unenviable list her peers couldn't wait to add another performer to. And maybe worse, once started, the procedures were progressive, until everyone's look became comically identical, that of carved feline features being pulled back by the g-forces necessary to reenter the earth's atmosphere.

She dared another half step closer to the mirror and, using her index fingers, pushed up the skin in front of her ears, tightening her jawline. It did look better, although it did little for her sagging neck. She was tired of trying to come up with combinations of turtlenecks, scarves, and shadowing collars to hide her age. She tapped the fold of skin under her chin with the back of her fingers and watched as it remained stubbornly unchanged. Maybe it was time.

Her agent had been getting a lot more calls since she had done the exposé of the FBI and the United States attorney's office in Los Angeles. True, it had been her manager's idea, but when she looked back on it now, it needed to be done. And Hollywood loved to target the FBI. If they and the U.S. attorney's office hadn't been so corrupt, why had their missteps been so easy for her to uncover? Maybe "corrupt" wasn't the right word. She had recorded agents and attorneys drinking on duty, frequenting prostitutes, and working out for endless hours at local gyms. There were actually some people fired, so it really had been a public service. And her peers obviously appreciated her efforts, because she was now getting called again.

She took a step back and put her hands on her hips. "Yep, I'm going to do it," she said out loud to make the decision binding. Pulling on a robe, she walked into her bedroom.

She didn't notice the man sitting in the chair until she saw him in the mirrored closet door. Spinning around, she grabbed at the front of her robe. "Who are you?" Then she noticed his gloved hands. In the left was a take-out cup of coffee. In the right was a gun, which hung indifferently. She tightened her grip on the front of her robe. "What do you want?"

He laughed noiselessly. "Certainly not that." She searched his eyes for any flicker of motive. They were gray and sad. Slowly the rage behind them became evident, not the sort that flashes for a moment, but the kind that doesn't burn out in a lifetime. There was little doubt in her mind how dangerous this man was.

She released her robe and let her hands fall to her side with a calming reassurance. Her voice mellowed. "Then what can I do for you?"

"Your story about the FBI brought me here. You really did a job on the agency."

"The story was true."

"Yes, you're a real patriot."

The remark seemed sarcastic, but she wasn't sure. His voice was emotionless, containing none of the contempt that ensured the depth of the insult. "The story was true," she said again, as if testing his ability to be rational, the repeated defense the only one necessary for a logical person.

"Careers were destroyed," he said. "How about your career? On the upturn, I would imagine."

"Who are you?"

"Someone who wonders why you hate the FBI?"

Even though he asked the question in the same flat tone, she felt an increased possibility of violence. "I—I don't hate the FBI. Why won't you tell me why you're here?" She stole a glance toward the door, measuring its distance and his range of fire from the chair.

He tipped the muzzle of the gun up at her. "Sit down on the bed."

Paralyzed by his sureness, she realized she wouldn't make it and did as instructed. Attempting a smile, she said, "Sure, whatever you say."

He took a swallow of his coffee. "I'm here for the same reason that you did your little story—to make the FBI pay."

"If we want the same thing, do you really think a gun is necessary?"

"Unfortunately, yes. I'm here to provide you with the means of really damaging the FBI."

"I don't understand. How?"

"I'm sure you believe in what you did. That it's critical to the well-being of the country to expose the FBI. And this has to be done no matter the cost. That is what you believe, isn't it?"

"Sure, I guess."

"See, we want the same thing. Only you're going to have to make the ultimate sacrifice for your—or should I say, *our*—cause."

"What, you think you're going to kill me?"

"Unless you can find some way to kill me. But since I'm the only one in the room with a gun, I seriously doubt that."

Her eyes locked onto him as her head tilted appraisingly. "You're from the FBI, aren't you? You were sent here to intimidate me. That's what this is really about."

He took the last drink of his coffee, tipping it up to ensure it was empty. Then, balancing the gun on his right leg and without taking his eyes from her, he pried the lid off the cup and set both down on the table next to him. With the gun back in his hand, he glanced at her, then carefully readjusted the cup's position on the table. "Not really. Women like you are too irrational to ever be intimidated."

"Women like me. You mean a *bitch*." She threw her head back and laughed as though trying to embarrass him with his inability to show emotion. "This is Hollywood, moron. Without the bitches in the middle of everything, this town's major export would be fat-free yogurt. From someone like you, 'bitch' is the ultimate compliment."

"In that case, you're the queen."

"Damn right."

Again his face mimicked laughter without a sound. Glancing once more at the cup, he rotated the automatic slightly until the ejection port was exactly where he wanted it. "Personally, I would have chosen a different epitaph, but who am I to argue with royalty?"

He fired once, striking her in the middle of the upper lip. She fell back dead as the ejected casing from the automatic arced through the air and into the cardboard cup. He walked over to the body and placed a blue piece of paper on her chest. On it was written "Rubaco Pentad." From his pocket he took a plastic bag containing a Q-tip and dabbed it in the blood that was trickling from her wound. Careful not to let it touch his skin, he resealed the bag.

He went back to the table, dropped the bagged swab into the paper cup, and pushed the lid back onto it. After looking around for any other trace evidence that might have been accidentally cast off, he slid the gun into its holster under his Windbreaker and walked out.

TWO

THE FBI WAS ABOUT TO PAY THE RUBACO PENTAD ONE MILLION dollars. At least that's what the group was supposed to think. Agent Dan West was being guided electronically to a location in Portsmouth, New Hampshire. Heading east, he crossed a wooden bridge, watching the river disappear into a turn that he knew had to be close to the ocean. Dusk and a warm summer breeze added to the serenity of the small seacoast town, making it an even more unlikely place to be the final twist in such a complicated and vicious crime.

For the first time since he'd left Afghanistan, a burning knot of fear was growing in West's stomach, something that had not happened in his three years with the FBI, all of which had been spent on a white-collar-crime squad in Boston. It had been mind-numbing work. He had tried to tell his bosses that because he was a former Navy SEAL, he needed something more confrontational than endless columns of numbers that never seemed to add up to the same total twice.

He checked the coordinates on the handheld GPS receiver—they now matched those given in the demand letter. He pulled into a small parking lot and got out of the Bureau car, a ponderous Crown Victoria chosen for its obviousness. A brief chill shuddered along his limbs as he stretched nervously. An unlit sign above the single-story building identified it. "It *is* the Kittery Point Yacht Club," he whispered into the microphone taped to his chest, confirming his location. Fearing the Pentad might be watching the drop site, the FBI had conducted only a satellite reconnaissance of the coordinates, revealing the yacht club as the likely destination.

"Copy," answered one of the dozen surveillance agents who had been following him at a discreet distance since he left the federal building in Boston.

West ran his tongue across his lips. The taste of salt air reminded him of his navy training, and that no matter what lay ahead, he was capable of handling it. His job was to drop the money and get out. The agents following him would deal with whoever tried to pick it up. The canvas bag he pulled out of the backseat was carefully weighted and shaped to give the impression it contained the full amount in hundred-dollar bills, but it contained only a thousand dollars, enough to make the crime a felony once delivered and retrieved.

Although the Rubaco Pentad appeared to be a politically driven domestic terrorism group, its demand for a million dollars was still technically extortion. And extortion, he had been taught during new-agents training, is simply a crime of intimidation at an anonymous distance. The victim has to be scared enough by the criminal's threat to do two things without question: part with the cash, and not contact the authorities. Each party has its own advantages. The extortionist has anonymity, while all law enforcement has to do is never lose contact with the money. Most cases wind up a draw: the criminal doesn't get the money, and law enforcement is unable to identify him. The would-be extortionist keeps from going to jail, and the Bureau justifies, in part, its budget requests. When the occasional arrest is made, it's because the extortionist thought he had come up with an original, foolproof gimmick to retrieve the money. "That's all there is to extortion," the instructor had declared. "There are no variations. The Bureau's been around for a century and no one has been able to figure out a way to do it differently."

But the Rubaco Pentad changed everything. After murdering a former Hollywood reporter a month earlier, it had demanded one million dollars to prevent the next killing. What was different about the Pentad's crime, other than the before-the-fact violence, was that the demand was made directly to the director of the FBI. In extortion or kidnapping drops, the Bureau always had at least some degree of surprise on its side, but the Pentad had taken that advantage away, leaving the agency unsure what to do next. The FBI was being told not only to come up with the money, but also to deliver it. Evidently the group felt its plan was so flawless that it could afford to humiliate the Bureau and still get away with the money.

The clear New Hampshire sky was full of stars; a half-moon hung distantly in the northeast. West looked around for some indication of what he was supposed to do next. He checked the coordinates on the GPS again. They matched those in the instructions exactly. Maybe he was just supposed to wait. He put the bag down and reread a copy of the demand note.

FBI,

Only your unconditional compliance with the following two conditions will prevent the next murder:

1. Delivery of $1,000,000 in hundred-dollar bills at precisely 9:42 P.M. on August 14 at **43.072N 70.546W.**

2. The public or media must not learn about the demand for money.

If either condition is violated, even by a "leak," the next person, a politician we have selected, will die. Although we doubt your ability to comply fully, we're willing to let the world-famous FBI try to get it right the first time. If not, this war will get progressively more expensive in terms of lives as well as money. Neither of which are we necessarily opposed to.

If the FBI continues to violate the rights of this country's citizens, the money will be used to finance much more drastic measures. More lives will be taken, and not one at a time. The FBI will be fully credited with the resulting mass destruction.

Make sure your delivery boy is a good swimmer.

The Rubaco Pentad

West checked his watch. It was almost nine thirty. Time was getting short.

Of course, he thought, the water. They wanted a good swimmer. He picked up the bag and walked across the parking lot tarmac and around behind the club. There was a waist-high fence that separated the asphalt from the grassy slope that led to the Piscataqua River. He vaulted over it and walked down to the edge. Music from inside the club lilted softly behind him.

Twenty yards to his right, he could see a faint optic-green glow among a cluster of large shrubs. Under them was a black tarp with a glow-in-the-dark arrow painted on top. The Pentad would probably have left it during the day when the paint would not have luminesced and been noticeable. The arrow pointed to a building on an island in the river, which was dimly silhouetted by the moonlight. It was a large white structure that, because of the notched turrets at either end, looked like a medieval castle.

The tide appeared to be out, making West wonder if he was supposed to swim across the river, roughly two hundred yards. He spoke into the mike on his chest. "Can someone find out what time low tide is here?" The entire operation was being monitored in the Boston office's major-case room.

After a few minutes someone said, "Nine forty-two P.M." That answered West's question about crossing the river. It was the exact time given in the instructions. Slack tide, the time of least current. Under the tarp were a scuba tank, fins, and a mask. At first glance the tank appeared old-fashioned, but it wasn't the tank. It was the harness that held it. Modern tanks come with a zippered vest or at least padded straps that divers can get in and out of easily. This one was fitted with excessively long black nylon webbing, crisscrossed unnecessarily, using far too much strapping. Some of it had been doubled in places that weren't necessary, and although it would be uncomfortable, it looked functional. Placed inside the mask was a wrist compass, which he strapped on. West explained over the radio what was going on. "Can you find out something about the building on the other side? It looks like that's where I'm heading."

West stripped down to his swimsuit. The "good swimmer" portion of the demand letter had been interpreted as an attempt by the Pentad to neutralize any FBI electronic devices, so the office technical agent had put a waterproof bag with a neck strap in a side pocket of the larger moneybag. Next to it was an underwater flashlight. Also a wax-sealed container had been jury-rigged by the head firearms instructor, who had placed a Smith & Wesson snubnose inside it.

It was now nine forty. As West started to slip on the fins provided, he found a folded piece of paper inside. "34°" was the only thing written on it. He held up his wrist and checked the heading to the "castle." It was exactly thirty-four degrees.

"Command, it looks like they want me to swim underwater straight to that building. Any idea what it is yet?"

"We've got the head resident agent in Portsmouth on the line. He says it's a hundred-year-old naval prison. Been closed for thirty years. That's Seavey's Island you're heading to. It's a secure naval shipyard now. We've got some of the surveillance units already at the main gate. They'll be on your land side by the time you get across."

"Just make sure they don't get me burned. That note sounds like these people would be just as happy if we screwed this up." He pulled the transmitter mike off his chest and packed everything into the watertight bag. As he stepped into the water, he took another deep breath and said, "Well, tough guy, this is what you wanted."

The water was cold, but the biggest problem was swimming underwater with the twenty-two-pound bag of fake money. The weight kept him deeper than he wanted to be. Some of the time he had to drag it along the bottom while keeping his eye on the compass. And the strange configuration of the harness webbing that was cutting into his waist and shoulders wasn't helping. Halfway across, the tide started coming back in and the current began picking up. It took him more than a half hour to get across the river.

As he got closer to the other side, he could see more luminescent green light. He felt the river bottom sloping up, so he set the bag down on it. Keeping a foot through the carrying straps, he surfaced to confirm his location. He was close to the prison now. Maybe too close. It looked black in its own shadow. And silent, making him want to hold his breath as if the building were a wounded animal he had stumbled across, its only means of attack to lure in those who believed it was dead. The structure was no longer two-dimensional, but seemed to wrap around the end of the island, and at the same time around him. Its west end had wings that ran north and south for hundreds of additional feet and at its tallest point was at least six stories high. So much for making the drop and leaving everything else to the surveillance agents. It looked like he was on his own.

He dove down and gripped the bag and saw that the green lights were a couple of glowsticks that had been attached to the underwater wall of the castle. When he got within a couple of feet, he snapped on the flashlight and could see the sticks had been laced through the remains of a metal gridwork that had once secured some type of conduit, possibly sewage, since the prison had been built when the country's rivers were considered nature's refuse solution. The underwater passageway was narrow, but he could fit through it. Taking a deep breath, he pushed the moneybag into the opening and followed it in.

A few minutes later he broke through the surface and found himself standing in a large stone room, the floor of which was bedrock except for the large rectangular access opening that he was now standing in. There were watermarks on the walls that indicated seawater filled the room to three-quarters at high tide. Toward the top of one wall were three heavy metal rings anchored into the stone and concrete, the kind that prisoners might have been chained to. He wondered if the U.S. Navy of a hundred years ago hadn't used the room for "retraining," taking the most uncooperative prisoners to the subterranean cell for an obedience lesson taught by two high tides a day and the flesh-nibbling crabs that rode in on them.

Pulling off the fins and mask, West shrugged out of the scuba tank and took out the snubnose. After turning on the transmitter, he spoke into the mike: "Any unit on this channel, can you hear me?" Because of the hundreds of tons of steel and concrete surrounding him, it would have been a miracle to get any reception. "Anyone hear me?" he tried once more. The only response was the hollow silence of the cavernous cell.

There didn't appear to be a way out of the room, but

then he noticed a trapdoor in the ceiling above the far wall. The height of the room was a good ten feet. How was he supposed to get up there?

He walked over to the wall directly underneath the trapdoor and shined his light up for a closer look. Just beneath it was a thick, rusty L-shaped hook embedded in the wall. In shoes, he could just touch a basketball rim if he jumped, ten feet. Barefooted, he could probably get up to the hook, but it didn't look like there was enough of it exposed for him to hold on to. He flashed the light around the room for anything that might help him reach it, but there was nothing except what he had brought with him.

Then it hit him—the webbing on the tank. That's why it was so long. The extortionists had used an excess of nylon strapping to rig the tank so he could extricate himself from this cell. It was some sort of test that they hoped the FBI would fail.

After stripping the strap out of the tank's frame, he quickly measured it using the nose-to-fingertip method. It was three lengths, about nine feet long. Great, he thought, nine feet to get me up ten feet and through the trapdoor. And with the moneybag. He let his sailor's knowledge of knots run through his mind for a while before the answer came to him.

He laid the scuba tank against the wall, and because it was round, he jammed the two wedge-shaped fins underneath it to prevent it from rolling out as he stood on it, getting him a foot closer to the hook. After knotting a simple loop in the middle of the strap, he tied a large slipknot at one end and threw it over the hook. Pulling it down slowly, he tied the moneybag tightly at the bottom end of the webbing.

As West started climbing, he realized how much the swim had taken out of him physically. He began to wonder if part of the Pentad's plan was to exhaust him. If it was, that meant a face-to-face confrontation could lie somewhere on the other side of the trapdoor.

Once he could stand in the knotted loop, he was able to straighten up and, with a full shove, push up on the door, causing it to rotate 180 degrees and slam against the floor in which it was hinged. West waited and listened. Still there was only silence.

The room he was climbing into was pitch black. He pulled himself up, drew his weapon, and got into a crouched firing position before turning on his light. It was some sort of holding room in a cellblock, about twenty feet by twenty feet. White paint was peeling off all the walls, and he could now smell it in the salty, damp air. Knowing how old the facility was and what the navy used for paint thirty years earlier, he was sure it was lead-based. An old dry-rotted ladder lay flat on the floor next to the trapdoor.

There was only one door in the room and he walked to it, turning off his light before opening it. He tried to do it carefully, but its rusted hinges echoed shrilly ahead of him. It opened to a narrow corridor. A hundred years ago the navy probably figured that whether on sea or land, a sailor needed only minimal width to move from compartment to compartment, so why waste money on aesthetics. At the far end of the corridor, he could see three more glowsticks fastened to a heavy stairwell door that had a small window of wired glass embedded in it. The sticks were shaped into an arrow pointing up. He went back to the trapdoor and pulled the moneybag up.

If he was going higher, maybe the transmitter would eventually work. He taped it to the small of his back and ran the mike up onto his chest, taping it in place. Then he put on his shirt to hide it. Jamming everything else into the bag, he headed for the glowstick arrow.

The stairwell was even narrower than the corridor. A metal railing ascended alongside the stairs. Peeling paint lined the deck and he could feel some of it sticking to the bottom of his feet. West turned off his flashlight. Of course they knew he was coming, but they didn't need to know exactly where he was. In the dark he put his hand on the railing and started up. There was a landing between each floor, and he stopped on each one, snapping on his light to check the next set of stairs. Then he turned it off and listened for a few moments. He heard nothing, though he knew they were there. He continued on up the stairs.

On each floor he checked the metal door to determine if it was where he was supposed to enter the prison, but they were all locked. The window in each had been covered with paper on the opposite side so he couldn't look through.

It took a few minutes to reach the top floor, the eighth if he had counted correctly. He tried the door and it opened. He turned on his flashlight and checked his weapon. He was now on a small landing with doors on either side. Shining a light through the glass windows, he could see they led off to different parts of the floor. Both were locked. Between them was a shoulder-width opening that looked down over an eight-story airshaft. All at once he could see the vastness of that part of the prison. Each floor was ringed with a catwalk accessing hundreds of cells. Underneath the railing at the edge where he stood was another glowing arrow, this time taped to the floor and pointing straight out. West leaned out through the opening without touching the ancient railing. On the deck one floor down was another arrow pointing back toward the stairwell. Was he supposed to rappel down to the next floor? He stepped back and tested the railing and, surprisingly, found it was rock solid. He leaned over again, trying to see what was on the landing below, but it was shadowed in darkness, and he couldn't get enough of an angle to use his flashlight. Quietly he tried his transmitter once more, but there still was no answer. He turned off the light and listened. Suddenly he felt the damp coldness that surrounded him, and shivered involuntarily.

Rappelling without a harness was chancy, but it was only about eight feet to the floor below. The nine-foot webbing was going to leave his descent a little short because of the four-foot-high railing and the knots at both ends, so he untied the bag, looping the webbing through the handles. Then, leaning as far over the side as he could, he swung the bag back and forth toward the landing below. When he was sure it would clear the railing, he released one end of the strapping, and the bag landed softly on the concrete deck below.

He pulled the webbing back up and tied it to the railing. Slowly he started to lower himself. When he came to the end of the strap, he could just reach the railing on his tiptoes. He took a moment to gain his balance on it and then let go of the webbing. As soon as his full weight transferred to the seventh-floor railing, he heard the horrifying sound of metal tearing. Both uprights supporting the crosspiece had been almost completely sawed through. He tried to grab the strap but it was already out of reach.

As he started to fall, he felt adrenaline explode through him. He turned himself in the air as best he could, hoping to catch a railing of one of the six remaining floors. But he was accelerating; it wasn't going to get any easier. He threw his hands at one of them, but because his body was askew, his right hand caught the railing before his left. With a sickening crack, his right shoulder dislocated as his left hand grabbed the railing, stopping his fall.

Blinding pain shot through the entire right side of his body, and he could hold on with only his left hand. Unable to pull himself up, he looked down, trying to count the railings below. The flashlight dangled from his useless arm as its beam swept the airshaft haphazardly. He was still three stories up. Something streaked by him and he thought it might have been the railing. Then he saw the cut and bundled magazine pages hit the ground and burst apart. The moneybag, now empty, floated by. Helplessly he watched his left hand, as if it belonged to someone else, come off the railing.

DAN WEST DIDN'T think he had been unconscious very long. The first thing he became aware of was footsteps. Help had arrived.

But there was something wrong with the approaching

steps; they were too slow. And they belonged to only one person. West tried to look around but the flashlight had come off his wrist and lay beyond his grasp, giving off only a small fan of light in the opposite direction. He was lying uselessly on his gun as his entire right side was all but paralyzed by the searing pain. Slowly so his movement wouldn't be detected, he reached back with his left hand and pushed the body recorder's button to the On position.

A man came up behind him and stood silently for a few seconds before walking around and standing in the flashlight's beam. Enduring the pain, West looked up as well as he could but still wasn't able to see his features in the shadows.

"Did you *want* to see my face?" he asked in a cold whisper that caused West to understand the consequences of being able to identify the individual. He picked up the flashlight and scanned the agent's sweating face. "You are young. That would explain the lack of self-preservation." He then shrugged and turned the light on himself. "Here you go."

West stared at the man's face, memorizing it. It was unremarkable except for his eyes; they were a stony gray but beginning to widen with pleasure. The agent tried to bring his injured right hand to his holster, but the extortionist easily kicked it away. "And they say the old BU was tougher. That must have been very painful."

Hoping the recorder wasn't damaged, West grimaced and said, "I don't suppose you'd want to tell me your name."

"What good would that do you now?"

"One last bit of satisfaction." He laughed painfully. "It's not like I've got much else to look forward to."

"And what's in it for me?"

"Come on. It's the ultimate act of control. Completely exposing yourself and then completely taking it away. For someone like you, that has to be damn near sexual."

The man's eyes narrowed in suspicion. "Someone like me?" the extortionist said, his voice amused but still in that hissing whisper. He then drew a black automatic. "I'm sorry, but we'd better move things along. I would imagine surveillance is getting close."

"I was hoping you'd stick around. Give them the opportunity to meet you and, with a little luck, shoot you to death."

"That's the saddest thing about being young—you actually believe there is such a thing as hope." He raised his gun and fired one round that hit Dan West in the right temple. The shot echoed metallically for a few moments, and the killer closed his eyes as if trying to prolong its sound.

When it was completely quiet, he scanned the floor with the flashlight until he found the spent cartridge. He picked it up and slipped out a side door.

THREE

ROBERT LASKER KNEW THAT IN WASHINGTON, D.C., THE QUICKEST way to have one's public-service résumé reduced to a one-line obituary was to get caught lying to the White House, especially if that individual happened to be the director of the FBI. But that was what he had just done. Anyway, he wasn't sure what the truth was, or whether he cared if, as director of the FBI, he ever found out. He told his driver that he needed to clear his head and would walk back to the office.

Pushing his hands deeper into his pockets as he walked along, he tried not to think about the meeting with the White House staffer who had summoned him because of the press the Bureau had been receiving about the Rubaco Pentad murders. "After three murders of well-known people, silence is not an option with the media. It looks like you're hiding something. You have to make some sort of statement," the staffer had said.

Actually, they were hiding something, not only from the public, and now the White House, but from most of their own agents as well. Lasker, without giving any details, told him that the investigation was at a critical juncture and the smallest miscalculation could cause additional deaths. The fear of the administration being dragged into the circle of responsibility for more murders was enough for the aide to back off, at least for the time being.

In truth, the FBI had not developed a single lead as to who was responsible for the murders or how to stop the killers from striking again.

Twelve hours earlier, the Rubaco Pentad had claimed its third high-profile victim, Arthur Bellington, a nationally known defense attorney who took particular delight in preventing or overturning FBI convictions, which he often followed with a press conference detailing the Bureau's ineptitude.

A month earlier, a former reporter had been murdered in her L.A. home. Within a couple of days, a million-dollar extortion demand was mailed to the FBI. When Agent Daniel West tried to deliver a dummy package of money to catch them, he too was shot to death. The Bureau had covered up the death, reporting it as a training accident, because of the Pentad's demand for secrecy concerning all monetary aspects of the case.

A couple of weeks later, Nelson Lansing, a Utah state senator who had coauthored a book about Ruby Ridge concluding that the Bureau had methodically executed members of the Randy Weaver family, had been shot and killed by the Pentad as he was leaving his Salt Lake City home early in the morning. To no great surprise, a two-million-dollar demand arrived at the FBI within a week. What followed then was anything but predictable. The letter also named the agent who was to make the delivery, Stanley Bertok of the Los Angeles division.

As instructed, Bertok, this time with the entire two million dollars, flew to Phoenix, rented a car, and took off on a four-hour drive to Las Vegas. The Pentad had warned about using FBI aircraft, which, like so many things in this case, indicated an uncommon understanding of Bureau procedure. The prescribed route was desolate and relatively free of commercial airline traffic so any plane would be spotted easily. Also, the terrain was flat and the roads were straight. Any trailing vehicle could be seen for miles. So the Bureau left it up to electronics, hiding GPS devices in the car and in the bag containing the money. Bertok was also given a cell phone with additional Global Positioning System abilities. Two and a half hours into the trip, the car, according to all three GPSs, stopped dead. Fearing discovery, the agents monitoring Bertok's movements waited almost another hour before closing in. When they arrived at the indicated location, the only thing they found was a fast-food bag on the shoulder of the road. Inside were the two GPS devices along with the cell phone. Bertok, the car, and the bag containing two million dollars were nowhere to be found. Twelve hours later, the rented vehicle was found at the Las Vegas airport.

Lasker continued his way back to the Hoover Building, forcing himself to walk slower. The weather was perfect and he took a moment to watch a couple of attractive young women pass him.

With the Pentad claiming its fourth victim the night before, it seemed improbable that the missing two million dollars was in their possession. If they didn't have it, the most plausible explanation was that Stan Bertok had just become America's newest millionaire. And that meant the FBI would soon receive another demand for money to prevent a fifth killing.

If an agent selling out wasn't bad enough, an even worse possibility existed. Just hours before, the lab had confirmed that all four victims, including Dan West, had been shot with the same weapon, a .40-caliber Glock, model 22. That particular gun was FBI issue and was part of Bertok's property. Coupled with the possibility of "insider info" with which the group operated, the thought had crossed more than a few minds that Bertok himself might have committed the murders to set up the extortion drop.

Involuntarily, Lasker shook his head at the ingenuity of the Pentad. Everything it did was carefully designed to defeat the FBI, especially its choice of victims. Not only were they high-profile individuals, their deaths instantly gaining national attention, but their murders took place in California, Utah, and Pittsburgh, implying that no one was safe anywhere. And maybe most important, each of the victims was known to have a conflicted history with the FBI, making the Bureau waste time either defending itself or planning circuitous avenues of investigation to avoid the appearance of any "further" impropriety. With the public not knowing why the victims were really being murdered, the confusion continued as to who was actually killing the "enemies of the FBI," as the media were now referring to them.

Most puzzling was how difficult the Pentad made it to

deliver the money. It almost seemed that they wanted the FBI to fail; in fact, that was exactly what one of the Bureau profilers theorized. "Their primary motive," he said, "is to disgrace the FBI. It is such an obsession with them that they consider murder nothing more than a necessary tool. They may not even want the money. Some people find self-validation in destroying institutions. They find power in destroying power. It's being done every day through lawsuits. But legal channels wouldn't produce the dramatic damage they feel they have a right to. And even though their methods would be considered by most as cowardly, they see themselves as great unsung heroes, defeating, in this case, an institution that the American people mistakenly see as heroic. The more times they can defeat it, the more heroic they are. And the more foolish we look. Do they want the money? Eventually they probably will. Greed is pretty dependable. But they're not going to be in any hurry to get it as long as they're beating us in these skirmishes. Waco and Ruby Ridge are apparently the justification of their actions. No one from the FBI was ever punished for those incidents, so they are taking retribution into their own hands. If Bertok did suddenly become a thief and take the money, they couldn't have hoped for anything better. It proves their point that the FBI is really corrupt and can't be trusted. And at some point they will reveal to the world that he took it. Again, to humiliate us. Not only do we have a dishonest agent, but we routinely cover up something like this. Which at the moment we are."

Lasker knew that whoever was pulling the strings, whether it was the Pentad or Agent Bertok freelancing—or both—the effect was paralyzing the Bureau's ability to go after them. That the FBI might be assassinating its enemies and blaming the killings on a fictitious group of terrorists was a ridiculous notion, but if the information about the Glock 22, the gun the Bureau had issued Bertok, became public, it might not seem so far-fetched.

At each of the crime scenes, a folded piece of paper with the same two words, "Rubaco Pentad," had been left on the victim's chest. Since "pentad" is defined as a group of five, the press felt safe in concluding that some sort of small domestic terrorism cell was committing the murders. And "Rubaco," they decided, was an amalgam of Ruby Ridge and Waco, two of the FBI's most enduring black eyes, especially among the more radical antigovernment groups, most of which would list the FBI as first-strike targets.

Seeking to further sensationalize the case, the press drew a more abstract but marketable conclusion: that each of the three known victims, because of his or her individual history with the Bureau, could be considered an enemy of the FBI. However, the two assumptions collectively formed a paradox. If the Rubaco Pentad were committing murders to save the world from the FBI, then why was it killing individuals who shared the same beliefs?

Because of the monetary demand, Lasker had initially assumed it was just another extortion with a different coat of paint, and it had been handled as such. Terrorists who demanded money were simply extortionists no matter what kind of rhetoric accompanied their demands. But after they left the hundred-dollar bills lying around Dan West's body, their long-range plans for the money suddenly seemed a more ominous possibility. If they were legitimate terrorists, there would be, as they had warned in their first demand letter, an irresistible irony to the idea of using secretly paid FBI money to commit mass murder, something for which the public would never forgive the Bureau.

FOUR

NEWLY PROMOTED DEPUTY ASSISTANT DIRECTOR KATE BANNON HAD never been in the FBI director's office before. While she and her boss waited for Bob Lasker's return, she took the opportunity to survey the room more closely. The lack of pretension in the decor was surprising. She didn't know what she had expected, but the offices of upper management she had seen usually looked more like small museums, lined with trophies, plaques, and photographs. Instead there were piles of documents littering the room, on tables and shelves, some of the taller ones leaning haphazardly. A few were starting to show a coat of dust, causing a dull mustiness that scratched at her nostrils. Only one photograph hung on the wall. It had apparently been taken during Lasker's Senate confirmation hearing. Shot from behind the soon-to-be director, it focused on the face of a bald senator whose scalp glistened with sweat and who for some reason was shaking an angry finger at the nominee. She smiled, suspecting that it had been placed directly behind the director's desk to remind everyone that whatever business had brought them there, he or she should remember that ultimately Lasker had to answer for what his agency did or failed to do.

The door opened and the director walked in. "You guys

been waiting long?" He fell unceremoniously into the chair behind his desk, grinding his eyes with the heels of his hands until he felt the tiny optic shocks that told him that was enough. He had gotten little sleep since the murders started, and the command performance at the White House had taken out of him what little was left.

Assistant Director Don Kaulcrick was sitting next to Kate. At fifty-three, he was the FBI's senior assistant director. He was tall with a disjointed thinness to his limbs. His hair had not started to turn gray yet and would have made his face look younger if it weren't for its being slightly lopsided, the right side of the jaw just noticeably larger than the left. It gave the appearance of a permanent sneer of skepticism, one that continually left subordinates trying to convince him of their sincerity, an advantage he had learned to exploit early in his career. But Kaulcrick noticed that Kate Bannon seemed immune to it, probably because very little intimidated her. So he did the only thing he could to combat her lack of regard for the privileges of rank; he handpicked her to be his assistant. That way he could personally rein in that freewheeling style that had caused her to rise through the ranks so quickly. "Not long, sir," he answered for both of them. "How'd it go?"

"Don, I was summoned to the White House," Lasker said. "That's like asking Marie Antoinette if the blade was nice and sharp. Kate, how are you?"

"Just fine, sir."

"They're not happy with us at 1600 Pennsylvania Avenue. I was told to stop screwing around and just go ahead and solve this thing. Thank God they've taken the gloves off—now we can start the real investigation. What a mess." Kaulcrick and Kate glanced at each other furtively, trying to determine if he thought they were considered responsible. "Someone please give me some good news."

After a few seconds, Kate said, "At the first three murder scenes, the killer or killers took the time to police up the casings. All we had were the slugs to identify the gun, but they got sloppy with this one last night. A forty-caliber cartridge was found near the body."

"That's it. That's the extent of the good news?" Lasker said. "I know I'm not as up on this stuff as you are, but why would you pick up the casing when the slug in the body can identify the gun?" the director asked.

"Maybe they were hoping that the slug would be damaged enough that it couldn't be identified. They used hollow points, which tend to deform a great deal more as they pass through the human body," Kaulcrick offered.

"I suppose," Lasker said. "What else?"

Kate said, "I'm not sure this is *good* news." She hesitated. Lasker gave her an unenthusiastic wave of the hand to continue. "So far, the people I sent to Las Vegas haven't been able to find any sign of Bertok having taken a flight out of there."

Lasker looked at the woman that he had heard male agents refer to as "too good-looking to be a female agent." She was tall with a figure that was both athletic and feminine. Her face would have had a blond, girl-next-door innocence to it if it weren't for the soft two-inch scar across her left cheekbone, a broken line that suggested a willingness for combat. In the past, he had noticed a nonchalance to the way she handled herself in a room in which she was the only woman. Lasker took a moment to lose himself in her confidence and then said, "I don't have to remind you how sensitive this is, Kate. I assume you've explained to everyone working this just how quiet it has to be kept."

"Yes, sir, I chose the agents carefully."

"All good investigators?"

"Not particularly. I went purely for obedience. As far as the investigation, I know what needs to be done, and I'm reading all reports to make sure it's getting done. I just wanted agents who above all else could keep their mouths closed."

"In today's Bureau? Please tell me how to accomplish that."

A corner of Kate's mouth lifted sardonically. "I picked only the most serious climbers." "Climbers" was a term street agents used to stereotype the most serious promotion seekers. "I told them if they did a good job, their name would be put on a priority list, but if this leaked out in any fashion, whether it was their doing or not, they'd seen their last promotion."

Lasker smiled. "Sounds foolproof." The director looked at Kaulcrick. "What else?"

He slid a report across Lasker's desk. "This is the latest analysis of the recording from Dan West's murder. The transcription is pretty much the same. That whispering voice the killer used makes it hard to distinguish. Like you suggested, the recording was played for Bertok's supervisor in L.A. to see if he could identify the voice. All he would say was it might be him."

The director turned to the transcription portion of the report. "And what about the language?"

Kate pulled out a different document. "Psycholinguistics said that a couple of phrases have definite overtones of someone familiar with FBI jargon, particularly 'BU' for Bureau and 'surveillance' instead of the more commonly used 'backup.' And due to the killer saying things like 'you are young' and 'the old BU was tougher,' the conversation has the subtlety of an older agent lecturing a younger one. But there's not enough to draw any definitive conclusions about the identity of the killer."

"So there's nothing to say it *isn't* Bertok."

"Unfortunately, no," Kaulcrick said.

"They seemed to know everything we tried to do at the New Hampshire drop. Does that take an insider's knowledge?" the director asked.

Kate said, "Not necessarily. Dummy packages have been used in the past, and it has been made public in court testimony. From the outset, they probably planned to commit two murders because they knew it would be a dummy drop. That way they could demand two million. As a side benefit, they can now argue that our ineptness caused not only murder number two, but the death of an FBI agent. I don't know, maybe Bertok was afraid that if he had tried to deliver the money, he would have wound up like Dan West, or worse. Maybe that helped him decide to take off. If he did," she said.

"If it is him, it's going to kill us when it comes out," Lasker said. "But for right now, the longer we can delay it, the more operating room we'll have."

"We still have to find him. What makes it so difficult is that we're looking for one of our own, and we can't even tell our own," Kaulcrick said. "Plus he knows all our procedures and has two million dollars to be creative with."

Lasker took a moment to consider what Kaulcrick had said and then asked, "Are we getting any closer to identifying this group? *Is* this really a group?"

Kate said, "It's been my experience that almost invariably extortionists who work alone will use plural pronouns like 'we,' 'us,' 'our.' It's part of their intimidation process to make the victim believe that the extortionist has more manpower than he does."

"So what you're saying is that this could be just one man."

"I'm saying it's a possibility."

"Is there any record of 'pentad' anywhere in our files?"

"Since the first murder, we have been running 'Rubaco' and 'pentad' every way possible," Kaulcrick said. "So far, nothing."

Kate said, "We've got a half dozen agents going through all the Waco and Ruby Ridge nut files. There's a few leads being generated, but nothing with much promise."

"For the moment, let's assume Bertok is not involved in the killings. Anyone have any theories why they picked him?"

Kate said, "He was a street agent who worked extortion cases. Maybe they ran into him somewhere or read his name in the paper. It might be another one of their ploys to make us think they know more about what we're doing than we do."

The director snorted a laugh. "So far it's working."

Kaulcrick said, "This could have been Bertok's operation from the beginning. With him and the money disappearing together, it would be shortsighted not to consider the possibility."

"If it is Bertok, why would he use a gun that is so recognizable as FBI issue?" Kate asked her boss.

"Nothing would cover his tracks better if he's caught and has to go to trial. He could then say, 'With a plan this well thought out, would I be stupid enough to use an FBI-type service weapon? Somebody wants you to think it's an agent who has done this.' If we're having these doubts, a jury certainly would. And then, at just the right moment, he would stand up and surrender his service weapon. 'Here's my issued handgun—check the serial number and test-fire it.' It would destroy the prosecution's case. Then he would only be looking at prison time for the embezzlement of two million dollars, which, with any reimbursement, carries a slap on the wrist compared to four murders."

"Assuming that's true, then what did he shoot the victims with?" the director said.

"A second, unregistered Glock 22," Kaulcrick answered quickly, as if he had expected the question.

"Do we know if he owns more than one gun?" the director asked.

"I checked his property card, and no, he doesn't," Kate said. "Not that he's told the Bureau about."

"I don't know, Don. If he has the money, then why this last murder?" the director asked.

"Sir, if all this was part of a planned defense, another killing would be proof positive that he had nothing to do with the murders. He just boogied with the cash, so the real killers had no choice but to find another victim and make a new demand."

The director collapsed back into his chair. "Anyone want my job?"

After a few seconds, Kaulcrick said, "I got something from the Chicago office this morning that might take your mind off this for a few minutes. May I?"

"Please."

Kaulcrick went over to a large television that sat on a corner table of the office and inserted a DVD. "I don't know if either of you saw this on the national news a couple of weeks ago."

A reporter came on the screen, microphone in hand, and started describing a hostage situation taking place at a suburban Chicago bank. Suddenly, the camera zoomed in on the bank's front door. A terrified woman opened it, and a gunman could be seen behind her shielding himself, his weapon pressed against the side of her head. The reporter said, "It looks like one of the gunmen is trying to negotiate some sort of deal." Just as the robber finished his demands and closed the door, one of the bank's front windows exploded as a man came crashing through it. He skidded across the sidewalk and lay unconscious.

The cameraman centered the shot on the body lying in front of the bank, and after another fifteen seconds, a second robber exploded through the adjoining window, landing on the concrete walk, dazed and unarmed. Immediately, customers and employees ran out of the front door as the police rushed forward to handcuff the two men. The screen went black.

"What happened?" Lasker asked.

"According to the report, witnesses said a customer, waiting until the two robbers were separated, disarmed them one at a time and then threw each of them through the windows."

"Who was it?"

"That is the strangest part to the story. No one knows. Whoever it was exited with the other customers and disappeared into the crowd."

"What?" the director said.

"The police and the media have been putting out pleas for him to call in, but so far nothing."

"What would make someone walk away from something that extraordinary?"

"I have no idea," Kaulcrick said. "Want to see how he did it?"

"Absolutely."

"Chicago sent me the surveillance videos from inside the bank." Kaulcrick shoved in another DVD. "This composite was put together from three different cameras. It starts with the first gunman being overpowered." He hit the Play button and it showed the bank lobby with customers scattered facedown on the floor. "See this hand here?" He pointed at the corner of the screen. "That belongs to our boy. Keep an eye on it."

"What's that next to it?" Kate asked.

"A watercooler. Keep an eye on that, too."

Kaulcrick pressed a button on the remote and the disk slowed to half speed. As the images rolled by, the hand on the floor reached up and took the bottle from the watercooler as its owner pulled himself from the floor. His grainy face came into view. He placed a hand on each end of the bottle, holding it in front of his chest just as the gunman realized he was up off the floor and turned toward him. The robber yelled something, but the man continued to move toward him, extending the bottle away from his chest and in line with the muzzle of the gun. The robber fired and the impact of the bullet ripped the bottle from the man's hands. Almost simultaneously, the man grabbed the barrel of the gun and twisted it outward in a move that Kaulcrick and Kate recognized as one they had practiced dozens of times during defensive tactics training. Once he finished twisting the weapon from the robber's hand, the robber swung at him, and the man used the gun to strike him in the head. Then, with relative ease, he hurled him through the glass window and immediately ran to the wall that separated the front door from the rest of the bank's interior.

"This is from a second camera," Kaulcrick said. The TV screen was filled with static for a second; then, from a different angle, the female hostage who had been held at the front door during the television report came around the corner, followed by the second gunman. The unknown man's hand flashed forward and shoved his weapon against the robber's neck. After a short hesitation, the bank robber dropped his gun, and when the man stooped to pick it up, he ran. But the man took a few quick steps and caught him immediately.

The robber struck him in the face to no effect. Before the robber could hit him again, the man punched him in the face, buckling his legs. Then the man turned and launched him through the second window. Looking up and realizing everything was being caught on camera, the man turned his head away and started herding the hostages out the door.

While the director nodded his head enthusiastically, Kate sat pensively. Noticing her lack of enthusiasm, he said, "Not impressed, Kate?"

She continued to look at the screen, which was again filled with static. "No, it's not that. . . ." She didn't finish her thought.

Lasker asked, "How'd he know there was enough water in the bottle to stop a bullet?"

Kaulcrick said, "I'm guessing he didn't."

"Why would someone do something like that?"

"Apparently, he has a screw loose."

"And they haven't found out who he is yet?" Lasker said.

"No. Chicago wants to release this to the local media. That's why they sent it to me, for authorization."

"Let me know who he is when he's identified. I'd be interested to know why he's so camera shy."

Kate said, "I think I know who he is."

"You do?" The director turned toward her.

"Sir, you haven't had the hand-to-hand training we have, but the way he took the gun from the first robber is an FBI move, one we have all practiced many times. That's what tipped me off. His hair's a little lighter now, but I think it's a former agent named Steve Vail. I was a security supervisor in Detroit for two years, and Vail was assigned there. Not on my squad, on the fugitive squad. And I'm pretty sure he was originally from Chicago."

"Former?"

"He was fired."

"Not given the option to resign?"

"They gave him the choice, but he refused to respond even though he knew he would be fired."

"So he could sue?"

Kate gave a quick, full-throated laugh. "I guess I'm not giving you a very clear picture of him. You're trying to figure him out by the experiences you've had with others. No, he's . . . probably the best word—the kindest word—is recalcitrant."

"He's a pain in the ass."

"Beyond that. They used to say he bit off his nose to spite his face so many times that he actually learned to like the taste."

"Then why was he fired? Apparently it wasn't for a lack of courage."

"He hated—no, that isn't right—he simply didn't recognize authority, at least not incompetent authority. That's what was so strange about his firing. He could have prevented it by giving up a thoroughly disliked assistant special agent in charge. It all started when a Detroit police officer was shot and killed in the line of duty. They didn't have any idea who had done it. Vail always had great informants, so he goes off on his own to contact them. At the same time, he's poking around the murder investigation, developing new sources. He finds this one local who, after a little, let's say, cajoling, names the shooter and also tells Vail that the gun used is at the killer's residence. Which was kind of a feat in itself because it turns out the informant was the killer's cousin. At the same time, because killing a police officer is a federal offense, the Bureau offers a twenty-five-thousand-dollar reward. Even though he would not have given up his cousin without Vail getting it out of him first, the informant decides that he might as well cash in and calls the same information into the FBI tip line. One of the ASACs at the time was Kent Wilson. Do you know him?"

"By reputation."

"Then you won't have any trouble believing what comes next. With the tip, Wilson has the same information as Vail—because of Vail's work on the street. Vail was always that guy you called when you needed to get something done in spite of the rules. All full of himself, Wilson has Vail come in and reads him the tip sheet. Then tells him to do whatever is necessary to get probable cause for a search warrant at the killer's residence. Vail leaves without saying a word. He already had everything in motion.

"Because the informant had no track record, his credibility for a search warrant wouldn't have been strong enough, so Vail calls one of his most documented sources and has him listen while he telephones the cousin and has him repeat the information. Then Vail has his old informant repeat it to him for probable cause on the search warrant. The Detroit police find the gun, get a confession and eventually a conviction.

"Wilson tries to take credit for the arrest, but the brass at the Detroit PD goes nuts because Vail had also been keeping them up to speed all along, since it was their officer. He didn't tell them about the sleight of hand with the sources. They call a press conference and give all the credit to Vail.

"The most amazing part is Wilson thinks it was all Vail's doing and calls in the Office of Professional Responsibility, telling them that Vail falsified information to obtain a search warrant. He gives absolutely no thought about how it could come back and collapse on him. Subsequently, Vail refused to talk to OPR.

"Because of the inconsistencies in Wilson's statement, they tell Vail what they suspected happened and even that Wilson had given him up. Still Vail won't answer their questions. Not even after they offered him a walk if he flipped on Wilson would he say anything. They even went to the trouble of tracking down Vail's old informant and threatened him, even tried to bribe him, but he wouldn't give up Vail."

"That's unbelievable. Why wouldn't Vail just give Wilson up? He's not exactly the kind of boss you'd waste loyalty on."

Kate leaned back. "Vail's not that easy to figure out, but there is one very practical reason. If he admitted manufacturing probable cause, OPR would have had to notify the state prosecutor's office, and the search, confession, and conviction would have been thrown out."

"So Vail let himself be fired so a cop killer wouldn't walk."

"I think it's even more than that. I don't know. He seems to have this resentment for the way the rest of us lack commitment or something. He didn't even show up for his last OPR interview, therefore insubordination."

"Too bad we lost him."

Kate sat silently considering something before she said, "Sir, Vail had this reputation for finding people. He handled all the federal fugitive warrants for Detroit homicide. They said whether someone was gone fifteen minutes or fifteen years, he'd find them. Like I told you, he wasn't on my squad, but everyone knew about Steve Vail. Funny thing was he seemed oblivious to any kind of notoriety, that anyone would be interested in anything he did. I always thought it was an act—until just now watching him sneak out of that bank."

"Are you suggesting we bring him into this?"

Kaulcrick said, "I don't think that's a good idea. We've got more than enough resources at our disposal. You can't bring a civilian into this. With each turn of this thing, it looks like we can't protect ourselves from ourselves."

"Just to find Bertok," she said. "Someone who doesn't have to tiptoe around like the rest of us. So far we've got nothing. It's pretty obvious that Vail can keep his mouth shut. What have we got to lose?"

The director pushed the Play button and watched again as Vail disarmed the two bank robbers. "Think you can get him, Kate?"

"Me? He despises men in authority. What do you think his reaction will be to a woman?"

"I think you'd better find out."

FIVE

STEVE VAIL SPLASHED SOME WATER ONTO THE MORTAR AND USED the forged steel trowel to turn it over, alternately using the knife edge to sink the moisture deep into the mixture. The late-morning sun felt good on the back of his neck. It had rained the night before, leaving one of those damp Chicago mornings that felt cooler than the mid-seventy-degree temperature. Moving back into the shadow of the large circular chimney he had been hired to rebuild, he picked up a brick and flipped it over so its wire-cut face was in position and buttered one end with the softened mortar. He pushed it into place, tapping the top with the butt of the trowel handle, and then used a backhand sweep to scrape off the excess mortar, flicking it into the joint just formed. His eye checked the brick's alignment as he reached for the next one.

The ladder he had used to get to the flat roof started tapping rhythmically against the top of the wall. Someone was coming up. Flicking the excess mortar off the trowel, he threw it, sticking it into the pine mortarboard. He peered over the edge of the roof and was surprised to see a woman coming up the ladder. She moved quickly, her hands and feet finding the rungs instinctively. She was wearing a pantsuit and small heels, which should have made the climb more difficult, but they didn't seem to slow her at all. Under her jacket, on the outside of her hip, he could see the bulge of a gun. Parked behind his truck now was a four-door sedan, one of those full-size government cars that were conspicuously nondescript.

Kate Bannon came over the top of the ladder and was surprised to find Vail leaning against the chimney, apparently waiting for her, his stare mildly curious. She brushed her hands against each other, wiping away imaginary debris from the ladder as she composed herself. "Hi," she said, extending her hand. "I'm—"

"Kate Bannon." He took her hand.

"How'd you know?"

"Detroit."

"I didn't think you'd remember me," she said. "To tell you the truth, I didn't think you knew I existed."

"I knew." His mouth tightened into a grin that she couldn't quite decipher.

"Even though I was some 'management bimbo' getting my ticket punched?"

He smiled more completely. "Even though."

"I would assume that's what most of the male street agents thought," she said. "And looking back, I'm not sure they were wrong."

"Brutal honesty, and so early in this little—what is it we're having, some sort of sales pitch?"

"At least give me the courtesy of pretending you're being fooled," she said. "And it's not about your performance at the bank last month if that's what you're worried about."

She was hoping to see some surprise from Vail that she knew he was the one who had disrupted the robbery, but his face had shifted into those unreadable planes she remembered from Detroit. "I'm not. I know they wouldn't send someone all the way from Washington just for that."

"How'd you know I'm at headquarters?"

"Five years ago, you were some 'management bimbo' doing your field supervisory time. I haven't been keeping track of the rate of promotion for women, but I would guess that's long enough for you to be at least a unit chief."

"Actually, I was just promoted to deputy assistant director."

"Really," he said. "You must be quite the agent because someone as brutally honest as you surely wouldn't accept a promotion simply because you're a woman."

She stared back at him, slightly amused. "Listen, Steve, if you're trying to convince me that you can be an SOB, I remember. You'll also find I'm not that easy to get rid of."

Vail laughed. "A deputy assistant director. And on a rooftop in Chicago. There must be a *really* big problem back at the puzzle palace?"

"There is something we'd like your help with."

"Unless you've got some bricks that need to be laid, you're in the wrong time zone, darlin'."

She looked at the chimney and the tools scattered around it. "You have a master's degree in Russian history from the University of Chicago. How did you wind up being a bricklayer?"

"Is there something wrong with being a bricklayer?" he asked, his tone half amused with the feigned indignation.

"It just seems like there would be easier ways to make a buck."

"Fair enough. It goes something like this. First you have to get fired, and then if you wait long enough, you start getting hungry. The rest of it just kind of falls into place."

"I would have thought that you'd have looked for something a little more . . . *indoors*."

"My father taught me when I was a kid. It's how I got through college. And if you're going to snoop around my personnel file, please get it right. *Soviet* history. It's an important distinction in case whatever brings you here depends on my ability to see into the future," Vail said. "Thus . . ." He waved his hand to encompass the surroundings. "Actually, I kind of like the work. It's real. There's something permanent about it, at least in human years. Handfuls of clay being transformed into complicated structures. And then, of course, it was the only house that the wolf couldn't blow down. Besides, there are too many bosses *indoors*."

"So you're never going to take a job that has a boss?"

"There's always a boss. The trick is to never take a job you can't walk away from. Especially when the bosses get to be insufferable, which I think is now a federal law."

"Is that what you did with the FBI, walk away when you didn't like the boss?"

"Seems like you've thought about it a lot more than I have."

"I've come with an offer that you can walk away from whenever you want."

He pulled the trowel out of the mortarboard and picked up a brick. "Then consider me walked away."

"I wouldn't be here unless we really needed your help."

"One of the things my departure from the Bureau taught me was that the FBI will never *really* need any one person."

"I'm impressed. You've maintained a grudge for five years. You rarely see that kind of endurance anymore."

"Thanks, but the credit really should go to my father. World-class scorn was the sum total of my inheritance. Enough of it can get you through anything." Vail started turning over the mortar on the board again.

"Do you want it in writing? The Federal Bureau of Investigation needs the particular skills of Steven Noah Vail."

"You'll find someone else."

Kate stepped in front of him. "I know something about you that maybe you don't even know."

"Oh good, I was wondering when we'd get around to managerial insight. Will I need something to write with?"

"You have to do this." Her tone was not pleading but accusatory.

He held up the brick between them. "I do *this* so I don't *have to* do anything."

Her eyes carefully searched his face. "My God, you don't know, do you? You really don't know why you do these things. Why you have no choice but to say yes to me."

"In that case, no."

"Stop being so *Vail* for a minute."

"Why is 'no' such a difficult concept for women? You demand we understand it the first time, every time."

"Do you know why you stopped that bank robbery?" Ignoring her, Vail spread a bed of mortar and pushed the brick into it. "Because no one else could," she went on. "Everyone else in the world is running around searching for their own self-importance, and you're cruising around ignoring yours." She smiled. "And let's admit it, if you're really that into revenge, what could be better than having the Bureau come crawling to you to fix some problem that all the king's horses and all the king's men couldn't?"

Vail stared at her like he was seeing her for the first time. He turned and went back to work on the chimney. For the next half hour neither of them spoke. She sat down on the edge of the roof and watched him. There was an economy of movement to his work that she supposed was necessary for any task so repetitive, but still there was something about the way he did it that she found intriguing. The way his large, veined hands flipped over the bricks and found the right alignment instinctually. The way when he applied mortar, it was always the exact amount needed, never dropping any, never needing to add any. The flow never interrupted. How he was transforming perfectly rectangular bricks into a perfectly round chimney.

The more she watched him, the more she realized he was working faster than he normally would. If the work was as rewarding as he had said, there should have been an occasional appraising touch or at least a glance when he finished a course, but instead he immediately reached for the next brick. She couldn't tell if he was just angry with her or if he wanted to get done so that he could be rid of her for good.

After the last brick was tapped into place and the joint scraped flush, Vail flicked the excess mortar off the trowel and then scraped both its sides on the edge of the board. She could finally see some reaction on his face. Even though the trowel was clean, he kept stropping it against the board absentmindedly. "What exactly is it that needs fixing?"

"I'm sorry, I am not allowed to tell you."

"Who is?"

"The director."

"*The* director?"

"That's the one."

"What is it that you think I can do that the other eleven thousand agents can't?"

"Most important? Be discreet. Last month's little bank robbery gave us a pretty good indication that you're not interested in getting your name in the papers."

"And less important?"

"You had a certain reputation in Detroit."

"For?"

"Hunting men."

"So you want me to find someone without anyone knowing that the FBI's looking for him."

"It's a little more complicated than that, but those are the main concerns."

"Other than getting to polish my neglected self-esteem, what's in this for me?"

"It's completely negotiable."

"Are you saying that as a deputy assistant director or as a woman?" As her face reddened slightly, the scar on her cheekbone started to glow white. He smiled. "That's enough of an answer for now. When?"

"I came in a Bureau plane. It's waiting at Midway."

Vail picked up a ten-gallon bucket and started shoveling the unused mortar into it. "Give me a half hour to clean up."

VAIL'S PICKUP PULLED up in front of his apartment with Kate's Bureau car close behind. He walked back to her as she opened the door. "I'll make it as quick as I can."

She got out. "Can I use your phone?"

"You don't have a cell?"

"I'd rather use a hard line."

"I wasn't expecting company."

Kate wondered how bad it was up there. She found herself intrigued at the prospect of peeking into Vail's personal life. "I'll keep my eyes closed."

Vail opened the door and let Kate walk in ahead of him. The small apartment was not what she expected. It seemed newer, better constructed than the rest of the building. The walls were unpainted Sheetrock. The taped seams were visible but had been smoothed with the expert touch of a trowel. In stark contrast, the dark hardwood floors looked like they had been recently refinished and were buffed to a high sheen. The furniture was sparse, and the few tables and shelves scattered around held a couple dozen different sizes and types of sculpture, mostly the kind that were found at garage or estate sales or dusty way-out-of-the-way antique shops. Strangely, all the human figures were of the headless variety and had apparently been purchased for the detail of the torsos. She wondered if there was another reason. "I'm still working on the walls, but I guess that's obvious."

On a worktable at the front window, to take advantage of the natural light, was an almost complete sculpture of a male torso formed by hundreds of thumb-size smudges of clay. "You live here alone?"

"If you're asking if it's mine, the answer is yes. And yes to living alone."

She walked over to the two-foot-high figure and examined it more closely. The upper portion appeared completed and was heavily muscled. She glanced around at the other works in the apartment to see if any matched the style. "None of the others are mine if that's what you're wondering."

"Do you sell them or give them away?"

"Actually, I throw them out when I'm done, or break them down so the material can be reused."

"Have you ever tried to sell them?"

"They're not good enough yet."

"Really, this seems like it has potential."

He pulled off his T-shirt. "That's probably why you're not working at the Guggenheim, and I'm a bricklayer. Beer?"

"Sure."

"Glass?"

"Please."

Her voice had an odd quality about it that Vail was drawn to. It was lilting, but at the same time gracefully incomplete, making him want to hear it again. "Not trying to be one of the guys drinking out of the bottle—refreshing." He handed her a glass and twisted the cap off. After opening his, he took a long swallow from the bottle.

She glanced at each of the sculptures again. "What's with the no-heads?"

He took another swallow of beer. For the first time that

day, she sensed a reluctance to answer a question, an evasion of the blunt answers that seemed to come naturally to him. "I find faces distracting. I'm always trying to figure out what the models were thinking about at the time, even what language they might be thinking in. Probably studying Russian and reading Tolstoy and Dostoyevsky all those years has scarred me for life. Besides, I've tried faces. They all wind up looking like they're from Middle Earth."

The explanation seemed superficially dismissive, one that he never quite believed himself. Remembering Detroit now, she wondered if there was a natural distance he preferred. Back then everyone assumed it was some sort of extension of his inexplicable modesty. Armed with this new insight, she looked around and could find no television or magazines or personal photos. Apparently not even pictures of faces were allowed. The real question, she supposed, was what had made him like that. "Even though you didn't say yes right away, I'm surprised getting you to come back to Washington wasn't more difficult."

"As you can see, my sculpting business isn't going that well. And the job I just finished was the only one I had scheduled."

Again, she detected a slightly hollow ring to his reasons. "You know, if you're interested in getting your job back permanently, that could be arranged."

"I'm not looking for permanent right now, just different."

She smiled and nodded, deciding to lighten the conversation. "I think I can pretty much guarantee that this is going to be different."

"Give me fifteen minutes. The phone's over there."

Kate sipped at her beer absentmindedly as she listened to the shower. She stood over the unfinished sculpture, admiring its virility. The shoulder and upper arm muscles seemed too large to be realistic, but it gave off a kind of primitive indestructibility. Then, closing her hand, she let her fingertips massage her palm, recalling the callused strength of Vail's handshake. She let the tip of her finger run lightly down the curve of the figure's spine like a drop of warm water.

SIX

AS THEY WERE BOARDING THE PLANE, KATE THOUGHT SHE MIGHT have a chance to find out more about Vail. That he had recognized her on sight had made her curious, even flattered. As far as she recalled, their eyes had never met in the year and a half they were in Detroit together. Now seemed like a good opportunity to find out why he remembered her.

Vail took the window seat without asking her preference, and by the time she got settled, he was sound asleep. He didn't wake up until the plane's tires chirped onto the tarmac at Dulles International. "Why are you looking at me like that, was I snoring?"

She smiled. "No, in fact for the first time today, you were perfect company."

"Is that how you like your men, unconscious?"

"My men? You make it sound like I collect scalps."

"Human beings are collectors by nature. Ownership, control. Breaching someone else's defenses. In one form or another, we all do it. It's part of the chase."

"Chase? What are we chasing?"

"That's what men—excuse me—men and women since Pythagoras have been trying to figure out."

"Pythagoras?"

"Yes, there were Greek philosophers before Socrates."

"The guy with the triangle?"

"The square of the hypotenuse. He believed that the soul was immortal. Do you think your soul is immortal?" Vail asked.

"Deputy assistant directors are not allowed to have souls."

"Or to collect scalps?"

"Actually that's a requirement."

He leaned close to her with mock intimacy. "Tell me something, Deputy Assistant Director Bannon, is that all I am to you—advancement?"

"Like you said, bricklayer, we all need something to chase."

THE DIRECTOR HAD given his secretary instructions to show Kate and Vail into his office as soon as they arrived. When they entered, Lasker was seated at his desk signing a stack of paperwork. Directly behind him stood Don Kaulcrick, taking each of the documents after it was signed and barely looking at them.

Lasker rose and offered Vail his hand. "Steve, thanks for coming, and on such short notice. This is one of our assistant directors, Don Kaulcrick." Vail shook Lasker's hand. The director waved Vail into a chair. "Your way of ending a hostage standoff is impressive."

"You'd think someone who did this job for a while would know better than to go inside a bank on Friday afternoon."

Lasker laughed. "Let me ask you something that's been

driving all of us around here nuts. After it was over, why did you just walk away?"

"I never really thought about it. But if it drove everyone nuts, especially around here, that's reward enough."

Lasker picked up a file that had Vail's name printed on the cover. "Is that a warning? In case you decide to help us."

"I would think after reading my personnel file that question would be unnecessary."

Lasker smiled. "I'm starting to understand why you were fired."

Vail laughed. "I can't see how it could have turned out any other way. It was a train wreck just waiting for the Bureau and me to be thrown in each other's way. No one especially wanted it, but at the same time no one cared enough to prevent it, most of all me. A bureaucracy has to have the ability to self-repair if it's going to be able to function. I've never done well knowing anyone has that kind of authority over me."

"So when you turned down a pass from OPR if you'd give up the ASAC, you weren't just being loyal?"

Vail turned to Kate. "I suppose Kent Wilson is an SAC somewhere by now."

"San Diego."

"Ah. At least they sent him to someplace with bad weather." He turned back to the director. "Let's just say I had other priorities."

"Like not letting a cop killer go free?"

Vail looked surprised, and Kate felt a small twinge of pleasure at uncovering something about Vail that he apparently hadn't wanted revealed. "I assumed that this command performance would be for some sort of more immediate problem."

"Sorry. Around here, constantly checking motives is necessary for survival. In that vein—while I know it's not necessary to say this to you—I have to ask that what you're about to hear not leave the room." Vail nodded. "You've heard about the 'Enemies of the FBI' murders."

"As much as I try to avoid the news, it'd be hard not to."

"Then I'm sure you know that a group calling itself the Rubaco Pentad is claiming credit for the killings. While they appear to be some sort of domestic terrorism group on a crusade, they have actually made large monetary demands to stop the murders."

"Who were they demanding it from?"

"The FBI."

"Not lacking confidence, are they? And you're not letting the public know about it because . . ."

"One of their demands is that if we do, they'll kill another prominent person. It's an ingenious tactic. Since we can't reveal their motives, it looks like we're the ones with the hidden agenda, as if it's just a matter of time before some vast governmental conspiracy is exposed. We're really handcuffed."

"I could see how you would be," Vail said. "Since I'm here, I assume things didn't go well at the drop."

"They turned it into a deadly obstacle course. It seemed like they didn't really want us to deliver the money. The agent making the delivery was shot to death."

"I assume the entire million wasn't in the money package?"

"Just a thousand dollars, and they left that at the scene."

"A warning that they'd be back," Vail said.

"Yes, it certainly was."

"Any decent leads come out of it?"

The director said, "Don, you've been handling that."

Kaulcrick said, "There was some scuba equipment used we're trying to trace, but it's almost impossible. And the prison was on a secure naval base, so we're in the process of finding out who's had access to it the last couple of months. It's literally thousands of people, so it could take forever."

"Sounds like somebody knows how to get you to burn manpower."

"Are you suggesting it's a waste of time?" Kaulcrick asked.

"Not at all. You never know what lead is going to be productive. But it sounds like they picked the base because the bigger and more complicated the location, the more time it takes to investigate. It seems that their major weapon is distraction. Leads like that need a lot of manpower but tend to never go anywhere."

"There's no question they know how to manipulate the investigation," Lasker said.

"So what happened at the second drop?" Vail said.

"Who said anything about a second drop?" Kaulcrick asked abruptly, glancing at Kate.

"The second and third murders did," Vail said. "Don, I'm here because I'm on your side."

"I have to apologize for everyone, Steve," Lasker said. "I've been so insistent that this not leak out, everyone has become paranoid about it. You've given your word and that's certainly good enough. What I'm about to tell you is even more sensitive." He then described the second demand letter along with its instruction for Bertok's role in the delivery of money. He detailed the route and the Bureau's inability to follow at an effective distance, and finally the disappearance of the agent and the two million dollars.

"So you want me to find Bertok."

"Yes. And should you recover the money, we wouldn't object."

"It couldn't have been an easy decision letting the full two million drive away."

"When you got the press holding you hostage twenty-four hours a day with the possibility of not stopping the next murder, it was a surprisingly easy call."

Vail became lost in thought. Kate waited a few seconds and then said, "I'm sure you've got a million questions."

"Nothing I need to waste everyone's time with right now. You haven't got the next demand letter yet, have you?"

"Not yet," Lasker said.

"Chances are the price will be going up. Do you think the delivery will be as difficult?"

"We hope not," the director said. "But I wouldn't bet on it."

Kaulcrick said, "We were hoping to identify them first."

"Any promising leads?"

Neither Kate nor Kaulcrick answered. Finally Lasker said, "Not really."

"That's too bad, but I guess it won't affect me finding Bertok, which, by the way, is not going to be easy."

Everyone was silent for a few seconds before the director said, "Actually the two problems may overlap. All three victims, and the agent at the drop, were killed with the same gun, a Glock model 22. That's the same model Bertok carried."

"There are thousands of those guns out there," Vail said. "Why would you think he could be involved?"

"Well, he was designated by name to make the drop, and whoever is doing this has a good knowledge of extortions, which Bertok worked. Plus he did disappear along with the money. I certainly hope he's not involved, but to be perfectly honest, we don't know."

"If it's him, why this last murder?"

Kaulcrick said, "In theory, he could be looking down the road for a defense. Why would he kill again if he already had the money? He's in law enforcement. He's used to seeing people getting caught when they thought they couldn't be. It's cheap insurance. Three murders or four, they can only give him the needle once."

"I guess it's possible, although that would take someone who is extremely cold—but I suppose two million dollars can get you to a lot of warm places," Vail said.

Lasker said, "So, Steve, will you help us?"

"If I agree, I have a couple of conditions."

"I'm certain we can work them out." The director opened a drawer, took out a black case with a gold FBI shield pinned to the outside, and slid it across the desk.

Vail opened the credentials and looked at his photo, which had been taken during new agents' training. "It's hard to believe I was ever that . . . *on board*." He closed the case and put it in his jacket pocket.

"Whether you find Bertok or not, I can make that permanent, with all the seniority, including the time you've been out of government service."

"I appreciate the offer, but it may be premature. I'm not here to find out if I can now be a good soldier. I know I can't. What you want me to do is difficult, which means, because of the methods I may find necessary, it's likely just a matter of time until you'll regret bringing me into this."

"Right now that's a chance I'm willing to take."

Vail smiled. "That's exactly what my last ASAC said to me."

The director forced a short laugh. "Okay, but if you don't want your job back, we'll have to pay you something. How about a percentage of any money recovered, or a flat amount for finding Bertok?"

"Which brings us back to the conditions. Two items. First, I'm sure at some point I'll have to get assistance from FBI field offices. Unless SACs have changed, they're not going to like taking orders from some imported street hump. So I'm going to need someone with enough capital letters in front of his—or *her*—name to make those guys nervous."

"Like Deputy Assistant Director Bannon?" Lasker said.

Vail looked at her. "How about it, Kate, think you can make the right men tremble?"

She felt herself starting to blush, but extinguished it with a sarcastic smirk. "Looks like *I'm* going to be the one taking orders from some imported street hump."

"And second?" the director asked.

"That I not be paid."

Confusion narrowed the director's eyes. "That doesn't make any sense."

Vail smiled. "If I'm being paid, sooner or later someone will consider me an employee and start giving me orders. We all know how that'll end. No, my payment is to not have to take orders from anyone. Maybe when we're done—if I'm successful—I'll add up my hours and you can pay me the hourly rate for a bricklayer."

"Then what's to prevent you from becoming a loose cannon?" Kaulcrick asked.

"Hopefully nothing."

"I have to tell you, I voted against bringing you into this," Kaulcrick said. "I'm sorry. There's enough confusion."

"If you keep being that honest, Don, you and I will survive. Even through the confusion."

Lasker said, "If you don't want anything more than a pittance, why would you take on something like this?"

Vail looked over at Kate. "Apparently, because I can."

SEVEN

VAIL SAT AT THE DESK IN HIS D.C. HOTEL ROOM READING FROM THE laptop computer Kate Bannon had given him. Everything from the Rubaco Pentad case, including crime-scene photos, lab reports, and surveillance logs, had been downloaded into it. For such a clandestine operation, an incredible amount of material had been reduced to writing. As he took another bite of the cold room-service hamburger, there was a knock at the door.

It was Kate. Although holding a briefcase with both hands in front of her, indicating her visit was official, she had changed clothes and was wearing a dress and heels. "Hi," she said, and walked in, looking around. "How's the room?"

"You've seen my apartment, how good does it have to be?"

"Good, good," she said distractedly. "Is there anything else you need?"

"What are you offering?" he said in a playful voice.

"Equipment, bricklayer, equipment. Like an agent's handbook or a pair of brass knuckles."

"I'm not the kind of person who thinks about his obituary, but I'd hate for it to read, 'He died because he brought a laptop to a gunfight.' "

"Okay, I'll get you a weapon," she said. "We'll need to get you to a firearms range to qualify."

"Do you really think there's time for that?"

"It's pretty much an unbreakable rule. You know, lawsuits."

"Isn't it my job to break rules?"

After a moment, she said, "Okay, I'll have it for you tomorrow. I've ordered up a Bureau plane. I assume we'll be flying to Las Vegas to try to pick up Bertok's trail."

"I was thinking more like L.A."

"Why L.A.?"

"I'm not exactly sure. Call it a hunch. And don't think that the Cubs having three games with the Dodgers this week has anything to do with it."

Kate studied Vail's face and found the same unreadable expression he presented when asked about anything he didn't want to answer. She was sure of one thing: his decision to start in Los Angeles had nothing to do with baseball or intuition. He had found some way to track Bertok that no one else had thought of. "You know this is going to be a lot easier if we don't keep secrets from each other."

"*Cosmo* says that a little mystery can keep a relationship from getting stale."

"There are only a few things in life that are unquestionable. That you've never read *Cosmopolitan* magazine is one of the most certain. Why L.A.?"

"First of all, it's about as far away from your boss as we can get. I know his type and I know my type. We've all seen how that movie ends."

"And second of all?"

"Simple math. How many times have each of the following locations come up in the case: New Hampshire, Pittsburgh, Utah, Arizona, and Las Vegas?"

"Once each."

"And Los Angeles?"

"I don't know, a half dozen?"

"Everything from the first victim to the postmarks on both demand letters to Bertok. Besides, I want to search his apartment again."

"Why?"

"The biggest mistake agents make is believing that because something was done once, it was done right." Kate nodded in agreement. "Now, what do we know about Stanley Bertok's personal life?" he asked.

"We've interviewed his supervisor. He described him as suffering from what he calls 'the dysfunctional twos.'"

"What's that?"

"Too much booze, too little money, and two ex-wives. He thinks Bertok may have seen an opportunity to downsize his problems and taken it."

"And psychologically?"

"Intelligent but brooding. No friends and not the world's most dedicated agent."

"But nothing to explain why our little band of terrorists picked him to make the drop. If they knew him well enough to ask for him, wouldn't they have to assume he was a risk to take off with the money?"

"Which leads us right back to him and the Pentad being one and the same, or at least being in it together."

"For something so well planned, this has some conspicuously dangling loose ends."

"Haven't you heard, there's no such thing as a perfect crime."

"Unfortunately, it doesn't have to be perfect to get away with it."

EXPLAINING TO KATE that he had been up the entire night reading the contents of the Rubaco Pentad file, Vail slept during the entire flight to Los Angeles. After they landed at one of the secure runways used by government planes coming into LAX, Kate had to wake him. As Vail stepped off the plane and into the blinding white light of the Southern California sun, he couldn't help but stretch himself against its silky warmth. The sky was a different blue than that of Chicago or even Washington. A thin band of gray-orange haze at the horizon separated it from the earth.

Parked a hundred feet away was a dark green sedan. A seemingly stoic man in his thirties wearing a tailored summer-weight suit was walking toward their plane. He had the practiced expression of someone whose first priority was that of confident congeniality, suggesting he was part of the office management team. He came up to Kate and offered his hand. "Allen Sabine," he said. Kate took his hand and introduced him to Vail. The two men shook hands. Sabine's dark hair had been carefully cut, and he stood with a practiced slouch that angled his face away to mask a long, sharp nose. He tried to take her bag, but she smiled graciously and said she needed the exercise. Sabine pointed at the sedan. "This is the vehicle we rented for you while you're here. It has the GPS navigational system you requested. We also put in a complete set of maps for most of Southern California. The SAC is available to meet with you anytime this morning."

"Okay," Kate said, "let's get it over with." She said to Vail, "The SAC is Mark Hildebrand. Ever run into him?"

"I don't think so."

"He seems okay, a little territorial on the phone when I told him we were coming out."

"Territorial's not all bad. Maybe he actually cares about what happens in his division."

"You're irritatingly positive after your nap."

"Sorry. Give me a few minutes with him, and I'm sure I'll be as good as new."

They got in the car, Kate in the front and Vail in the back. She handed him a Glock model 22 encased in a holster, with two extra clips. Then with just enough ceremony to be sarcastic, she handed him an operation manual for the weapon. "I thought you should at least know how to load it."

"You could have given me this before we took off."

"You were asleep. Plus, I was curious whether you'd ask for it, and since you haven't been checked out, I didn't want you practicing your quick draw on the plane and accidentally shooting me or the pilot."

"I would have been careful not to shoot you. I can imagine the paperwork involved." She handed him a credit card and then a cell phone. "Speaking of paperwork, don't I need to sign for all this?"

She lowered her voice. "After your little speech to the director about it being just a matter of time until you ran amok, I thought it would be better if none of these items were traceable to you, or more important, us."

"Sometimes you scare me."

"If only that were true."

They were now proceeding north on the 405. The traffic was heavy, so they moved in and out of bottlenecks. When an opening presented itself, everyone drove as fast as possible. Vail couldn't help but notice that the cars were in remarkable condition. The vast majority of them had no fading of paint, no rust, not even dirt. It was a different world; even the highway was clean and perfectly landscaped. The few pedestrians he had seen from the freeway were jogging or biking, wearing the minimum of clothing. Like everything else in Southern California, there seemed to be a subliminal theme of eternal youth, or at least its quest.

Sabine said, "I guess the reason I was sent to pick you up is that I'm Stan Bertok's supervisor. At least I was. So fire away."

Before Kate could say anything, Vail said, "*Was?*"

"Well, I guess technically I still am, but I seriously doubt he's just going to walk in one of these mornings, sit down at his desk, and go to work."

"I suppose not," Vail said.

She said, "Tell us about him."

"He wasn't—isn't—much of an agent, at least from my standpoint. Everything he did I had to keep a close eye on. He was a pretty heavy drinker. I got a call one night from the LAPD; they had stopped him driving drunk. I had to go down and drive him home. And he has some financial problems. A couple of ex-wives will do that, I guess. And I get a call occasionally from bill collectors."

"Do you think he took off with the money?" Vail asked.

"I don't want to convict the guy in absentia, but if he didn't, where is he?"

"So if he took the money, you wouldn't be shocked?" Kate said.

"I suppose not."

"Where do you think the Pentad got his name?"

"I have no idea."

When they got to the office, Sabine led them to the special agent in charge's office. "Boss, this is Deputy Assistant Director Kate Bannon and . . . I'm sorry."

"Steve Vail," Kate said before Vail could answer.

The SAC was tall and trim with a dark tan. His thick blond hair peaked low across his forehead, and he was wearing a medium-blue shirt with a contrasting white collar. The cuffs, also white, were set off by large gold cuff links.

He shook Kate's hand first. "Mark Hildebrand. We spoke on the phone." He repeated his name when he shook hands with Vail. "Please, have a seat." He instructed Sabine to shut the door as he left.

Kate watched Vail examining Hildebrand before saying anything. "Mark, we appreciate your letting us come in here and run this operation. The director has all the confidence in the world in you and your division; it's just that this case is running from coast to coast, and he feels it's best if we chase it, you know, for continuity."

"What exactly is it that I can do for you, Kate?"

Vail said, "We need to search Stan Bertok's apartment discreetly."

Hildebrand was surprised at the presumptive authority in Vail's voice. He looked at Kate, but she exhibited no interest in asserting herself. "I'm sorry, Steve, you didn't say where you worked. Are you with OPR?"

"A man can only dream. No, I'm just the deputy's gun bearer on this."

Hildebrand stared at Vail, trying to get a better read on him. Kate broke the silence. "Is there a problem, Mark?"

"No, it's just that we've already searched the apartment—with a warrant. With all that's going on, we're being overly judicious. I don't see what searching it again will accomplish."

"Look at it this way," Vail said, "when we don't find anything, you can say 'I told you so.'"

"Somehow I don't think you believe that," the SAC said, still trying to figure out the source of Vail's authority.

Kate said, "Mark, we've been exposed to a completely different set of facts in this case than your agents. We'll see it from a different angle. Or if you prefer, call it a lack of imagination. If you think we're second-guessing you, I apologize, but we're going to need to take another look."

Kate could see that Hildebrand resented being told what to do in his own backyard, and liked it even less that he had no choice. Vail had been right about the resistance he would receive, especially with his seemingly intentional lack of tact. The SAC grinned artificially. "We can use the same AUSA, Tye Delson."

Kate said, "Mark, I know I don't have to say this, but the

last thing we need right now is someone leaking this to the press. This Delson, we can trust him, right?"

"*Her.* And yes, you can. Unfortunately she's leaving the United States attorney's office soon. Too bad, too. You just can't find prosecutors like her anymore. The agents here love her. She's invited to more of our parties than I am. She'll probably have your warrant in a couple of hours. She's already got all the boilerplate from the first search, and she knows the right judge to get it signed in case the probable cause isn't as clear-cut as they'd like."

"We'll want the affidavit sealed," Kate said.

"That's what she did before. Do you have time to go see her now?" Kate nodded and Hildebrand picked up the phone. After a brief conversation, he hung up. "She's in her office. I told her you're on the way."

Vail asked, "Do you have a good lock man here?"

"Why?" the SAC asked, and Kate could tell by the intentional flatness in his voice that he intended to question anything Vail requested from now on.

"We still want to do this quietly, probably in the wee hours of the morning," Vail said.

"We will get you in."

Kate and Vail stood up, and she shook hands with the SAC. "We appreciate the help, Mark. I'll let you know how we do."

Once outside the SAC's office, Kate said, "Boy, you and management, talk about a match made in heaven. How did you last three years?"

EIGHT

TYE DELSON OFFERED KATE AND VAIL A SEAT IN HER CRAMPED OFFICE. Although there were overhead lights, the only illumination came from a small brass lamp on her desk. The assistant United States attorney was slender and wore a long midcalf black dress that failed to reveal a single curve. Her hair was dark brown and cut short, framing her face symmetrically. Her skin could have been described as flawless if it hadn't been for its ghostly lack of color. Her lipstick was a waxy brown-red, which Vail thought an unflattering choice. She wore glasses and was one of those rare women who were more attractive because of them. Her eyes were overly made up, which, coupled with the magnification of the glasses, made them appear to be oversized, like one of those Keane paintings of innocent but somehow damaged children. And they had a quick intelligence about them that was almost lost because of a vague nervousness that flickered through them. Her voice, however, was perfectly confident, allaying any fear that she might not be up to the rigors of hacking her way through the legal mazes necessary to put men or women in federal prison.

Vail noticed a framed quote by Martin Luther on her wall: *Each lie must have seven lies if it is to resemble the truth and adopt truth's aura.* "I don't think I've ever seen that before."

Tye said, "This is a business of lies. The police lie to suspects to get them to confess, and defense attorneys lie to juries to . . . well, because that's what they get paid to do."

"And prosecutors?"

"We're the biggest liars of all. We tell ourselves that we're making a difference," she said. "Sorry. I know how cynical that sounds. That's a big part of the reason I'm leaving the United States attorney's office. I'm thinking about practicing real estate law, where lying is not only assumed, it's profitable."

Instead of seating herself behind the desk, she spun her chair around and sat on the windowsill, using the seat for her feet. Vail could see it was a technique that had been used before, and he appreciated that someone who had attained the lofty position of assistant United States attorney had developed the courtesy of not "holding court" across her desk with those who had come for her help. She pulled the window up a couple of inches and lit an unfiltered cigarette, inhaling deeply, the paper pulling at her thin lips with a surprising sensuality.

"I know, I know, all federal buildings are smoke-free. Forgive me my one vice. Well, my one admitted vice." She grinned a little self-consciously. "So you want another warrant for Stan Bertok's apartment. Can I assume the search for him isn't going well?"

"You can," Kate said. "And we want to go in after midnight."

"It'll take a little more probable cause, but it seems like

a prudent approach. I've got the basics from the other warrants. What exactly do I list as the object of your search?"

"Two million in cash," Vail said.

Tye laughed with an erotic huskiness, apparently the byproduct of her "one vice." "Wouldn't that be nice. Something tells me that even Stan Bertok would be a little more discreet than that."

"So you know him," Vail said.

"We've had a couple of cases together."

"What did you think of him?"

"I don't know how accurate any of my judgments might be in hindsight."

"No one's keeping score. We're just trying to find him," Vail said.

"Fair enough. Well, he was a guy who seemed to be mailing it in, you know, as if his mind was someplace a lot darker. He was always wired—no, that's the wrong word. It was more like he was ready to explode. Maybe a closet depressive. He'd go off in a corner at parties and pound down the liquor. If someone tried to keep him from driving home, he'd want to fight them. He got the reputation of being a mean drunk, but I think it went deeper than that."

The use of the noun "depressive" struck Vail as an overly clinical choice of words and caused him to wonder what made her so familiar with psychological problems. "Were you surprised when he disappeared with the money?"

"To tell you the truth, I was more surprised he accepted the assignment without protest. After all, the last agent was shot to death, right? Stan was not a team guy. And he certainly wasn't looking for any medals."

"So you weren't surprised he vanished with the money?"

"Are you sure he did?"

"Is that the old 'innocent until proven guilty'?"

"That's the old 'as soon as you give me some proof I'll be glad to hang him,' but in the meantime . . ."

"Is he a smart guy?"

"Do you mean, to stay one step ahead of you, or was he smart enough to put this extortion together?"

"Both."

She stared into Vail's eyes and let her voice drop a half octave. "Actually, I don't know how hard you are to stay ahead of, but measuring him against everybody else around here, it wouldn't be that difficult."

When Vail smiled in response, Kate interrupted. "And the extortion?"

"The one thing I've learned on this job is never to underestimate a man's capacity for evil. Even a *good* man's."

"And a woman's?" Vail asked.

Her mouth shifted to one side artfully. "Men are mere amateurs by comparison."

"What about him being a murderer?" Kate asked. "Did he have enough evil in him for that?"

"I know the press is trying to intimate that agents may be involved in these murders, but that's just today's journalism. I would find it hard to believe that any agent could do that. But then every time a serial killer is caught, invariably the next-door neighbor is on the news saying what a nice guy he was. That's not why you want this search warrant, is it? For murder evidence?"

"We wouldn't want to exclude any possibility. If we did and missed something, we'd be crucified later," Kate said. "Especially with this 'Enemies of the FBI' thing gaining momentum."

"If you're going to gather evidence that could be used in a murder trial, the probable cause for your search warrant has to be one hundred percent accurate. This is the first legal step to that end, and as such has to be carefully vetted. The fruit of the poisonous tree falls from this point forward. Keeping that in mind, what evidence do you have indicating that Agent Bertok is involved in these murders?"

Vail said, "Disregarding supposition, the only link is that he was issued the same make and model of gun that was used in the murders, as were thousands of other agents."

"So nothing," Tye said.

Vail said, "We were told that 'nothing' is usually not a problem for you."

She took a last drag on her cigarette and flipped it out the window. She stood up and closed it. "Let's simplify everything. We won't accuse him of anything. I assume he has certain items in his possession—credentials, gun, handcuffs—which were issued to him. Since he has abandoned his job, and his whereabouts are unknown, the government needs to recover its property. Possibly he has returned to his apartment since his disappearance and left them behind."

"Impressive. Nothing up your sleeve and—poof—a search warrant. It's nice having a legal magician on our side for a change," Vail said.

"Only for a month or so, so abuse away. But both of you remember, there is no magic, just illusion, and with that goes the magician's oath."

"Which is?"

"Never reveal how it's done."

"Believe me, there's no one more qualified to keep illusions secret than an FBI agent," Kate said.

"Good," Tye said. "So now anything found incidental to the search of the missing agent's apartment will be admissible in court, provided you don't overstep the limits of the warrant."

"Such as?" Kate asked.

"If you're looking for an automobile, you can't go looking in dresser drawers."

"Credentials could fit almost anywhere," Kate said.

"Nice how that works out, isn't it?" Tye said.

"Then we're all set?" Vail said.

"There's one small problem. Because the purpose of the search warrant is so routine, and his apartment is apparently abandoned, there's no justification for a nighttime entry. But a suggestion—sunrise is a little after five thirty, which is a time when most of his fellow apartment dwellers will be deep in REM sleep."

THE ONLY SOUND in the dimly lit hallway was the metallic scratching of Tom Demick's lock picks as he raked the tumblers of Stanley Bertok's door lock. Vail had been surprised by the technical agent's appearance when he had been introduced to him. His hair and full beard were pure white and made him look much older than his fifty-one years. He was stocky with a belly that hung amply over his belt. Vail supposed that because he didn't look like anyone's preconceived notion of a clandestine-operations agent, it gave him the perfect cover should he be interrupted. Demick's hands, especially his fingers, were thick and stubby, like those of a second- or third-generation fisherman or some other occupation that required digital strength and leverage rather than quick dexterity. However, they worked precisely with no wasted motion. It took less than three minutes before Demick straightened up and carefully rotated the lock cylinder open. He looked at Kate to see if she needed anything else. She gave him a silent salute of thanks, and he lumbered off toward the rear parking lot.

Vail opened the door and stepped in quickly. Kate followed him, and while he locked the dead bolt, she placed a copy of the search warrant on the rickety kitchen table. There was still a copy of the first one executed by Los Angeles agents almost a week and a half earlier.

The one-bedroom apartment was sparsely furnished, and although its occupant hadn't been there for a while, the acrid stink of cigarette smoke was still in the air. On a table next to a threadbare sofa was an answering machine; alongside it sat an ashtray with half a dozen butts in it. Kate handed Vail a pair of evidence gloves.

Although the light wasn't blinking, the display on the answering machine showed three messages that had been heard previously but not erased. Vail hit the Play button and listened as one of Bertok's ex-wives threatened him, in a routine voice, about his child-support payment being late again. The second message was the same woman not so patiently demanding an immediate call. The last one was someone who identified himself as Josh and asked for a call back. Kate said, "That's probably his brother in Minnesota."

Vail picked the handset out of the cradle and turned it over. A small screen on the back of it revealed an Incoming Calls button. He pushed it and scrolled through the numbers. "612 area code. That sound like Minnesota?"

"I think so," Kate said. "He's been interviewed, and we're pulling his toll calls once a week just in case."

Vail continued to scan the missed calls. He took out a small notebook and started writing the numbers down. "This is interesting. Do we know what time Bertok disappeared?"

"Not exactly. I don't think anyone noted the exact minute that the car stopped moving. It was a little before three o'clock in the afternoon on the seventeenth."

"There's a bunch of incoming calls on the day of the drop, all from the same number. It looks like they were calling every fifteen minutes or so. The last one was at two thirty-eight P.M. Whoever it was never left a message."

Kate walked over to Vail. "What's the number?"

"It's a 310 area code. Wait, I've seen this number." He flipped through his notebook. "It's the cell phone Bertok was given to take along on the drop and was left behind with the tracking devices. He was calling his own phone."

"To check his messages."

"I suppose it could have been routine, bored with the drive or nervous about what he was about to be put through."

"Is calling every fifteen minutes routine?" She looked

at Vail, who shrugged his shoulders. "Let's assume for a minute that he had intended to steal the money. If he was calling that frequently, maybe it had something to do with his plans to get away."

"Maybe."

Kate went back to searching the drawers in the kitchen while Vail finished noting the calls. When Kate was finished, she said, "You done in here?"

"All set. Let's search the bedroom. Nine out of ten times, that's where the goods are found," he said.

"That sounds very Freudian."

"Who knew more about human beings hiding stuff than Freud?"

They went into the small bedroom, and while he looked under the mattress, Kate started searching the slim dresser. He said, "I've got the bathroom." After pulling back the shower curtain, he checked the medicine cabinet. Other than shaving material, toothpaste, and aspirin, it was empty. The sink was set in a white vanity. He pulled open the single door and saw that it was empty. He started to leave when he noticed the side of the vanity. On the edge along the wall were faint gray smudges arranged in a pattern as if fingertips had left them. He forced his fingers into the crack between the cabinet and the wall, pulling it out about six inches. Wedged in an unfinished cavity of the wall was an accordion file with an elastic band around it. He took it into the bedroom and sat down to open it.

"What's that?" Kate asked.

"The goods. Apparently Freud was wrong." Inside were a dozen documents of differing sizes. Shuffling through them, he took out a metal document seal press and a writing tablet, both of which he handed to her. She flipped open the cover on the tablet. There was nothing written inside, but two-thirds of the top page was precisely torn off. And it was blue. "My God," she said, staring at the tablet.

"What is it?"

She turned the torn, blank page toward Vail. "I guess you were right about doing things a second time." The size, color, and texture of the blue writing paper were identical to those of the neatly torn pieces used for the Pentad notes. She looked back at Vail, who continued to go through the documents methodically. She had learned not to expect any type of reaction from him, but she was amazed that even this piece of evidence didn't seem to excite him.

The top four sheets of paper Vail now had in his hands were blank applications for a U.S. passport. The next was a Florida birth certificate. The name at the top had been carefully whitened out, and the name "Ruben Aznar" had been typed over it. Under the document were three more full-size copies that, through the careful use of a copying machine, had eliminated any evidence of the Wite-Out. Vail felt the seal embossed into the bottom of the page and then held it up to the light to read the raised letters. He turned over one of the documents and pressed the metal seal into a blank space. Holding it up at an angle, he said, "That's what I thought. It's not the Florida state seal. It's a notary public for the county of Los Angeles. Unless you really look at it, you think it's a certified original document." There were a half-dozen copies of the birth certificate and an application for a Florida driver's license with a Miami address.

"How long did Bertok know about the drop before he flew to Phoenix?"

Kate said, "I'm not sure, maybe two days. Would that have been enough time to get all this together?"

"I suppose if you know the right people. Most agents working criminal cases do."

"If this is the blue paper used in the notes, the lab should be able to match it." Still Vail showed no reaction. "Why do you think he chose Miami?"

"He's got two million dollars in hundred-dollar bills and knows the serial numbers have been recorded. He needs to get it dry-cleaned. With Miami's drug history, it's not exactly a stranger to that type of transaction. Plus, it's the gateway to the Caribbean, Cayman Islands, Panama, the Bahamas, Netherlands Antilles, and a half-dozen other governments specializing in laundering money and helping Americans evade taxes. Between the secrecy of the banking laws and the individual governments' interests in keeping the United States out of their business, I'd say it's a high-probability destination."

"This looks like the break we've been looking for. You don't seem very fired up about this."

"We've found a few pieces of paper, nothing more."

"Excuse me for getting excited, but if you had been on this from the beginning, this would look like the Second Coming of Christ," she said. "Are we done here? I've got to get the Miami office on this."

"Can you pack everything up while I take one last look around?" Vail asked. "I want to check all the nooks and crannies."

Kate reached over on the bed and pulled the lone pillow out of its case and then started to fill it carefully with the cache of evidence. "Look who's been promoted to gun bearer."

He smiled. "The death of chauvinism has been greatly exaggerated."

"And they say all the really great pickup lines have been used."

"I assume you'll get this hand-carried back to the lab."

"I will. What'll you be doing?"

"I'll try to get the United States attorney's office to authorize a pen register on this phone in case Bertok starts calling for messages again."

Kate hadn't considered using the device. It would list all the activity on Bertok's line including incoming calls that might be traced back to him. "And if they won't authorize it?" she asked.

"Then I'll have to."

"FIND ANY *Bureau property*?" Tye Delson asked.

"You know," Vail said, "this would be a lot easier if we didn't have to read between each other's lines."

"So you want to know if I'm a stand-up gal."

"I guess that's what I'm asking."

"Do you know why lawyers follow the rules, Steve? It's not that they believe in them—in fact their biggest weakness is probably that they feel rules don't exactly apply to them. No, they follow the rules simply because they've seen too many people get caught who didn't. I have this fairly well-researched idea that at some point in their life, every sociopath dreams of going to law school. Unfortunately, too many of them get through."

"Are you calling yourself a sociopath?"

"We're all sociopaths. The only variable is whether we control it or it controls us. What I'm saying is that I don't need to follow all the rules all the time. And I can keep a secret if it's for the greater good, but at the same time I don't want to be given up by someone who pledged allegiance and then got faint at the sight of his own blood."

"Just because I'm hanging around with a deputy assistant director doesn't mean I want to be one."

"The little bit I've been around you, you're not like any of the other agents I've worked with. You have an obvious disregard for protocol, almost like you don't work for the government. How long have you been on the job?"

Vail looked at his watch. "Almost two days."

"Meaning this isn't your first time around."

"I used to be an agent. Years ago."

"And now they've rehired you?"

"More or less. Just for this case."

"You must be quite a guy. What is it that makes you so valuable?"

"I don't get faint at the sight of my own blood."

She laughed. "Then it appears we have the makings of a grand conspiracy. What did you find at Bertok's apartment?"

Vail told her about the hidden folder containing the identification documents in the name Ruben Aznar.

"That alias is a good choice for the Miami area. It's vague

enough where it could be either Hispanic or some other unidentifiable origin because Bertok does not look Latin."

"We found another potential lead. On his phone's incoming calls. Just before they lost contact with him during the drop, he called his apartment from a cell phone. It looks like he was checking his messages."

"Any idea for what?"

"Coupled with those Miami documents, we're hoping travel arrangements or some contact to launder the money. But those aren't necessarily high-percentage guesses."

"Does that mean you think this entire thing is his doing?"

"No stone unturned, counselor."

"It's hard to believe that an agent could be behind all this."

"We're open to alternate theories," Vail said.

"I know the evidence is piling up, but still."

"Either way, we've got to find him. I was thinking about a pen register on his apartment phone. If he was checking for some critical message, maybe he'll call again and we can track him that way. A long shot, but at this point everything is."

"I understand that you've been out of the Bureau for a while, but pen registers take a mountain of paperwork, and probable cause. And it's getting worse every time I turn around. I have a feeling that you're a person who could find alternative means."

"All right, we never talked about this."

"Did you forget, Steve? I can keep my mouth shut."

"Just trying to keep the list to a minimum."

"What list?"

"The one entitled 'Also Named in the Indictment.' "

WHEN VAIL GOT back to the FBI office, he was directed to a room that had been set up for Kate while she was in Los Angeles. The door was closed and he could hear her on the phone. He knocked twice and walked in. "Yes, sir, he just came in. I'll call you back." She hung up. "That was the director. They've just received another demand letter. . . ."

Vail could see the concern in her eyes. "And?"

"Three million dollars. He wants you to make the drop."

NINE

KATE STOOD OFF TO THE SIDE, NOT WANTING TO BE NOTICED AS she watched Vail. They were in the L.A. FBI's major-case room. Tom Demick, the tech agent who had so deftly opened Bertok's apartment door, was taping a microphone wire to Vail's bare chest. He looked over at her briefly and rolled his eyes in silent prediction that the Pentad's ingenuity during the first two drops had already rendered the predictable device a waste of time. She smiled back obligingly and continued to search his face and body language for any sign of fear. His hands hung loosely at his side as Demick clipped the radio's body into the back of his waistband. Vail turned back toward her, and she could see his heart beating against the lean muscle of his chest. She timed it—about forty beats a minute. She thought about the moment he had been asked to make the drop, even though West had died and Bertok had disappeared; he had shown no surprise or apprehension, almost as if he had expected it.

Vail leaned closer to the tech agent. "Did you get the pen register on Bertok's phone?" he asked quietly.

"It's up and running. I'm checking it as often as I can. Other than the ex-wife and brother, you want to be notified of any calls, right?"

Abruptly the door opened. The SAC, Mark Hildebrand, walked in and stepped to the side to allow Assistant Director Don Kaulcrick to pass. Kate and Vail looked at each other. Neither of them had any idea he was coming.

The two men were followed by three other people, one a female agent. She had in her hand one of two straps that were connected to a large canvas bag. A male agent, who stood well over six feet tall and was powerfully built, held the other. They both had on suit coats which rode up over holstered handguns and spare magazine pouches. Evidently the three million dollars had arrived.

The other man was older, almost completely bald, and dressed in a pair of slacks and a golf shirt. There was an air of confidence about him. He was carrying a large brown leather carryall the size of a small suitcase. Demick introduced everyone as Vail pulled on his shirt and buttoned it. The older man in casual clothing was a technical agent from headquarters and was introduced only as "Bob." He asked Vail, "You're making the drop?"

Vail looked at the athletic-looking agent holding the bag and then at Kaulcrick. "Unless the assistant director knows something I don't."

"You're making the drop, Steve. But as a matter of fact I do know a little something that might change the way we're going to do this." Kaulcrick pulled a folded document from his coat pocket. "The lab has matched not only the paper from the pad you and Kate found hidden in Bertok's bathroom to the last Pentad note, but its torn edge as well."

"Then this is all Bertok," Kate said.

"That seems like a fairly safe bet."

Vail said, "So the money is just a way to catch him."

"Can you think of a better way for us to get our hands on him?" Kaulcrick said.

"Does this mean we can go public if we catch Bertok?" Kate asked.

"The director, being a former federal judge, doesn't want to take anything for granted. If we gave a big, splashy news release, the Pentad might kill someone else just to remain in character. If there is a Pentad beyond Bertok. Plus the demand note is very specific should anything go wrong. But let's not worry about that until we get him into custody." Kaulcrick handed Vail a sheet of paper. "This is a copy to keep with you."

FBI,

Your agent's greed has complicated everything, so contingencies have become necessary. If you fail to deliver $3M, the sum will be increased to $5M, and that would mean we owe you two more bodies. Two prominent D.C. area newspeople have been selected. As before, should any of this find its way to the media, there will be two less of them to write about it.

34.344 N 118.511W *at 7:17 P.M. on September 2. Look in the sub.*

No guns. No cell phones.

The Rubaco Pentad

"So I am going to drop the full three million?" Vail asked.

"Again, the director doesn't want to take any chances, so yes. Make the drop, and the agents covering you will take care of grabbing Bertok."

Vail looked at the headquarters tech agent and pointed to his bag. "Is there something in there for me?"

"Because of what happened in the past, we want to be overly cautious. That transmitter you've got on has a GPS capability, but I've brought two other items for you to carry in case they try to render the primary transmitter inoperable. The first time a river was used to neutralize it. Who knows what it'll be this time." From his case, he took out what looked like a wallet. "This is also a GPS transmitter, very new, very micro. If you're patted down, it looks and feels just like a wallet. It'll tell us exactly where you are at all times. And it's waterproof." Vail took out his own wallet and handed it to Kate, and then put the transmitter in the same back pocket. "Also, we used canvas to fabricate the moneybag because of its thickness. There's an overlapping seam at the bottom that's hiding another GPS, which has the same microtechnology as the wallet. It's even thinner because it doesn't need the leather to disguise it. The hope is that because this bag weighs almost seventy pounds, the bad guys won't be picking it up over their heads to check the bottom. Even if they do, it's extremely difficult to detect." He reached into the side pockets of the bag and took out three items: an underwater flashlight, a knife with a regular blade and an equally long saw blade, and a low-light monocular.

"What's with the knife?" Vail asked.

"If nothing else, it's a backup weapon. The letter said

no guns. We thought we'd include one with the saw blade because who knows what you're going to run into. It was developed for clandestine military units."

Vail snapped the flashlight on and off and opened both knife blades. He took his own lock-back knife out of his pocket and handed it to Kate. Opening the mason's knife and seeing its honed sharpness, she said, "I'm surprised you thought you needed a gun."

Vail was reading the demand note and didn't appear to hear her. "Is that 'sub' as in submarine?" he asked.

Tom Demick pulled out a map and laid it on a desk as everyone gathered around. "We've reconned the area only by satellite and map. Didn't want to go stumbling around there with GPSs. It's in West Hollywood. As close as we can figure, it's this clear area right here between Lucas Avenue, South Toluca Street, and Beverly Boulevard. There's no water or submarines around there, but I'll keep working on it."

Kate said, "Seven seventeen is the exact minute of sunset, so you will be working in the dark."

"I'll hope that's not a metaphor."

"This is the FBI—everything's a metaphor."

VAIL LAY HIDDEN in the tall grass between two overgrown shrubs that were against a ten-foot-high chain-link fence. It surrounded a huge vacant lot. According to his wallet GPS, he was still about a hundred yards short of the exact West Hollywood coordinates given in the demand note. He had crawled as far forward as he could. Using the low-light monocular, he searched the area in front of him. When he radioed the information to the major-case room and the covering surveillance cars, he heard Kaulcrick's voice. "What's inside the fence?"

"Nothing I can see worth protecting. It looks like a giant vacant lot, maybe the size of one and a half football fields but shaped like a triangle."

"Do you see anything inside?"

"Nothing."

"Can you get in?"

"There's barbed wire coiled all along the top as far as I can see. But the ground inside is not overgrown, so the kids around here probably have a way in and use it to play ball. I guess it's time to let whoever's waiting see me." Vail tucked the monocular into the moneybag, which he hoisted onto his shoulder once he stood up. He started skirting the fence. About sixty yards from where he had parked the car, next to a small footpath that had been worn through the underbrush, he found a hole in the chain link that had been snipped away from the post. He reported what he had found on the radio. "Hold on, Vail, we're trying to get a satellite picture of the area," Demick said.

Technology, while providing remarkable advantages to law enforcement, had a crippling side. It could make investigators lazy, keeping them from remaining flexible. Vail was worried that the agents surveilling him were finding it much easier to track him through the GPS monitors in the major-case room than trying to follow him through the dark, irregular terrain. And those were the kinds of vulnerabilities that the Pentad somehow understood and exploited. He pulled back the corner of the fence, pushed the bag in ahead, and squeezed through.

He took out the wallet GPS again to check his position. The destination coordinates had been locked in and an arrow on the screen pointed toward a thirty-foot rise in the ground still almost a hundred yards ahead. He picked up the bag and started toward it. The radio's earpiece crackled with Tom Demick's voice. "I think I've figured out where you're going. I should have thought of it before when I heard Toluca Street. It's the Toluca portal to the old Pacific Electric Railway. I pulled it up on the Internet. It stopped running in the fifties. It used trolley cars. The kind that had the poles that reached up to the overhead electric lines. You're at the beginning of a mile-long tunnel that was built to circumvent traffic back then, but both ends were sealed off years ago. Located at your end is Substation 51. That's got to be the 'sub' in the note."

"Very nice, Tom. I'm on my way."

One of the surveillance teams came up on the radio. "Command, this is One-three, we're at the fence, and it doesn't look like we can follow the package without being made. The terrain is too open."

Vail answered, "I'm good here. The last thing we want is to get burned. I'll let you know if I need anything."

"Copy," One-three answered.

In the major-case room, Kate looked at Kaulcrick. "I don't like this."

"Uncertainty is exactly what Bertok wants. Quit worrying. Vail wanted to do this. We've got him surrounded. It has to be far enough away that we won't be made. We're in far better shape than that debacle in New Hampshire. And we've got three monitors up here, each one tracking the different GPSs. Nothing can go wrong."

Vail's voice interrupted. "I'm at the substation. It's a small square building, every inch covered with graffiti." Involuntarily, his hand went to where his gun should have been, but then he remembered he wasn't armed. "Let's go to radio silence until I see what's inside." He carefully stepped up onto the landing in front of the door and then moved against a wall as he listened. He couldn't hear anything. He peeked inside.

Three glowsticks formed an arrow like he had read about in the naval-prison report. Next to it were two others holding down a sheet of paper. The room was otherwise empty. He went in and picked up the note. Underneath it was a walkie-talkie with the transmission key soldered into a permanent transmission position. The extortionists were now listening to him. He read the note:

> **Do not transmit one more word on your radio. Take this radio, clip it to your belt, and leave yours here. Follow the arrow.**

After carefully folding the note and putting it in his pocket, Vail opened his shirt and peeled the microphone from his chest, pulling the Bureau radio from his waistband. He dropped it loudly on the floor so the extortionist's radio could hear it being discarded and then attached their radio to his belt. That answered the question why they didn't want him to bring a cell phone—it could be used for silent text-messaging.

The arrow was glued to a couple of rocks. It pointed toward the sealed entrance of the railroad tunnel. But the rocks used seemed to have a secondary direction. Their difference in height also made the arrow rise, almost as if it was pointing to the top of the tunnel. Vail stepped out of the building and stood still for a moment, making sure the satellites could once again lock onto the two remaining GPSs. He started walking slowly toward the entrance to the tunnel.

"Steve, what's happening?" Kate said into the mike. "Steve?"

"Something must have happened to his radio," said the agent watching the monitor for the GPS on his body transmitter. "Even though he's moving away from the substation, the monitor shows the radio's still in the building."

The headquarters tech agent had been hovering between all three monitors and said, "They must have had him take it off and leave it there. It's okay. That's why we gave him two backups. They're still working fine."

"But we can't communicate with him," Kate said.

Kaulcrick spoke into the radio mike. "One-one, do your people have the area surrounded?"

"As best we can without getting too close."

"Just make sure if he leaves that fenced-off area, he can't get by you."

"I don't like this," Kate said again. "At each turn, we're losing more control."

Vail had reached the mouth of the tunnel. The arched entrance was an almost perfect half circle about twenty feet high. It had been sealed up with cinder block and coated with a concrete plaster. Like the substation, it shimmered electrically with graffiti of all colors in the low light.

The glowstick arrow in the substation indicated that Vail was supposed to go to the top of the opening. Around the left side of the entrance was a small pathway up the steep grade. It ran between the huge concrete frame of the tunnel and the chain-link fence. He shifted the heavy bag more toward the middle of his back and maneuvered up the thirty-degree grade. At the top of the structure, he started walking, following the tunnel's spine along its mile-long length, looking for the next instruction.

Seventy-five yards farther he found another glowstick, attached to a small metal door in the ground. It appeared to be a hatch for maintenance workers if access became necessary to work on the electrical lines that ran along the tunnel's ceiling. A rusty padlock that had secured the hatch had been cut and lay next to it. The thick metal door was ajar. Judging by the piles of dirt and stone around it, the entrance had been covered over and somehow the extortionists had found it and dug it out.

Under the glowstick was another note.

Remove the other tracking device and leave it next to the opening. Then take the money and enter the tunnel.
Do not use lights—tunnel rigged with explosives and photocell trigger.

Once again, the Pentad had anticipated more than one tracking device. Vail took out the low-light monocular and scanned the surrounding area to determine if any of the surveillance agents were close enough to observe where he was going. He couldn't see any.

Down inside the hatch were individual U-shaped ladder rungs that were anchored into the concrete wall. Below them, another glowstick arrow sat flat on the floor, pointing toward the remaining mile of the tunnel. Vail then used the monocular to look more closely at the floor of the tunnel. He could see small glints of light surrounding the luminescent marker. Taking a handful of pebbles that had been cleared from around the hatch, he tossed them in as long a pattern as possible. The sound of stone plinking off metal echoed lightly from below. He refocused the monocular to get a better look and could now see that the floor was booby-trapped with long nails hammered up through boards.

Vail wondered if it was a bluff that the tunnel was rigged to explode. The glowsticks wouldn't give off enough light to trigger a photocell, so he had no choice but to assume it was true. The one thing that was certain was they wanted him to proceed in the dark. Was it so he would jump down onto the punji boards? Or was there another reason?

He eased the GPS wallet out of his back pocket and set it down carefully to mark where he was last aboveground for the surveillance teams. Then he lowered the bag through the hatch ahead of him and started down the metal rungs. Once he was completely clear of the hatch, he pulled both straps of the bag over his head so they sat cross-chest and then shifted the weight completely behind him.

He stepped down two more rungs, and as he was testing the next one, the hatch was slammed closed. Then he heard a lock being snapped shut. It was followed by dirt and gravel being shoveled back over the hatch.

IN THE MAJOR-CASE ROOM, the headquarters tech agent watched the monitors intensely. "What happened? We've lost transmission for the GPS in the bag. He must have dropped it and the weight of the money disabled it. Wait, the wallet device is still moving."

"Which way?" Kaulcrick asked.

"It's moving east."

"All units, the package is moving east from the last location," the assistant director barked into the microphone. "Can someone get an eye on him? Don't lose that money!"

"This is One-four. It's pretty dark, but I see something moving. Let me try to get over there."

"Don't get too close, we don't know who's around."

The tech agent, watching the grid on the monitor, said, "He's now walking up Emerald Street."

"Does anyone have him?" Kaulcrick asked, his voice starting to rise. No one answered. "Does anyone have him!"

Again all the radios were silent. The tech agent said, "He's turned onto West Second Street."

"One-four," Kaulcrick called, "have you caught up to him?"

"Not yet, sir."

"One-one, flood that area with your people. Find him. And that bag."

TEN

VAIL STEPPED DOWN, BUT HIS FOOT COULDN'T FIND THE NEXT RUNG, so he reached twice as far, thinking maybe they had cut off a rung hoping to get him to slip and fall onto the punji boards, but he couldn't find the next one either. Apparently, they had cut the rest of them off.

So he was unable to go up or down. Then he remembered the agent in the underground chamber at the naval prison, seemingly trapped, but a means, although not obvious, had been left for him: the length of webbing. The reason for the maintenance hatch had been to service the overhead cables that had once carried the electricity to power the trolley cars. He climbed as high as he could on the rungs and ran his hand out toward the center of the tunnel until it hit a braided steel cable. It was about an inch and a half thick, and he wrapped his free hand around it, pulling to test its ability to hold him and the extra seventy pounds of money. Satisfied it would, he let go of the ladder rung and swung out over the twenty-foot drop. Hand over hand he proceeded, testing each new forward grasp to make sure it would hold him before committing his weight.

KAULCRICK BARKED into the radio, "Can anyone see where he is?"

Again, the only response was silence. Suddenly, the tech agent said, "He must have gotten into a vehicle. The transmitter is moving at a car rate of speed now. He just got onto the 110 northbound."

"Did you hear that, One-one?" Kaulcrick asked the surveillance supervisor.

"I've got cars heading that way."

HANGING TWENTY FEET in the air, Vail had traveled about eighty feet horizontally along the electrical cable that paralleled the tunnel floor, which he had to assume was still covered with punji boards. His shoulders and arms were beginning to burn with fatigue. He blocked it out and went another thirty feet before the pain had all but paralyzed him. Suddenly it no longer mattered—he had run out of cable. Unable to go back or forward, he had no choice but to drop to the floor. Were the boards under him? Willing up what little strength remained, he screwed his grip around the cable with his right hand and pulled the bag across his head with the left, dropping it into the darkness with as much accuracy as possible directly below him. He hung for a moment longer trying to readjust his balance in the dark without the extra weight. In the event the floor was still booby-trapped, he was going to try to drop directly on top of the bag without falling off and onto any of the surrounding nailed boards.

From the way he had released the bag, he calculated it

was a foot or so off to his left. Swinging slightly to his left, he let go and fell the remaining fifteen feet, hitting the bag with both feet at the same time. But the currency inside had shifted during his "walk," so he fell off farther to the left. As he lost his balance, he prepared for the pain of the nails as he hit the floor, but the spiked boards weren't there. Instead he hit the earthen floor.

He shuffled his feet around to explore the ground, but there were no more boards. He picked up the bag and found two boards stuck to it. Directly under the cable, the floor had been booby-trapped, but not to the sides. That meant he was supposed to pierce his feet only. While that would incapacitate him, he would still be able to deliver the money. He examined the bag and discovered that the Pentad's overkill approach had paid an unexpected dividend: the GPS sewn into the bottom of the bag had been pierced and probably rendered inoperable.

Something scampered along the wall. Vail hoped it was only rats. But then he thought about how if he had landed on the nails, he would now be leaving a bloody trail for whatever it was to follow. Up ahead, he could see another of the Pentad's luminescent arrows, leading to, he was relatively certain, some other unpleasantry.

"HE'S LEFT THE 110 and is taking the 101 west," the tech agent called over the major-case room's radio.

"One-one, do you have him?" Kaulcrick asked.

"I think so. It's a dark green pickup truck. There appear to be two white males inside the cab."

"Can you see Vail?"

"Not from this distance."

"Crossing Santa Monica Boulevard," the tech agent called out.

"That's the right vehicle then," the surveillance supervisor said. "We're right there."

"Then stay on him." Kaulcrick leaned back uncomfortably in his chair.

"We've got to make sure that's Vail," Kate said.

"Who else could it be?"

AFTER ANOTHER HUNDRED yards Vail found the next arrow and continued to follow it farther into the tunnel. He could now see the next glowstick in the distance, but it didn't appear to be an arrow. It was an X placed on another cinder-block wall. Vail calculated that he had not come more than half a mile, so the tunnel must have been previously sealed off in sections. When he got closer, he could see that the X was attached to a thick nylon rope, the kind used by mountain climbers. It had a snap-link tied to the end. A note simply said to place the extortionists' radio inside the moneybag and attach the bag to the rope.

The rope disappeared into a square hole cut in the base of the wall just large enough for a person to squeeze through. Vail got down on the floor and tried to look into the hole, but it was pitch-black. Out of the side pockets, he took the flashlight, folding knife, and monocular before placing the radio inside the bag and looping the rope through both of its straps, locking the snap-link back onto the rope.

Feeling the movement on the rope, someone started pulling it almost immediately. Vail let it go, knowing it would not go through the hole without his help. The bag turned slightly sideways and couldn't get through. The rope strained and then went slack as whoever was pulling on it tried to free the bag. Finally Vail turned and pushed the canvas container, guiding it through the two-foot-square hole.

Once it was through, he could see a small amount of light coming in from the upper part of the other side of the opening that the money was pulled through. Whoever was up there was using a concentrated-beam flashlight, he supposed, to ensure the bag was not getting hung up anywhere else. As he watched the money disappear, Vail noticed a newspaper on the floor, half opened and standing tented about four feet directly in front of the hole. It seemed odd that it would have remained upright during the years that the tunnel had been sealed. He looked a little more closely at it. It was not yellow or faded. He couldn't quite make out the date at the top or the headline.

Then he thought he saw a smaller cord being pulled up after the bag. The last thing Vail noticed before it went dark was a two-foot square of plywood on the other side of the opening lying flat on the floor butted up against the hole cut in the wall. Then he heard the same sounds he had when he descended into the tunnel: the hatch being shut and padlocked, followed by the scraping of dirt and rock to cover it over.

"WHERE ARE THEY NOW?" Kaulcrick asked.

"Just passing the Encino off-ramp."

Kate pulled the microphone away from Kaulcrick. "Can you get someone up there to make sure it is Vail?"

Kaulcrick grabbed the mike back. "Hold off on that, One-one." He turned to Kate. "You've got to calm down. If they get burned, this could all be for nothing."

"You don't know if it's Vail, which means you don't know where the bag is."

Her words set off panic in Kaulcrick's eyes. "Okay," he said, and keyed the mike: "One-one, maybe you had better get someone up there and make sure it's Vail." He shot a bitter sideways look at Kate. "Very discreetly."

VAIL RESTED with his back against the wall, trying to figure how he was going to get out of there. That's why they had insisted that he could not bring a gun; he might have been able to shoot through the hatch and destroy the lock that sealed it.

He heard something again along the tunnel's walls, getting closer, apparently attracted by his scent and lack of movement. He decided that the rats weren't necessarily meant to attack him, but to provide a constant distraction with the possibility, keeping him from thinking about any other traps that might have been set.

Maybe he should just wait for the cavalry. But they wouldn't know about the photocell-triggered explosives—if there were any. The irony of them opening the hatch and detonating it with their flashlights would certainly appeal to whoever was doing this, plus it would destroy any evidence. Then he thought of something even more alarming: they had him leave the wallet GPS so they could use it to draw the surveillance away from the tunnel. With both entrances covered over, he was virtually buried alive, and no one had any idea where.

The only choice left to him was to crawl through the opening and see if he couldn't somehow get that hatch open. He eased his shoulders into the hole, being careful not to break any planes on the other side. Pushing out on his shoulders and bringing his arms up to the sides to fill the opening as much as possible so no light would leak back into the section he was in, he snapped on the flashlight. The chamber was no more than five feet to the opposite wall, which was also constructed with cinder blocks. Against it sat the newspaper that was open along its center fold and sat, inexplicably, in a foot-high tent on the dirt floor. Its newness reminded him that it had to be hiding something. Then Vail noticed that the dirt around it wasn't hardpacked like everywhere else in the tunnel. It had been dug up and then hastily tamped down again. A small spine of dirt led from the newspaper back to the plywood board, which was now less than an inch from the tip of his flashlight.

And the plywood wasn't completely level. Something was underneath it. Because of the telltale rise in the dirt that ran from the newspaper to the board, he had an idea what might be under the paper—a Claymore mine. Claymores contained hundreds of steel balls and C-4 explosive, and were completely directional. Someone struggling through that small hole headfirst and leaning on the board that covered the plunger would have their head vaporized. It seemed like something that the Pentad would consider a perfect ending.

"THEY'RE STILL WEST on the 101. Going through Thousand Oaks," the tech agent said, now sitting at the monitor tracking the GPS's movement.

Finally one of the surveillance units said, "I went by and got a good look at the two occupants. Neither of them is our guy."

Kate looked at Kaulcrick, who appeared to be frozen by indecision. She leaned over him and keyed the mike. "One-one, have your people stop that pickup and search it."

FIVE MINUTES LATER, the surveillance supervisor came up on the air. "Command, someone tossed the wallet GPS in the back of the truck, probably when it was stopped at a light on Second Street in West Hollywood. There's no bag and both of the occupants look like working humps."

Kaulcrick slammed both of his fists down on the radio console. "Okay, One-one, have someone bring them both to the office to be interviewed," Kate said. "The rest of your people I want back to that railway yard. Use that wallet GPS, and we'll guide you to the spot where we lost contact with the bag."

STILL WEDGED IN THE HOLE, Vail carefully picked up the end of the board. Under it was a Claymore plunger.

The mechanism was designed to fit in the hand and took only a couple of pounds of pressure to generate enough electrical current to detonate the blasting cap at the other end. Within the plunger was a simple safety device, a square wire loop, that when in place blocked the plunger's path, making it impossible to squeeze. To arm it, the wire was simply rotated down out of the way. That's what the cord Vail had seen being pulled up after the bag was for, to ready the mine for firing. The weight of the bag being pushed through the hole would have been enough to depress the plunger and set off the mine, blowing up the money, so the safety had to be on. The extortionists had run a doubled cord through the safety and after extracting the money pulled the loop flat, arming the device. It was then ready for an exhausted and possibly injured agent to crawl through the opening and put his entire weight on the plywood.

Vail slowly extended his hand to the plunger and re-engaged the safety by rotating the loop back up under the handle. Once he did, he turned off his light and crawled into the smaller chamber. Inside, he took the piece of plywood, tipped it up on end, and pushed it flush against the hole in the wall as a light seal. He opened both blades of the Special Ops knife and jammed the knife blade into the dirt and the saw blade into the board to hold it in place.

After turning on the flashlight, he stood as far to the side of the newspaper as he could and carefully lifted it. The Claymore was sitting on its metal scissor legs, elevated to get as many of its projectiles delivered as accurately as possible at the opening. Behind it, on a plastic spool, was about a hundred feet of wire. Taking his time, Vail extracted the blasting cap from the mine's body.

At the same time Vail was climbing the rungs that led up to the hatch through which the money had disappeared, six of the surveillance agents, led by GPS directions from the major-case room, were only twenty yards from the hatch where Vail had originally entered the tunnel. Had he known this, he would probably have worked a little quicker in case the entire underground structure had been wired with explosives. When he reached the hatch, he found it tightly locked. Climbing back down, he retrieved the mine, then took it back up to the hatch and forced the scissor legs into the joint formed by the small door and the metal frame it fit into. That way the blast would be concentrated at the lock. Slowly he screwed the blasting cap back into the mine's body and let the wire spool unravel. Turning off the flashlight, he took the plywood board from the hole and crawled back through. Then tipping the board kitty-corner, he was able to shimmy it through the opening. He pulled the spool in after him and then felt around until he found the plunger. Before reconnecting it, he pushed the plywood up, covering the hole, and leaned his back against it. Even though most of the blast would be directed at the hatch, it would give off light in all directions. With the board in place the detonation flash would be contained. He hoped.

"I'VE FOUND SOMETHING over here," one of the surveillance agents yelled to the others. "This dirt is fresh." He dropped down on his knees and started moving it with his hands.

"There's a door here." The rest of the agents came running over to help.

The surveillance supervisor came up and looked at the hatch. "Anyone got bolt cutters?" he said to them, as well as into his handheld radio.

"This is One-four. I've got a set in my trunk. I'm just pulling up outside the fence. I'll be there in two."

VAIL TOOK A MOMENT to run through everything in his mind again. Taking the plunger in one hand, he flipped the safety wire out of the way and squeezed.

"COMMAND, WE'VE GOT an explosion a couple hundred yards to our north." The surveillance agents started running toward it.

ELEVEN

KATE WALKED INTO THE EMERGENCY TREATMENT ROOM AT THE hospital, nodding at the two surveillance agents who stood conspicuously at either side of the door. Inside, a doctor was stitching up a wound in Vail's back caused by a chunk of plywood from the explosion. "Are you all right?" she asked, putting her hand on his forearm and squeezing it without realizing what she was doing.

"I'm about to get up and walk out of here. Any time you can do that after tangling with a Claymore, you're having a pretty good day."

The doctor taped a bandage in place and said, "You're all set. Just watch the stitches." The doctor handed him a prescription slip. "You're going to need this for the pain when that local I gave you wears off."

Kate picked up Vail's shirt and held it for him while he put it on. A jagged hole was surrounded with drying blood. "I guess we owe you a shirt."

"Since I lost the three million, why don't we call it even."

"Hildebrand has the whole office out at the tunnel. The LAPD bomb squad is checking the main section, but it's going to take a while, since they can't use lights. Because of the device at the exit, they're taking the entrance warning as gospel. They have to use night-vision goggles to go in. Actually I think they're making entry where you blew the hatch and are working backward. One of the sergeants is going to call me once they find out what they're dealing with."

"That's another reason I asked for you to come along."

"Which is?"

"Because you're a handsome woman, you can get favors *outside* the FBI."

"Handsome?"

He had finished buttoning his shirt and took a step closer to her. His voice softened. "Do you think I should have said . . . beautiful?" He was looking into her eyes now.

It took a moment for her to compose herself. "I think that painkiller has worked its way up into your brain."

Carefully, Vail started tucking in his shirt. "How's Kaulcrick taking all this?"

"Not as well as you are. In his mind, he got bested by Bertok."

"Maybe," Vail said.

"What does that mean?"

"It means there are an awful lot of moving parts to this thing to be only one person. I have to think about it for a while." As they walked out the door to the parking lot, Kate saw him discreetly slip the pain prescription the doctor had given him into a trash receptacle.

Once they got to the hotel, she walked him to his room. "Sure you're all right?"

"If I'm not, what did you have in mind?"

"The standard stuff—CPR, tourniquets, a kidney."

Vail smiled. "Thanks for the ride."

"I'm glad you're okay."

As he turned to put his key in the lock, surprising even herself, she gave him a light kiss on the cheek, but immediately regretted it. He was the last man in the world she wanted to think of her as an emotional female. She reminded herself that Vail, however, was not most men. And maybe it was a good thing to show him that she was capable of a certain degree of intimacy. If nothing else, it would keep him from figuring her out as easily as he did everyone else. "There's a conference call with the director at nine A.M. If you don't feel up to it, I'm sure he'll understand."

He stared at her for a second. "Thanks for hanging in on my side. I know that people like Kaulcrick see it as being disloyal."

"That's all right, I plan to do a lot of sucking up to him over the next few days. And should push come to shove, I'll give you up in a heartbeat."

"If you do, I'll tell him you kissed me."

"He said, she said, bricklayer." She turned to go. "I'll see you in the morning."

NO SOONER HAD VAIL gotten his shirt off than he heard a soft knock on the door. Thinking Kate had returned, he was surprised to find Tye Delson standing in the hallway.

"Hi," she said. "Came to see if you're all right."

"I'm good. How'd you know?"

"The pickup truck that was used to lead your surveillance crew away. They needed a search warrant."

"I'm sorry, come on in." He opened the door wide and stepped back.

She gave the room a quick look and said, "Thought maybe you could use a drink." She pulled a silver flask out of her purse and held it up with ceremony. "I've brought bourbon. The shopkeeper told me it is the traditional celebratory for a near-death experience."

"So we're celebrating?"

"Actually he said it was good for calming the nerves, but if I thought you were that kind of man, I probably wouldn't be here."

"Let me get some glasses." He opened a drawer and pulled on a T-shirt.

"How many stitches?" she asked when she saw his back.

"It felt like seven or eight." He walked over to a side table and picked up two glasses. "Do you want ice or water?"

"This is twelve-year-old Kentucky sipping whiskey. The clerk insisted that it not be defiled with California groundwater." Vail came back, and she poured a couple of ounces for each of them. Then she took out a pack of cigarettes. "Do you mind?"

"It won't be the first time I smelled smoke tonight."

After she lit one, she held up her glass and said, "To surviving." They both took a healthy swallow. "So how bad was it down there? In the tunnel."

"It wasn't the best of times; it wasn't the worst of times."

"How very non-Dickensian. From what they told me,

it sounded pretty bad. They don't know how you weren't killed."

Vail studied her for a moment, trying to figure out why she was there. The first time they had met, she admitted liking to hang out with agents, but this seemed more than that. She was wearing a dark workout suit that, unlike the long, loose dresses he had seen her in at the office, revealed an amply feminine figure. Was he a curiosity to her, someone who seemed so uncontrolled by the Bureau, yet the person called when there was a problem? "Is this a California thing, where the AUSAs make house calls?"

"No," she said mischievously, inviting more questions.

"Then why?"

"Just to make sure you're okay. Sort of."

"Sort of what?"

She took a long drag on her cigarette to make him wait for an answer. "You know, to see what you're like away from work. You're interesting. No, that's a little overused. You're enigmatic. I don't get much of that."

"Funny, I seem to be getting too much of it lately."

She pulled a piece of tobacco from her lip. "How do you and Kate get along?"

"She's been a good boss on this."

"I don't know you real well, but from what I've seen, you're not the kind of person who allows himself to have a boss. Is that what happened before? Why you *used* to be an agent?"

"That observation would hardly qualify you as clairvoyant. So that's it, I'm enigmatic? That's why you're here?"

She stared at him for a moment searching for any hidden

motive and then laughed. "You really don't have any idea of the effect you're having on people around here, do you? You've been here—what—two days, and you've already found all that evidence in Bertok's apartment, virtually solving the case, and then tonight, you survived death, apparently with great casualness. You're becoming quite the celebrity, so I thought I should try to get here before the crowds get too large." She took another sip of her drink. "I was hoping you might need some company. You know, all that testosterone stirred up and looking for an outlet." She brought the cigarette up to her mouth and used her tongue to slowly moisten the entire circumference of the unfiltered tip before taking another deep drag, her eyes never leaving his.

"I've heard of picking off the weak and wounded from the herd, but never the overstimulated."

"Sooner or later overstimulation leaves a man weak."

"Is that something you picked up from Stan Bertok?"

Tye laughed. "I can honestly say I never had the pleasure, or displeasure, depending on your point of view," she said. "Oh, I see. You're wondering if I'm some sort of Bureau camp follower. Well, I'm not. This is a very limited offer."

She drank the rest of her drink and poured another ounce into her glass, holding up the flask to him. "No, I'm good."

"On the drink or my offer?"

"I know in the not too distant future, I'll regret this, but both."

Vail could see a sadness flood through her, not one of rejection, but of having to be alone.

She threw back the remaining bourbon and swallowed it. "That's very diplomatic, but please don't take that tack. I doubt I would find you nearly as interesting if I thought you were the kind of man who was capable of regret."

TWELVE

WHEN VAIL GOT TO THE OFFICE THE NEXT MORNING, HE FOUND KATE busy at her computer. He sat down across the desk from her while she continued to type. She looked up briefly and nodded, a little too casually, he thought. Maybe she was trying to undo any feelings exposed the night before. He smiled to himself and then became lost in the efficiency of her hands. Like her, they were athletic, quick but unhurried. When she finally pushed away from the keyboard and looked up, she said, "How'd you sleep?"

"On my stomach."

"I meant, did you sleep?"

"I think so."

"How's the back?"

"Actually a little less sore than my shoulders and arms."

"Your little ceiling walk was pretty impressive. A lot of people around here are talking about it."

He laughed a single grunt. "When the director calls, I'm going to make a suggestion that the next drop we use million-dollar bills."

"Do compliments embarrass you or are you just annoyingly modest?"

"I've found people who have their heads turned by compliments have them turned by criticism."

"So you don't want anyone to say anything to you."

"I'm sorry, I meant *annoyingly modest.*"

Kate laughed. "Do you need some coffee?"

"I'm good," Vail said. "On the way up here, I checked the pen on Bertok's phone. Nothing. What's going on out at the tunnel?"

"LAPD did find explosives at the entry hatch. And on a photocell trigger. C-4 packed with some of those two-inch nails they used to make the punji boards."

"That's probably why it didn't detonate when I set off the Claymore at the other end. Too far away. I don't suppose they were considerate enough to leave any evidence."

"No latents, but we're working on the boards and nails, trying the lumberyards around to see if someone ordered the pieces cut to those lengths. We're also checking to see if there have been any recent thefts of Claymores or C-4."

"That would be a little too easy."

"They are an inconsiderate bunch," Kate said. "I didn't want to ask you last night, but what was it like in the tunnel?"

"Dark, but enlightening."

"How very paradoxical," she said playfully.

"I was just going for cute."

"Enlightening, how?"

"It's interesting how much you can learn about an adversary when your life depends on anticipating his—*or her*—next move."

"Now, *that's* cute."

Don Kaulcrick walked in, followed by the SAC and Allen Sabine, Bertok's supervisor. Kaulcrick said, "The director hasn't called yet?"

"No," Kate said.

"I'm sorry, Steve, how are you feeling?"

"I'm fine. How are you doing?"

Kaulcrick forced a smile. "Other than being three million short for the week, I'm okay."

The phone rang and Kate pushed the speakerphone button. "Kate Bannon."

"Good morning, Kate," Bob Lasker said.

"I've got you on speakerphone, sir."

"Please tell me who else is in the room."

There was something insistent in the director's voice that told her he wasn't simply taking roll. She started with Vail and then listed everyone present in descending order of rank.

Lasker said, "Steve, I called the hospital last night but you had already left. How's the back?"

"It's superficial. I'm fine."

"That was an incredibly courageous thing you did."

"I'm not sure self-preservation is all that courageous."

"I'm too pleased to argue semantics. Let's just say I've never been so impressed by self-preservation. Or happy to give away three million dollars. So someone bring me up to date on what's going on out there. Let's start with the tunnel."

The Los Angeles SAC spoke up, telling the director what the agents at the scene had found so far. He then filled him in on the minimal evidence that had been recovered and what the LAPD's bomb squad had found.

"Explosives, that's new," Lasker said. "Steve, do you think it has any significance?"

"I think whoever is responsible for this is trying to keep us off balance. It keeps a pattern from forming. Patterns can be analyzed and eventually turned into names and addresses, and the Pentad has been very good at preventing that so far."

"Hopefully, the money being delivered means the end of the killing. Mark, tell me what else your agents are doing."

"Well, sir, we're doing neighborhood investigations all around the tunnel. The group had to find and dig out those entrances. Hopefully someone saw them. We're tracking down the kids who we're told play in that lot regularly. We're sending the punji boards back to the lab. Also we're checking with the hardware stores and lumberyards in the area to see if anyone ordered boards cut to those specific lengths or a large quantity of the particular nails used."

"Sounds like you've got everything covered. Keep at it. Hopefully, now that they have the money, they'll go on the run. Chasing people is our strength."

"Yes, sir."

"And now, if you don't mind, I've got some headquarters business I need to discuss with Don and Kate. Steve, you may as well stay."

The SAC motioned to Sabine that they were leaving. Once the door closed, Kaulcrick said, "Yes, sir."

"Do you need anything—more manpower, lab services, anything?"

"Right now there's just not a lot to go on, so, no, we don't need any help. When we get a break, I won't be shy about asking."

The director didn't say anything for a few seconds. "That's not exactly encouraging, Don. I was hoping once we paid them, there would be leads. Steve, have you got anything on Bertok?"

"We're working on a few things."

"Like what?"

Vail glanced at Kate. "Stuff," he said, the reticence in his voice a warning.

"Ooookay," Lasker said, hesitating a few moments to consider the possible illegalities that were being kept from him. "Well, people, this is where we wanted to be. Without a threat of someone else being murdered. This is where I say, pull out all the stops and catch them. Are there any stops to pull out?"

"I guess that depends on whether you want to reveal this to the media or not," Kaulcrick said. "If you do, hopefully we can get the public back on our side."

"It's not an easy call. With all the evidence against him, we know that Bertok is involved, but what we don't know is whether he's acted alone. Maybe there is a Pentad. Maybe it's just one other person, but it could be ten. Nothing was ever said about us letting it out after they got the money. I don't want to risk them using it as an excuse to start killing again. Later, if we're getting nowhere, we can think about going public. I don't know. Steve, what do you think?"

Vail felt his phone vibrate. He looked down at the screen. "711" was typed in. It was the code he and Demick had agreed upon. Someone had called Bertok's phone. "I'm sorry, sir, Kate and I have to go."

THIRTEEN

WHEN VAIL AND KATE WALKED INTO THE TECH ROOM, TOM DEMICK was on the telephone, apparently with one of his contacts. He looked up and pointed at the pad of paper in front of him. A single phone number was written on it. "Yeah, Tony, I appreciate it." He wrote down an address. "Friday, right, and this time I'm buying. . . . Okay, but I'm buying the liquor." He hung up and tore the sheet of paper off the pad. "The call to Bertok's phone came from West Hollywood, a Laundromat, less than a mile from the subway tunnel."

"Hopefully it was him," Vail said. "Not exactly a home address, but it'll give us a place to start."

"Do you want me to go out there with you?" Demick asked.

"Thanks, Tom, we'll take care of it," Vail said. "Can you get all the outgoing calls from the Laundromat phone for the last two weeks?"

"That shouldn't be a problem, but there'll probably be a bunch. I should have them by the time you get there."

"For now, can we keep this between the three of us?" Vail asked.

"The three of us?" Demick said. He leaned closer to Vail in mock confidence. "You do realize that one of us is a deputy assistant director. Who exactly are we keeping it secret from?"

"Okay, let's keep it between the two of us."

ONCE THEY WERE IN the car, Kate said, "I know you were kidding back there, but you don't actually think I'd ever give you up, do you?"

"I'm just passing through your career. You'd have to be a fool not to."

"Then I'm a fool."

"Right now we're in a vacuum, operating with impunity. The director knows we're doing something less than legal, and he says do whatever you have to do to protect the public. Breaking rules becomes noble, even heroic, so whatever I do, you're on my side. But what if you're suddenly standing in front of a federal grand jury and they ask you about committing illegal acts. And don't think they'll be concerned about the common good. Are you going to perjure yourself and risk prosecution?" When she didn't say anything, he continued. "You're not a fool."

"I am still on your side."

"I know you are, but the problem is only a fool can be *just* on my side. So sometime in the near future I may have to do something alone."

She stared ahead in silence. "Has that always been effective for you?"

"What?"

"When you feel yourself getting too close to someone, you treat them like they're not worth your time."

"Unfortunately, that tactic doesn't seem to work as well as it once did."

"I'm not amused."

Vail pulled to the curb. "This is the address."

When she still didn't say anything, he said, "Isn't one of my *assets* being able to break rules without anyone knowing, so everyone else can swear on a stack of Bibles? You can't be in on all the good stuff while innocent of all the bad stuff, because the good and bad are usually inseparable."

"Okay, okay. It just seems like you're a little too eager to keep everyone outside the great wall of Vail, and by 'everyone' I mean me."

He laughed. "You think too much of me. I'm no white knight. I do what I do mainly because I have a pathological need to settle all scores, and in spades. Take those two bank robbers. I had them disarmed and all but unconscious, but I threw both of them through the windows for good measure. Anyone who would do what they did to that poor old woman they threatened to shoot deserved a few moments of someone treating *them* without boundaries. So, yes, I do have issues."

"Meaning you're blaming your father."

"I can blame him only for getting me started. I'm the one holding on to it. I guess I like the way it drives me."

"That's your rationalization for not trusting anyone?"

"I'll tell you what, from now on I'll do my best to trust you without reservation."

Kate knew how difficult a concession that was for him, how difficult any concession was for Steve Vail. "And I'll do my best not to give you up to the federal grand jury," she said.

They both got out of the car and went inside. The place was empty. The only sound was from one of the dryers, which hummed as a load tumbled inside, a button occasionally clicking against the metal drum. Next to the folding table, two pay phones were mounted side by side on the wall. Vail checked the numbers and pointed at the one on the right. "This is the one used to call Bertok's machine." He took a step back and looked around. Kate sat down on one of the plastic chairs bolted to the floor and waited. Vail's eyes finally went back to the tumbling dryer. "What time did Demick say that call was made?" he asked her.

She glanced at her watch. "Almost two hours ago."

"The load in the dryer is large, and the way it sounds, it's dry. Maybe its owner was here two hours ago. Let's wait." She waved her agreement, and he sat down.

A couple of minutes later, the dryer snapped to a halt, and almost as if on cue, a customer pushed open the front door. A woman in her sixties, she walked carefully by Vail, giving him a suspicious glance. As she eased the dryer door open, he said, "Excuse me." He stood up and drew his credentials, opening them for her inspection.

"FBI? I'm washing clothes, not money."

Vail smiled appreciatively. "You're pretty quick." He could see how she would have been very attractive as a young woman. Mischief glinted in her eyes, and there was still a trace of Midwest in her speech, but not enough to tell on which side of the Mississippi it had been ingrained.

"Do you like fast women, Agent Vail?"

"What man doesn't . . . ?"

"Anna."

He turned to Kate. "Do you have that photo?" She handed him Bertok's credential photo and smiled at the woman. "Hi, I'm Kate Bannon."

"You're FBI too?"

"Actually, she's my boss," Vail said.

She examined Kate's face. "You have a good look. I mean photographically. The camera would love it. You have that skin that glows on film. Even that scar seems to work." She leaned in toward Kate and, in a loud-enough whisper for Vail to hear, said, "The help looks pretty good. Hope you're taking advantage of your position." She leaned back and smiled at Vail, the idea of shocking him dancing in her eyes.

"Unfortunately, she's not," Vail whispered back. He held up the photo of Bertok. "Have you seen this man in here today, Anna?"

"You're asking for my help? Maybe I should take advantage of my position."

"A good-looking woman like you, I'd be honored."

"You sound more like a casting director than a cop." She took the photo and turned it, holding it up to the light. "I'm still too vain to carry my glasses." She tilted it through a couple of more angles to catch the light before handing it back. "There was a guy in here making some phone calls, but he was pretty covered up, like the Unabomber. Sunglasses, baseball cap, hooded sweatshirt pulled over the hat and tied so you couldn't even see the color of his hair."

"Any idea how old or tall?"

"I've been around here long enough to know if a guy dresses like that, you're safer watching his moves than trying to get his vital statistics. He was up to something; I just wanted to make sure it wasn't me. Especially when he asked for change."

"How much did he need?" Kate asked.

"Lots, I guess. He had to be making long-distance calls. First he holds up a hundred-dollar bill, so I get the impression he's trying to see what I had in my purse. But it looked like there was something wrong with the bill. It looked kind of raggedy."

"Raggedy, how?" Vail asked.

"I don't know, kind of torn, not on the edges, in the middle."

"Like holes had been poked into it?"

"The nails," Kate said under her breath.

The woman looked at Kate uncomprehendingly and then said, "Yeah, I guess it was holes, but it had to be bogus or something because then he says he'll take twenty dollars for it so he can put it in the bill changer." She pointed to the large silver box hanging on the wall at the other end of the laundry. "That's when I knew it was a scam."

"Did you say he made the calls?"

"Yeah. He takes the hundred and feeds it into the changer, so I knew it wasn't real. I guess the machine read it as a twenty because about twenty bucks in quarters drops down."

"Then he made the calls?"

"Yes."

"Did you hear any of the conversation?"

"No, the whole time he's turned to the wall, mumbling."

"How many calls?"

"I stopped paying attention. I don't know, two or three, maybe. I don't know."

"How long did they last?"

"Not long. I'd be guessing less than a minute, I suppose," the woman said.

"Then he left?"

"Yeah."

"In a car?"

The mischief returned to her eyes. "Yes."

"Anna, you little minx, you know something."

"Yes," she repeated. "Give me your best offer."

"My undying gratitude."

She put the last article of clothing in the basket. "You carry my basket out to the car, and I'll tell you something about when he left." Vail picked up her laundry. "He left in a car, a green midsize. Toyota or Honda, I can never tell them apart. Like I said, I knew he wasn't right, so I watched him through the window. He drove down the block and pulled into that motel." She walked over to the window and pointed.

"You've been a big help, Anna. Let's get you out to your car."

She took his arm formally, and as they walked out, she said, "This suit looks good on you, but do you know what you'd look even better in?"

"No, what?"

"My shower." She looked back at Kate and said, "Sorry, doll, you snooze, you lose."

When Vail came back in, Kate asked, "Did you get her number?"

"Hey, you never know. I might get a day off while we're out here."

"You construction guys," she said, shaking her head in feigned disgust. "I got ahold of Demick. He's sending out an evidence team. You know what this means."

"Let me hear what you think it means."

She looked surprised that there might be different interpretations of what they had just learned. "If Bertok has the bills that were damaged during the three-million-dollar drop, he's got to be the Pentad."

"Possibly," Vail said.

"*Possibly?* Is anything ever a sure thing with you?"

"Why be in a hurry to make assumptions? Let's just keep following the yellow brick road until we find the guy behind the curtain," Vail said.

THE CONQUISTADOR MOTEL rented rooms by the hour. It appeared to have thirty to forty rooms on two floors. It was U-shaped with all the parking directly in front of the rooms. The marquee advertised special weekly rates with free adult movies. Kate stood at the Laundromat window waiting for the evidence team and watched as Vail walked into the motel's office.

Down the street in the opposite direction, not visible through the Laundromat window, sat a green Toyota, its driver watching Vail. Keeping his hands below the dashboard, he released the magazine from his Glock and, after checking it, rammed it back into the grip of the weapon, fully seating it, and then chambered a round. Lowering the visor and flipping up the cover on the mirror, he looked at himself, trying to decide whether he was recognizable behind the sunglasses, cap, and drawn-up sweatshirt hood. He peeled off his sunglasses. His gray eyes looked tired but clear. They began to widen with anticipation.

VAIL CAME THROUGH the Laundromat door, his expression urgent. "We got to go."

"What happened?"

"They're gone."

"They?"

"Our boy and his rented significant other. The manager didn't know her, but he was sure she was a hooker."

"Did he make Bertok's photo?"

"Said he never saw him. She rented the room."

"Phone calls?"

"None. But the manager wrote down his plate on the registration card."

"What about waiting for the evidence team?"

"We don't have to protect the scene for them. They just have to retrieve that hundred-dollar bill and dust for prints. The way that guy was covered up, I doubt he's going to leave prints, and nobody's going to get to that hundred until the owner comes down and opens the machine." As they hurried to the car, Vail handed a slip of paper to her and she dialed the office, asking for the radio room.

After a few seconds, Kate said, "It's registered to a local car rental agency. I'll call them." Vail started the car. After a couple of minutes of conversation, she hung up and said, "The person renting the car is an Alan Nefton at 2701 Spring Street, Los Angeles. It's a Toyota Camry." Kate repeated the address as she entered it into the car's navigational system.

Vail had a map out and found the address. "It's not far," he said.

Kate called the radio operator again. "Check Alan Nefton's driver's license for a description." Vail pulled away from the curb. After another minute, she said, "There's no record on file for any Alan Nefton." Kate disconnected the line. "Well, let's hope the address isn't a phony too."

Kate watched the car's navigational screen without saying anything to Vail, who, once seeing where the address was on a map, didn't refer to it again. When they were within two blocks, he said, "That should be it there, the small house with the bars on the windows and door."

"It looks abandoned," she said.

"Probably because it's wedged between those two industrial properties that are abandoned." Both businesses were large and dwarfed the tiny residence between them. One appeared to be an old flour factory, faded black letters on its whitewashed wall proclaiming "Stabler Milling Company Est. 1883." The other looked to be an automobile graveyard, its eight-foot fence keeping its exact contents hidden. "Probably the look he was going for."

"And he doesn't have to worry about the neighbors sticking their noses in his business."

"Keep an eye out for the car. I'm going to drive by at a normal speed. Because it's on my side, I'm not going to look at it. If anyone is looking out, they'll watch me to make sure I'm not checking it out, so you have to memorize all the windows and doors." Vail hung his arm out the window and, staring straight ahead, took off slowly.

Kate looked as straight forward as possible. "Okay, the west side has one window at the back with bars. The front, one barred door and a barred window on either side of it. The east side has a window toward the front but no bars."

"That just leaves the back," Vail said. "We'd better get surveillance out here." They were a block and a half past the house and Vail was looking for someplace to turn around when he spotted a green Camry coming at them. "Okay, here we go. Don't look at the car." With his peripheral vision, Vail could feel the driver scrutinizing him. He leaned over and placed his palm on Kate's face. Snarling, he pushed her head away roughly. Before she could react he said, "Sorry, he was eyeballing us."

In the rearview mirror, Vail tracked the Toyota as it pulled up in front of the house. He turned into a driveway and parked so his car was difficult to see. They watched the driver get out. Kate said, "That's him!"

"You recognize his face?"

"No, he's too far away, but that's the same Unabomber getup the woman at the Laundromat saw."

Vail watched him go into the house. "Okay, let's go."

"Let's go? Don't you think this is a job for SWAT?"

"See that gate on the front door?"

"What?"

"It's not closed all the way."

"So?"

Vail put the car in reverse and backed out into the street.

"Chances are he didn't lock it because he's leaving right away. We don't have a choice." Vail was now driving toward the house. "When I pull in, go along the east side of the house. Be careful going past the window." He was close enough to see the property in detail now. "There's a Dumpster in the back for cover, and it's off to the side. You can watch both the back and the east side of the house from there. I'll go in the front."

"What about the window on the west side?"

"It has bars on it, remember? He can't get out that way."

"Okay. I guess."

"It'll be fine. Just make sure you get some cover. Take your cell phone. As soon as you set up, call in the infantry."

Kate drew her automatic and pulled the slide back far enough to make sure there was a round already in the chamber. Vail turned quickly into the driveway and was out of the car before her. Keeping low, she sprinted around the side of the house to the Dumpster, then straightened up behind it. There was only a single door in the back of the house and it was covered with another iron gate.

Giving her a few seconds to get into position, Vail now swung open the front door. It was dark inside, and he knew he would be silhouetted if the Camry's driver was in position to shoot. He drew his Glock and dove through the opening. As he did, an explosion lit up the room. Vail heard two rounds thud into the wall behind him. In the flash of light, Vail saw a dark figure standing in an interior doorway.

Now it was dark again. The door was slammed and some sort of heavy lock was thrown. Hugging the wall, Vail worked his way over to the door. A board creaked under his feet. A burst of three rounds ripped through the solid wooden door. Without standing completely in front of it, Vail kicked at the edge of the door just above the knob. It didn't give at all. He had kicked in enough doors to know that this one was heavily barricaded and it was going to take more than foot-pounds to open. Moving back along the walls, he exited the front of the house. "Kate!" he yelled.

"Yeah," she called back.

"You all right?"

"Fine. You okay?"

"He's barricaded himself."

"LAPD and our people are on the way."

"Just hold your ground. He can't get out."

Vail could already hear sirens in the distance. As they grew louder, he heard a single gunshot, this time muffled. He knew what that meant.

FOURTEEN

AN LAPD CAR SWERVED INTO THE DRIVEWAY, AND VAIL WAVED THE officers to the front porch. The driver went to the trunk and took out a shotgun, jacking a round into the chamber as he trotted to Vail's position. Vail asked him, "Can you go and cover the back? There's a female agent there with a handgun, but I'd feel better if it were covered with a long gun. Go along the east side of the house. There's a window, but he's barricaded in a room on the opposite side." The officer didn't hesitate, taking off in a low trot.

Within seconds, Kate joined Vail. "Did he shoot at you?"

"Yeah, but that last round wasn't fired through the door."

She looked at him in surprise. "Suicide?"

"If I were a betting man . . ."

An hour later both LAPD and FBI SWAT teams were in the small parking lot of the abandoned auto salvage yard that crowded up against the west side of the house. After a short disagreement as to how to broach the room that the gunman had barricaded himself in, the PD team agreed to take the perimeter while the Bureau made entry. First, bullhorn pleas were made for him to surrender. The only response was silence. Vail told the team leader that he didn't think the standard battering ram or pry bar was going to be enough to open the inner door. "Well, let's give it a try and see what happens," the agent said.

Vail and Kate waited outside while the team leader gave the go-ahead. They could hear the battering ram thudding against the door. After almost a minute, there was a metal clang as the ram was dropped on the floor. One of the SWAT team members came out and got an explosive kit and took it inside. Within a couple of minutes the team backed out of the house, the leader holding the detonator attached to wires that ran back inside. "Everyone stand clear of the windows and doors," he yelled. He waited a few seconds for all movement to cease and then yelled, "Fire in the hole." He pressed a button. An explosion erupted and the team ran back inside.

Vail followed them in. A heavy metal rod ran from the floor two feet inside the bedroom door to just below its knob, anchoring into heavy metal plates at both ends. The door was twisted and hanging from one hinge. Vail stepped into the room.

In the corner lay Stanley Bertok, a nine-millimeter hole neatly torn through his right temple, a single trickle of blood less than two inches long now dry against his skin, his face recognizable in the sunlight that was coming through the barred window. Vail studied the body for a while before carefully touching the blood from the wound. It had already crystallized. Bertok's mouth was open slightly, and without anyone noticing, Vail bent over to smell his breath. In Bertok's curled hand lay the most sought-after gun in recent FBI history, his Glock model 22.

VAIL WATCHED as the evidence agent, using a cordless saw, carefully cut out a small section of wall that contained one of the bullets fired at him. It was the fourth one the team had recovered in addition to the five ejected shell casings. The fifth bullet, they decided, had been fired out the open front door and would probably never be found. It didn't really matter; one was all that would be needed to match the gun taken from Bertok's hand. The day's events had left little doubt in anyone's mind that it would match the four slugs extracted from the Pentad's murder victims.

Assistant Director Don Kaulcrick and the SAC came through the door. "Everybody okay?" Kaulcrick asked.

"Not counting Bertok, everyone's fine," Vail said.

The assistant director looked down at the body. "At least he did the right thing."

"Maybe." Vail's voice was a little more displaced than usual, encrypted.

"I would have thought that you of all people would be happy. Your assignment was to find him. You did it and did it well. I would have preferred you cut us in on it before the fact, but . . ."

"When we got the call about the Laundromat, it sounded like a dead end, so we thought we would waste only two agents' time."

Kaulcrick nodded in agreement but his look seemed questioning. "That's fine, Steve. The important thing is we got Bertok. Any sign of the money?"

Kate, listening from the kitchen area, walked in. "We

didn't want to contaminate the crime scene, so we've just given the house a cursory search. So far, nothing."

Kaulcrick walked over to the evidence agent. "How much longer are you going to be?"

The agent pulled out the section of the wall he had been working on and placed it in a cardboard box. "We're pretty much done. The only thing left is the car."

Kaulcrick went over to the SAC and put his hand on his shoulder. "Mark, I want someone reliable to immediately carry all this ballistics material back to the lab. Take your Bureau plane. I want it in the examiner's hands before sundown, eastern time. I'll call ahead and have someone waiting to go to work on it."

"What about the slug from the body?"

"There's no hurry on that. As soon as the M.E. can get it out, we'll send it back. The thing we need to know right now is whether Bertok's gun is the one used in the murders. Unfortunately, given the circumstances, he's left little doubt."

Kate held up a clear plastic envelope sealed with red evidence tape. Inside was a sheaf of hundred-dollar bills. "These were in Bertok's wallet."

Kaulcrick took the envelope from her and examined the bills. "What are these holes?"

Vail said, "From the punji boards when I dropped the bag in the tunnel."

"So these bills are part of the three million."

"We haven't checked the serial numbers yet, but they should match," Kate said.

Kaulcrick took out a three-by-five card and made a note. "So it was all Bertok. Let's tear this place apart."

"There's really not much to search," Kate said. "The house is small, no attic, basement, or crawl space. No furniture. I've been through the rooms a half-dozen times looking for hidden boards and compartments—nothing."

"When ERT finishes, let's get some fresh eyes in here, Mark," Kaulcrick said to the SAC. "Have them check the walls, floors, and ceiling. Let's go take a look at the car. If the money isn't in here, it's the next best bet."

Outside, Kate took out another evidence envelope and shook out a set of keys with the rental tag attached. She slid one of them into the trunk lock and opened it. There was a collective "Yeah!" as everyone recognized the large canvas bag that, when last seen, had contained three million dollars. The head evidence agent stepped forward and, pulling on a fresh pair of plastic gloves, unzipped it. Inside were a few banded stacks of hundred-dollar bills, pierced with nail holes.

"Where's the rest of it?" Kaulcrick asked. "How much is in there?"

The agent counted the stacks. "If there's a hundred bills in each stack, we've got only fifty thousand dollars here." Sticking out from under one of the bundles, he saw something shiny—a key. He pulled it out. The number 14 was stamped into it.

"What's that for?" Kaulcrick asked.

"I don't know," the agent said.

Someone said, "Could be for some kind of storage facility."

Kate looked over at Vail. His attention had once again drifted elsewhere.

Kaulcrick turned to the SAC. "Obviously, the money is wherever this key fits. How many men can you put on it?"

"I can deploy the entire office if you want."

"We need two things. First, a couple dozen copies of the key. And then a list of storage facilities in the city. Have someone list them by proximity to this location. The closer, the higher the priority. What was the alias he was using for the car registration?"

"Alan Nefton," Kate said.

"They can also check that name and the name from the Florida driver's license. . . ."

"Ruben Aznar," Kate said.

Kaulcrick made another note on his three-by-five card. "Also, Mark, I want you to handle the media. Have a news conference and tell them only that, tragically, an agent has committed suicide. Nothing about the Pentad, nothing about any money, terrorism, or extortion. Don't give them anything specific why he might have killed himself. 'On-going investigation,' et cetera. If someone does make the connection between Bertok's death and the Pentad, deny it unequivocally." Kaulcrick turned back to everyone there. "If there is any leak of this—any leak—there will be more Bureau polygraphers in this division than falsified time sheets. Now get going."

As the group around the car started to disperse, the assistant director said, "Well, Steve, I guess you can head back to Chicago."

"What are you talking about?" Kate asked.

"He was asked to find Bertok, and he's done that. This is all drone stuff now: go to the rental places and show the key. It's just a matter of time until someone stumbles across it. I think we can take it from here. I would think you'd find that boring, wouldn't you, Steve?"

"Actually, the director asked me to find Bertok *and* the money. You wouldn't mind if I hang around until you do find it, would you? I promise not to get in the way."

"Does that mean you don't think we will find it?"

"It means I'm curious, nothing more."

"Sorry if I'm a little defensive. I'd like to think that the Bureau could solve at least part of this case." There was something strained about Kaulcrick's attempted humility.

"I'd just like to see how it turns out. I'll keep my hands off," Vail said.

Kaulcrick stared at him for a moment. "Are you sure that's possible?"

Vail smiled. "Probably not."

THAT NIGHT VAIL watched the SAC on the early news. He stood at the lectern and read from a prepared statement. "Special Agent Stanley Bertok of this division, a twelve-year veteran with the FBI, committed suicide earlier today in this city. Agent Bertok had not reported to work for the last several days, and agents from this office had been searching for him. One of those teams finally located him and discovered that he had killed himself. This office is continuing to investigate the matter. Once that investigation is completed, our findings will be made public."

The statement, short by design, caused the reporters to

start firing questions at Hildebrand. “Any idea why he killed himself? Was he depressed?”

“I’m not a psychiatrist, but I believe depression is involved in most suicides. If he was depressed, we had no indication of it prior to this.”

Another reporter asked, “How hard were you looking for him? Why wasn’t there a public plea for help in locating him?”

The only answer that occurred to Hildebrand he knew could open Pandora’s box. He looked back past the lights for some signal from Kaulcrick, who sat in his chair passively. “Like any organization, on rare occasions,” Hildebrand started, “we have employees who are out of pocket for short periods of time. And when they are located, the explanations are usually quite innocuous. We had no reason to believe this was any different.”

Then someone asked, “Was there any connection between the suicide and the unsolved murders committed by the Rubaco Pentad?”

Again the SAC looked at Kaulcrick, who gave no indication that he had even heard the question. “No, there was absolutely no connection,” Hildebrand said. “I’m sorry, I’m late for another meeting.”

The reporters, smelling blood in the water, fired their questions on top of each other as the SAC picked up his notes and hurried out of the room.

FIFTEEN

AT NINE O'CLOCK THE NEXT MORNING, VAIL TAPPED ON TYE DELSON'S office door before pushing it open. She was leaning over a half-dozen law books that covered her desk, lost in her reading. "You got a minute?"

She looked up, and it took a moment for her to remember where she was. "Oh, Steve, sorry. I was trying to figure out something."

"Is this a bad time?"

"No, no. Shut the door, will you. I could use a break." She shoved up the window behind her desk until it was completely open, drew a cigarette, and lit it. "Please, sit down." She sat down on the sill.

"You've heard, I assume."

"About Stan, yes. They called me for a legal opinion for a search of the house and car. After the fact, I'm guessing."

"What do you think about Bertok's involvement now?"

"If you remember, the first time we met I told you I didn't think he could be involved in any murders. They said he shot at you. I guess I've always been better with books than people."

"I'm not sure that's true. I want to ask you a people question—which has to stay in the room."

She took a drag on her cigarette and blew out the smoke pensively. "That seems to be a standard tagline to any conversation with you."

"Does that mean you want to go back to your law books?"

"God, no," she said. "Please, I'm begging you, implicate me."

"I'm not sure that this extortion was a one-man job."

"There's an awful lot of happy FBI bosses who think otherwise."

"Self-congratulating management—is there any bigger canary in the mine that something is wrong?"

"I wouldn't argue with that," she said. "Do you have any proof?"

"The timing at the tunnel isn't right."

"Are you sure? Stress can distort time, especially when you're going through something as sensory depriving as you did."

"I'm not talking just about inside the tunnel. I checked all the logs, the time that the GPS started away from the tunnel, and the time of the explosion when I blew open the hatch. Last night, I went back out there and timed the walk from the tunnel to where the truck was intercepted. Anyone coming back from that would have run into the surveillance agents. And whoever it was would have had to come back to pick up the money."

"So you think Bertok had a partner?"

"One person couldn't have done it alone, no. So, is there anyone you know that could have been in this with Bertok, if it was Bertok?"

"*If* it was."

Vail chose not to explain. "Yes, if it was."

"Well, you're the guy he was shooting at, so if you want to give him the benefit of the doubt, who am I to argue? I assume you mean someone in the FBI."

"Yes."

"Why are you asking me instead of people at the Bureau?"

"I don't want anyone there to know that I'm not buying the Bertok-alone theory. That's why I want this kept quiet for now."

"If you have doubts about his involvement, why another agent?"

"I've taken a look at Bertok's phone records. There were no calls to anyone other than his brother in Minnesota, and his ex-wives both here and in Arizona. That suggests someone he had regular contact with, like at work. Again, that's why I'm here; I don't want to ask the wrong person in the office."

Tye took a long drag on her cigarette. "I hate to point any fingers, but there is one person Bertok worked with on occasion. Vince Pendaran. And he is sort of connected to the enemies list."

"How?"

"The first victim—Connie Lysander, a former reporter turned whistle-blower. You know about her?"

"Just what's in the file."

"She made a lot of allegations around here, most of which were false. However, there were some firings, most notably the United States attorney, who was a good guy. There were also some suspensions, one of which was Pendaran for using the services of prostitutes. I don't know why he wasn't fired. He seems to be one of these guys who continually fall through the cracks."

"What's he like?"

"Different. He worked undercover until he got caught stealing from a UC project. Again, I don't know why he wasn't fired. Instead, they transferred him to Bertok's squad. If you haven't picked up on it yet, it's a dumping ground for problems in the office. The word is that the supervisor, Allen Sabine, never complains, so they keep handing him the problem children. Anyway, Pendaran came up here a couple of times with Stan when they needed the okay for an arrest that was a little shaky. There's something about the way he looks at you. I don't know, it's cold, like he's trying to figure out where your buttons are. I'd see him at parties. Very taciturn until he got the requisite number of drinks in him, which I think was one. Then you'd find his hand on your ass. Everyone pretty much treated him like he had the plague, you know, an OPR incident looking for a place to land. That is, everybody but Bertok. For some reason Pendaran seemed to respond to him. You know, Stan could get him to do some work even if it was only as his gofer. And to a degree, socially as well. He'd take the effort to drag him into conversations at office functions. I guess even the most downtrodden needs the occasional project to ensure there's at least one person below him on the food chain."

Vail's cell phone rang. It was Kate. "We just got word. They matched Bertok's gun to the four victims and the shooting yesterday."

"Does that include the shell casing from the third murder?"

"Yes," she said. "Why is that important?"

"I'll explain when I see you. Will you be available to take a ride a little later?"

"Sure."

"I'll see you in an hour or two." Vail hung up. "As you could probably tell from that call, they matched Bertok's gun to everything from the first homicide to yesterday's shooting."

"Then are you still interested in Pendaran?"

"Yes."

"Interesting," she said. "I assume you'd prefer someplace away from the office to converse with him."

"Like where?"

"It came out during the Lysander exposé, his trips to professional ladies were almost daily. That's why he was so easy for her, and OPR, to catch. The names and addresses are in the DOJ file."

"Where is that kept?"

She stubbed out her cigarette on the outside sill, tossed the butt into the six-story air shaft, and pulled the window closed. She sat down at her desk and typed on her keyboard. "I *obtained* a copy of it for my own private edification, trying to find a loophole for the old United States attorney when he was under fire for not properly leading the troops. Unfortunately, like the FBI, we have strict rules about showing files to outside agencies, so you can't see this." She gave him a crooked smile. "I'm going to lunch. Do me a favor when you leave, shut down my computer."

"I owe you one, Tye."

"That's a funny thing, Agent Vail. I keep hearing that

around here, but no one ever seems to pay up. Care to be a trendsetter?"

Vail smiled noncommittally and watched as that vague loneliness seeped back into her eyes.

AS VINCE PENDARAN exited the Swedish Academy of Massage and walked to his Bureau car, Vail watched him, trying to decide whether his gait was the same as that of the man who had walked into the house on Spring Street the day before. As he put the key in the lock, Vail walked up behind him silently and measured his height and weight. "I guess you don't have to worry about going to these places now that Connie Lysander is dead."

Pendaran spun around. His sweaty black hair hung low on his forehead, his eyebrows thick and lowered in disdain. He was powerfully built, his stance now angry. "Who are you?"

Vail pulled out his credential case with the gold badge on the outside. He didn't bother opening it.

"You OPR?" Pendaran asked. "I was just seeing a source."

Vail laughed. "That's it? You've been hit for this once before and that's as creative as you can get? Let me give you a tip: get a better story because the next time OPR comes for you, they're bringing machetes."

Pendaran's eyes darted around the lot before he said, "Why don't we talk in the car."

Vail went around to the passenger's side and got in. "I'm Steve Vail."

"The guy from headquarters that Stan is supposed to have tried to shoot?"

"Supposed to have?"

"Stan was a friend of mine, and I know he did some out-of-bounds stuff, but shooting at people, that wasn't him."

"Money can change people in a hurry."

"You'd have to prove it to me."

"Was he a good enough friend that you might want to get something going on the side?"

Pendaran's head snapped toward Vail. "I hope you're not saying what I think you're saying?"

"Actually, I am."

"Oh no, not me. I don't know anything about any murders."

"Weren't you two partners?"

"On the job, sometimes. And that was all."

"If you didn't help him, who else could have?"

"Why don't you get out of my car."

"And if I don't?"

Pendaran smiled viciously. "That would turn a very mediocre afternoon into a very pleasant one."

"Then, between you and Bertok, that would make you the violent one."

"Do yourself a favor and leave before you find out."

"Not the way I would have played it, Vince, but then I never murdered anyone." Pendaran glared at him, and Vail stared back with an amused calm. "At least not in cold blood."

Vail got out and watched as the Bureau car sped out of the lot.

SIXTEEN

WHEN VAIL CAME THROUGH THE DOOR OF KATE'S OFFICE, SHE SAID, "Where have you been?"

"Out looking for the guy on the grassy knoll."

"You think someone else is involved?"

He told her about his time analysis at the tunnel.

She took a moment to consider what he had found. "What about—no, that wouldn't work." She took a few more seconds to consider other possibilities. "It sounds like he couldn't have done it without help."

"Bertok worked with a guy named Vince Pendaran. He's got some speed bumps in his personnel file. One of them was Connie Lysander. I just caught him coming out of a full-service massage parlor. I put some angst on him but not enough to get a good read."

"And?"

"He's not the right size for the guy that we saw going in the house yesterday, and his walk was different. Just the same, keep his name in the back of your Rolodex."

"What do you mean, 'not the right size'? I thought Stan Bertok was the perfect size to play the role of Stan Bertok."

"Really, I thought he was a little too tall."

"What are you talking about?"

"Patience, Bannon, all questions will be answered during this afternoon's field trip. Hopefully."

"Oh, yeah, this has promotion written all over it," she said. "This Pendaran, where did you come up with him?"

"Tye Delson."

"That's getting to be a regular stop on your little errands list."

"I'm becoming addicted to secondhand smoke."

"So, this ride we're taking, I assume it has something to do with your undetected co-conspirator?"

"Are you ready?"

She pulled on her jacket and tapped her hip, verifying she was armed. "Gun, check." Tapped the breast pocket of her blazer. "Credentials, check." She opened her mouth and ran a finger behind her back molar. "Cyanide capsule, check." She picked up her briefcase. "To the Batcave."

As they got in the elevator, Vail asked, "What's going on with *Money Search L.A.*?"

"For a reality show, it's pretty surreal. It's an all-hands production. Kaulcrick and Hildebrand are running it from the major-case room. If they've got anything going, I haven't heard about it." When he didn't say anything she glanced over at him. His eyes had become unfocused, and she knew that he hadn't heard her. She leaned back against the wall and waited. When the doors opened in the basement, he finally looked at her. "Why did the killer pick up his casings after the first three murders but not after the fourth?"

"Oh, I know this one," she said facetiously. "Because it

doesn't matter. Everything has been matched to Bertok's gun."

"I know you can't answer every little question about a crime, but this one doesn't seem to be that small to me."

"I don't know," she said. "The more crimes a person commits, the more mistakes he makes. Maybe he got scared off the fourth time. Maybe he couldn't find it. Maybe he had a plane to catch. Is it really that big a deal?"

"By itself, it's not. But why pick them up at all? He was leaving the slugs behind, which are much more incriminating and easier to identify."

"After the first two, we announced that the slugs matched, so the killer knew we could identify the gun. He probably figured if we matched the slugs, why bother picking up the brass?"

"If they didn't want them matched, then why use the same gun?" Vail said.

"I suppose they wanted everyone to know that they were responsible for all of the killings."

"Exactly. If they wanted the world to know, why pick up the casings in the first place?"

Kate finally took a moment to consider the inconsistency. "That's a good question."

They got to the car, and Vail put his briefcase in the trunk. Kate could see a shotgun case and a long silver-colored pry bar in the trunk. "What's that?"

"A Halligan. It's a fire department tool. I like to think of it as an all-purpose key."

"Just so I'm clear, you intend to use it on a door, not on a person."

"Where's your spirit of adventure?"

"And where did the shotgun come from? And more important, why do you think we'll need it?"

"It's a new option from the car rental company. They call it their hunter-gatherer option."

Then she noticed a large square black case that she hadn't seen since the advent of the Bureau's Evidence Recovery Teams. "And an evidence kit?"

"Chance favors the prepared mind."

"In other words, if you find evidence, you can keep all your hole cards hidden."

"And to think I was reluctant to bring you along," Vail said. "Keep it up and I'm not going to let you be my girlfriend anymore."

"When we get on the freeway, let me know when you get up to eighty so I can dive into oncoming traffic."

Once they cleared the garage, Vail drove for a while without speaking. Then he said, "Okay, let's look at this. Why did Bertok go to that house on Spring Street? The money wasn't there. Nothing was there. It seems like a major mistake, since he used that address to rent a car. Especially after such an extraordinarily well-planned series of crimes."

"Also a good question."

"That's two good questions too many."

"Can I assume we're going back to Spring Street?"

"Yes, you may," he said. "I'm curious about one other thing. How come you're not helping Kaulcrick find the money."

"Have you noticed any changes in the assistant director in the last twenty-four hours?"

"I haven't noticed any changes other than he's let it become a little more obvious that he has an ego."

"Well, you're right, he does have an ego, and usually he's pretty good at keeping it in check until after he delivers the coup de grâce. But I think he's getting tired of trying to navigate through your vapor trail. He knows that you and I are working together, so I'm sure I'll be the last to know anything that might give you an advantage."

He smiled at her. "Then I guess we'd better find the money ourselves."

"Why am I suddenly getting the feeling that you don't think that money is in locker number fourteen?"

"Human nature is to be lazy," Vail said. "I'm always suspicious of things that seem too easy."

"And, of course, you'd never bother Kaulcrick with your suspicions."

"I have already told him, and everyone else, that the biggest obstacle in this case is distraction. They listen, nod their heads in agreement, and then go running after the first shiny object."

"Funny how, once again, that leaves you all alone to do what you want."

"There is one basic tenet of metaphysics that guided my career as an agent: If they're there, they ain't here."

"Ever think that may be why your FBI *career* was only three years long?"

"I only think how great those three years were."

After another fifteen minutes, Vail pulled up to the house that the day before had been overrun with law enforcement personnel and now stood deserted. The only reminder was the yellow and black tape that crisscrossed the front door. Kate said, "I know this is a stupid question, but did you notify anyone in officialdom that we were coming out here?"

"You're right, that was a stupid question." He got out and went to the trunk, lifting out the pry bar. "But I got Mr. Halligan's permission, if that helps. Come on, let's take a walk around first."

They started on the east side of the structure. "The front-room window has no bars on it," Vail said. He inspected the construction on either side, running his hand along the siding. "There were bars, but they were removed. You can see where the holes have been repaired. Looks fairly recent, too."

Kate stepped closer. "Why would anyone do that?"

"Yet another good question. Here's another one: why have bars on all the other doors and windows but take them off of this one?" Vail walked to the back of the house and after checking the wrought-iron gate protecting the back door asked, "Where did you take cover back here, behind the Dumpster?"

"Yes." She pointed at the bin twenty yards off the northeast corner of the house. Vail went over and stood behind it. "It provides perfect cover. It's also the ideal position for watching the rear door and the east side of the house at the same time. Exactly what we needed at the time." Vail walked around the Dumpster, inspecting it. "I was at the front of the house, so that leaves just the window on the west wall of the house. Let's take a look at that."

"What exactly are we looking for?" Kate said.

"I don't exactly know."

When they got to the other side, Vail seemed more interested in the ancient wooden fence that surrounded the industrial property than in the house or the bars on the bedroom window. Kate tugged on them. "These seem to be in good shape."

Vail was still inspecting the wooden fence that surrounded the auto scrap yard. "It's not more than ten feet from the house to this fence," he said to no one in particular. Finally he walked over to the window. He took the bars in both hands and jerked on them with his entire weight. They moved about a half inch. He pushed and pulled, moving them back and forth several times. "They shouldn't do that." He took a couple of steps back. "These are newer than the others." Again he grabbed them, and now using all his strength he tried to pull them out of the wall, but they would move only the same fraction of an inch. Vail leaned in and inspected the bars where they were anchored into the siding.

"Meaning what?" Kate asked.

"I'm not sure yet. Let's go inside."

"Yet" was one of those little signs Kate had learned to pick up on with Vail. It meant that he probably knew what was going on, but, as with everything else, he saw no advantage in letting the rest of the world in on it.

He took a quick look around the neighborhood before inserting the claw end of the Halligan bar into the frame of the gate and in a quick, smooth pull, popped it open. He didn't bother using the tool on the front door. After testing the knob, he swung his hip into it, snapping it open. Kate followed him back to the bedroom where Bertok had died the day before. He pulled up the window sash and yanked on the bars again, watching the points where the metal ends were anchored into the outside wall. Stepping to the right side, he inspected the casing that trimmed the inside of the window. "Did you bring any evidence gloves?"

"Very subtle, Vail. Give me the keys, and I'll get the evidence kit."

When she came back in, she set the case down and opened it. She handed him a pair of gloves. "You do remember that this place has been processed?"

"Only in the places that fit the story."

"*Story?* That's what happened."

"Take a magician—are his illusions the truth or are they fiction? What you *believe* you see is fiction. Only when you know how the trick is done does it become truth."

As much as Kate had come to expect miracles from Vail, this seemed too far-fetched even for him. "This was all some kind of trick?"

"Let's start with the way we traced Bertok to this place. Anything bother you about that?"

"What do you mean? I thought it was a nice investigative string that led us to him."

"That's just it, *a nice string*. I've never seen one fall into place so neatly. The call to Bertok's apartment leads to the Laundromat, then to the motel and the DMV and finally here. All in less than two hours. And of the more than eight thousand hours in a year, all three of us show up here at the same moment. It was almost like one of those training exercises that Quantico dreams up for new agents out at the combat village."

Kate considered Vail's refusal to accept the obvious. She wondered if it was a discipline, or a reaction to a demanding father whom he had once referred to as the sire of his "world-class scorn." Either way, the result was Vail's ability to find his way through a maze that everyone else failed to realize existed. And while it was an extraordinary thing to witness, Kate wondered if it wasn't a coping mechanism. "I see your point about it all falling into place nicely, but doesn't that occasionally happen? Ballistics has confirmed that Stanley Bertok shot at you, barricaded himself, and then committed suicide with his issued handgun, which was also used in four murders."

"It wasn't Bertok," Vail said without the least bit of uncertainty.

"What?" Kate said, her volume unintentionally incredulous. "I'm pretty sure the guy in the morgue is Bertok."

"It is, but that's not who shot at me and is probably not who committed the murders."

"Based on what?"

Vail ignored the question. "Don't you think it was very convenient that he came into the Laundromat just after the woman we talked to arrived, almost like he was waiting for a witness. He made sure she noticed him with all that hassle about the hundred-dollar bill. And the bill happens to be one of the punctured ones from the drop, so there's no doubt about its origin. But he's all covered up to the extent that she can't identify Bertok's photo. Then he conveniently pulls across the street to the motel in plain sight of her."

"But he had the identical clothing on when SWAT broke in here and found him."

"Did you take a look at the body?"

"Not really. I mean I saw it, but I haven't been around enough of that sort of thing to know what to look for."

"First of all, he didn't have cigarettes on his breath. I checked the evidence sheets last night. He didn't have any cigarettes or a lighter on his person. Remember his apartment, what a heavy smoker he was?"

"Maybe he quit."

"Maybe, but it would have been a pretty stressful time to start worrying about lung cancer. But more definitively, the blood coming from his temple had completely dried and crystallized."

"Meaning?"

"It takes a while for that to happen. Longer than the time between the shot and SWAT breaking in."

"Are you saying he was already dead?"

"Yes."

"Then who shot at you?"

"Whoever was at the Laundromat, and we saw coming in here."

"So when we were driving by here, Bertok was already in here, dead."

"Right."

"Okay, this look-alike shoots at you, locks himself in this room, fires a shot to simulate the suicide shot."

"Probably while holding the gun in Bertok's hand in case of a residue test. Yes, that's right."

"That's right?" Kate asked. "Then when SWAT broke in here, where was he? With the bars on the window, the only way out is the door where you and I and the L.A. cop were waiting to light him up."

Without answering, Vail pulled on the evidence gloves. First he felt along the left edge casing, and after apparently not finding what he was looking for, he tried the right side. As he slid his hand along it, he found a gripping point and pulled the casing off. Inside was a metal plate into which were anchored the ends of the bars. He pushed the plate up and, reaching through the window, pushed the cage open. It swung out on the hinged edge of the other side. Vail put the casing back into place and pushed on it until it snapped into place. He climbed out through the window. Once on the ground, he swung the bars back into place, and a soft metal snap sounded when the bars reseated themselves in the hidden metal plate. He pulled on them to make sure they had locked into place.

"Those bars on the living room window were removed so anyone covering the back would have to also watch that side because escape was possible through that window. The Dumpster was probably put back there for cover so whoever went to the rear would be screened from this side of the house. This side would be ignored because the window was barred, which is exactly what we did."

"But where did he go once he was outside?" Kate asked. "We were in the front and the cop with the shotgun was in the back."

Vail walked over to the fence and tested several of the wooden boards until he found two next to each other that were not nailed at the bottom. He angled the lower ends away from each other and, half squatting, squeezed himself through the narrow opening. "I'll be back in a few minutes." He let go of the boards and they swung back into place.

Ten minutes later, he came back through the fence. "It's just a short walk to the other side of the property. There's a side street where he could have had another car parked."

"How'd you know about the bars?"

"I didn't, but when I felt the bars move back and forth and saw that pin-and-loop construction that could act as a hinge, it seemed like the only possibility. See, all those years in the construction trade weren't wasted after all."

Kate let all the implications run through her mind, trying to synthesize them into a logical explanation. "But Bertok's gun was used in the homicides, three of them before he even disappeared. So how can it *not* be him?"

"The answer to that will require a call to the firearms unit at the lab."

She had no idea what Vail meant but opened her cell phone and dialed FBI headquarters. Once she was put through to the lab, she asked for the examiner on the case and hit the speakerphone button. "Hi, this is Deputy Assistant Director Kate Bannon."

"Mike Terry," the examiner said.

"I'm calling on the Pentad case. I'm going to put on an agent named Steve Vail. Please answer any questions he might have."

Vail took the phone. "Hi, Mike. You got a match on all the slugs with Bertok's issue weapon, is that right?"

"And the casings. The one from the fourth murder and all those recovered at the house where he died."

"Where is the gun now?"

"I've got it right here. I was just finishing my report."

"Other than ballistics, did you do any examinations on it?"

"Not really. Assistant Director Kaulcrick called and said the comparisons were to be done immediately. At the time I was right in the middle of an examination for a customs agent who had been shot, so I went back to that once I had completed the Bertok tests."

"I'd like you to take a look at the barrel of that Glock. It should have a serial number." The examiner didn't answer right away. "Mike?"

"Sorry. I was looking at the gun. It definitely has some wear. But the barrel, it looks much newer."

"I thought it might."

"But the casings matched. And they have nothing to do with the barrel. This has to be the gun used in the homicides."

"Good enough. I'm just tying up some loose ends. Let me have the serial number on the barrel. For the office records." After writing it down, Vail hung up and handed Kate the phone. "Call the armorer at Quantico and see if this is the barrel that was in Bertok's gun when it was issued to him." He handed her the slip of paper with the serial number on it.

Kate called Quantico and was put through to the armorer. She read him the serial number and, after five minutes, said thank you and hung up. "You were right. That is not the barrel that was originally in Bertok's weapon. It all makes sense. Whoever did this committed the first three murders with a Glock 22 of their own, kidnapped Bertok, took his issue gun, and switched the barrel from the first three murders into his Glock. Then they committed the fourth murder with Bertok's gun and left the casing because it would now match. Shot at you with the gun before escaping out the rigged window, and they had already placed Bertok's body in here. Then they just had to leave the gun behind, which tied up all loose ends." A look of revelation creased her features. "Which means that if all this was staged, the key in the moneybag can't be anything more than another wild-goose chase."

She looked at him to confirm her theory, but he was taking out fingerprint powder and a brush from the evidence kit. He dusted the white window frame with black powder. "Nothing there," he said.

Then he took off the casing and dusted the metal release mechanism. "And nothing there. So much for a quick solution."

Vail packed up the kit and took it out to the car. They got in and Kate asked, "What do we do now?"

"Do you have any contacts at ATF?"

"I could make a call to headquarters and find one."

"We need a factory trace on the barrel."

"Then what?"

"We'll have to see where that leads us."

"Is it me, or are we losing ground?"

"Well, let's see. We now have five murders, we're short four million nine hundred thousand plus, and we're still being played like a whorehouse piano." He smiled. "I'd say we've got them right where we want them."

SEVENTEEN

THEY HAD BEEN DRIVING FOR ALMOST A HALF HOUR WHEN KATE cracked her window to let the warm sunny air stream across her face. It felt good against the cool artificial flow being pumped so uniformly throughout the car. She needed some sort of sensory feedback to separate the real from the staged. She, like everyone else, had been taken in by the Pentad's plan to blame Stan Bertok for the murders. She let her mind find its way through the twists and turns of the case, looking for any inconsistency that the FBI would eventually have picked up on to lead them to the truth. She was not sure there were any. In the end, the money would not have been found, and the search for it would have become no more than a frustration eventually downgrading to a mild curiosity as everyone thankfully moved on to new priorities. She closed the window and looked back at Vail. He glanced at her with an absentminded smile. He didn't seem to appreciate what he had done. Then a more immediate downside of the discovery hit her. "Do you want to tell Don about Bertok or should I do it?"

"You're the one who has to keep him happy."

"We swallowed the Pentad's frame hook, line, and sinker. I'm pretty sure that's not going to make him happy. Until a half hour ago, this case, minus the money, was solved. Now we've got another murdered agent, no suspects, and not the slightest idea where the money is."

"Then give him Pendaran. If he has someone to go after, it'll take some of the sting out of being wrong about Bertok."

"What about tracing the gun barrel? We can't really tell him about Stan Bertok without explaining what we've found out about his gun."

"Give that to him too."

She looked at him quizzically. "You're suddenly generous." She let it hang in the air to see if Vail would respond. When he didn't, she said, "I know you like to keep the best lead to work on yourself. Giving up both Pendaran and the gun will leave you nothing. Unless you're keeping something from me."

"Maybe it'll get you back in his good graces. Besides, tracing the barrel is piecework; doing it doesn't interest me. Just let me know what they find out. Besides, like you said, we have no choice—it's part of exonerating Stan Bertok. And Pendaran is going to need surveilling. That's not a one-man operation, not twenty-four hours a day. I've never had the patience for surveillance."

"Okay, then tell me, while we're doing the light lifting, where will you be?"

Vail pulled up in front of the federal building. "Even bricklayers are entitled to a little downtime. Union rules." Vail glanced at his side-view mirror.

"Just on the off chance that you've got something going on, please keep the stupid stuff to a minimum."

He checked the mirror again to make sure the car that

had been following them since they left Spring Street was still there. "Define 'minimum.'"

"You know, anything that causes a lot of paperwork, blowing up tunnels, shoot-outs, honking off assistant directors." She squeezed his hand before she got out. He took a moment to enjoy her rhythmic walk in the dazzling sunlight. *Not now, Vail*, he admonished himself. Once she was inside the front door, he checked his mirror to make sure the car was still with him. He wasn't positive but he thought there was now a second vehicle.

Once a seam formed in the traffic, he pulled away from the curb. He had to assume they were the Pentad. But why were they following him? They had their money and as far as anyone knew, Bertok was being blamed. They had been on Vail since he left Spring Street. Was there something else there they were afraid he'd find?

If he had told Kate about being followed, she would have wanted to bring in the troops, and as careful as these people had been, they would have been gone long before anyone could have gotten near them. He decided if he was going to sneak up on them, he'd have to go back to Spring Street alone.

At a light, he drew his automatic and set it on the seat next to him. When the light went green, he checked his mirror again. There was definitely a second car, and they were keeping a block's distance between themselves and him. One was a dark gray two-door Dodge and the other a gold Honda. The Dodge was the one he had originally spotted and apparently had called the Honda for help.

Vail drove at a leisurely pace, slowing down for lights so

they wouldn't lose him. The drive back took about a half hour. Reholstering his weapon, he got out and went to the trunk. Slipping the monocular into his suit pocket, he lifted the evidence kit out of the car along with the Halligan bar. He set the evidence kit on the front porch and pushed open the door. Hiding in the shadows of the front room, he used the monocular to look out the window. Half a block away, the Dodge had pulled to the curb. He assumed the Honda was hanging farther back.

Going out on the porch, Vail took several items out of the evidence kit. Pulling on a fresh pair of gloves, he walked back to the Dumpster and started dusting, occasionally ripping off a piece of clear tape and apparently lifting a print, which he then attached to an index card. He repeated the process two more times before returning to the house.

The driver of the Dodge lit a cigarette. His gray eyes narrowed as he tracked Vail's movements. "Vic, he's back inside the house," he said into his cell phone.

VICTOR RADEK SAT in his Honda almost a hundred yards farther away. He wondered if all his planning was going to be ruined by the man's voice he was listening to. Had he made the mistake that was going to enable the FBI to identify Radek or the other members of his gang? "I don't like this. This is the guy from the tunnel, so he's no fool. Are you sure you wiped down that Dumpster, Lee?"

"I'm sure. Whatever prints he found aren't ours. They could be anybody's, probably the cops or FBI."

"You're sure?"

"I'm positive."

"And inside the house, you're also positive?"

"I wiped everything down before I went out the window."

The first time Radek saw Lee Salton in prison, he immediately recognized his usefulness. Always boiling just below the surface was a brutal, hair-trigger violence, which was common in a place like Marion. But Radek also detected an unusual weakness that rarely accompanied homicidal ability, something that made Salton exploitable. Salton needed someone else to be in charge, which in turn allowed him to rationalize not being responsible for his actions. Salton, as deadly as he was, was not a psychopath. When acting on his own, he invariably suffered self-recrimination afterward. When directed to violence by someone else, he suffered no such guilt. One night they got very drunk on prison hooch, and Salton told him that his mother had been a Bible-thumping lunatic, while his father was an alcoholic over-the-road trucker who, when returning home, would invariably re-mark his territory by beating the hell out of both of them.

Salton had been the ideal instrument to carry out the Pentad murders. He was efficient, dependable, and, as he proved in setting up the Bertok suicide, fearless, and he could follow the most complicated instructions. Best of all, he kept Radek from having to get his own hands dirty. And, most important, Radek knew that Salton was incapable of ratting him, or anyone else, out.

The agent in the house had become a threat. First surviving the tunnel, then the shoot-out the day before. Now he had crossed paths with Radek again. He couldn't know what they were doing there, but there he was. Why did he keep going back to the house? Radek feared it was only a matter of time until he discovered the trick bars on the bedroom window. If he did, the FBI would again be trying to figure out who was responsible for the murders instead of just chasing their tails looking for the money. There was only one thing to do.

"Is he still in the house?"

"Yeah," Salton answered.

"What's he doing in there? They did all their crime-scene stuff yesterday."

"You don't think he can figure out that trick window, do you?"

There was something uncertain in Salton's voice. "Why, Lee? What if he does? Didn't you wipe the plate down before you closed it up?"

"I'm almost positive I did."

"That's not good enough."

"He was trying to kick the door in and shoot me, remember?"

"If he finds any one of our prints, we're through."

"What do you want me to do, Vic?"

"Think you can take him out?"

Salton leaned across the front seat and picked up a Heckler & Koch submachine gun from the passenger-side floor. "As much trouble as this guy has been, try and stop me." He chambered a round.

"Once you put him down, we've got to destroy the evidence he's collected. Just torch the house so we don't have to worry about it again."

Salton put the car in gear. "My pleasure." He pulled up a little past the house, closer to the salvage yard than to the one-story structure, and got out, leaving the engine running. Cutting across the lawn on an angle so he couldn't be seen as easily, he pulled himself up on the front porch silently and flattened against the wall. He could now hear Vail moving around inside. Counting to three, he spun himself in front of the door with the MP5 positioned on his hip ready to fire. Vail was in the bedroom doorway, putting the door back up over the opening. As soon as he saw Salton, he pushed it closed.

Salton took three quick strides toward the bedroom and opened up, firing full automatic, low through the door in case Vail had hit the floor. And if he was still standing, the raking burst would take his legs out from under him. After firing all thirty rounds in the magazine, he slammed in a second clip and moved to the door. Raising the weapon to his shoulder, he kicked open the door. The room was empty and the bars on the window had been swung open.

Behind him, Salton heard Vail's voice. "You would think that if there was one person who wouldn't fall for that it would be you."

Vail watched Salton's neck muscles tighten with decision and knew what was coming next. Salton started to turn, firing before he could see Vail, hoping that the spraying rounds would cause the agent to take cover.

Vail stood his ground and fired one shot, hitting Salton in the side of the head just above the ear. The machine gun went silent and Salton's lifeless body hit the floor. Vail moved to the wall next to the front window and peered out carefully, looking for the Honda. He could see it now. It had moved up to where the Dodge had been sitting.

After a few seconds, the silence was interrupted by a cell phone ringing. Vail patted down Salton's body and found the phone. He answered "Yeah" as anonymously as possible.

"Did you get him?"

Vail was surprised by the matter-of-factness of the voice. "Yeah," Vail answered, trying to keep the single syllable unrecognizable.

There was a hesitation and then the voice ordered, "Say something else."

Vail knew he had been discovered. "Looks like you're going to need new business cards. I'm thinking something like the Quartet Rubaco, or the Rubaco Tetrad has a nice ring to it, you know, for continuity, since the Pentad has been reduced by one member. Personally—"

The line went dead. Vail moved back to the window and watched as the Honda turned around in a driveway and disappeared from sight. He dialed the office on Salton's phone and looked down at the body. "Don't worry, it's a local call."

When Kate answered, he told her what had happened. She started to ask a question, but he cut her off, telling her there was at least one more member of the gang in the area, and then hung up.

He turned back to the man he had just killed. Rolling him over, he searched his pockets. He didn't have a wallet, but he did have a thick wad of hundred-dollar bills in one of his front pants pockets. He was wearing a black turtleneck, not a logical garment for such a hot L.A. day. Vail pulled down the neck, revealing a tattoo that was hidden just beneath the collar. The faded letters said AT YOUR OWN RISK. Tiny drops of blood in red ink dripped from the letters. The quality, Vail knew, was jailhouse. He pushed up one of the sleeves, revealing more tattoos of institutional inferiority. He was about the right height and weight of the individual who had fired at him the day before. Even though he was dead, there was still something about him, some kind of potential for violence. It was the eyes, Vail decided. They were still open and full of hate.

Vail walked out to the car, which was still idling. The front and back seats were empty. He reached in and turned off the ignition, taking the keys. Watching the street in case the Honda returned, he opened the trunk. A heavy cardboard box was the only thing inside. It was bigger than a large suitcase, tightly sealed with nylon filament tape. Vail took out his lock-back knife and slit along the seams. Packed in heavy-gauge plastic and wrapped with the same tape were neat stacks of banded hundred-dollar bills.

EIGHTEEN

KAULCRICK AND KATE ARRIVED IN THE SAME CAR. VAIL WAS HALF sitting, half leaning against the Dodge's trunk. "You okay, Steve?" she asked before she was all the way out of the vehicle.

"I'm good." Kaulcrick didn't say anything but just looked at him. Vail pointed down, indicating that the assistant director should look in the trunk.

Once he did, he said, "Do you know how much is in there?"

"From its weight, I'd say roughly three million."

Kate said, "What happened?"

Vail explained how he thought he was being followed when he dropped her off at the federal building. He didn't mention that he had first noticed the sedan when they had left Spring Street. He explained how the confrontation between him and the dead man inside had happened.

After closing the trunk, Vail led the three of them into the house. Kaulcrick squatted over the body. "Any idea who he is?"

"I gave him a quick pat; I couldn't find anything. He isn't a domestic terrorist. Check his neck and arms. That's institutional ink."

Other FBI cars along with LAPD started arriving, shutting down their sirens as they got out. Kaulcrick said, "Kate explained about Stan Bertok, which I was having a hard time believing until you called with this. So all of this was a straight-up extortion."

"A lot of colored smoke and strobing lights, but that would be my guess. And this guy is about the right size for Bertok's stand-in yesterday."

"Was he acting alone?" Kaulcrick asked.

"I don't think so. There was a second car following me."

"You're sure?"

"We had a brief telephone conversation when he thought he was talking to his co-worker here. Sounded like he was the guy giving orders."

"Well, we know it wasn't Pendaran. Surveillance just found him coming out of the same massage parlor. Which doesn't mean that he isn't part of this."

"There's still two million dollars missing," Vail said. "Somebody's got it. And unfortunately, it isn't us."

"We'll get this man fingerprinted and find out then who he and his friends are. Kate, take Steve back to the office so he can give his statement regarding the shooting. Give her your gun, Steve." Vail handed it over and knew it would be gone until the investigation of the killing was completed.

When they went out to the car, Kate insisted on driving, which Vail took as not being a good sign. Once they were on the freeway, she said, "So, you first noticed we were being followed when?" Her tone indicated she knew the answer.

"I *thought*—possibly—we were being tailed when we left the house."

"So you're back to not trusting me."

"What exactly is it that you think you missed out on?"

"I'm sure I would have been scared to death. Maybe that's what I missed out on."

"This case isn't some little hothouse laboratory to see where your limits are. These animals have murdered five people *so far*, two of which were FBI agents. They just tried to make it three. And I've got a feeling they're not done yet."

"I can handle it."

"You probably can, but I don't want to be there if you can't. You told me I do this because I can, because I'm built for it."

"Am I that big a liability?"

"For me, everyone's a liability. Do you think if you were in that bank with me, I would have done what I did? Instead of throwing caution to the wind, I'd be worried about you getting hurt. I can't handle that kind of responsibility. No faces, remember?"

"What do you want me to do, sign a waiver? I need to know that I can do this. Not like you, but that my career hasn't been some illusion fueled by affirmative action or because men find me attractive."

Vail closed his eyes and leaned his head back onto the rest. After a few moments to let the immediacy of their emotions dissolve, he said, "Without looking at the mirrors, Kate, tell me if we're being followed." She looked over at him and, seeing his eyes closed, stole a glance at the rearview mirror, searching the highway behind them. Although he still hadn't opened his eyes, she suspected that he knew she had looked. He said, "Are you still sure you want all the way in?"

VAIL'S SHOOTING STATEMENT took over three hours. He was interviewed by the office legal agent, who made him repeat the story over and over to eliminate any inconsistencies before it was reduced to writing. "Usually shooting reviews can take up to three months before a decision can be made as to whether it was justified or not," the agent said, his voice as flat as if he were reading him his rights.

Vail laughed. He knew it was a good shooting and there were no witnesses, but what he found amusing was that by the time this decision had worked its way through the hallowed halls of the Hoover Building, he would be back laying bricks. When the agent asked him what was so funny, he waved apologetically and signed the statement without reading it.

Vail was then led to another interview room, where two detectives from the LAPD were waiting. They were given a copy of the statement. After reading it, they interrogated him for two more hours. When they were done, he headed to see Kate. He was thinking about the ride back to the office. Not a word had been spoken after his asking about being surveilled. He decided that he had been too hard on her. Whatever her reason for being angry, she was a more than capable agent, and just as important, she had not once chosen her career over his reckless resistance to all things FBI. And as unaccustomed as he was to giving in to his feelings, he liked her, probably more than he wanted to admit.

Her door was ajar and he knocked twice before walking in. She was on the phone and motioned him to come in and sit down. Behind her in the corner was a newly arrived steel safe, the kind that looked like a filing cabinet except it weighed six hundred pounds and the top drawer had a combination dial embedded in the center of it. The box containing the better part of three million dollars sat on the floor next to it.

He took off his jacket, throwing it onto a chair. There was a newspaper there and he picked it up. The front-page article was about Bertok's suicide. He started to read it out of habit, but then remembered that between the SAC's press release and today's discoveries, none of it was true. He put it down. Kate glanced at him and he pursed his lips deferentially as a peace offering. A thin smile lit her eyes. After another minute she hung up. "How did it go with LAPD?"

"They didn't say, but it didn't seem like they were out to get anyone," he said. "For what it's worth, I was out of line with some of that stuff in the car."

"And some of it you weren't. When you get to the DAD level you become spoiled and don't think you should be denied anything. It's just that ever since we sent you to that tunnel to make the drop, I've felt like a hypocrite. Giving orders, making things happen, but not really risking anything. You could have been killed, and I was sitting in the major-case room drinking coffee. You've got to understand, I don't want to feel like a phony. And every time you do something like this it makes me feel that way."

"If there's one thing I can spot, it's a phony. Believe me, you're woefully underqualified. And as far as these situations, when they come up, I never know what's going to happen. I never have a plan or calculate the odds of surviving or anything else. It just works out. One day it probably won't. Maybe that's why I don't mind being a bricklayer. A surprisingly small number of us get shot. At least not on the job."

She smiled and took another Glock automatic out of her desk drawer, the same model as the one he had surrendered. She handed it to him. "I went down to the firearms vault and drew this for you."

"And I didn't get you anything. How about I buy dinner?"

"You're on, but it's probably going to have to be carry-out. We got an ID on the guy who spent the last two days shooting at you—Lee Davis Salton. Recent graduate of the Marion Federal Correction Institution. Long list of bank robberies, plus a particularly nasty little kidnapping in which a man hired him to torture and maim his wife without killing her. Wanted her to suffer for a long time, I guess. I don't know how these people find one another. Plus, just before Salton got out, they liked him for killing an inmate named Michael Vashon, but they couldn't make the case. The prison is e-mailing photos of his social circle. Hopefully one of them will be your contestant number two."

"I wish I had gotten a look at him."

"The names will be a starting point anyway," she said.

"How's Kaulcrick reacting to all this?"

"I don't think he's had time to feel bad about it. On the one hand, he's got three million dollars of the Bureau's money back. On the other hand, it wasn't him who recovered it. He can't even claim he directed the operation. So I think he's attempting to find some redemption in proving Pendaran is involved. They've completed a factory trace of that barrel found in Bertok's Glock. It was part of a shipment that went to a gun shop in Lynwood, California, on April 21 this year. It was sold to an individual named Galvin Gawl."

Vail could tell by the sway of her speech that the surprise ending she was apparently building up to was going to point to someone known to them. "Who is?"

"Don't rush my big finish. We checked Bureau indices and there is a Galvin Gawl. Turns out it's a former undercover identity for Vince Pendaran." Vail didn't have any apparent reaction. "Okay, what's wrong now?"

"What's Kaulcrick doing with this?"

"Like you said, surveillance, and I'm sure he's getting search warrants. You're the guy who came up with Pendaran. Now you don't think it's him?"

"Pendaran was not the second guy in the Honda, remember?"

"So maybe he's part of the group. Is this just you being contrary or is it because an assistant director is calling the shots?"

He smiled. "You read my file. Did it mention anything about me working well with others?"

"Wait a minute. You're not afraid of Kaulcrick beating you; you're using Pendaran as a stalking horse."

"A stalking horse?"

"You want it to look like the FBI is biting on Pendaran so you can look somewhere else."

"Next time I'm asking for a deputy assistant director who spends more time shoe shopping," Vail said. "It has to appear to whoever's left in this gang that the official FBI is buying the Pendaran strategy so we can sneak around and try to figure out who's who. These people are too smart, too well informed, for us to try and fake that."

"*We?* Meaning I'm back to keeping things from my boss."

"If career is your choice, all you have to do is go see Kaulcrick and tell him that I'm sandbagging him. No hard feelings. It's your call."

Kate considered the offer for a moment. "Tell me, what are you going to do next?"

"Sorry, no hedging of bets. With every turn of this, there are fewer people to trust with information. What I need right now is some blind loyalty. Either you're all the way in, or all the way out."

Kate sank back in her chair and sighed. "Why not? I've probably already been promoted beyond my level of incompetence." She looked at her watch. "I've got to go. Don called a meeting that started five minutes ago. He told me to bring you along if you were done with your statement."

"Tell him I'm not done yet."

"And you'll be—what—here brooding?"

"I like to think of it as post-shoot-out quiet time."

"You sure you're all right?"

"I'm sure."

"Then I should go."

Vail went over to the small table he used as a desk and picked up his laptop.

"Where are you going?"

"To the hotel. I'm going to reread the entire file."

"Why?"

"The first time I read it, I was looking for Bertok. It'll be interesting to see if I can find anything behind all the misdirection."

Kate said, "You've got to admit, it was pretty impressive how they set him up."

"It was, and it also gave them one very large additional benefit. Five million dollars all in one shot was a lot to expect the Bureau to pay, so they made it look like one of our own took off with two million. Then their request for three million to stop the killings didn't seem all that unreasonable," Vail said. "They definitely know what they're doing. They don't just come up with a scheme and stick to it. They continually tweak their plan, changing it on the fly. They find a chink in our armor and exploit it in the next step."

"I guess we're pretty lucky to get the three million dollars back."

"Speaking of which, are you going to leave it there?" Vail asked.

"Oh God, I forgot about it. A couple of the accountants were supposed to come up and count it, but they're all on some fraud special, so it might be a day or two before they can get to it. That's why they brought the safe up. I checked a few of the serial numbers and they are from the tunnel drop. I guess we shouldn't leave that much money lying around." Opening her desk drawer, she took out a piece of paper and handed it to him. "Here's the combination. Would you mind?"

He looked at the numbers and handed it back to her. "If

it's not here when you get back, promise you'll give me a twenty-four-hour head start."

A strand of hair had fallen over her face. With a coffee cup in one hand and a notebook in the other, she tried to blow it to one side. "Only if you promise to send for me."

NINETEEN

KATE QUIETLY CLOSED THE DOOR BEHIND HER AND LOOKED AROUND the SAC's conference room. The briefing had begun and Kaulcrick shot her a deadpan glance in reaction to her tardiness. He was sitting at the head of the table, and the SAC, Mark Hildebrand, sat to his right. She was surprised to see Tye Delson there, who nodded and gave Kate a half smile. Kate also recognized a couple of the supervisors, one of which was Allen Sabine, who had the enduring misfortune of supervising not only Stan Bertok, but Vince Pendaran, the new focus of the extortion investigation. Also sitting at the table was an agent from the Evidence Recovery Team. Off in the corner, as far from the table as he could get, Tom Demick sat in a chair against the wall, trying to remain unnoticed.

Kate pulled out a chair, and Kaulcrick asked, "Where's Vail?"

"He went back to the hotel. I think he just needed a little downtime."

"Just as well." A young agent walked in and handed the SAC a sheet of paper, which he glanced at and then handed to the assistant director. Kaulcrick read it, setting it on the table in front of him. "Kate, we were just discussing where we wanted to go next. The evidence has become fairly strong that Pendaran is part of this."

"Don't take this the wrong way," she said, "but I think we have to be careful. Remember how strong the evidence was against Stan Bertok."

"Okay," Kaulcrick said, slightly annoyed, "let's review, Kate. Pendaran had a grudge against the first victim, Connie Lysander—motive. Someone had to come up with Bertok's name for the Pentad—opportunity. He purchased the gun barrel used in the murders with his undercover name, Galvin Gawl—means." Kaulcrick held up the sheet of paper that had just been delivered. "And now this. Remember those documents you found hidden behind the vanity in Bertok's bathroom, the Florida birth certificate with the whitened-out name? Well, the lab was able to remove the Wite-Out, and the Florida Bureau of Vital Statistics has confirmed the original document was applied for using the name Galvin Gawl—method. And there's been a strong indication from the beginning that the Pentad has been operating with inside information. I think we're safe in assuming that Pendaran is part of this." He turned to the AUSA. "Miss Delson, I assume that'll be enough to obtain search warrants for his apartment and car and anything else we'd like to get a peek at."

"It's more than enough, but I'm not sure that the 'inside information' is *legally* quantifiable. It could be argued that everything the Pentad knew about this case, they could have gotten through criminal experience, books, movies, or newspapers. The defense could easily demonstrate that at trial. Let's not give them any help. Everything else is very strong."

"As long as we can get a search warrant, you can leave out whatever you want," Kaulcrick said. "Now, does anyone have any ideas how we can identify the one other member of the gang, the one driving the Honda?"

Hildebrand said, "Salton and Pendaran are the only known connections to him. Since Salton's dead, Pendaran is our only hope. Once we take him into custody, we can threaten him legitimately with the death penalty. If he didn't commit any of the murders, we can offer him a deal to give him up."

Kaulcrick turned to Tye. "Which means we're going to want those search warrants as soon as possible, but I'd like to give surveillance another twenty-four hours to see if he'll lead us anywhere or to anyone. How's this time tomorrow look?"

She looked at her watch. It was almost 6 P.M. "We've got plenty of probable cause for nighttime entry. Have an agent in my office at four P.M. tomorrow to swear to the affidavits."

Kate leaned back in her chair. There seemed to be an undercurrent of self-congratulation in the room. The mood was almost giddy. Pendaran was going to be charged in the case even though the evidence had unfolded in a manner not unlike it had for Stan Bertok. Yet no one seemed wary of that. The FBI was finally about to win, and everyone could claim to be part of the success. Kate suddenly realized that she was developing Vail's need to look beyond the obvious. Because everything had fallen into place so neatly, Pendaran, she decided, was in all likelihood not involved.

VICTOR RADEK SAT on the motel bed trying to ignore the room's sour odor, which was made worse by a cheap, flowery deodorizer. A box containing the remaining two million dollars sat next to him. Two million dollars and he had to hide in this dump. He punched the box relentlessly until he noticed that his knuckles had started to bleed. Then he began pounding it harder.

How had this happened? He closed his eyes and could hear that agent's voice on Salton's cell phone, mocking him, telling him he'd now have to rename the Pentad because there was one less of them. He was the problem, Radek decided. He had failed to die in the railroad tunnel. And he had somehow killed Lee, taking back the three million dollars they had worked so hard for. There had to be a way to get that money back. He considered the possibility of another high-profile murder, but by now they had identified Salton, meaning they were one step closer to finding out who he was. There wasn't enough time to plan another murder. And with Salton gone, he doubted that any of the remaining members of his gang could pull it off. Again he could hear that agent's voice, so insulting, so defiant—he was the one who had brought the FBI one step closer to finding him. Before Radek could make any move to recover the three million dollars, he had to kill him.

IT WAS A LITTLE after 5 A.M. when Kate was awakened by a knock on her hotel room door. Before she could get up, a second one came. She reached for her automatic on the nightstand. As quietly as possible she walked to the door, not wanting to alert whoever was on the other side. Through the peephole she saw Vail and unlocked the door.

She sat down heavily on the bed and put her gun back on the side table. "Guess you were still sleeping," he offered as an apology.

She was wearing a short nightgown and noticed that Vail had discovered its thinness. "You should see me in this with my hair combed and some makeup."

A quick flash of red rose and disappeared from his face. Even the slightest embarrassment in him pleased her. "I've got time," he said.

"Is that why you came?"

"If I say yes, what happens?"

"Sorry, no hedging your bets."

"Ahhh, yes," he offered.

"Oooo, so close, but not quite sincere enough."

He walked over to a chair where she had left her robe and handed it to her. "In that case . . ."

She pulled the robe on and tied the belt loosely. "You don't look like you've been to bed."

Vail rubbed the stubble of his day-old growth. "Not yet. I just finished rereading the file."

"And?"

"What's the most logical way to investigate this case?"

"It's a little early for a pop quiz, but I don't think it's by going after Pendaran. I don't know, I guess you have to dig into Salton's history, see who he was tight with inside and look for anyone he might have hooked up with when he got out."

"That's logical, but it's one of those things where there

are just too many possibilities. While he was in prison, thousands of prisoners came and went."

"I suppose then you have to go back to investigating the murders, separately and as a group."

"And that's what the Bureau's been doing. But it's not working, because whoever is responsible was using that investigation to lead us to Bertok and Pendaran. The murders are not the key."

"Then what is?"

"The drop locations. While the selection of the murder victims can be almost random, the drops are much more critical because they are the most vulnerable phase of the extortion. They're the only time when the Bureau and the criminals have to be in the same place at the same time, so the Pentad has to be familiar and comfortable with them. There are three locations. The Arizona highway, which is just too long to reveal anything. And we know that the group is centered in Los Angeles, so for them to have knowledge of that railroad tunnel and the area in general doesn't help us at all. But the naval prison in New Hampshire may be a way into this."

"Do you think that one of them was a prisoner there?"

"It's been closed for thirty years, so probably not. But that island is more than a prison. It's a naval base with a lot of civilian employees as well. It has a hospital, a hotel, and everything in between. It's a small city."

"How does that narrow it down?"

"It doesn't. But with Salton identified, it looks like there's a reasonable chance we're dealing with career criminals. Federal ex-cons. New Hampshire is a small state, less than a million people. Social Security numbers issued to residents begin with 001 to 003. Can you get ahold of someone at the Bureau of Prisons and get a list of everyone with a New Hampshire Social Security number who was released within the last year from Marion? Then two years, up to the last five years. Five lists."

"I assumed you checked Salton's."

"New Jersey."

"That sounds like it still could be a lot of people. With just the two of us sneaking around, it could take forever," Kate said. "I assume you've come to me with this because we are going to be sneaking around."

"I prefer 'parallel investigation.' It'll sound better at your trial board."

"So what do we do with this list of people with New Hampshire Social Security numbers?"

"Our target extortionist is now living here, and if I've learned one thing about Los Angeles, it's that you can't live here without driving. When you get the list of the New Hampshire names, run them for current California driver's licenses."

"That makes sense. I'll get on it as soon as I can get dressed. What will you be doing?"

"Well, I could stay and watch." She started pushing him toward the door. "Then I'll be sleeping."

EVEN THOUGH HALF AWAKE, Vail let the phone ring three times before he reached for it, hoping it would stop or go to voice mail. "Hello," he said, trying not to reveal the sleep in his voice.

"I'm sorry, did I wake you?" Kate said.

"Funny." Vail looked at his watch; it was 10:30. "What's up?"

"For one, the Bureau of Prisons. Fortunately, they're three hours ahead of us, and I got them to run the New Hampshire numbers. Then I had those names checked for California driver's licenses."

"How many?"

"Fourteen."

"That's more than I would have liked, but we can probably narrow it down by city, age, crime, anything like that."

She smiled to herself and hesitated a moment to enjoy what she was about to say. "No need."

Vail pulled himself up to a half-sitting position. "Aren't you the little overachiever this morning?"

"I called the agent in charge up in Portsmouth, where the first drop was. They've been quietly conducting an investigation up there since Dan West was murdered. The big employer there is the shipyard. I had them check their list of old employees, and guess what?"

"One of your fourteen worked there."

"Worked there as a welder when he was eighteen. Before he went to prison the first time. Victor James Radek. White male, thirty-eight years old. Released from Marion nine months ago. Did fifteen years for robbing an armored car. Supposedly he was the brains behind a gang that actually hit eight different cars, but the government could prove only the one. None of the money was ever recovered. He was incarcerated in Marion at the same time as Salton."

"That's nice work, Kate. For a—"

"Woman?"

"I was going to say deputy assistant director, but woman works equally well."

"Apparently your tongue is wide awake."

"We can start with the address on his driver's license."

"I'll pick you up in a half hour," Kate said.

WHEN VAIL GOT into the car, she handed him a container of coffee. "Thanks. Anyone going to miss you in the office?"

"They're too busy congratulating one another about Pendaran." She handed Vail two different photos of Radek. "He was arrested three months ago by Alameda PD for DUI. They e-mailed that to me after I talked to you. The other's from Marion."

Vail took a long look at the mug shots of Victor James Radek, memorizing the inner trapezoid of his features, from the outer corners of his eyebrows to the underline of his lower lip. In the local arrest photo, anger had reduced his eyes to slits and his lips were drawn back in defiance. His expression was that of an experienced criminal who didn't like being caged no matter how briefly. His shoulders filled the frame, and his lean jawline suggested that he was not only fit, but capable of explosive brutal force.

His prison photo was different. He had been in the system for a while when it was taken and had learned that invisibility was the surest path to early release. Prison officials referred to it as "Caspering" after the cartoon ghost who was almost invisibly transparent while just trying to be everyone's friend. Radek's expression was as neutral as humanly possible. And there was something about the production quality that left the photo generically stark, washed out not only in color but in depth, eliminating any other clues to the person behind the mask. Vail looked a little closer and thought he could detect the slightest smirk at the corner of the convict's mouth, as if the world were about to end and he was the only one who knew about it. "Sounds like you don't think Pendaran's involved."

"At that meeting yesterday, I listened to the evidence against him, and it suddenly came to me that this is Stan Bertok all over again. Radek and his merry men put this in place just in case we saw through Stan and the suicide. I was surprised that Tye Delson didn't question it. I thought she was a little smarter than that."

"Maybe she was embarrassed because she's the one who first came up with Pendaran's name."

"You're making excuses for her? You know what that's a sign of, don't you?"

"Oh, how I'm going to regret this. *What?*"

"She's got a thing for you. And you like that."

"I'm not sure that's true."

Kate laughed. "Then maybe it's you who's got a thing for her. I know there's a thing in there somewhere."

Vail said, "Is this important to you, Kate?"

"No!"

"*Kay-tee*," he teased.

"It's not," she said quickly, and realized how unconvincing she sounded.

"That's too bad."

His tone made her look at him, and she could see he was no longer joking. *Too bad*. What was that supposed to mean? She told herself she couldn't care less. She didn't have time to peel the layers off Vail's motives. All she could do was pretend the remark didn't register. But of course it had. She adjusted the rearview mirror unnecessarily, as if she were extra vigilant, since they had been followed the day before. Reading men's intentions, at least the more basic ones, had never been difficult for Kate, but Vail, from the moment he knew her name on that Chicago rooftop until this latest overture, confused her. "So what's the plan when we catch up with this guy Radek?"

"First, hope he's not at this address."

"Why?"

"If he is running this operation, he's smart enough to never have lived at an address listed on a state identification card. At least not since he's been in the extortion business."

The address was in Inglewood, and when they got there Kate pulled up under the shade of a tree a half block away. "Do you see what I see?" she asked.

Vail had already taken out the monocular and was examining the gold Honda in front of the address. "That looks like the same car."

"I used to own the same model."

"Congratulations on your good taste. I'm sure this guy steals only the most reliable means of getaway."

"Does that mean he's there?"

Vail picked up the radio mike. "Call Demick and have him get a phone number for the place while I run the plate."

Kate got Tom Demick on the phone and gave him the address. He said he would call her right back. When she hung up, Vail was writing down the registration information from the radio operator. "Comes back to a fifteen-year-old Oldsmobile station wagon. Registered owner lives in L.A."

"Which means the car and the plates are both stolen," Kate said.

"But why leave it in front of an address that connects him to it?" Vail asked.

"Maybe he's inside."

"Hopefully we'll find out as soon as we get that phone number."

"Maybe—since you got Salton—he figured you were coming for him, so he just dumped it here and took off in his own car." Her phone rang. It was Demick with the phone number. She wrote it down and, after hanging up, held it out to Vail.

"You call. A woman will be less suspicious if he answers."

"What do you want me to say?"

Vail got a look of mischief on his face. "Since you can't ask for him, ask for Steve. But you got to do it in a sexy voice if this is going to work. Let me hear you."

Impishly, she shifted herself in the seat and, turning toward him, leaned in. In a throaty whisper, she said, "Hi . . . is *Steeeve* there?"

"Very nice, but you need to pucker your mouth a little more."

"He can't see my lips on the phone," she said playfully.

"It's called method acting."

She leaned a couple of inches closer and puckered her lips. "Hello, I'm looking for big Steve Vail. Is he there, cowboy?"

Vail leaned back and closed his eyes. "Once more with more emphasis on 'big.' "

She turned forward and dialed her phone. "If you want more, it's twenty dollars a minute."

She put it on speaker and Vail listened as the phone rang four times before a beep sounded to leave a message. She hung up. "Apparently nobody's home." Vail opened the car door. "Where are you going?" He went to the trunk and took out the pry bar, holding it up to her as an answer. "Dr. Halligan, I presume," she said.

"Call me on my cell if anyone shows up."

"You sure you don't want me to come with you?"

"Only if you promise to call me big Steve the whole time."

"I hope he is in there, waiting for you."

"Then how about 'cowboy'?"

"And heavily armed."

FIFTEEN MINUTES LATER Vail got back in the car. "Anything?" Kate asked.

"Not a thing. No furniture. There's nothing touching the floor except a cell phone in a charger. It's either a mail drop or safe house." He punched 911 into his cell phone and, after identifying himself, requested that a marked car be sent to their location. "I got the VIN number. When they get here, we'll have them run it and get it towed to where we can search it without being surprised."

"Why don't you have the office run it?"

"If Kaulcrick or the SAC hear that we've found a stolen gold Honda, our little clandestine operation will be over."

"Which reminds me, while you were *hunting-gathering*, Kaulcrick called and left me a voice mail. They're going to execute search warrants on Pendaran. He wants me there."

"You want to go?"

"And what, ruin my career as a lookout?"

WHEN THE TWO Inglewood police officers arrived, Kate and Vail got out and flashed their credentials. "Thanks for coming out so fast," Vail said, and handed the driver a slip of paper. "That's the VIN on the Honda. Could you run it? We're pretty sure it's stolen."

The driver had that threadbare look of an experienced cop. "FBI working stolen cars now?"

Vail smiled. "We think it's tied to some homicides."

"In Inglewood?" the cop asked.

"No."

The cop gave him one last evaluative look and turned to his onboard computer, punching in the VIN number. Almost immediately, it came back as stolen. "Out of L.A.," the cop said. "What do you want to do?"

"Any chance we could get it towed to someplace a little more private than this?"

The cop smiled. "Sure. We wouldn't want anyone breaking into it. You know, illegally or anything."

TWENTY

ARE WE GOING TO COMPLETELY PROCESS THIS CAR?" KATE ASKED as she continued to drive, her eyes lazily following the towed vehicle in front of them.

"At this point, we're just looking for leads to find Radek, so we'll give it a quickie and then have Inglewood store it. There's no immediate need to be concerned about trace evidence. At some point we'll want ERT to give it a good going-over in case it was used to transport Bertok. But I'd be surprised if someone like Radek would be driving a car that had that kind of evidence in it."

"So this little *reconnaissance*, it's supposed to never have happened."

In a soothing voice, Vail said, "You're getting drowsy. Your eyelids are heavy."

They pulled around behind the Inglewood Police Department, and the tow truck driver waved them into a parking space marked Visitor. Then he backed his truck into a large garage before unhooking the Honda. Vail took the Halligan bar out of his trunk, and he and Kate walked inside the building. The truck driver came up to them. "Do you need anything else?"

"Can you slim-jim the door for us?" Vail held up the pry bar. "I don't want to use this unless I have to."

"These newer models are a little more resistant, but I'll get it open. The department mechanic's off today, but he made this tool specially for these push-button door releases."

Kate said, "If he gets the door open, you won't need the Halligan. There's a trunk release alongside the driver's seat."

The driver went to a workbench and came back with a thin steel rod that had a series of severe angles welded together smoothly. He inserted it between the door glass and the frame and then manipulated it while feeding more of it inside, making the tip change direction until it hovered over the door lock button. He carefully pulled it toward him a fraction of an inch, and the electric lock inside the door thumped open.

Vail pulled on a pair of evidence gloves. Carefully he leaned inside the vehicle, opening the console compartment without sitting in the driver's seat. He could smell the vague odor of air freshener masking an odor of gasoline. "Do you smell gas?"

"We're in a garage."

"No, it's definitely inside the car."

"Is it important?"

"I don't know."

"Yes, I guess so. Do you want me to start dusting the outside?" Kate asked.

"Ah, no. Why don't you hold off for a minute?"

"Something wrong?"

"In a minute." Walking around to the other side of the car, he opened the passenger's door. Across the carpeted mat on the floor he could see lines of recent vacuuming. The mats in the back were also freshly vacuumed. "This car is cleaner than when it was new."

"Is that unusual? I thought a lot of ex-cons were neat freaks because of living in such a small space."

Vail didn't say anything but walked back around the car and leaned into the driver's seat area again. Using a flashlight to check several locations where fingerprints couldn't help but be left, he said, "There are no prints. Neat freak or not, this car has been dry-cleaned."

"Meaning what?"

"Meaning he was expecting it to be found," Vail said.

"So what if he was? There'd be nothing to lead back to him or the murders."

"That makes sense except that he parked it directly in front of his house."

"Enough. We've got the car. Search it, and if there's nothing in it we'll move on. Pop the trunk," she said, and then looked down at her hands. "I tore my gloves. I'll go get another pair." Vail reached down and pulled up the release, and the quiet click of the trunk opening came from the back of the vehicle.

Something didn't make sense about the car. Everything throughout the case had been carefully planned and executed. Why leave a stolen vehicle in front of his house, especially after Vail had seen it?

Kate walked back in and came up to Vail, pulling on a fresh set of gloves. "Helloooh, can you open the trunk?"

Absentmindedly he said, "I did."

She looked back at it and then reached around him and pulled the lever again. When she didn't hear it release, she examined it again. "This one doesn't pop open nearly as high as mine." She started back toward the trunk.

Kate took hold of the trunk lid. *"Hold it!"* he yelled. She ripped her hand away as if the metal had been white-hot. She had never heard that much urgency in his voice before. He took her by the arm and pulled her back from the car.

"What's the matter?"

"How high does that lid usually come up?"

"I don't know, six to eight inches."

"Stand here." Vail stepped to the side of the trunk. Kneeling down, he shined his flashlight in the one-inch opening between the lid and the car's body. "I can't see in."

"What's the matter?" she repeated.

"Maybe nothing."

"Yes, there is."

"I just don't want to take anything for granted with these guys."

"You think the trunk could be rigged?"

"I don't know. Maybe the lid not coming up is just a malfunction."

"I've got that LAPD bomb squad sergeant's card, the one I met after the tunnel drop. I could give him a call."

"First I'd like to be sure."

"The backseat folds down. You can see into the trunk that way. Just pull on the top of the seat."

Vail took hold of both her arms firmly. "I know you're going to want to give me a hard time about this, but I need you to go wait outside the building."

"What are you going to do?"

"Find out what's in the trunk."

"Don't. Let me call that sergeant."

"If there's the slightest chance someone will get hurt, their protocol is to blow everything in place."

"What's wrong with that?"

"Normally nothing, but any evidence that might be in that trunk will be gone, and frankly, I'm out of ideas. Now, please go."

"Steve, there's nothing I want more right now than to turn around and sprint out of here, but if you're going to do this, I'm staying." He still had ahold of her arms and searched her eyes for resolve. "I am staying."

"You know I'm the one paid to do stupid things."

She laughed nervously. "Considering the size of your paycheck, that's only fair."

"An irrefutable argument." With her standing outside the rear door he carefully climbed in and knelt on the rear seat. "Ready?"

"Fire in the hole," she whispered.

Vail frowned at her and then ran his hands along the seam where the top of the seat met the rear ledge. When he couldn't feel anything that shouldn't be there, he pulled evenly and the seat back came down smoothly. Carefully he shined the light into the trunk's interior.

"Anything?" Kate asked. He backed out of the car slowly and took her by the arm, leading her out of the garage. "What's in there?"

"A lot of gasoline and some other stuff I'm not sure of. It's set to do something. You'd better call that sergeant."

They got in their car, and after Kate finished her call she asked, "How did you know about the trunk?"

"It just didn't make any sense. Why leave a stolen car at his known address, and at the same time clean it of all evidence? Suddenly it occurred to me that Radek was using it as a warning device. If we got onto him, his driver's license address would be the first place we'd look. But he wouldn't know unless something newsworthy happened like an explosion or fire or whatever those things in the trunk are supposed to cause. Then when the lid didn't come all the way up, it seemed like too big a coincidence."

Vail turned on the Bureau radio. The traffic slowly volleyed back and forth between the various units executing the Pendaran search warrants. It sounded as though the assistant director and the SAC were both at Pendaran's apartment. And judging by the casual, amused voices of the agents, it was going well. Then the SAC's voice burst loudly across the air. "Central, call the United States attorney and let him know that we have located a gym bag filled with banded hundred-dollar bills. And they have punctures in them. We're checking the numbers now. Tell him we'd like authorization to arrest the subject."

Kate checked Vail for a reaction. There was none. "Could Pendaran be involved?"

"Funny how only the punctured money keeps showing

up. I don't know how much there is, but I know you can't get two million dollars in a gym bag."

"I guess that's my reward for hanging around with you. They get the money, and we get the bomb," Kate said.

Vail smiled at her. "Am I a good time or what?"

SERGEANT MIKE HENNING of the Los Angeles police bomb squad lifted off his helmet, wiping his hand across his sweating forehead. Like so many people in L.A., he seemed almost too attractive for his job, as if he were an actor shooting a movie. With his dark, waxy hair combed straight back and his thin, sculpted mustache, he could have been a figure in an art deco poster from the thirties. "It's shut down," he said to Kate and Vail.

"Then it was a bomb," she said.

He peeled back the Velcro straps that fastened his protective suit. "Well, it's a device. But there's no explosive. It's more of a flamethrower than a bomb. I've never seen anything like it. Whoever built it wanted somebody dead, and in a fashion that would have made a very loud statement. If you had yanked the trunk open—barring a malfunction—you'd have been incinerated. Come on, I'll show you."

The trunk lid was now fully open. Henning wiped his forehead again. "A flamethrower is made up of a fuel supply, a compressed-gas source, and a striker, all contained in a delivery system." He pointed into the trunk. "This is absolutely deadly. Not just regular deadly, agonizing deadly. Somebody doesn't like law enforcement." Henning looked at Vail. "I assume this was done by your friends from the tunnel."

"Because of similar construction?"

"Because of its deadliness. Whoever put it together had his heart set on killing human beings, but not until they'd suffered a great deal of pain. I'd love to set this off to show you just how serious these people are, but that would make a mess." He leaned over the trunk. "What makes it so ingenious is that the trunk is the delivery system. And it's completely disposable. One use only. As a side benefit it destroys all trace evidence at the same time it's inflicting casualties."

"Exactly how was it supposed to work?" Kate asked.

"See the liquid bladder lying on the bed in the trunk? It looks like about a ten-gallon bag. Made of some sort of polymer. They're commonly used as extra fuel cells, usually on boats. They're durable, puncture-resistant, and fit anywhere. But see these?" Henning pointed to six evenly spaced plastic plugs along the back end of the bladder closest to the trunk opening. "Those were cut into the bag by your friends. They then epoxied those blowout plugs and their seatings into it. At the moment, there's a minimum of pressure on them from the gasoline, so they will stay firmly in place, preventing the gasoline from escaping. Now take a look at the other side of the bladder. The hole with the metal plate reinforcing it, that's how you fill the bag up with gasoline. Only, after filling it, they used the coupling to attach that compressed-air cylinder bolted down behind it. And as you can see, the cylinder has a quick-release nozzle and handle. The wire that connected the trunk lid to the quick-release handle was just long enough so when you got the lid half open, all the compressed air was released at once. It's driven through the bladder, blowing out the six plugs and shooting the gasoline straight up into the trunk lid. The curve of the lid would channel it out through the back, deluging whoever was standing directly behind the car."

Henning shook his head with admiration. "Now this is even more impressive. When the fuel hit the lid, it would jerk it up fully, causing the strikers on either side to spark, creating a delay effect." Vail recognized the strikers. They were used by welders and looked like giant safety pins with a metal bottle cap at one end. "In other words, first you're soaked with the fuel, and a split second later it's ignited, ensuring the target is turned into charcoal in less than three seconds." Henning pointed to the back of the bladder. "There was a little of the fuel spilled around the intake plate. That's probably what you smelled, Steve. It isn't just gasoline, it's napalm. It'll stick to you. I've never believed in evil genius, but this comes close."

"Napalm? Can we trace something like that?" Kate asked.

"It's probably homemade. You just dissolve common Styrofoam in gasoline. It's been used since the sixties, but it'll stick to you just like the expensive spread."

"Is this safe for us to search now?" Vail asked.

"Just let me get some photos of it. Then I'll cut back those trigger wires and it'll be completely inert." Henning pulled a camera from his case and started taking the photos.

When he finished, he used a small pair of wire cutters to trim the rest of the three wires hanging from the underside of the trunk lid that had been attached to the two welding strikers and the gas cylinder before he disarmed them.

For the next fifteen minutes, Kate and Vail searched the

car while Henning watched. Vail suspected that Henning was watching Kate more than him. But then he was sure that's why the cop had come out in the first place. Vail stole a glance at Kate as she moved from the front seat to the back, putting herself in awkward but candid positions. She straightened up quickly and caught Vail. Not knowing why he was watching her, she asked, "Did you find something?"

Vail pulled at his gloves, slightly embarrassed. "Not yet."

"Where does this leave us?"

Vail bent down and picked up the compressed-air tank, turning it upside down. "There's a serial-number plate on this. Manufacturer is in Minnesota."

"I know the ASAC there. We were on the inspection staff together. Should be a one-phone-call lead. Are we done here?"

"I am. Why don't you make that call, and I'll talk to someone about storing the car."

Kate walked over to Henning. "Thanks, Mike, you've saved the day."

"Any time, Kate."

"Come on, I'll walk you to your van," she said. "This doesn't have to go into a report right away, does it?"

"Would it be better if there was no report?"

Vail watched her hook her arm through his as they started out of the garage. "That wouldn't cause you any problems?"

Vail turned his attention back to the air tank. They had found no fingerprints, no hairs, fibers, or blood anywhere in the trunk. But a traceable serial number? Even if the deadly device had been ignited, the digits engraved in the metal plate would likely have survived. Were they trying to distract the Bureau again by pointing them in a new direction, one that could also be deadly? Even if they were, it didn't matter; he and Kate had no choice but to follow it.

Kate came back and Vail looked at her, amused. "What?" she said. "He's a nice guy."

Vail smiled. "And very *Maltese Falcon*."

"Is that bad?"

"Let's see, at the end of the movie, the woman is arrested for killing one of the detectives. That gives me a fifty-fifty chance. I guess you can't ask for better odds than that these days." Vail wrote down the manufacturer and serial number off the tank and handed the slip of paper to her. "Please call your friend in Minneapolis."

"Okay, ahhh . . ."

"What?"

"Do you think it's time to go to Kaulcrick and tell him what we've got? Get some manpower to start looking for Radek?"

"Again—our best shot at solving this case right now is if we have two investigations going at the same time: one in the direction Radek wants, and one in a direction that he doesn't know about."

"How sure are you about all this?" Kate asked.

"How sure do you need me to be?"

"To keep my sanity? Absolutely positive."

"Then Agent Bannon, you are in serious trouble."

"APPARENTLY YOU HAVEN'T HEARD, Don, but J. Edgar Hoover is dead. The FBI no longer calls the shots. Your agency is under the auspices of the Department of Justice, not the other way around."

Del Underwood was the United States attorney in Los Angeles. He was in his midforties and was athletically trim, a noticeable anomaly among the notoriously sedentary population of lawyers. He also wore large wire-rimmed glasses that were popular in the seventies as though trying to recapture some past image of himself. He adjusted them as he leaned forward, placing his elbows on his desk to send the message that he was ready for the fight that was apparently brewing across the assistant director's face.

"This is not about who's in charge," Kaulcrick said. "This is a national case that has literally taken the FBI from the Atlantic Ocean to the Pacific. We've had two agents murdered, and we're about to arrest another for being one of the people responsible. We have a great deal more invested in this than the United States attorney's office does. And the director thinks if Pendaran's arrest was released as national news in Washington, it would have much less of an impact on the Bureau's image."

"If you're so worried about your image, maybe you should have fired someone like Pendaran when you had the choice."

"What really worries me is when political appointees start examining everyone else's ethics."

"What does that mean?" Underwood said, his voice rising.

"It means that you're the United States attorney simply because your party is in the White House. If that changes in the next election, you'll be gone to some fat-salary law firm, and we'll still be here dealing with your self-serving decisions."

"Why, because we won't let you hog the credit?"

"We solved the case."

"And we have to take this into a courtroom and prosecute it, your mistakes and all."

"Who do you think is closer to the attorney general, you or the director of the FBI?"

"The local United States attorney always makes the press releases concerning arrests in his or her jurisdiction. Let's call the AG and let him decide."

"Fine. While you're calling him, I'll call the director."

Out of deference to the two men's positions, Mark Hildebrand had not said anything, but now he decided it was time to interject himself. In a calm tone, he said, "If I may. Calling bosses will give them the wrong impression about your ability to handle your duties. A compromise will serve everyone much better. I can see both sides of this because I work for Don, but I work more regularly with you, Del. So how about this? We'll have the news conference here in Del's office. He can make the opening statement, a kind of 'The Los Angeles United States attorney today announced the arrest of . . .' Then Don, representing himself as someone out of Washington, can give all the details and make it more of a national release like they would have in Washington, telling how the entire FBI, coast to coast, has worked to uncover one of its own gone bad. That way it's both local for the United States attorney's office here and national for the FBI."

Kaulcrick looked at the SAC, somewhat surprised at his diplomatic skills. Then he glanced at the United States attorney to see if he would agree. Underwood crossed his arms in front of his chest and leaned back in assumed contemplation. Finally the assistant director said, "I guess I can live with that."

Underwood pondered it a few more seconds for effect and then said, "So can I. Exactly how much of the evidence are you going to reveal?"

"I know you've got to prosecute this, Del, so I don't see a need to reveal any specifics."

"I've gone over it with the lead prosecutor. He said while the gun barrel and birth certificate being traced back to Pendaran are great pieces of circumstantial evidence, he'll need more to ensure a murder conviction."

"We also found fifteen thousand dollars in his apartment. The serial numbers matched those from the three-million-dollar demand."

"The prosecutor is aware of that. It's still not the complete smoking gun he'd like. What's the read on Pendaran? Think he'd make a deal to avoid the death penalty?"

"We've tried that. At first he was denying everything, even offered to take a polygraph. But when we started threatening him with the death penalty, the only word out of his mouth was 'lawyer.'"

"Are you doing anything to find the money? It would certainly tie everything together. Then we wouldn't need to bargain with him."

"That's *all* we're doing. Mark's got every available agent

working on it, trying to trace Pendaran's entire life. As soon as we know anything, you will, because we will still need search warrants."

"Fair enough."

Standing up to leave, Kaulcrick said, "I'll see you this afternoon at the news conference."

TWENTY-ONE

THE ASAC IN MINNEAPOLIS CALLED KATE BACK IN LESS THAN AN hour. The manufacturer of the compressed-air tank used in the jury-rigged flamethrower had a former agent as its head of security, and he was able to access their computer records from home, since it was after five o'clock. She wrote down the information and thanked the ASAC. "The tank was sold to Outside Zsport Company, 2121 South Alameda in L.A. I'll call and make sure they're still open." After a short conversation, she hung up. "They close at ten P.M."

"It's not far."

"Did you wonder about how they were financing all this? I mean the apartment, the house on Spring Street, everything?"

"I was until you said they never recovered the money from Radek's armored-car robberies."

"That's what I was thinking," she said. "The total haul was almost a million and a half."

"Apparently, even criminals have figured out that it takes money to make money."

The traffic was light and it took only twenty minutes to get to the sports store. "I'll go find out where we're going next."

She watched him walk inside and felt a rush of anticipation. To distract herself she started scanning through the FM stations on the radio. By the time she found one she liked, he was getting back in the car. "Amazing how fast they can find something when it's closing time." He started the car and, after checking a map, made a U-turn.

"Where are we going?"

"West Seventh Street. They sell those tanks for paintballing. The name the buyer used was Thomas Carson, with this address." He handed her a slip of paper.

"Think the name's a phony?"

"If it isn't, it'd be the first one. Why don't you call someone at the office anyhow and have them check indices. Also ask them if there's an employee by that name. Just in case."

Kate called the Los Angeles office and was told that no one by the name of Thomas Carson worked there, and indices also failed to find any record of it. "Nothing," she said after hanging up. "I hope that doesn't mean the address is no good."

"So far, every time we have run into an alias, the address has been good. If it is this time, you know what that means."

Kate said, "You think this is an ambush?"

"I'm hoping so." The surprised look on her face asked the question. "Because we're not going to get any closer if it isn't. Unless you've discovered a way to make an omelet without breaking eggs."

She leaned back and closed her eyes. "I'm starting to wonder if there is such a thing as an omelet."

THE WEST SEVENTH STREET address was in a commercial neighborhood that in recent years had begun to be gentrified. The structure was a seventy-five-year-old office building and was thirteen stories, taking up a city block. Neglect and the hydrocarbons of Los Angeles's automobile culture had left the structure stained and unappealing. But apparently someone had recognized not only the subtle architectural qualities of the building but also its easily alterable construction and dimensions and was spending several million dollars rejuvenating it. The stone pediments that accented the top two floors had been sandblasted back to their original spotless beige. The upper-floor windows had been removed, and the spaces were now covered with heavy-gauge clear plastic awaiting energy-saving replacements. Scaffolding hung from thin cables a hundred feet long. A heavy tarplike material surrounded the three lower floors to keep debris from falling. A temporary walkway with a protective overhead had been constructed along the sidewalks that surround the building. "This is different," Vail said.

"Different how?"

"The prison and the tunnel were abandoned sites. This building's being rehabbed."

"It's nice to see that the Pentad's found a more glass-half-full place to try to kill you."

"Not me, darlin', *us*." Vail turned the corner. "Let's see if we can find the construction entrance. We'll set up on it for a while and see what happens."

Vail drove slowly around the building. It was a little after 10 P.M. and there was little traffic. Kate was leaning forward searching the enormous structure through the windshield. "Is that it down at the end of the building?" she asked.

"Unpainted plywood doors with a padlock on it. Looks like it, but let's drive all the way around and see if there is any other way in."

As they drove by, Kate could see the door had been pried open and left slightly ajar. "Looks like someone is already here."

"Let's get an eye on it and see if anyone else shows up."

He parked the car as far away as he could while still being able to see the door. Both of them slouched down in the seat. For the next half hour they watched the building. Occasionally a car drove by, but none stopped. Then a man on foot rounded the corner and, under the shadows of the protective overhead, slipped into the building through the jimmied door. "Did you get a look at him? Was it Radek?" Kate asked.

"I couldn't tell."

"I know you're not going to agree, but maybe it's time to call for some help. I know that means Kaulcrick. But if we're looking at the big finish here, will it matter?"

"That's still a fairly good-sized if."

"Maybe they've got the money hidden in there, or they're in there splitting it up so they can run."

"I don't know what's in there, but I know they wouldn't leave a trail to the money."

"So do we wait, or do we call in the cavalry?"

"Unfortunately, we have no choice. The two of us can't surround this place."

"What do I tell Don?"

"I suppose you've got to tell him the truth. Just minimize it by telling him we didn't know if Radek was involved for sure until we discovered his car, which—without any bomb squad details—led us here. And now that we know that Radek's probably involved, we didn't want to try to arrest him until he got here."

"That's pretty thin," she said.

"Then tell him we didn't want him involved because we thought he'd screw it up."

"Much better." She dialed Kaulcrick's cell and, when he answered, explained how they had identified Radek as a possible leader of the Pentad and then found his car and the booby trap, which led them to the building they now sat watching. Vail could tell by the long pauses during which Kate listened that the assistant director wasn't buying their "stumbling" across another member of the Pentad crew.

When she hung up, Vail asked, "I'm guessing he didn't take it like a man?"

"I think you actually have to be a man to take it like a man. He's getting ahold of the SAC, every available agent, SWAT, and I think he said something about the Marines. And of course he said under no circumstances are we to do anything until he gets here."

"With that kind of call-out, we'll be lucky if they're here in an hour."

"I'm guessing it'll be closer to two."

"No LAPD?"

"I don't think he wants anyone stealing what's left of the thunder."

She looked over at Vail and could see he had shifted

gears. "I don't like sitting here waiting," he said. "They're not going to stay in there forever."

"If I have to hold you at gunpoint, we're not going in there until everyone gets here." Then recognizing that look in his eyes, she said, "Steve, I'm begging you, don't."

Vail put his head back and closed his eyes. "Okay, then you've got first watch."

She studied him as he sat there. His breathing slowed and she could tell he was already half asleep. She just shook her head in wonder.

For the next fifteen minutes, she busied herself with writing down the license plate numbers of passing cars. She knew it was an exercise in futility, but she hoped it would help the time pass. Then a full-size sedan pulled up to the construction door, a blue light flashing on its dashboard. She nudged Vail. "Is that an agent?"

Vail put the monocular up to his eye. "I don't recognize him, but that doesn't mean much. It does look like a BU car."

A man in a suit and tie got out and, after turning off the light and drawing his weapon, carefully opened the construction door and slipped inside. She said, "Damn! Someone must have put out an 'agents need assistance' call at this address. We have to stop him." Vail got out quickly and went to the trunk.

Kate hurried after him. He took out magazines and put them in his jacket pockets. "What are you doing?"

"Either someone at the office put out the wrong information or whoever's inside found a way to lure an agent in there. They knew we'd see him and chase after him. He's bait for us."

"You don't know that for sure."

"Are you willing to take that chance? Call the office and let them know. When they get here, you can follow me in."

"I'm going with you."

"Wait until somebody else gets here."

"You did hear yourself use the word 'bait,' didn't you? I won't allow you to go alone."

Vail stared at her for a second before a short burst of laughter escaped from his mouth. "Then you'd better make that call quick." As she took extra magazines herself, he shoved a flashlight in his back pocket. They started walking toward the building. She dialed the office. In a low tone, she explained the situation and that every available agent should proceed to the West Seventh Street address immediately.

They reached the door and Vail said, "When we get inside don't say anything or move around. Just stand there and let your eyes adjust to the darkness. There should be enough light coming in off the street for us to be able to see. If you're going to shoot, make sure of your target. A construction job this big should have a night watchman."

"You're not going to use the flashlight?"

"We'll be enough of a target." They stepped inside, and he eased the door shut as they both listened.

Kate said, "What now?"

"If that guy was an agent, we just have to listen. Are you familiar with the expression 'Ride to the sound of gunfire'?"

"Who said that?"

"Custer." He turned and walked toward two dots of white light across the darkness.

"Very reassuring."

"Stay directly behind me."

As he suspected, the two tiny circles of light were the Up and Down buttons for an elevator. He pushed Up. "How do we know what floor?"

Vail said, "They'll find a way to let us know."

"Again, reassuring."

The elevator came and they got in. Vail pushed the buttons to all the floors and then drew his automatic. Reaching up, he used the muzzle to break the single lightbulb and the car went dark. Kate took her gun from the holster and wrapped both hands around it. He said, "Don't hold it with both hands. It makes it too hard to maneuver. You're probably going to be ducking a lot sooner than you'll be shooting."

The car jolted to a stop and then swayed back and forth slightly as the doors to the second floor started to open. As soon as they were wide enough, a body in a gray uniform fell through the opening. It was tied to an eight-foot-long two-by-six to give the corpse enough rigidity to lean against the door. The handle of a large screwdriver was sticking out of the guard's chest. Vail checked his throat for a pulse. "I'm going to guess they know we're here."

Kate stared down at the body. The brutality with which he had been killed and displayed released a panicked surge of adrenaline through her bloodstream. In the dark, quiet surroundings, it seemed dreamlike, vivid but not real, something that would surely go away if she closed her eyes for just a second or two.

Vail grabbed her roughly by the arm. "You're going to need to focus, otherwise you're a liability." He picked up the body, carried it out of the elevator, and laid it down with a surprising gentleness.

Kate shook her head as if trying to come out of a deep sleep. "I'm here, I'm here."

"Good," Vail said, pressing the button to close the elevator doors.

"You don't think they're on this floor?" Kate asked.

"They're going to be closer to the top."

"How do you know that?"

"Because it's their MO to wear us out before we get to . . ."

"The Little Big Horn?"

"Close enough."

As the doors opened at each floor, she caught herself holding her breath. With each stop, she understood the odds were increasing dramatically that the next time the doors opened, they would be waiting. Then she realized she was letting happen exactly what Vail had warned her against—the group psyching her out. But how was it possible not to be intimidated by this? She glanced over at Vail, who appeared as matter-of-fact as usual.

Whether it was Vail's composure or fear's tendency to eventually diminish itself through logic, by the time the doors opened on the eleventh floor, the terror she felt was at a level only high enough to give her a combative edge. She stared into the darkness, ready. Again there was nothing. As the doors started to close, Vail grabbed one of them and pulled it open. "What!" she whispered.

"Smell it?"

She started to say no, but then she did recognize something. "Garlic?"

"Overpowering garlic."

"So?"

"That means someone had their dinner up here. Which means they've been here for a while."

"Waiting for us?"

"Once Radek found that car gone, he knew that it would only be a matter of time until we worked our way here."

"Can you explain to me how you know that?"

"Not *now*, dear."

She regripped her automatic. "Are we getting off?"

"Let's go up one more floor."

"Why?"

"I don't know. Maybe the garlic isn't intentional." He let go of the door and it closed. "These people have played with our minds so much that logic has become a handicap. We just have to go with instinct and hope we can react quickly enough when the time comes."

"Wasn't that Custer's plan?"

"And it worked every time but one."

The door opened on the twelfth floor. Vail and Kate could see an office straight ahead at the far end. A single light illuminated its half-glass walls. The man they had seen exiting the automobile with the flashing blue light and enter the building sat in a chair facing them. His mouth was gagged and his hands were pulled back behind him and immobile. He spotted them and started nodding his head furiously. Vail let the doors close without getting off. "What are you doing?" Kate asked.

He took out his lock-back knife. Opening it, he handed it to her. "Be careful, it's like a razor. You go to him slowly, and I mean slowly. I'm going to walk backward right behind you. Once you get to him, cut him loose."

"Do you think they're here or down a floor?"

"I wish I could tell you a floor down." He pushed the button and the doors opened. Vail grabbed Kate by the arm, pulling her into the relative darkness. She felt his back against her. She tried to slip her finger onto the trigger but realized she was gripping her gun too tightly. She loosened her grip until it felt more familiar. With the knife in her left hand, she started toward the gagged man. Vail followed gently against her back.

After a few steps, she remembered the garlic and tried to see if the odor was present, but she couldn't smell it. In fact, she couldn't smell anything, not the mustiness of the building or the distinct smells of construction and its crews. Apparently, her sense of smell had shut down. She hoped that the myth about the loss of one sense increasing the others was true. She turned her head to one side and then to the other trying to see into the darkness surrounding them.

Now she was close enough to see the man's eyes. Although his mouth was covered she tried to recognize him from around the office. He didn't look familiar. She watched his eyes closely, thinking that if the others were around, he would signal her by shifting them in their direction, but they were locked on her.

Once she got through the office door, she moved quickly to him. Vail stood in the doorway searching the black stillness behind them. She held the knife up to indicate to the man that she was going to free his hands when she noticed that his feet weren't bound to the chair.

He burst upright and she could now see his hands were free. In his right hand was a revolver. Instinctively she slashed at the hand with the knife in her left hand. The sharp blade tore through the tendons and muscles of his wrist, paralyzing his hand. She felt the sickening resistance as steel struck bone. The gun now hung precariously, dangling from his useless trigger finger, which was caught in the guard.

He started to transfer it to his left hand, but Kate's right hand was faster. She shoved her automatic against his chest and pulled the trigger twice. He fell to the floor dead.

A burst of automatic-weapons fire raked the office, exploding the windows. Kate felt something slam into her. She spun to the floor and felt the coolness of blood escaping from her side. At the same time, Vail dove to the floor, firing a single shot over her head, putting out the desk lamp. Everything went black. She heard him crawling to her through the shattered glass.

"Are you hit?" he asked in her ear.

"I think so. My side," she said a little louder than she wanted to.

He slid a little closer and gently put his hand up under her blouse, his fingertips immediately finding the entry wound. Although it stung a great deal, she was reassured by Vail's hand exploring it. She felt him reach back, identifying the exit hole. "It's through and through. The bleeding isn't bad. Looks like it may have bounced off a rib." He took out his handkerchief and opened it. "Just keep this pressed against both holes."

She did as instructed, and as with any traumatic wound, her touch made it less threatening.

Vail dragged the dead man over to the wall and leaned him against it on his side. He then pulled Kate over and had her lie next to the body. "That's an assault rifle. It'll shoot right through this wall, but I don't think it'll get through him too, so stay right here." He handed her the flashlight and took a coin out of his pocket. "When you hear this quarter land out there, stick your arm straight up and snap the flashlight on and off over the top of the wall. Then pull your arm down even faster."

Silently Vail maneuvered back to the corner of the office and stood up invisibly in the deep shadows. Kate held her breath, not wanting to miss the sound of the quarter hitting the floor. She understood it was her job to draw fire. It seemed like it was taking Vail forever, and at the same time she hoped she'd never hear the coin land.

But then the quarter struck something metallic. She held the light straight up, even rising from behind the corpse to ensure that the light went over the bottom half of the wall. She snapped it on and off and then pulled herself close behind the body. Immediately automatic fire raked the wall. She felt at least two rounds thud into the body in front of her. Then, illuminated by the flashes of his Glock as he fired three times, Kate saw Vail's face, stoic, workmanlike, as if he were at the range. She heard a body fall, and then there was nothing but more of the black, horrid silence. She waited a few seconds before asking in a strained whisper, "Is that it?"

"One more," he answered.

Had Vail seen another man during the exchange? Kate thought back. The door had been jimmied when they arrived, meaning someone was already inside. They had then watched two more arrive, including the "agent." Two of them were now dead.

Vail took a quick step out of the shadows and dove through the shattered office window. Three gunshots skidded after him. During the brief bursts of light, he was able to locate the gunman and the obstacles that lay between them. He still couldn't tell whether it was Radek. The shooter was barricaded behind a large wheelbarrow used to haul cement. Vail doubted that one of his rounds would pierce it, especially because of its curved surfaces. But he had spotted something immediately off to the gunman's left side, a steel beam exposed by the construction work. He needed to get another look at it to confirm the angles of its surfaces. He decided on a position to move to and fired another burst in the general direction of the last gunman to keep his head down.

Once there, he fired again, moving behind a three-foot-high pile of drywall and at the same time noting the steel beam's details. He was now in a better position for what he was going to attempt.

In the vague blue light coming in the windows, he could see exactly where the beam was and the angle of its surfaces in relation to the final gunman. Quietly, he slid a full magazine into his Glock and stepped from behind the Sheetrock pile. Standing up tall, he took a two-handed grip on the Glock and sighted it on the beam. He started firing slowly, watching the sparking impact of each round on the steel beam, adjusting his aim slightly after each one. The slugs ricocheted closer and closer to the man's position. Finally one hit him, causing him to grunt deeply. Somewhere in the torso or legs, Vail judged. He moved his point of aim higher on the beam, and the gunman, realizing he had nowhere to go, reached his hand up over the wheelbarrow and fired blindly, trying to get Vail to stop shooting. Vail took aim at his hand and fired one round, striking either the hand or the arm. He stepped back behind the drywall stack and shoved another magazine into his automatic. The sound of sirens racing toward them now penetrated the building. For once, the troops had arrived at the right time.

He knew that with his quarry wounded, he could simply walk toward him and shoot intermittently until he was safely over him, then take him into custody if he chose to surrender. If not, killing him was not a disagreeable alternative. Vail took a single step and then heard a shotgun racking a shell into the chamber. He turned and dove back behind the drywall. The gunman fired three blasts and then Vail could hear him moving toward the elevator. He started to look over the stack of building material when another explosion of double-aught buck slammed into the front edge of Vail's concealment.

The elevator opened and Vail stood up to fire. He caught a glimpse of the man dragging his bleeding leg into it and fired one more shot into the car just before the doors closed. Vail didn't know if he had hit him. He considered looking for the stairs, but by now the building was surrounded. And running around with a gun in his hand didn't seem like a good idea. More important, Kate needed attention. Her wound hadn't looked bad, but he had examined it in the dark. He hurried over to her. "He's gone," he told her.

Kate stood up, still pressing Vail's handkerchief to her

side. He took the flashlight from her and checked the wound.
"Will I live?" she said, forcing a smile.

He dabbed at the wounds analytically and then had her again hold the handkerchief against them. "Unfortunately, deputy assistant directors are not that easy to kill."

Suddenly the floor shook with an explosion. Vail shined the light over at the elevator. Dust and debris billowed out from the crack between its doors. Kate said, "I guess that was meant for us. Good thing you never pressed the Down button." She looked for a reaction from Vail, but his mind was once again racing ahead.

TWENTY-TWO

VAIL LEANED ON THE FENDER OF THEIR RENTED CAR AND WATCHED Kate come out of the hotel entrance. Her gait was measured and she listed a little to the left. He opened the passenger door for her. "Did you check your stitches?"

"No more blood on the bandages. How did you make out with LAPD last night?"

"They were pretty decent about it. I was there two, two and a half hours. They want to get your statement today."

Once she was in the car, Vail went around and got behind the wheel. "How'd you sleep?"

"Off and on. I was pretty wired up," she said.

"I'm usually the same way when I knife and shoot a guy."

She tried not to laugh. "How'd you sleep?"

"Fine, until the two A.M. messenger arrived."

"The two A.M. messenger?"

"It's when I go to bed with something on my mind. Sometimes my brain does the work and wakes me up, usually at two A.M."

"With the answer?"

"Always with an answer; sometimes it's even the right one."

"Can't you make your mind do that during daylight hours?"

"Usually not. It has this obstinacy. I know, I know—where could that possibly come from?"

Kate held her side. "Please don't make me laugh." She straightened up. "And what problem did it resolve this time? Was it the same one that was bothering you when that elevator exploded last night?"

"Actually, the elevator exploding was my problem."

"You don't think that was meant for us?" she asked.

"Only if we survived the shoot-out. I think there's a high probability it was meant to take out whoever survived. Otherwise, why didn't it explode on the way up?"

"I don't understand. I thought it was Radek who was killed in the explosion."

"The legal agent met me over at LAPD last night so I could give both statements at once. He said that the body was so badly damaged that they might have to go to DNA to identify it. If they can even come up with Radek's DNA from other sources. He wanted to know if I had any ideas, which I didn't."

"So it'll take a while, so what? It's not like he's going anywhere."

"I don't know."

"You don't know what? You don't think it's him?"

"We have to consider the possibility. You have to admit he's no dummy. Why would he get in an elevator knowing once it started down, it was going to blow up?"

"Maybe it was an accident. You shot him twice. Maybe he's not as smart with a couple of bullets in him."

"Maybe."

"Do you ever get the feeling that the two A.M. messenger is just screwing with you?"

"Almost always," Vail said.

"I got a call first thing this morning," Kate said. "There's a briefing in the major-case room at ten A.M. Maybe it'll put some of your demons to rest."

"Who called you?" Vail asked.

"Some clerk. It wasn't Kaulcrick, if that's what you're asking."

"I imagine your boss is not pleased with our lack of *sharing*."

"A deputy assistant director wounded in a shoot-out with murderers? He can't land on me with both feet. Not today anyway."

"You know what your real sin is? When you guys go back to Washington, you'll have the better stories at cocktail parties."

"And all I had to do was get shot."

"But do I get thanked?"

"Thank you."

"You're welcome. And since you're being gracious, what do you say I take you out to dinner tonight? *Out* out, not something that comes in cardboard containers."

"That depends."

"On?"

"Do you want to take *me* to dinner, or is this something you do for all the women who get shot around you?"

"Usually I just drop them off at the emergency room and keep going."

"When you make me feel that special, how could I not accept."

They pulled up to the federal building and could see that both the front and garage entrances were swarming with reporters and their news vans. "If I let you off at the corner, do you think you can sneak by the media without stopping to show them the bullet holes?"

"I'd be lying if I said yes."

WHEN VAIL AND KATE walked into the major-case room, a smattering of applause erupted. There was nowhere left to sit, but a couple of agents got up and offered Kate their seat. Vail said, "This is typical. Where's my chair? I shot somebody, too."

Kaulcrick and the SAC were at the front of the room. "Okay, if we could have everyone's attention," Hildebrand said. Everyone turned toward them. "As I'm sure most of you know, last night, Deputy Assistant Director Kate Bannon and Steve Vail were involved in a shoot-out with three of the individuals who were responsible for the murders of five people, two of whom were our own. Assistant Director Kaulcrick and I feel that these three men along with Lee Davis Salton, who was recently killed, and Vince Pendaran made up the group calling itself the Rubaco Pentad, which was responsible for extorting five million dollars from the United States government. Sewed into the lining of the jackets of two of the men were false IDs. Through prints, we discovered their true identities, Wallace David Simms and James William Hudson. Both of them, along with Lee

Davis Salton, were convicted bank robbers who served time together in the federal prison at Marion, Illinois.

"We believe the fifth man, the one killed in the elevator explosion, was Victor James Radek, the leader of the group, also incarcerated with the others at Marion. Unfortunately the body was so badly damaged by the blast, we're having trouble positively identifying him. Along with the phony identification, we found about ten thousand dollars on both Simms and Hudson. All hundred-dollar bills. The serial numbers matched those from the extortion. Also in the lining of their coats, Simms and Hudson each had deposit slips from a New Hampshire bank in the amount of six hundred thousand dollars. After we recovered three million dollars two days ago, that left two million to be split three ways, since Pendaran is in custody. Which, with the amounts already recovered, would come to roughly six hundred thousand a man."

Don Kaulcrick stepped forward. "As you can imagine, we were pretty excited about finding out where the bulk of the remaining money was, so we contacted the Boston office, who rousted out the bank's president in the middle of the night. He found that the slips were indeed from his bank, but the account numbers were phonies. It turns out the slips were forgeries. So it seemed we were back to square one. But we did have some good fortune. Tracing phone numbers that were called from a cell phone we found on Simms's body, we were able to locate an apartment Victor Radek was using. A search of that apartment revealed the blank deposit slips that he used in preparing the forgeries. There was also another cell phone in the apartment. We're presently pulling those records. Keep your fingers crossed. We have two evidence teams there right now processing the entire place. Radek was originally from New Hampshire, so he could have had connections at that bank. The Boston office is looking into it. We are working under the assumption that Radek was looking to eliminate his partners, and at the same time, a couple more FBI agents. We figure he gave the members of his gang the deposit slips to convince them that their share had been deposited for them. Then whoever survived the gun battle, whether it was his people or ours, was supposed to die in the elevator."

Someone asked, "Then why did he use the elevator?"

Hildebrand said, "We asked the same question. So we had Sergeant Mike Henning from the LAPD bomb squad give us a hand at the scene as he did at the tunnel drop. Mike."

Henning stood up from a front-row seat. "The device was really overkill, so we're having trouble reconstructing the triggering mechanism. It was wired to the floor-button panel, so we think there may have been a way to disarm it from inside the elevator car, something as simple as a three- or four-digit code typed into the panel. Either it malfunctioned or the person we believe is Radek, having been shot in the leg and hand, forgot the code, or maybe he simply panicked and punched in the wrong one. Steve Vail fired a shot into the elevator just as the doors were closing. Maybe the shot fatally wounded him. It could be a week or more before we have a better idea." Henning wrote his pager number on the board. "I strongly suggest you call me before executing any more search or arrest warrants in this case. These people have a history of booby-trapping everything. You're aware of the tunnel and the elevator. And I understand that Kate and Steve ran into a car that had its trunk rigged, so don't hesitate to call." Henning shot a smile at Kate as he sat down.

"One other thing we found at Radek's apartment," Hildebrand said, "was a complete set of identification in the name of William Thompson, no middle initial. Since Radek convinced the others that the money had been deposited in a bank under aliases, we feel there's a possibility that he has all of it stowed in a bank under that alias either in accounts or in a safety-deposit box or boxes. So ladies and gentlemen, we're going to wear out some shoe leather. We're sending out instructions to every office in the Bureau to contact every bank. Our division will be searching most of Southern California, unless someone feels they have a better idea." When no one spoke up, Hildebrand said, "Okay, see your supervisors for assignments."

Kate looked back at Vail and sensed that the briefing had not answered all his questions. Kaulcrick walked up to them. "Kate, how are you feeling?"

"I'm fine, Don."

"LAPD homicide is in the SAC's conference room. They're going to need your statement."

She got up slowly and said to Vail, "I hope you didn't rat me out."

"Yeah, like you're not about to give me up."

When she was gone, Kaulcrick said, "I need to talk to you, Steve. How about in Kate's office in a half hour?"

Vail couldn't tell what the assistant director had in mind.

That he wanted to talk to him alone was probably not a good sign. At least it had never been in the past. There usually came a point with Vail when enough had been accomplished, and the unfinished balance wasn't worth the disruption of having him around. That time may have arrived.

"I wouldn't miss it."

WHEN KAULCRICK WALKED IN, he found Vail sitting behind Kate's desk, pushing 9mm rounds into a magazine for an older-model Sig Sauer automatic that was sitting on the desk beside him. He had just drawn it from the firearm vault. Kaulcrick sat down and Vail set the clip aside. "So what's up?"

"I'm wondering why you and I are never on the same page."

"Don, if you're going to cut me loose, I understand. I'm the one who predicted it, remember? So let's skip the hand-wringing search for the reasons."

"Nobody's cutting you loose. I am genuinely curious why you don't come to me when you find something."

"We told you about Pendaran, and we called you last night, but things just got out of hand when it looked like an agent was in trouble."

Kaulcrick smiled and shook his head slowly. "In both instances, you were conducting your own investigation and called only when you couldn't take it any further. Steve, I just want the truth."

"Do you want me to be honest? Before you answer, think about it."

Kaulcrick was sitting with his legs crossed and tapped his index finger on his thigh in brief contemplation. "Yes, I do."

"Okay," Vail said. "The FBI's large bureaucratic structure, especially in this case, is what the Pentad targeted. Knowing how you did things, they were able to use it to their advantage. Recognizing this, I let you follow the Pentad script of false leads to lull them into a false sense of security. With them thinking the Bureau was falling for it, I was able to work behind the scenes and find a few of their weak spots."

"So we were nothing more than a decoy for you."

"You were following the logical leads. Which had to be done."

"I don't like being a decoy."

"No one does."

"And given the least provocation, you'd do it again, wouldn't you?" Vail shrugged, implying he wouldn't contest the assistant director's assumption. "Can you think of any circumstance that would allow us to work together to find this money?"

"I was brought into this precisely because I am not a team player."

"What if I found a way to make you want to work with me?"

"I'd be interested in hearing it."

"What if I developed the best lead to recover the money?"

Vail laughed. "Then why would you come to me?"

Kaulcrick smiled caustically. "I said 'developed the lead,' not that I had figured it out completely."

"You found something at Radek's apartment."

"Yes."

When Kaulcrick didn't say anything else, Vail said, "Am I supposed to guess?"

"No, I'll tell you on one condition."

"Which is?"

"I'm with you every step of the way."

"How good a lead is it?"

"Does it matter?"

"No, I guess not," Vail said. "Agreed."

Kaulcrick handed him a clear plastic evidence envelope with a slip of blue paper inside. On it was written: "2M-8712."

Vail looked at it and turned it over, finding the back side blank. "Is that the same paper as the death notes, the tablet that was planted at Bertok's?"

"It looks the same. We found it hidden in a book that was on a shelf over his desk."

"And no one has any idea what it means?"

"None. But it's got to be important. Why else hide it like that?"

Vail didn't answer right away. "The first demand note had the amount written out in numbers. The second note shorthanded the three million dollars as a dollar sign with a 3 and an M. The 2M could mean two million dollars."

"What about the four numbers? Could they be an address, like he knows the street but wants to make sure he remembers the numbers correctly?" Kaulcrick asked.

"Possibly, but he knew how to get there, and it's unlikely that he would trust anyone else enough to send them to get the money."

"On the off chance it is an address, I could get some analysts to start running through the reverse directories just looking for those four digits."

"This is a big city. There could be a hundred of them," Vail said. "What was on the desk?"

"At his apartment? Just a cell phone in a charger."

"Since he was keeping the piece of paper that close to the phone, it could be a phone number."

"But it's only four numbers."

"Salton had a cell on him, and at least one of those guys last night had a phone. And I saw one in a charger at that house where we found the Honda. They're probably all throwaways with the preloaded minutes. Why don't we try all the exchanges on them with 8712?"

"If you're right and we wind up with a dead guy's cell phone number, how's that give us a location?"

"One thing at a time. Let me get Tom Demick up here. Can you have someone bring us those three phones?"

A half hour later Demick sat at Kate's desk examining the three cell phones, scrolling through Menu options. He wrote down their phone numbers. Two of them had the same exchange. Vail then turned one phone on and dialed it from Kate's desktop landline. It rang four times before a beep sounded without a greeting to leave a message. He hung up and dialed one of the phones that was not turned on. It rang once before the beep. He then dialed the exchange of the two that matched followed by 8712. He held the phone away from his ear so the other two men could hear. "The number you have dialed is no longer in service." He dialed again, this time using the other cell phone exchange followed by the same four digits. He held it out as it rang four times before the beep. "It's turned on." He looked at Demick. "So far, so good."

"I don't get it," Kaulcrick said.

"If this is the number Radek was referring to in the coded note, it means the phone is still turned on, hopefully on a charger like the one they found at his apartment and at the house where he had his car. Correct me if I'm wrong, Tom," Vail said, "but as long as it's turned on, we can ping this number."

"We should be able to."

Now Kaulcrick understood. "So the cell's GPS, which they're all equipped with for emergencies, will tell us where the phone is located."

"Tom, can you get the phone company moving? We'll get Tye Delson on the court order and search warrant. All we'll need is the address," Vail said.

As everyone stood up, Kate's phone rang. Vail answered it. "It's for you," he said, handing it to the assistant director.

Kaulcrick listened for a while. "A complete match, both prints and DNA . . . excellent." He hung up. "That was Hildebrand. When they processed Radek's apartment, the only identifiable prints they found were his, which were everywhere. They also took a few items for a possible DNA match, including his toothbrush. The agents ran everything over to the state lab, and they just confirmed that the prints were Radek's and his DNA was a match with the body from the elevator. Let's keep our fingers crossed that the money is at this phone number."

TWENTY-THREE

NORMALLY THE INDUSTRIAL STRETCH OF NINTH STREET WOULD HAVE been relatively deserted, but now the street, the ends of which were closed off by uniform cars, was crowded with LAPD and FBI vehicles. In the middle of the block was the object of the activity, a one-story brick building which had been built as a steam laundry almost a hundred years earlier. Presently, it was believed to contain Victor Radek's cell phone. Several businesses had occupied the structure since its construction, the owner of the last one painting the exterior khaki green with red trim to match the color of its low tile roof. The glaring midday sun cut cool black rectangles and triangles into its recesses.

Located through tax records, the real estate agent stated that she had rented it to an individual who had taken a six-month lease on it. After being showed a copy of the search warrant, she identified Radek's photo as the man who had rented it using the name William Thompson. The only other thing she could remember about him was that he had paid cash.

The bomb squad van sat thirty yards from the front of the building. Inside the vehicle, Sergeant Mike Henning sat watching a TV monitor as he guided a wheeled robot through the back door of the building. Standing behind him were Kate, Vail, Kaulcrick, and Tye Delson, who had been asked to come along in case the phone led to another location that needed legal access.

As Henning guided the robot with a joystick, the monitor showed four different pictures being transmitted from the device's four cameras. Although each could be deployed in different directions at the same time, they were now all pointed straight ahead. The four streaming images were similar, but everyone who was watching shifted their eyes from image to image, hoping to spot something. There was scattered refuse on the floor inside the building, but on the worktables were power tools and what appeared to be board scraps. "When we get in there it'll be interesting to see if any of that stuff could be from the punji boards you ran into at the tunnel, Steve," Henning said.

The robot continued to slowly search the first floor of the building, turning through the walled-off workspaces, which were all connected through a series of doorways and short corridors. Most of them had worktables and stools bolted to the floor. Henning would crane one of the cameras up from the robot's low position to inspect whatever material was on the table and then explore the debris on the floor. After almost a half hour the device was back at the door it had entered through, indicating it had gone full circle. "What are we looking for again?" Henning asked.

Vail said, "To start with, the cell phone we got the GPS reading from. It's in there somewhere, probably plugged into an electrical outlet. I didn't see it."

"And let's not forget about the money," Kaulcrick added.

"Hold on a minute," Vail said. He walked to the back door of the van and leaned out. "Even though there are no windows below the first floor, it looks like there could be a basement. That door you went by next to the men's room, think the robot could open it?"

Henning spun the robot around 180 degrees and backtracked. It got to the door and did a sharp right turn. The bomb squad sergeant jockeyed it back and forth until the mechanical pincers on the arm closed around the doorknob. Everyone watched as the arm rotated. They could hear a click as the striker cleared the plate. Slowly Henning backed it up, pulling the door open. The robot then moved forward around the door, and Henning flipped a switch. A small spotlight came on. There was a narrow descending staircase. "It is a basement. But that's too narrow for the robot to make the ninety-degree turn halfway down the stairs. And it may be too steep for the treads."

Vail took out his cell phone. "Can you turn up the audio on the robot?" Henning twisted the volume control to its maximum level. Vail dialed the phone number that had led them there. Everyone listened, and after a few seconds the robot's microphone picked up a faint ringing. "How much does your friend weigh, Mike?" Vail asked, closing his phone.

"That model is almost two hundred pounds. Are you thinking about carrying it down the stairs?"

"I'd have to tip it on end, but I should be able to get it down to the basement." Vail picked up a flashlight that was sitting on a makeshift desk.

"Steve, I really think one of my people should do it," Henning said.

"So do I, but do you have someone who's used to wrestling that kind of weight?"

Henning nodded at the agent's logic. Vail stood up and stripped off his suit jacket. "Let's at least get you in a protective suit," Henning offered.

Vail laughed. "If there is anything to trip over down there, me in one of those outfits will make sure that I do. But let me go see what's what before we decide anything."

Everyone sat in silence as Vail stepped down from the van and made his way around the back of the building. Tye Delson said, "I know I'm just a lawyer and don't understand every little thing that you guys do, but why does Steve always get to *volunteer*?" Her voice seemed to have a slightly emotional edge to it.

Kaulcrick turned toward Kate and they exchanged questioning glances. Then he said to Tye, "Did you hear anyone ask him to go?"

She asked the assistant director, "Is that how you justify not going yourself?"

Kaulcrick turned around and stared at the monitor, holding back his anger. He reminded himself that the important thing right now was recovering the money.

Kate watched him and knew that he wouldn't forget the slight. He never did.

Henning had reversed one of the robot's cameras and it captured Vail walking into the building. He stepped around the device and became visible on the other three quadrants on the screen. The beam of his flashlight lit the stairs as he tested the first step with his weight before descending. Once he made the turn halfway down, the cameras lost sight of him. At the bottom, he found a light switch and turned it on.

Half the basement looked like the bowels of a hundred-year-old building, unpainted, dank, abandoned, but the other half was finished. The walls were paneled and half of the area was covered with thick rubber matting, the kind that is found in gyms to absorb the impact of dropped weights. Four folding chairs sat near a minifridge. In the corner was a card table; on it was a cell phone, its charger plugged into the wall. The matted area was covered with weight-lifting equipment, benches, bars, dumbbells, and large steel plates. Vail hit Redial on his cell and the phone on the table rang. He disconnected the call. He checked the refrigerator and there was only a single can of beer in it.

He stepped back and tried to imagine the group's traffic through the area. Obviously, someone used it to lift weights. A lot of men become addicted to the intensity of it in prison. The equipment upstairs indicated that they used the place as a workshop for making the punji boards. The basement was probably where they sat around drinking beer and planning whatever came next. But Vail's eye for construction told him that something was out of proportion. Then he saw what it was—the matting, almost as if it were meant to be a distraction.

Teeth, like dovetail joints on well-made furniture, held the two-foot squares together. Vail did a quick count along two adjoining edges, determining that there were sixty sections, far more than were needed for the amount of weight equipment present. He started walking across them, looking for any further indications that they might be hiding something. In the middle of the floor, he knelt down and tried to get his fingers in between the pieces to pull one up, but it was almost impossible to get any kind of grip. He thought that one of the criteria which Radek would have set for himself was immediate access for a getaway. Maybe one of the outer pieces.

Letting his eyes trace the edges as he moved over them, he noticed an inch or so of cloth sticking out from under a stack of four twenty-five-pound plates in the corner. Vail restacked the weights to one side, exposing a sturdy foot-long black strap sticking up between two of the squares. Slowly he pulled on it. It was anchored under the middle of one of the tiles, which popped up. Under it was plywood. Vail pulled up the adjoining pieces of matting until he exposed the entire piece of wood. It was covering a three-foot-square hole cut into the concrete.

Vail lay on his stomach and lowered his face as close to the edge of the board as possible. He turned on his flashlight and lifted the plywood slightly. Under it he saw a large metal box. Slowly he lifted the cover out of the way. Scattered around the steel container were a half-dozen handguns and two canisters of what appeared to be pyrotechnics. He couldn't tell for sure because they were wedged behind the metal chest, which had a heavy padlock on the front of it. There were also a number of boxes of different-caliber ammunition stacked around it.

Vail walked back upstairs and asked the SWAT officer at the back door to get him the largest bolt cutters they had. He then went out to the bomb unit's van and told them what he had found.

"Well, let's get it open," Kaulcrick said.

"If anything's booby-trapped, it's that box," Henning said. "Think you can get the robot down those stairs, Steve?"

"I think so, but I'm going to have to cut that lock, unless R2 can."

"Unfortunately, it can't. But once you do, don't open the box. That's the robot's job."

A SWAT officer came up to the van with the bolt cutters. "Don't worry," Vail said, "I can still see that flamethrower."

Vail went back down to the basement, and after cutting the lock and carefully removing it, he went back upstairs to the robot. "Mike," he said into its microphone, "how about retracting the arm as much as possible." Once Henning had, Vail stood it up on its back end and bear-hugged it up off the floor. With short, measured steps he walked the device down the stairs, squeezing past the turn and then all the way down onto the concrete floor. "Okay, we're all set here. Fire it up."

The robot came to life, its cameras adjusting forward and the spotlight turned on. The arm extended forward with a motorized whir. Vail got in front of it and pointed at the hole in the floor. The arm and its camera craned down toward the metal box. "All set?" Vail asked.

The arm gave a short up-and-down motion, and Vail headed for the stairs. Before leaving, he walked around the first floor looking at the tools and board scraps, trying to figure out whether this was the building used to make the punji boards. If it was staged, the gang members had done a good job, because there was sawdust on the floor where the boards would have been cut. In the corner was a plastic twenty-gallon trash container. He took the lid off, hoping to find the nails used with the boards or, more likely, the boxes they came in. Immediately the strong odor of garlic became obvious. It was as pungent as the night before in the building on West Seventh Street. He put the lid back on and dragged it out the door.

In the van, everyone was even more closely gathered around the monitor, but Henning was waiting to make sure that Vail had cleared the building before going ahead. When he stepped back up into the van, Henning said, "Okay, here we go."

He maneuvered the robot back and forth until it was at the edge of the hole and its arm was directly over the hasp from which Vail had cut the lock. With microscopic movements on the joystick, Henning closed the pincers around the hasp. He raised the lid a quarter of an inch and stopped, taking his hand completely off the joystick so he wouldn't accidentally raise it any farther. He put his hand back on the control, raising it an inch, this time keeping hold of the stick. They still couldn't see into the box. He raised it another two inches and then maneuvered the spotlight into a lower position. The lowest camera's image on the screen became the most vivid with the increased light. Fully illuminated were the strongbox's contents. It was filled to the top with strapped bundles of hundred-dollar bills wrapped in the same heavy plastic and tape as the recovered three million dollars.

A small cheer went up inside the van. Henning continued raising the lid. Suddenly Kate said, "What's that on the side, a wire?"

Henning tried to reverse the robot's arm to close the lid but it was too late. The screen went blank. "What happened?" Tye asked.

The sergeant checked a gauge on the control panel. "That's weird. It's shorted out. Must have been wired to fry whoever opened it."

"What do we do now?" Kaulcrick asked.

"I'll have to suit up and go down there."

Just then gunfire erupted from inside the building. The SWAT officers stationed around the perimeter pulled back and took cover where they could. "What's that?" Kaulcrick said.

Henning said, "There's no one in there. That electrical charge must have set off the pyrotechnics Steve saw around the metal box, heating up the ammunition."

Everyone scrambled out of the van and watched the building. Dark gray smoke started escaping around the door and window frames. Henning tilted his head back slightly and sniffed the air. "Metallic. That might be thermite," he said ominously.

"What's that?" Kaulcrick demanded.

"Thermite grenades are used by the military to destroy enemy equipment in a hurry. They burn at two thousand plus degrees centigrade. It'll burn right through a tank and melt everything around it."

"The money!"

"If that is thermite, all you're going to have is a pile of ashes."

"Why would anyone store something like that next to money?" Kaulcrick said angrily.

"They probably had it in the cache ready to destroy the guns and ammunition in case they were raided. They put the box in there and electrified it, thinking if they had to get out in a hurry, all they had to do was shut off the juice, grab the box, and set off the thermite to destroy all the evidence. The electrical current must have set off the thermite unintentionally."

"What do we do now?" Kaulcrick asked.

Tye Delson lit another cigarette and, her reserved composure regained, said, "Call the fire department."

TWENTY-FOUR

KAULCRICK ORDERED EVERYONE BACK TO THE OFFICE FOR A TWO o'clock meeting and asked Sergeant Henning to join them when he was done at the scene. Kaulcrick knew he had to break the news to the director that they had just incinerated two million dollars of Bureau money and realized there would be technical questions he wouldn't be able to answer. Besides, it was the LAPD's robot that had destroyed the money. And if push came to shove, Kate had actually spotted the trip wire and tried to stop it.

Kate got behind the wheel and told Vail she'd drive. She looked up and said, "I think we're being followed." She adjusted the rearview mirror to get a better look at the blue-gray trash can sitting on the backseat.

"It's nice to see that watching two million dollars burn didn't dampen your sense of humor."

"Hey, life is good. All the bad guys are dead and the money is *accounted* for, unless your friend in the backseat has a different opinion."

Vail reached over the seat and pried open the lid. Immediately the odor of garlic filled the car. "Ring any bells?"

"Funny, I suddenly have an overwhelming premonition I'm about to be shot."

"Exactly. Just like last night."

"I know you're big on tying up all the loose ends, but hunting down whoever overseasoned a meal is a little obsessive, even for you."

"Ever notice, every time you drive we have an argument?"

"Yeah, me driving, that's the problem."

"Maybe it's low blood sugar. How about some lunch? No Italian, I promise."

KATE AND VAIL sat at an outdoor table. She was nibbling on a single taco while he worked his way through a combination plate that looked more like an entire station at a buffet. She said, "You know, this isn't the last meal the Bureau's going to pay for."

"You've just answered the one question that's been on my mind."

"Which is?"

"Why you're not married."

"Are you saying I'm too critical?"

"Oh, no, dear."

"Sorry, it's just that it's kind of fun to find little things about you to pick at. Were you really wondering why I'm not married?"

"For a good-looking, only slightly neurotic woman, I think that is the presumed path."

"You do know how to turn a girl's head."

"Okay, an attractive, confident, fearless woman."

"Fearless? Does that mean you think marriage takes a certain amount of courage?"

"No, I think marriage takes a lot of courage. More than I have."

"Actually, I question whether I do." Her eyes hooded in a new level of contemplation. "My father traveled a lot, on *business*. On one occasion, after returning home, he passed along to my mother a sexually transmitted disease. By the time I got to high school, she had left him. Since then, the few guys I could have been serious about couldn't pass the fidelity tests I ran by them. So here I am, career woman. Hear me roar."

"What kind of test?"

"If I let that out, then someone could cheat it. Besides, I've come to realize that if I've got to give someone the test, he's already failed."

"So it's going to wind up just you and your retirement check, a little too much of which will go for cat food."

She smiled, trying to deny the tiny flicker of sadness in her eyes. "If the cats will have me."

Vail said, "You were probably wondering why I've never been married."

Kate burst out laughing, launching a small bite of her taco into the air.

"Then again," he said, "maybe not."

VAIL DROVE BACK to the office, and when they pulled into the garage, Kate asked, "You are coming to the meeting, right?"

"I don't know if you saw the look on Kaulcrick's face

when he came out of that bomb van, but I've seen it before. This case is wrapping up. I'm just a matter of hours away from being two thousand miles east of here with a brick trowel back in my hand. Me being at that meeting will just make everyone uncomfortable. My presence has a way of getting in the way of a good rationalization, which several people in that room are going to need. Besides, it'll be best for you to be seen in public without me tagging along."

Kate knew she was probably wasting her time trying to convince him. "I'm sure the director will want to thank you personally."

"Which will make it even worse."

"You mean for me. Any credit you get will be less for Don, and he'll see me as part of that."

Vail gave her a half smile. "We burned up two million dollars today. Any credit being passed around may not be the kind you're expecting." Vail pulled up in front of the federal building.

"When the dragon's slain, no one asks how many federal dollars it cost," she said and pivoted toward him. "Why won't you stay with the Bureau?"

"I guess because it is the Bureau."

"We'll have dinner tonight?"

"Does that mean you're giving me one last shot at the brass ring?"

Kate leaned over and kissed him on the cheek. "What makes you think you had any shot, bricklayer?" She got out and disappeared through the door.

THE MEETING STARTED at a few minutes before two o'clock. Tye Delson asked, "Where's Steve Vail?" Everyone was sitting around the table in the SAC's conference room.

Kaulcrick turned to Kate. "Where is he?"

"To tell you the truth, I have no idea. You know Vail."

"I'd be surprised if anyone knows Vail."

The phone rang and Kaulcrick hit the Speaker button. "Don Kaulcrick here."

"Hello, Don." It was the director. "Please tell me who is present." The assistant director first introduced Tye Delson. "She's been with us through this whole thing, giving legal opinions and making sure our search warrants were valid." The director thanked her, and then Kaulcrick went around the table, naming the SAC, Kate, and the two ASACs. Finally he introduced Mike Henning as the sergeant in charge of the LAPD bomb squad unit that had helped at the tunnel and again today at the steam cleaners. "Mike has the technical savvy about the robot and what happened with the money, sir."

"Mike, as always, the FBI is indebted to a local police department. I know your chief fairly well, and he'll hear from me about your assistance. I cannot thank you and your people enough. Can you give me a rundown on what happened out there today?"

Henning detailed the attempt to recover the two million dollars, and how the electrical booby trap set by Radek detonated the thermite device accidentally.

Lasker said, "How do we know there was two million dollars in the box?"

"Before I tripped the device, we saw the stacks of banded

hundred-dollar bills, and the box was full. It was the general consensus, based on the three million recovered, that it was about the right size to contain the missing two million dollars."

"Where is the box now?"

"Your Evidence Recovery Team is packing it up. There's not much of it left."

"What about the contents?"

"Just a fine ash now, sir."

The director said, "Don, I want everything carefully preserved. There are two agents from the lab on their way. They tell me that with microanalysis and spectroanalysis they can determine what was burned inside that box and how much there was of it. I just want to be sure the money is gone when I explain this to the White House. I know they'll ask."

"I'm sorry about the money, sir, but I don't see any way that it could have been prevented," Henning said.

"There's absolutely nothing to be sorry about. You've all performed impressively during an impossible situation. You've recovered more money than you've lost, and two million dollars does not make a dent in what we would have had to spend if this went on any longer. We would probably have offered a million-dollar reward for Victor Radek alone."

Kaulcrick leaned back. "That's very generous of you, sir."

"And, Mark," Lasker said to SAC Hildebrand, "I'm going to try to get out to L.A. next month. I'd like to meet with all your people who were involved."

"They'd be honored."

"So where's Steve Vail?"

Kaulcrick hesitated, and Kate said, "Oh, you know how much he likes to be thanked, sir."

"Take me off speaker, please, Kate. Again, everyone, well done."

Kate picked up the handset. "Yes, sir."

"Where is he really?"

"It's like I said, he really doesn't like to be made a big deal of. I think it embarrasses him."

"From what I've been able to read between the lines, he's mainly responsible for putting this group out of business. Am I correct?"

She glanced at Kaulcrick and then carefully said, "A good deal of it, yes."

"He's too valuable to this organization to let go. I want you to offer him this permanently. He can go off anywhere he wants and work any case he wants. He can work directly for me."

"I'll do my best."

"Everything considered, it looks like you already have. You, too, have my appreciation. How are your injuries?"

"I'm fine, sir."

"And tell Vail, even if we can't figure out a way to keep him aboard, I will find some way to thank him."

"I'll threaten him with that."

The director laughed. "How much longer will you and Don be out there?"

"I would guess we'll be done with the evidence and reports in three to four days."

"Come see me when you get back."

TOM DEMICK had provided Vail with a rarely used alcove in a remote corner of the office's technical services section. He was wearing evidence gloves and going through the trash container from the building on Ninth Street. It seemed too pat that the extortionists had advertised themselves as a pentad. Now five people, including Pendaran, had been identified, and everyone was assuming that because the body count had reached that number, there could be no one else involved. Why would they give away their strength up front?

He had started listing all the container's contents on a pad of paper. Maybe he could, through content, fingerprints, or DNA, separate them by the person who had deposited them, allowing him to determine that there were more than five people. After processing a few items, he realized it would be an impossible task. It was time to cut the Gordian knot.

He reached in and shifted the contents around until he found the source of the garlic odor. It was an order of linguine with red clam sauce in a foil carryout container with a plastic top, which was in a paper bag stapled closed with the receipt attached. The top of the bag had been torn open and the lid pushed to one side. It appeared that the meal hadn't been touched. Vail leaned a little closer and sniffed the sauce. There was far too much garlic in it for anyone's taste. Now fascinated, he set it on a dusty desk beside him.

There was a good chance that whoever had set the meal in the trash did it so it would be noticed. But why? Would he have noticed it if he hadn't smelled the odor of garlic so prominently the night before? Was this meant to lead the FBI away from something again? Or to something?

He dug around in the old desk and found a staple puller. He eased out the fastener and unfolded the receipt. Unbelievably, it was dated the afternoon before and was paid for with a credit card. It was for two orders of linguine. The restaurant, Sargasso's, was located on West Seventh Street, less than three blocks from the building where the shootout the night before had occurred, and less than two miles from the building they had searched this morning.

Vail wondered if he was supposed to follow another investigative chain from the staged meal. Then it occurred to him that every time he discovered one of these pieces of evidence—from the flamethrower car to the dead bodies to the burned money—another clue was left behind to follow up on, which in turn led Vail into another deadly situation. Was this another trap Radek had set in place before his death, or was someone else afraid Vail would discover his involvement and was trying to kill him? Like everyone else, Vail had assumed Radek was the mastermind behind the murders and extortion. But maybe he wasn't. Vail's cell phone rang.

It was Kate. "I thought you were taking me to dinner tonight."

"What makes you think I'm not?"

"I haven't heard from you in a while. I thought maybe you were hiding out on some rooftop in Chicago. You're not, are you?"

"Let's be European and eat late. Pick you up at nine?"

"You need time to fly back here, don't you?"

"Something like that." He hung up and thought about going upstairs and telling her what he was doing, but the night before he had given in to her and then she'd been shot. And if it had been the late Victor Radek who left the garlicky meal for him to find, Vail was chasing shadows. He put the credit card receipt in his pocket and headed for the garage.

SARGASSO'S WAS ONE of those small tucked-away restaurants that use crisp white linen tablecloths and hand-washed crystal that pulse in the low light to create quiet, intimate dining. A man stood with his back to the door inspecting the dining area with proprietary authority. "Excuse me," Vail said, pulling out his credentials.

The man glanced at the identification but took a few more seconds to size up Vail. Then he held out his hand. "Armand Sargasso. I'm the owner, Agent Vail." He had just a touch of an Italian accent left, as if he had come from Italy as a young boy. There was also a noticeable New York corruption of the hard consonants. "What can I do for the FBI today?"

Vail handed him the credit card receipt. "Yesterday, someone got carryout in the middle of the afternoon."

"I'll get my receipts. Would you like something? Espresso? No, no, it's too hot. How about some nice gelato? I've got hazelnut."

"Do you make it?"

"We even roast the hazelnuts ourselves."

"Maybe a small dish."

The owner disappeared into the kitchen. A few moments later a young man came out with the dish of ice cream topped with some kind of whipped cream and a waffle biscuit wedge, set it in front of Vail with a spoon, and nodded respectfully.

By the time Sargasso came back, Vail had finished all of the dessert.

"How was it?"

Vail pointed at the empty dish. "It was awful."

The restaurateur laughed. "I've got a lot more stuff you won't like. You should come back for dinner, my treat."

"How about I come back, and it'll be the government's treat?"

"Even better." He handed Vail the original credit card receipt.

It was signed "Andrew Parker." "Who waited on him, do you know?"

"We do a pretty fair carryout business. It could have been any of my waitstaff. I was at the market yesterday afternoon."

"This guy ordered both meals buried in garlic."

"Oh, him. That would have been Nina. When she told the chef, he wanted to take a cleaver to the man. I heard about it when I got back. "

"Is Nina here now?"

"She's working tonight. You come back for dinner. I got some beautiful veal this morning."

"Then how about a reservation for two, nine thirty."

As soon as Vail got in the car, he called Tom Demick.

"Do you know who has the office contact for MasterCard?"

"I'm sure it's on one of the white-collar squads. I could find out."

Vail read him the information off the credit card receipt. "If you could verify the name as Andrew Parker and get the address on the account, I'd appreciate it."

"Since you're asking a lowly tech agent to do this, I assume the fewer who know about this, the better."

"Notice how that isn't even a question."

TWENTY-FIVE

THIS PLACE IS NICE," KATE SAID. "HOW DO YOU KNOW THE OWNER?"

"Do you want a really nice dinner, or do you want the truth?"

"Pass the Chianti and start lying."

"Let's see . . . the concierge at the hotel recommended it. She said a date brought her here, so I stopped in this afternoon. Armand is one of the guys who after a minute and a half treat you like they've known you their whole life."

"What did she say about the food?"

"I don't think she remembered."

"Then why—in your little *narrative*—did she recommend it?"

Vail tilted his head suggestively. "I think, by the end of the evening, everyone was . . . *satisfied*."

"Exactly what kind of dining experience did you ask her about?"

"You certainly are asking a lot of questions."

"Sorry, just trying to keep my honor intact."

"As an occasionally honorable person, I can tell you it's overrated. Besides, you're freshly wounded."

"What does that have to do with it?"

"I wouldn't want to be responsible for ripping open your stitches."

Kate laughed musically. "You must be quite the athlete. And an even bigger optimist."

"You're the one who started it."

"Me?"

"You're wearing a dress, and unless my eyes are going, it's a little shorter than the last time."

She blushed and looked down at the menu. "I wanted to look nice for you."

"Accomplished."

She let her eyes drift up to him slowly. "Thank you."

"This isn't a sympathy date, is it? You know, because I'm about to get fired?"

"I thought you were better at reading people than that."

"Only when it comes to evil intentions. When it comes to the good stuff, I don't have a clue."

"That would imply a lack of exposure to the good stuff."

"Finally someone to show me some compassion," Vail said. "I'm ready to leave right now."

"Slow down there, Secretariat. First things first. Since the government is paying for this meal, let's get the paid advertisements out of the way up front," Kate said. "The director asked about you this morning."

"Next time you talk to him, tell him Steve said 'Hey.'"

"He wants you to stay on board. He said you could work any case you want, anywhere in the country."

"The work's not the problem. It's the bosses."

"You would report only to him."

Vail laughed. "You're becoming quite the salesman, aren't you, saving that last little tidbit to ambush me because you knew it would be my final line of defense."

Kate interlaced her fingers and rested her chin on them. "Go ahead, Steve. I want to see how creative your excuse is for not accepting."

"How about 'I'll think about it'?"

"Legitimately?"

"Legitimately."

The waiter came, and they both ordered the veal. Vail asked him, "Is Nina here?"

"She's in the kitchen. Did you want to speak to her?" he said, pointing to the back.

"That's all right. I can go back there." When the waiter left, Vail asked Kate, "Did you bring the photos of Radek and his crew?"

"Now?"

"Sorry."

Kate took the mug shots out of her purse and handed them to Vail. "When you called and said you wanted them, I figured it was for tomorrow. I'm beginning to find your concierge story a tad suspicious."

Vail refilled her glass with the thick velvety wine the owner had sent over. He got up and leaned over, touching his cheek to hers. He let it linger a moment. Then he turned his head until his lips were just touching her ear and whispered, "Would I lie to you?"

A shudder of pleasure ran through her and she shrugged her shoulder toward her ear in an unconvincing gesture of modesty. Then, as though trying to neutralize Vail's surprising effect on her, she said, "Considering the primary directive of all men—absolutely."

Vail laughed. "You're not leaving me much room to operate." He walked up to the front of the restaurant, where the owner was lining out a reservation. He extended his hand. "Thanks for the wine, Armand."

He shook his hand and smiled. "For you, I send over the stuff that doesn't come from a box."

Vail noticed that Sargasso's accent had shifted from Brooklyn back a little closer to Italy, apparently something the customers found authentic. "It's very nice," Vail said. He looked back at Kate. "I hope it's as strong as it is good."

The restaurateur stared at Kate appreciatively. "*Molto bello*. Maybe I send another bottle to make sure." Sargasso wagged his eyebrows.

"Thanks, but I think you've done enough. Is it all right if I go in the kitchen and talk to Nina? I promise to stay out of everyone's way."

Sargasso looked back out the door to make sure no one was coming in and said, "Come on." Vail followed him into the kitchen and introduced Nina, a thickset woman whose hands were julienning vegetables with a practiced consistency. "This is the man from the FBI I told you about who was asking about the Garlic Man. Please help him if you can." Sargasso slapped Vail on the shoulder and went back out through the swinging door.

He took out the pictures of Radek, Simms, and Hudson. Since Salton was dead and Pendaran was in custody at the time, they couldn't have purchased the meals. Vail laid the photos on the counter in front of the sous-chef as she continued to cut the yellow and green vegetables. She blew a long strand of graying hair away from her eyes. "The one on the right, that's him," she said. It was Victor Radek.

"Did he say anything other than giving you the order?"

"When I told him that was an awful lot of garlic, he said the weirdest thing. He said, 'Only if you're going to eat it.' "

"That makes more sense than you know. Anything else?"

"No, that was about it. Paid with a credit card. Gave me the creeps the way he smiled at me."

"How so?"

"It wasn't real, like he had never smiled before."

"Thanks for your time." Vail went back to the table, where a fresh bottle of wine had been delivered. Kate nodded toward it. "Quite the operator, aren't you? Another bottle with the owner's compliments." She held up her glass as if to toast Vail.

"I told him I was getting nowhere with you sober."

"So this Nina, is she my competition?" she said playfully.

"As if anyone could compete with you."

"There isn't enough wine in this entire place to get me to swallow that line."

Vail sat down. "I told you I wasn't very good at this."

"Don't panic just yet, bricklayer, you're doing all right."

"That's a little teaser to get me to tell what happened in the kitchen, isn't it?"

She tilted her head coyly. "Is it?"

Vail stared at her as if making a decision. "Okay, on the off chance that this will help close the deal, here's what I've been doing. Remember the trash can in the backseat of the car?"

"A story that starts with a garbage can and winds up in a kitchen doesn't sound like it's going to be very interesting."

"That's the good thing about it, it's not interesting at all." The waiter brought their veal, and when he was gone, Vail said, "It would probably be more exciting talking about what we're going to have for dessert. Or for dessert after dessert."

"Hmmm, methinks he protests too little. Maybe you better give me the boring details."

Vail told her about Nina's identifying Radek as having come to the restaurant the afternoon before, ordering the two heavily seasoned meals, and saying they were not for eating. "So then he puts one where he hides the two million dollars and the other in the building last night."

"Why?"

"He wanted them to be noticed. The one from last night set up our noticing the one today. In case we survived last night."

"That means he expected us to find the laundry. Would he leave the money there and then direct us to it?"

"He didn't plan on dying. If we did somehow survive the shoot-out, he would have gone to the laundry and taken the two million out and left the metal box to electrocute one of us. And just in case that didn't happen, he left the second garlic clue."

"To lead us where?"

"Does it matter? He's dead."

"Well, something good did come out of the money being destroyed."

"What's that?" Vail asked.

"If there were doubts that Radek was dead, there's no way he would have let it burn up if he were alive."

"I hadn't thought of that."

"But DNA already said he was dead. Why did you chase down this clue?"

"My only reason for checking this out was to make sure it was Radek and not somebody else we didn't know about," Vail said. "That's why I wanted the photos."

She smiled. "Let's see, the Pentad minus five bad guys, and five million minus five million—we're back down to double zeros, just the way the Bureau likes it. I believe I'll have another glass of that unbelievably inexpensive wine."

Vail poured them each another glass and held his up to hers. "To the bureaucratic goal of zero."

Kate's cell phone vibrated on the tabletop. She picked it up and looked at the screen. "It's Kaulcrick."

"Don't answer it."

"You know I have to."

"Okay, then have a lie ready. You have a fever; you think your stitches are infected. Come on, Kate, you should really be on light duty," Vail said. "*You're drunk.*"

"This is the first time I can ever remember being so attracted to a desperate man. Hold that whimper." She answered the phone. "Yes, Don." She looked at Vail and started deliberately taunting him with the vagueness of her responses. "Uh-huh . . . okay . . . sure . . . uh-huh . . . okay, I'll be there." She hung up and waited a couple of seconds before bursting into laughter. "You should see your face. He was just letting me know that the lab confirmed that the residue from the steel box was consistent in both weight and components of paper and ink with forty to forty-five pounds of U.S. currency. I believe that's what two million dollars of hundred-dollar bills weighs."

"Did he say—"

"I'm sorry, Steve, that's it. I'm off duty. I just want to spend the rest of the evening without the FBI. Besides, I normally require a forty-eight-hour turnaround after being shot, so let's just have a nice, boring dinner."

TWENTY-SIX

"I THINK I HAD TOO MUCH WINE." THEY WERE STANDING IN KATE'S hotel room and Vail had put his arms around her.

"Already auditioning excuses for the morning?" he said. "I find that most encouraging."

"I thought you were worried about my stitches."

"I promise to take you straight to the ER afterward."

She pushed him to arm's length in a halfhearted tease. "So you like my dress."

"Do you think at this particular moment I'm going to say no?"

She pulled him back to her and tilted her head slightly, inviting a kiss. He opened his mouth slightly, barely touching his lips to hers. She pressed forward and he pulled back an equal distance, keeping the touch light and increasingly arousing. She pulled her head back. "I thought you didn't know anything about the good stuff."

"Must be beginner's luck."

She put her head on his shoulder. "Mmmm," came from somewhere deep in her throat. "I seriously doubt that," she said. "Do you know what the nicest thing about tonight was?"

"*Was?* I was hoping the nicest thing hadn't gotten here yet. I didn't miss it, did I?"

She raised her voice slightly to override Vail's attempt to dismiss the poignancy of what she was about to say. "That we were able to spend a couple of hours without a single word about work."

Before Vail could say anything, the hotel phone rang. She looked at her watch; it was almost 1 A.M. She went to the nightstand. "Hello."

"Kate, I hope it's not too late." It was Tye Delson and she sounded drunk.

"Too late for what?"

"I've been trying to find Steve. I've left messages on his cell phone and on the hotel voice mail. You know where he is?"

"Is something wrong?"

"I just need to talk to him."

"Hold on." Kate held the phone out to Vail.

Vail craned his head back slightly in surprise. "For me?"

"Tye Delson," Kate said.

He took the phone and Kate sat down on the bed. "Tye, what's wrong?"

"Oh, Steve." He heard her voice crack with emotion. "I've been on the phone for the last two hours trying to find you. I was afraid you had already left." She was talking loud enough that Kate could hear her.

"Left for where? What's wrong?"

"Can I come and see you?"

"Now?"

"It's just that I don't want to be alone. Just for tonight."

Vail looked down at Kate, who stared straight ahead, her face somber. "Tye, I don't think so."

"I know last time I came uninvited, but now I'm asking. Please."

Vail saw one of Kate's eyebrows arch involuntarily. "That wasn't a good idea then, and it isn't now."

"Can you come here then?"

"What you need is to go to sleep."

"Please, Steve."

"I'm sorry, Tye, no."

"You're going back to Chicago or wherever, aren't you?" The emotion was rising in her voice as though she was on the verge of tears. "The case is over, isn't it, Steve? All of them are dead, and you're disappearing like men always do?"

"Tye, how much have you had to drink?"

Suddenly she sounded as though she was trying to get control of herself. "I'm making a fool of myself, aren't I? I just want to know if you'll be leaving L.A. now."

"I'm not sure."

She didn't say anything for a long time. "I'm going to bed now. Promise you won't leave until you come and tell me good-bye—in person."

"Sure, but for right now, get some sleep." Vail hung up, and it took him a few seconds before he dared look at Kate. When he did, she pursed her lips and tilted her head, inviting an explanation. "After the tunnel drop, she showed up at my room."

"And?"

"There is no 'and.' We had a drink and she left."

"If you discouraged her then, why is she coming back for more?"

Vail exhaled through his nostrils. He leaned down and

kissed Kate on the cheek dutifully. "Thanks for a nice night."

When he got to the door, she stood up. "Steve, I'm sorry. I'm not really doubting you."

"I know," he said, smiling sadly. "But we are our fathers' children." He turned and walked out.

THE NEXT MORNING as Vail was getting out of the shower the phone rang. It was Tom Demick. "I got that address from MasterCard you wanted. I tried your cell, but you must have had it turned off, and I left you a message on your room phone to call me. Didn't you get it?"

"Sorry, I was out to dinner. It was late when I got in."

Demick gave him the address. It was a post office box in Aqua Dulce. "Where's that?"

"It's about an hour north of here. Take the 101 to 170."

"Thanks, Tom." Vail hung up and looked at the blinking light on the phone. He had ignored it when he came in, thinking it was Tye Delson. He pushed the Message button. The first one was Demick asking Vail to call him. The remaining three were from Tye, each a little more drunken, a little more desperate. He turned on his cell phone and there were the same number of calls from both Demick and Tye. He took a deep breath and hit Tye's callback number.

"'Lo," answered a voice almost unrecognizable with sleep.

"Tye?"

"Oh, God, Steve." Vail could hear her sitting up. "I'm so embarrassed."

He laughed. "You should be. Are you all right now?"

"I wish I could say I was too drunk to remember, but unfortunately I do. You must hate me."

"Yes, that's why I called."

"I'm so sorry." Vail could hear her walking with the phone and then opening a door. "There is an explanation, not that there's anything that could excuse what I did."

"I don't need an explanation."

"Maybe I'll hate myself a little less if I can give you one."

"Then fire away."

She didn't say anything for a few seconds. "Great, that's just great."

"What?"

"The morning paper. It's as bad as I thought."

"What is?"

She sat down with an audible sigh. "You know I've been planning to leave the United States attorney's office. I mentioned it a couple of months ago to a reporter who was covering one of my cases. Last night I stopped at one of the local watering holes to have a drink while the traffic cleared. And this reporter's in the bar. Looking back on it now, I'm not so sure it was accidental. We start talking. Somehow he heard that I had gotten search warrants in the Pentad case, so he starts asking me about it. A couple more drinks and he tells me he'd like to do an article about me leaving the U.S. attorney's office. As you've probably figured out by now, my judgment isn't the best when I'm drinking. Eventually I started complaining about the Department of Justice, the United States attorney's office here, and—I'm sorry, Steve—about how poorly, overall, the FBI conducted the investigation. That is until you got here and then repeatedly risked your life without a second thought or a bit of thanks. The article comes off as if I've got this big crush on you. By the time I got home last night and started sobering up, I realized what direction the reporter was going to take the article and wanted to give you a heads-up. I tried to reach you, and when I couldn't, I started drinking until I finally found you, and by that time I was a mess."

"Is that going to hurt you at work?" Vail asked.

"That's your only concern?"

"In a couple of days I'll just be one of the great unwashed in a place where they don't read Los Angeles newspapers."

"Can you ever forgive me?"

"For being concerned about me—I think so."

"With a little bit of luck I'll never have to face Kate again. She must legitimately hate me. I hope I didn't cause any problems last night."

"Kate's a good person. And she also will be leaving L.A. soon."

"I'm getting out of here too," Tye said. "Do you think there's any chance I'd like Chicago, Steve?"

He hesitated so she would understand what he was about to say had two meanings. "I'm afraid you wouldn't find it much different from Los Angeles."

She gave the kind of disheartened chuckle that came involuntarily after a failed long shot. "Sorry, Steve, I had to give it one last try."

TWENTY-SEVEN

THE CLERK AT THE AQUA DULCE POST OFFICE HAD GIVEN VAIL DIRECTIONS to the old Franklin Movie Ranch. "It's on Stanfield Road off Hope Creek Road." The name on the box rental was the same as on the credit card receipt, Andrew Parker, with an address of simply Franklin Movie Ranch, Stanfield Road. The property had been used as a movie set back in the forties when the studios were turning out westerns every couple of weeks. As far as the clerk knew it hadn't been used in more than half a century.

As Vail drove along Hope Creek Road, he wondered if he was wasting his time looking for anyone else who could be involved. And more important, if he was, why? Wasting time was something he hated. Somebody else could have been involved in the murders, but that didn't seem likely. Radek needed the power that came with being in charge. It was a big part of why he was a criminal. If there was someone else, it had to be an underling who had gone unnoticed. But there was also a practical reason for his pursuing Radek's last clue. If a booby trap had been set, it should be located and neutralized.

Vail turned onto Stanfield Road, which then climbed along the barren foothills, through large boulder-sized outcroppings that he recalled were ever present in the old cowboy movies. Finally at the peak of one of the hills, he saw a rutted dirt road off to the right that wound down around some large rock formations. A simple nailed cross of wood crudely lettered said, "Franklin Ranch." He turned in and drove slowly, trying to keep the car from bottoming out in the ruts. Once he circled below the boulders, he could see three dilapidated buildings in the flats below. He stopped and got out into the scorching sun. Using the monocular, he scanned the area, looking for any indication of recent use. The single-story structures were less than two hundred yards away. He decided to go the rest of the way on foot.

He opened the trunk and slipped off his suit jacket, tie, and shirt, leaving him in his T-shirt. The shotgun case contained a canvas bandolier of shells with a Velcro closure, which he wrapped around his waist and secured. There were scattered shells in the case, and he loaded five of them, alternating the double-aught buck and deer slug. He racked the first one into the chamber and clicked the safety on. His cell phone rang. The caller's ID was blocked. "Hello."

"Hi." It was Kate. She waited for his response.

"Everything all right?" he asked.

"I guess that's what I'm calling to find out."

"Other than a long, icy shower I had to take last night, we're fine."

"I didn't sleep much."

"Only someone who didn't care would."

"Thank you," she said. "Where are you?"

"Sightseeing."

"That sounds evasive."

"Apparently not evasive enough. I'm in Aqua Dulce. It's an hour north of L.A."

"This is the part where I try to pin you down with a series of escape-proof questions."

"Fair enough. The credit card used at Sargasso's came back to an Andrew Parker at the Franklin Ranch in Aqua Dulce. I just got here."

"Does that mean you think there's someone else involved?" Her tone had that impatient "here we go again" charge to it.

"It is a very small loose end, and you know how they drive me crazy."

"Should you be out there alone?"

"All the black hats are gone, remember? I just want to see if there's something out here Radek might have rigged that'll hurt someone if they stumble across it."

"Were you going to tell anybody about it? What happens if you get hurt?"

"There's no urgency here. Anything suspicious, I'll call in the locals."

"Promise?"

"I promise."

"I'd come out there myself, but I'm buried in paperwork. I've been making a list and so far I'm up to almost thirty 302s to dictate. And that isn't counting the evidence and lab transmittal letters. Let me send somebody out?"

"I'm standing here looking at the place. This is just a walk in the park. By the time they get here I'll be headed back."

There was a hesitation and then Kate said, "Have you seen the morning paper?"

"No."

"Tye's kind of doing an exit interview in it. You might want to get a copy."

"I hope that's not you being mean."

"So you have seen it."

"I talked to Tye first thing this morning. She wanted to apologize. She wanted me to pass it on to you because she figures she could never face you again."

"Interesting. I would never have guessed that a man who could so casually throw bank robbers through windows would be so protective of someone who had embarrassed him."

"What makes you think I'm embarrassed?"

"I guess *that* was me being mean. I'm sorry. How about I buy you dinner tonight?"

"Do you know who Sisyphus was, from Greek mythology?"

"With great apprehension I'll have to say no."

"For offending the gods, Sisyphus, a man of many indulgences, was sentenced to Hades, where he was to roll a boulder up a steep mountain, with one small catch. Just as he was about to reach the top, it would always roll back down, forcing him to start over. He was to do this throughout eternity."

"And you think that's us."

"It did seem like the gods were conspiring against us last night."

"I say we try shoving it up the mountain one more time to make sure we are actually in hell," she said.

"Sometimes understanding the futility of our fate is the only form of happiness we're allowed."

"Funny, I've always found the struggle to be the real reward."

"That confirms something I've long suspected—you're a better person than I am. If you want to again risk the wrath of the gods, I'll be back this afternoon."

He hung up and let his eyes trace the twisting road leading down to the ranch. There was little shade; in fact, there were only a few scrawny trees scattered across the property. Vail glanced at the sun for position, its unrelenting glare warning that it was going to be another hot day.

Vail took his time getting down to the three ancient, colorless structures. They were nothing more than shades of gray, as if permanently in an old black-and-white movie. They had been built side by side without any space between them, and the way the outside walls leaned made them appear to be holding one another up. There was a wooden walkway in front of all of them, with a corrugated metal sheet overhead. The outer ones were smaller and had flat roofs, but the middle structure had a peaked roof and looked like it was the only one used in the last fifty years. A hand-painted wooden sign over the door said "Last Chance Saloon." Whether it was a movie set or someone had tried to make a business of it after the western movie business dried up, he couldn't tell.

Kicking up dust as he walked down the road, he cautiously approached the first structure. The door was half open, and he could tell by the debris on the floor that no one had been in there in years. Instead of going in the middle building next, he went to the third one and found it in a similar condition.

That left the "saloon." It was much cleaner inside and along one wall was a homemade bar. It looked only a few years old. The rest of the long room was relatively empty except for some fast-food containers scattered on the floor.

He examined it again, this time searching for anything that might have the attraction of a trap, but couldn't find anything. He walked back onto the front walkway and looked beyond the building. Then he thought he heard something up on the ridgeline where he had parked. Stepping back into the shadow of the saloon, he watched and listened for a few minutes but heard nothing else.

Fifty yards farther into the property he could see a foot trail disappearing into a stand of low trees. He started to follow it, and when he was halfway to the tree line, he saw a white paper bag, a twig driven through it holding it to the ground. He bent over and picked it up. It was from Sargasso's restaurant and it smelled of garlic. Next to it was a 30-06 casing, untarnished by the weather.

As Vail bent over to retrieve it, a shot rang out from behind him on the hill. He dove to the left and rolled, holding on to the shotgun. From the sound of the shot, he could tell it was a heavy-caliber hunting rifle, probably a 30-06.

He half crawled, half ran back to the dilapidated buildings. That's when he felt the wetness against his shoulder. He reached up and brought back his hand with blood on it. He felt the wound again; his trapezius had been nicked. Three inches to the left, it would have severed his spine.

As he worked his way behind the buildings, he tried to remember if he had loaded the deer slug first or the buckshot. The slug could reach two hundred yards, but with the shotgun having only a bead on the end of the barrel, it would take lottery luck to hit anything that far uphill. The buckshot would be useless at that distance.

When he got to the edge of the structure, he pumped all the rounds out of the gun, then picked up the three slugs off the ground and reloaded them along with five more from the cartridge belt.

Peeking around the corner, he tried to find a route to the top of the ridge with at least some cover. There were a few boulders, but they were thirty to forty yards apart. The advantage Vail had was that if the rifle did have a scope—which the difficulty of the first shot indicated—it would be hard for the shooter to get a bead on him if he kept moving and changing direction. And it probably was a bolt action, meaning it took a second or two to chamber each round, something, with a little bit of nerve, Vail could use to his advantage.

He snapped off the shotgun's safety. He stepped out from behind the building and counted, "One idiot, two idiot, three idiot," then jumped back behind the building as another rifle shot rang out.

He ran, zigzagging. He dove behind a rock just as another round hit somewhere behind him. Although he still hadn't seen the shooter, Vail knew that he was in the outcroppings near where Vail had left his car.

Taking a deep breath, Vail raised the shotgun over the rock he was hiding behind, took a quick sight along the barrel, and fired. As he started running to the next spot, he heard the oversize slug he had fired ricochet off the rocks somewhere in the vicinity of the sniper.

Another rifle shot came from above, again exploding into the ground ten yards to his left. It meant that the shooter was firing wildly, more concerned with pinning Vail down than with hitting him.

The reason Vail had chosen this route was that he figured once he had reached the spot where he was now, the sniper could no longer see him moving. The shooter, realizing that, may have taken that last shot out of desperation. Either way, Vail could work his way up the hill without being exposed to the sniper's line of sight. He ejected the rest of the slugs and reloaded with double-aught buck from the bandolier. If the single-shot rifle was the only weapon that the sniper had, the closer Vail got, the more effective the spray of .32-caliber pellets would become. But first he had to get up there.

Snaking through the outcroppings, Vail maneuvered his way up toward the ridge, being careful not to expose himself. Of course, the shooter could move and possibly surprise Vail, something he had to remain aware of.

Vail heard another shot, somewhat muffled. And then another.

It took him another ten minutes to reach the top. The sniper was gone, but behind Vail's car, he could see another set of tire tracks in the loose dirt. The last two shots had taken out Vail's rear tires.

While he waited for the rental company to send someone to tow him to a gas station, he checked his wound. It had almost stopped bleeding. Draping a handkerchief over it, he slipped his shirt and jacket over it. A tow truck arrived and took him to a gas station, where both tires were repaired.

An hour later he was on the 101 heading south toward L.A. Apparently there were more than five people in the Pentad. Today's shooter was number six. Although Radek had set up Vail with the Italian dinners, someone else was trying to kill him now. Which didn't make any sense. All the money was gone and the accomplices were dead. Why call attention to yourself by doing this? And why Vail? Did he know something that would reveal the identity of the last person? It was the only reasonable possibility. Was there actually someone from the Los Angeles FBI involved? It wasn't Pendaran, because he was in custody. Obviously it was someone comfortable with firearms, because the heavy-caliber rifle had a punishing kick to it. Plus, it took a certain confidence to hunt a man in the open.

VAIL PULLED INTO the hospital's emergency room parking lot and walked in. The doctor who had stitched up his back after the tunnel drop was again on duty. "You do understand we don't give frequent-flier miles."

Vail laughed. "This one wouldn't even get me to the airport." He took off his shirt.

"Gunshot?"

"Walked into a door."

"Thank goodness," the doctor said sardonically. "Otherwise I'd have to report it. You make me wish it was possible to short-sell life insurance on certain individuals."

The doctor cleaned the wound and started putting a thick bandage on it. "Do you have anything a little less noticeable?" Vail asked. "I've got a date for dinner."

The doctor put a thinner square of gauze over the laceration and taped it tightly into place. "Hold on a minute and I'll take those stitches out of your back, or do you think you'll be back in a day or two?"

"I know every waiter in L.A. is actually an actor, but I didn't realize the doctors were comedians."

"What's frustrating is all the sick people that keep coming in here. Talk about no sense of humor. And comedy, after all, is all about feedback. Around here I get almost no reaction." When he had taken the last suture out, Vail started putting on his shirt. "Do you want anything for pain?"

"I'm good, thanks."

The doctor gave him a spool of tape, some extra gauze bandages, and a tube of ointment. "You can use these to dress the wound yourself. Or just save them for the next time you get shot."

TWENTY-EIGHT

"THIS LOOKS NICE," VAIL SAID.

"I hope you like Chinese."

The restaurant was large and busy. The waiters spoke a minimum of English and the busboys none. The noise level was considerably higher than Sargasso's. He wondered if Kate had reconsidered her offer and was sending him a message. She ordered a diet soft drink, apparently not wanting to test her resistance to both Vail and alcohol again. It was probably for the best anyway. If he should have the opportunity to take his shirt off later and she saw the bandage on his shoulder, a new round of trust disputes would be sparked.

"You've seen me eat. Do you think there's anything I don't like?"

"Somebody in the office suggested it," Kate said. "So there really wasn't anything out at that ranch? Maybe the garlic clue was supposed to take you in a different direction."

"Like what?"

"I don't know. It was left for a reason. If there was no trap at the ranch, then I don't know."

"Another one of life's unsolved mysteries. How are the paper wars going at the office?"

"Mind-numbing. You owe us a few reports, you know."

"302s are for court testimony. The last I knew, dead men aren't usually prosecuted. Or is the United States attorney's office low on stats?" he asked.

"I don't know about conviction rates, but they're soon to be short one assistant USA."

"Tye?"

"They've suspended her until the case can be reviewed. It isn't looking good."

"Aren't they the courageous bunch. She was leaving anyhow. That was the reason for the article."

"You like her, don't you?" Vail shot her a look. "No, I mean as a person."

"I didn't hear anybody complaining when we needed a friendly legal face."

The waiter came and they both ordered.

Kate said, "Have you thought any more about the director's offer?"

"Yes, but I don't know how seriously. I need to go back to Chicago and work for a while and see how everything feels. I'm not sure making a decision right now would be in anyone's best interest."

"When are you going back?"

Vail thought about being shot at. He wasn't going to let that go. And he wasn't going to tell Kate. "I'll stick around for a couple of days. Make sure I didn't leave any loose ends hanging. Mostly I'm doing it so I can ignore your orders that I do paperwork."

THE EVENING ENDED matter-of-factly with Kate and Vail saying good night to each other as he got off the elevator one floor below hers. He guessed there would be no third attempt to roll that rock up the hill. He lay in bed trying to read. The night before had been perfect until Tye called. Tonight couldn't have been any more ordinary. Last night they had tried to be two relatively normal people, looking for physical companionship. Tonight the real Kate and Steve showed up and proved they were who they were. And that last night's little drama-comedy was a one-night-only engagement.

He tried reading the same paragraph again but became distracted by the image of her laughing over the white linen tablecloth at Sargasso's, her hand absentmindedly caressing the wineglass, her skin flawless in the candlelight. He set the book down and turned off the light. He suspected it was going to be a night without much sleep.

After a few minutes of staring into the darkness, the phone rang. "Hello," he answered quickly.

"Vail . . ." It was a male voice that he couldn't quite identify.

"Yes."

There was an unnatural laugh. "Sorry I missed you at the ranch today."

Vail was speechless. It was the voice he had heard the day he killed Lee Salton—Victor Radek's. "Apparently we're both hard to kill."

"We'll see." The voice now became amused. "Guess why I'm calling."

"Well, there is a rumor going around that you've had

a couple of financial setbacks. I could lend you a couple of bucks if you wanted to meet me."

"You do get a quick read on people. I am calling about money, but I was thinking more like three million bucks."

"I'll have to go to an ATM, but okay. Where and when?"

"Actually I was thinking you could go to the FBI office and get it there."

"The funny thing about that is the FBI actually thinks it's theirs."

"That's why you're going to have to steal it."

"I hope you've got a plan B."

"I'm sticking with plan A." Vail then heard him say to someone in the room with him, "Say something."

When there was no response, he heard a violent slap. Then, "Steve, I'm sorry." It was Tye Delson.

Radek came back on the phone. "Do you still need a plan B?"

"No."

"Good. Here's the way it's going to go. I'll call you at midnight on your cell phone. Make sure you have the money by then. If you don't . . . well, you know the rest of it. I'm going to put you over a few hurdles to make sure you're following all the rules."

"And those are?" Vail asked.

"No one knows about this. If you try to backdoor me, I'll know. Ask yourself how I know what hotel you're in, or that the money is still in L.A., or how I knew to grab your girlfriend here at her apartment. Also, I've set a number of obstacles along the course you'll have to follow, so if anybody else from the FBI is involved . . . well, you know those clowns, they'll stumble over them and cost the princess here her life. Then we'll both have to start looking for a plan B, which for someone with my limited imagination starts with more bodies. Funny thing is I was going to be satisfied with just killing you this morning, and then I saw the article about the prosecutor."

Vail suspected Radek was trying a little too hard to prove he had someone on the inside. He could have found out about Vail's hotel from Tye or her cell phone. It had been only a couple of days since the recovery of the three million dollars, and with all that had been going on, it was a pretty safe bet the money would not have been taken back to Washington yet. As far as getting Tye's home address, someone as streetwise as Radek would have no trouble conning a clerk or secretary from the USA's office into giving it up, especially after her embarrassing article in the newspaper. Or he could actually have someone in the FBI feeding him information. Vail decided he couldn't take the chance. Especially since Radek was right about the others stumbling through the exchange. The tunnel had proven that.

"I'll be alone."

"I know you will. You're a loner. You could have called for help when we were following you that day, but you took Salton on by yourself. Same thing at the ranch this morning. If nobody else is around, you might get a chance to kill me, is that it?"

"You'll have to admit, you do need killing."

Radek brayed a cold, angry laugh. "I could make the same argument. You've been ruining the beauty of this operation since the tunnel. I should have killed you then, but now all I want is my money so I can get out of this stinking country."

"It might be worth three million to get rid of you, but one question, the guy in the elevator."

"Benny? He was one of my dummies from prison. We were all in his apartment when I sent the three of them to that building to kill you. After they left I took his toothbrush and put it in my apartment where you'd find it."

"You have them take all the chances, and then you send them out to die. I can see why you don't want anyone to know you're still alive—they might somehow get the idea that you're a coward."

"Run your mouth one more time, Vail, and me and the princess here are going to start getting more friendly. I like them with a little more meat, but as a special consideration for everything you've cost me . . ."

"Okay, okay, I'll get the money."

"Midnight, hero. And no guns. Just your cell phone and a flashlight. And don't waste your time trying to trace this phone." Vail heard something heavy smash the phone just as the line went dead.

VAIL WALKED into Kate's office carrying his suitcases, both empty. He tried the handle on the safe drawer. It was locked, which meant the money was still in there. She had said something about the accountants working a special and not being able to get to it for a few days. He dialed the combination and it opened. Two of the drawers were brimming with packs of hundred-dollar bills just the way he had stacked them. Quickly, he filled the suitcases.

VICTOR RADEK kneeled over a large sheet of steel plate. He had a welding mask on and was attaching the last of four metal rings to it. When he was finished, he turned off the hissing torch and heard the muffled complaints of a woman. They were coming from the baby monitor next to him. The transmitter unit was inside the sealed wooden box a few feet away. It was roughly the size of a small coffin. He got up and went over to the box, kicking it viciously. "This is the last time I'm going to tell you to shut up, and then I'm going to take a cutting torch to the box." The monitor fell silent.

"I'll tell you when to start moaning for help."

He went over to the wall and pushed a button, which activated a crane that lifted the steel plate into the air. He nodded with satisfaction at the way the huge plane of metal was balanced.

TWENTY-NINE

VAIL SAT IN HIS CAR OUTSIDE HIS HOTEL, WAITING FOR RADEK'S call. He checked his watch again; it was after 2 A.M. The suitcases were secured in the trunk. He couldn't believe he was delivering three million dollars to a murderer for the second time.

The phone rang. "Vail," he answered.

"Do you have the money?"

"Yes."

"There's a boarded-up factory on Keller Street where it dead-ends at the river. Around back you'll find a black trash bag next to the fence. Be careful with it, there's a laptop inside. It's already on, so just open it and wait for my instructions."

It took Vail less than twenty minutes to find the factory. He turned off his lights and listened, but the only thing he could hear was the occasional rush of distant traffic. As instructed, he had left his handgun in his room. He got out and went to the trunk, taking out the suitcases. Around the back of the building he found the plastic bag where Radek had said it would be. Inside was the laptop, a couple of small green lights indicating it was running. A wireless Internet card protruded from the left side. He opened the lid and immediately heard Radek's voice.

Vail then noticed the webcam at the top of the computer. Radek was now able to watch him, but the screen was black which meant Radek was keeping his camera blocked so Vail couldn't see him. Because of satellite technology, it was impossible to tell where he was. "In the bag are a change of clothes. Set the computer on the ground and step back so I can see you completely. Then change clothes just in case there's something hidden in yours that will track you." Vail did as he was told, and when he was done, Radek said, "Over against the wall are two large duffel bags. Bring them back here, and then let me watch you transfer the money—slowly. And riffle through the stacks when I tell you to so I can be sure it's all there."

Vail complied with the instructions and when he was done closed and secured the bags with the clips at the end of the shoulder straps. "Okay, now where's Tye?"

"Come on, Vail, would I have made it that easy?"

"The money is staying right here until I hear Tye's voice."

"How about a compromise." Radek kicked the wooden box and then held the baby monitor up to the computer speaker.

Vail heard a woman's voice heavily muted, seemingly pleading for help.

"Okay, where to?" Vail asked.

"Get your flashlight and cell phone." Radek watched as Vail transferred the devices to the pants he had been given. "Okay, climb over the fence. At the bottom of the incline is a set of railroad tracks. Follow them north for about three-quarters of a mile until you find yourself on a small overpass bridge. Below will be another set of tracks. When you get to that point, turn on the flashlight and hold it up. Then turn in a full circle so I'll know you're there."

Vail tossed the two bags ahead of him and climbed over the fence. The incline was steep but not long. He half slid, half walked down until he was at the tracks. They ran alongside the narrow Los Angeles River. With the track bound by a waist-high retaining barrier, there was no room on either side of the rails to walk, so he had to step from wooden tie to tie and watch each step as the thirty-plus pounds of cash in each hand made the balancing act that much more difficult.

When he reached the overpass, he was soaked with sweat. He set the bags down and looked around, trying to figure out if Radek was around or just running him through a gauntlet to break him down physically and mentally. There were a few dots of yellow light scattered in the distance, but no apparent hiding place in the vicinity from which Radek could be watching him. As instructed, Vail switched the flashlight on and held it up, slowly turning in a complete circle. Immediately his cell rang. Wherever Radek was, he could see Vail. "Yeah."

"Get down to the rail line below and follow it to the right." Vail looked down and it appeared to be about a fifteen-foot difference in elevation. He released one of the bags over the side and then the other before letting himself drop to the track below. He picked up the bags and followed the track as instructed. It immediately crossed over the river and turned sharply south, back in the direction he had come from but on the opposite bank of the concrete-walled waterway.

This track seemed even narrower and he began to wonder if a train was scheduled, another obstacle that it would have been like Radek to throw in. Fifteen minutes later he found himself passing under the same road he had traveled beneath when he started out. He was back to where he had started but on the other side of the river, the shadow of the factory up on the rise.

His phone rang. "Yes."

"Flashlight."

This time Vail shined it only in the direction of the factory to see if that was where Radek was. "You're in position now," Radek said. "Get across the river and bring those bags to the roof of the factory."

"And then what?"

"Meaning, where is your woman? All your questions will be answered when you get up there."

"How do I get to the roof?"

"I wouldn't use the front door." Radek hung up.

Vail lowered himself from the track and walked down to the angled concrete bank of the river. It was about fifty yards wide at that point. The water appeared, by the debris in it, to be a couple of feet deep at the most. He slid down the embankment and half fell into the water. It was waist-deep and its coolness felt good. The current was surprisingly strong, and as he walked, he held the bags above it. On the other side he waited for the water to drain from his clothes before climbing the equally steep embankment.

Tossing the bags over the fence that had been scaled a little over an hour before, he vaulted himself over. The laptop was gone but his clothes were still there. After changing, he wondered about Radek's warning to not use the front door.

Above the entrance to the building was an engraved stone anchored into the brickwork above the door identifying it as the Y. P. Androyan and Sons Wire Works, established in 1913. It was a four-story brick structure whose footprint was triangular. One end of the building was not much wider than its double door, but the far end was close to a hundred feet wide. Probably the original piece of property had dictated the design of the building. Located less than a hundred yards from the Los Angeles River and with a rail line on either side, it looked like, at one time, the area had been a prime industrial location.

Between the second- and third-story windows was a faded blue and white sign that read "For Lease." A heavy steel gate protected the front door, but it was ajar, like at the house on Spring Street. And Radek had warned him not to go in that way, probably more to protect the three million dollars than Vail. He decided to look for another way in.

Along the street side of the building was a fire escape, which ran from the second floor to the roof. Vail drove onto the sidewalk and parked directly underneath the steel lattice of ladders and landings. He got out and could see that if he stood on the roof of his car, even with his best vertical leap, he would still be a foot or two short of the fire escape. He went to the trunk and took out the Halligan tool. After patting his pockets to make sure he had his flashlight and cell phone, he decided to take along the low-light monocle, since the building appeared to be completely dark inside.

He had figured out how to get himself onto the fire escape, but the two bags of money were going to be a problem. Remembering how Dan West had negotiated his way out of that naval prison cell, he took his knife and, pulling out each of the seat belts to its maximum length, cut them free. Knotting the ends as tightly as possible, he had a length of strapping almost twenty feet long. He threaded it through one bag's handle and tied it to the other.

After climbing up on top of his car, he fed the pick end of the Halligan up through the fire escape's grated floor and pulled himself up. Once he swung himself up onto the landing, he lifted the tool and money up after him.

As quietly as possible, he started making his way up to the roof. The windows he passed were a common factory type, the kind that after turning a handle inside, the bottom of the frame rotated outward. On the third floor he noticed that the pane directly above one of them was broken. A few small pieces of broken glass were on the outside sill, indicating that it was not the result of kids throwing stones, but broken from the inside. A little too convenient. He regripped the pry bar and bags and headed up the final ladder.

Once he stepped onto the roof, the only thing visible was an eight-foot-high structure along the back edge that housed an access door for the building's stairwell. He looked over the side and let his eyes trace the railroad tracks he had walked. Radek must have watched him the entire time from there, making sure that no one else was anywhere near.

Sitting on the tarred surface next to the access structure, he could see something emitting a small green light. Halfway across the roof, Vail could hear a woman's muffled voice coming from it. When Vail reached the source of the light and sound, he discovered it was a baby monitor. Because of the limited range of the device, it meant Tye had to be inside the building. Underneath it was a note, which simply stated, "Leave the bags here."

He set down the bags and tried the doorknob. It was locked. He pushed the adze end of the Halligan between the door and the frame just above the lock. It sank in just far enough so he would be able to get some leverage on it. He took a half step back and pulled evenly on the tool's shaft. The door shifted inside the frame but the pry bar started tearing through the edge of the wooden door. Vail pushed the tool's head deeper into the widened gap. Again he pulled back, and this time the door sprung open with little sound.

He had no idea what lay ahead. Other than his knife, he had no weapon, so the Halligan would have to do. He started to take out the flashlight but then remembered the photocell trigger in the tunnel. Instead he closed the door behind him, which enclosed him in darkness. He stood perfectly still while his eyes adjusted. After a moment, he could see some light at the bottom of the stairs on the fourth floor, possibly coming through the windows from the streetlights.

The stairs were wooden and creaked with almost every step. He took his time, listening after each one, and at the same time feeling ahead for any wires or rigged construction. It took twenty minutes to descend the three floors, and his legs were starting to feel the exhaustion of the last couple of hours.

At the bottom of the stairs was a door. It was locked. To his left was a hallway that skirted the outside of the first floor. The main part of the floor was most likely a factory workspace. Halfway down the corridor was another door. Vail tried it, but it was also locked. At the end, the corridor turned right toward the building's main entrance. There was light from the street coming through the double door windows. To his right was a large open door that led to the floor's workspace.

Then he noticed, sitting six feet from the entrance door, an object that was four feet tall and three feet wide. He stepped slowly toward it. It looked like an industrial-size cable spool for heavy-gauge wire. After another step, he could see that it was coiled with hundreds of feet of barbwire. It didn't make any sense until he looked at the core. It was packed with something light in color. Thin electrical wires ran out of it toward the door. Carefully he stuck his finger into the center of the spool. The material had the consistency of C-4. He was afraid to move any closer, but instead took out the monocular and traced the wires visually. They ran to two electrical contacts, one on each of the front doors, like a burglar alarm. As soon as either door was opened, the electrical signal was interrupted and the blasting caps at the core of the spool would be detonated. Any person or persons entering through that door had no chance of survival.

Ever so slowly, he pulled the blasting caps out of the C-4. Stepping around the spool, he laid them on the floor. Not wanting to get any closer to the doors, he took the sharp, claw end of the Halligan and drove it accurately into the wooden floor, severing both wires, one with each side of the claw. He picked up the caps and tossed them down the hallway as far as possible. Blasting caps were relatively inert. Even if they went off at that distance, they couldn't detonate the stable C-4. Vail knew the bomb was not for him, but rather for any FBI cavalry should they somehow be tracking Vail's movements. If there was an "obstacle" for him, it lay somewhere else.

He pulled the Halligan out of the floor and looked through the inner door into the workspace. The windows had been drywalled over. Only a thin slit of a window at the back end of the room allowed any light at all. Using the monocular, Vail could see a dozen or so dark shapes of uniform size placed irregularly along the floor. The pattern seemed to be random, but Vail could see that it was arranged so that eventually, in the dark, anyone walking through the room would bump into one of them, and possibly with the same consequences as entering through the front door. After memorizing their positions, he gripped the Halligan at its balance and stepped into the room.

Immediately he heard a woman's desperate moans. She was somewhere inside the large room. Straining his eyes to confirm the location of the objects along the floor, he slid each foot forward, testing for trip wires while continuing to move toward the voice.

Halfway across the room, he stopped and took out the monocular. He could see the outline of a coffin-shaped box along the far wall where the muffled syllables seemed to be coming from. This was where he was supposed to become emotional and charge toward it. He stopped, took a deep breath, and blocked out the muted pleas.

The objects placed between him and the box containing her turned out to be eighteen-inch-high wooden cubes. He could now see a small green dot of light up on the wall, and he suddenly became aware of an almost inaudible hum, an electrical hum. The transmitter for the baby monitor? He took one more step forward and felt the floor give way slightly, causing a distinct mechanical click underfoot.

A small spotlight snapped on, illuminating what housed the green point of light. It was a motion detector, the kind used in home security systems, and its green light had changed to red, indicating it was now armed. He froze. Illuminating it meant that Radek now had him trapped and wanted him to know.

He was standing on a two-foot square of plywood, which had been painted flat black to make it unnoticeable. He suspected that the click heard under it might have done more than turn on the light. Vail turned his attention back to the sensor. Ordering himself not to move his head, he used eye movement only. A snarl of wiring surrounded the monitor. It was hooked into a larger cable, which ran up the wall and then overhead toward him, finally disappearing behind a large black void above his head.

Imperceptibly, Vail moved his head upward slightly to determine exactly what was above him. It was not a void at all, but a huge steel plate hanging ten feet over his head. His mason's eye estimated it to be approximately sixteen feet square, and he was at its dead center. Printed in large chalked letters on its underside was a note:

> **VAIL—**
> **EM wired to pressure release and motion sensor.**
> **Good-bye.**
> **Vic**

That's what the hum was, an electromagnetic crane used to move stock around. And it was double primed. Two systems to make sure he couldn't move. Either the sensor or the pressure-release switch he was standing on would shut it off and drop the steel on him. He couldn't see how thick the plate was, but the thinnest he was aware of was three-sixteenths of an inch. A sixteen-square-foot piece of that thickness had to be close to two thousand pounds.

An urge to laugh at his own insolence started to rise up in him. He would gladly have given in to it to relieve some of the tension if he hadn't feared it would set off the motion detector. His contempt for anything meant to control him, even if it was concocted by Radek, was about to take his life. Insolence had always been a trusted, if expensive, ally, but never this costly.

His self-recrimination was interrupted by another burst from the wooden box, now only twenty feet away. It reminded him that more than his life was at stake. He had to find a way out. Trying to gauge the speed needed, he doubted that he could make it beyond the edge of the steel plate before it crushed him. However, it would be close. The eight feet to the edge looked like a hundred.

Then he remembered that he was still holding the Halligan tool in his left hand, a possible solution to the ton of impending death hanging over him. The pry bar was three and a half feet long and the shaft was one-inch-thick steel alloy. Primarily it was manufactured for fire departments, so its strength had to be exceptional.

Running and diving straight forward was the best chance, since turning in any other direction would add an additional split second. Once he took that first step, he would have to flatten out as horizontally as possible and at the same time move the bar behind him, turning it vertical with the claw downward. That way, if he didn't make it to the edge in time, the Halligan would stick upright in the wooden floor and absorb the initial blow of the steel. He hoped. If he ever needed to take a deep breath it was now, but that pinpoint of red light reminded him that if he did, it would probably be his last.

He closed his eyes and could feel his heartbeat pounding against his eyelids. He forced himself to slow his breathing. Inside his head, he visualized what he had to do: flatten out and at the same time move the bar into position and behind him. He waited until he could no longer hear his heart. One more time he closed his eyes and watched himself perform the intricacies of the long eight-foot dash.

He exploded forward. At the exact same instant, the hum of the electromagnet crane above him stopped. Everything became slow motion, and the last thing Vail remembered was the first gray light of dawn coming in the small, slotted window.

THIRTY

AS KATE BANNON RODE UP IN THE ELEVATOR, SHE TOOK A SIP OF HER coffee. It was too hot but she took a mouthful anyway, hoping the sting might bring her to life a little more quickly than just waiting for her system to metabolize the caffeine. Again she had not slept much, if at all. The night balanced at the tipping point between suspected sleep and dreamlike wakefulness.

She was the only person in the elevator and tried to distract herself by listing out loud the things she had to do today. After a few items, her thoughts returned to Vail and how awful their dinner had been last night. The night at the Italian restaurant had been the most fun she had had in years, until the call from Tye Delson. She had been wrong to let it come between them. Even though she had apologized to Vail, he seemed to understand her behavior better than she did and accepted it as the only way things could be between them.

The elevator doors opened and she stepped off. After punching in the security code, she pushed open the door and headed to her office. Two agents were sitting across from her desk. The older one was overweight and his suit was worn and ill-fitting. The younger one didn't seem old enough to be an agent. He was thin and wore wire-rimmed glasses. His suit was new but too heavy for the Southern California climate, giving her the impression he was just out of training school. They both stood and introduced themselves as being from the accounting squad. "We're finally here to take the three million dollars off your hands," the older one said with a certain amount of boredom.

"Believe it or not, with everything going on, I forgot it was here." She pulled open her desk drawer and took out the safe combination, handing it to him. While he bent over the dial, she opened another drawer and handed a sheaf of papers to the younger one. "This is a list of the serial numbers from the third drop. We'd like to verify that they are the same."

He took it from her and adjusted his glasses as his eyes slid quickly down the list.

The older agent pulled the drawer open and said, "Which drawers is it in?"

Kate jumped up. She looked down into the empty drawer and then started opening the other three. They were all empty. How could she have been so stupid to leave the combination in her desk and the office door unlocked? She grabbed the phone on her desk and ordered the two accountants away from the safe so as to not further contaminate any physical evidence that it might hold.

"Don, the three million's gone."

VAIL DIDN'T KNOW how long he had been out, but the first thing he heard was a woman's sobs. Back over his shoulder he could see the silver Halligan holding up one corner of the two-thousand-pound steel plate. It was bent, and the claw had been driven into the floor three or four inches, but it was holding. His legs were still under the plate but they weren't pinned. He pulled himself forward until he was clear. Standing up, he felt pain in his right shoulder blade. The plate must have caught him there just as he was diving to its edge, slamming his head into the floor and knocking him out. He touched his aching cheekbone. It was scraped raw.

He looked around for something to pry open the box. The voice became louder now that she could hear him moving around. He found a claw hammer on the floor behind it. "Hold on, Tye." There were a dozen nails on both sides, and he sank the claw between the top and side, working the hammer along the seam until he could get his fingers in between. The crying became louder with relief. With one great pull he tore the lid up.

The woman inside sat up immediately. It was not Tye Delson.

DON KAULCRICK stared down at the empty drawers. "When's the last time you saw the money in here?"

Kate said, "The day Vail put it in there. The day the safe was delivered. Actually, I never saw it in there. I was late for a meeting and had him secure it."

"Who else knew the combination?"

"Tom Demick changed it before bringing it down,

so just him, Vail, and me. But," she continued, her voice anxious, "foolishly I left the combination in my desk drawer."

Kaulcrick turned to the SAC. "I want a list of everybody who hasn't been to work in the last couple of days."

"I assume you'll want to talk to Demick, too," Hildebrand said.

"Yes." He looked at Kate. "Where's Vail?"

"I haven't seen him today."

"Get him in here now."

VAIL WAS ABLE TO CUT AWAY the flex-cuffs that bound the woman's hands and feet without much trouble, but the duct tape wound around her mouth and head took more time because of her hair. When she was finally free, she told him that she had been coming out of work late and was in the building parking garage when she was abducted at gunpoint. She was brought to this factory, bound, and gagged and placed in the box. Vail showed her a picture of Radek and she said he was the individual who had kidnapped her. "Who are you?"

"I'm with the FBI."

"Why are you alone?"

"You're safe now, that's all that's important."

"How'd you find me?"

"I paid three million dollars."

"I don't understand."

"You were supposed to be someone else."

She noticed his cheek for the first time. "Are you all right?"

"Other than being short one assistant United States attorney and some hundred-dollar bills, I'm fine." Vail's cell rang. It was Kate. "Hello."

"Steve, where are you?" she asked in a tone edged with panic.

"Sounds like something is wrong."

"Somebody took the three million dollars from my safe."

Radek still had Tye. He had told Vail that no one could know about it, and he wasn't sure that just because the money had been delivered, he could tell anyone. Maybe Radek wanted to hold on to her until he got away completely. "I'm sorry, Kate," Vail said, and hung up, turning off his phone.

"Something wrong?" the woman asked.

"Let's get out of here." He led the woman up the stairs. On the second floor, he walked over to a window that was marked as a fire route and opened it. He helped her out onto the fire escape and followed her.

Once they were in his car, Vail said, "I'm going to take you to the nearest police station. I want you to tell them what happened." He wrote down the address of the factory and Radek's full name and handed her the paper. "Tell them there's a large bomb at the front door that's been disarmed, but they should still go in through the second-floor window we came out of just in case."

"Aren't you going with me?"

"I'm going to be straight with you. There's another woman's life at stake, and it's better that no one know about her or me until I can find her. So if you don't give them a good description of me or tell them I'm an FBI agent, it would buy me some time."

"Are you really with the FBI?"

"Yes." He showed her his credentials. "But not for much longer."

"THAT'S IT, *he's sorry*," Kaulcrick said. "I guess we don't have to look any further."

They were in Kate's office. "There's got to be a reason," she offered.

"Yes, there is. He wanted three million dollars."

"You know he'd never do that."

"Then why didn't he give you an explanation?"

Mark Hildebrand recognized the charged tone and knocked on the door frame as a formality before entering. "Don, the United States attorney just called me. He's been trying to get ahold of Tye Delson since that article came out, and they can't locate her."

Kaulcrick looked at Kate angrily. "Maybe we just found his motive. Quite a coincidence, the two of them and the three million all disappearing at the same time. Mark, get the entire office on this. We need to find both of them. Two separate investigations. Call the USA back and get a warrant for Vail. Theft of government property. See if he can't find a way to get one for Delson too. Go!"

THIRTY-ONE

AFTER WALKING THE WOMAN INTO THE STATION AND POINTING OUT the desk sergeant, Vail turned to leave. She started to thank him, but he held a finger up to his lips, and she understood the only thanks he needed was her promise to keep him as anonymous as possible.

There was only one thing that mattered for Vail now—finding Tye Delson. Back in the car, he started driving. There was one unexplored possibility. And it was a long shot. When Vail had asked Radek who had been killed in the elevator, he had said "Benny," from prison. And they had all been at Benny's apartment before he sent his crew to kill Vail and Kate. Maybe that's where he was holed up. It wasn't likely Radek would give away any information that would help, but then he expected Vail to be dead by now.

When Kate and he had identified Radek through prison records, there was a report being assembled on his associates from the Bureau of Prisons. It was supposed to be e-mailed to him and Kate. But he never checked, because they had identified Radek and immediately began focusing on finding him.

The problem was that Vail's laptop was still in his room at the hotel, and by now it was likely that the entire Los

Angeles division of the FBI was hunting him. That meant, in all probability, there were agents waiting for him in his room. But he had no choice. Making a U-turn, he headed for the hotel.

When he arrived there, he drove around the block at a normal speed looking for Bureau undercover cars. He couldn't see anything that indicated any type of outside surveillance, probably because they were afraid he would spot it. Ahead, across the street from the hotel, was a ten-theater cineplex. Perfect, he thought.

After parking in the lot, he went up to the ticket seller. When he told her it didn't matter which movie, she gave him a strange look. "Don't tell me you've never had people come in to hide out for a few hours." She replied that if they did, they never discussed it with her. Vail was now sure she'd remember him and the open abrasion under his eye, which made his performance a little more sinister. The model for what would happen within the hour had been played out at the Biograph Theater in Chicago sixty-five years earlier when the G-men had to surround the neighborhood movie house to wait out John Dillinger rather than risking a shoot-out and endangering innocent civilians.

Vail had read the undisclosed but accurate accounts of the termination of the bank robber's life one night after he had spent three days locked down in the bowels of the University of Chicago's archives while finishing his master's thesis, a period he found as dreary as one of the Russian gulags he had repeatedly read about. The special agent in charge of the FBI office, after missing Dillinger during a shoot-out at the Little Bohemia Lodge in northern Wisconsin which left three civilians and an agent dead, didn't want any further embarrassment. So that night at the theater he went to the ticket office to see what time the movie ended. While they waited, he nervously made several more trips back to the box office with the same question to reverify the time. The ticket seller became so worried about a robbery that she called the Chicago police, who had been intentionally omitted from the case because it was feared that they couldn't be trusted.

Vail knew that as soon as the FBI traced his cell phone call, someone would go up to the cashier and show her his picture. She would remember him and tell them about his "hiding out" comment. Hopefully, like with Dillinger, that would draw in all available agents, including those at the hotel.

Inside the theater, he found a hallway away from the mainstream and turned on his cell phone. He checked the GPS function and it displayed all zeros. The office had been "pinging" his phone trying to determine its location, which is why he had it turned off immediately after talking to Kate. It was how they had found Radek's two-million-dollar cache. He dialed the hotel number and asked for the manager.

"This is Tom Mallon. I'm the manager, how can I help you?"

"Tom, this is Mark Hildebrand. I'm the special agent in charge of the Los Angeles FBI. How are you?"

"Fine, Agent Hildebrand."

"Some of my agents are over at your hotel on a surveillance, and we're not sure which rooms they're in. I need to talk to them on a landline. Could you tell me where they're located? We want to make sure they're in place before we go ahead with another part of the operation. I appreciate your continuing discretion in this matter."

"One moment, sir." The manager came back on the line. "Agent Hildebrand, that's room 431. I'm told there were three of them. Would you like me to connect you?"

"Thank you, no. I'll have someone call them on one of our security phones." Vail hoped the manager would be distracted enough by the wonder of what kind of technology could do that, that he wouldn't have any afterthoughts about whom he had actually talked to. Vail walked down the corridor until he found a large trash can outside one of the theaters, and dialed the weather. As soon as he was connected, he dropped the phone in the receptacle and walked out to the parking lot.

Vail judged he had at least a few minutes, maybe as much as a half hour, before they pinged his phone and reacted. He parked his car in a private garage across the street behind the hotel. In the trunk, he opened his briefcase, took out his handcuffs, and ripped off a couple of Post-its from their small yellow pad and put both items in his pocket. He used the rear entrance of the hotel and walked through to the lobby. He found a chair that was out of the foot-traffic area so he wouldn't be noticed by anyone rushing out of the building. He settled down and waited.

Vail's room was 432. Three men in the room across the hall was fairly standard. They would take turns watching his door through their peephole, a task that Vail knew from experience could be done effectively for only fifteen to twenty minutes before eyestrain and stress set in. The others would watch TV in between. If Vail did enter his own room, two of the agents would step into the hallway to intercept him while the third called for backup.

He also knew that because of proximity, these agents would be called first to respond to the theater until reinforcements could arrive.

Vail figured he needed no more than thirty seconds in his room, enough time to retrieve his handgun, hidden on top of the TV cabinet, and the laptop.

Not twenty minutes later, the elevator doors opened and two agents came hurrying through the lobby, not taking the time to maintain their anonymity. Vail got up and went to the house phone and dialed the operator, asking for room 431. "Hello," the voice answered inquisitively; Vail could hear the television on in the background.

"Yes, sir. This is room service. The manager has instructed me to call you and offer you a complimentary lunch. We have a very nice chicken parmigiana today on a bed of angel-hair pasta."

Of the thousands of rules in the FBI, there was only one that had yet to be violated: Never turn down a free meal. "Sure, that would be great."

Vail wanted to make sure he had the head count right. "How many orders?"

"The other two guys had to run out for a while. Can they get something when they come back?"

"The chicken is very good, but not when it's cold. I'll put two orders aside. Call when they're back. Anything to drink?"

"A Coke?"

"Yes, sir. It'll be about a half hour."

Vail hung up and headed to the stairwell. He stopped at the second floor looking for a maid's cart. On the third floor, he spotted one. She was busy in the room's bathroom. He took two hand towels, two bath towels, and a steel-handled dust mop and disappeared back into the stairwell.

Before entering the fourth floor he tied each of the bath towels around the ends of the steel shaft. Out of his pocket he took out the Post-its and peeled off the top one. Quietly he moved to room 431. First he stuck the yellow tab across the peephole so the agent would have to come out to discover him there. Chances were that with Vail being "located" at the multiplex, the remaining agent's vigilance would be intermittent, leaving him watching television more than the peephole.

Vail then slipped one of the hand towels around the door handle. He took out his handcuffs and hooked them around the handle and squeezed the strands tightly against the cloth. Raising the mop handle horizontally, he adjusted the positions of the bath towels so each rested against one side of the doorjamb. He wrapped the last hand towel thickly around the middle of the steel bar and tightened the other cuff to it. Now the door could not be pulled open.

Immediately he turned and used his key card to open the door to his room. The Do Not Disturb sign was still hanging from the knob. He reached up to the recessed top of the TV cabinet—his automatic was gone. They had already searched the room. The laptop, however, was still in place. If he came back, they probably wanted him to have the initial impression that no one had been there. He unplugged the computer and, as he wrapped the cord around it, opened his door. As he started to close it quietly, he saw his handcuffs on the door across the hall strain against the mop's shaft. The agent inside was trying to get out.

Vail ran to the stairwell and down to the first floor, exiting through the back of the hotel. Just as he walked into the garage's first floor, he saw a Bureau car come slicing around the corner behind him. Then another. Fortunately, they hadn't seen him. He was going to have to hole up for a while.

He had parked on the third level in an end spot. Hopefully, once the search at the theater was abandoned, they wouldn't think to look for him so close by. He turned on the Bureau laptop that was equipped with an internal wireless Internet card, but because of the garage's construction, he couldn't get a signal. It would have to wait.

Suddenly he realized he had not slept in thirty-six hours, the night after his first dinner with Kate, and then not very well. He crawled into the backseat and was asleep in minutes.

THIRTY-TWO

VAIL SLEPT LESS THAN TWO HOURS AND THEN FITFULLY, AWAKENing at the sound of any vehicle passing by in the covered garage. He got out of the car and walked down to the street, where he watched the traffic for fifteen minutes from a shadowed doorway. When he was satisfied that there was no longer a search being conducted in the neighborhood, he went to his car and drove out.

When he finally found himself a safe distance from the hotel, he pulled over. After turning on the laptop again, he waited while his e-mails downloaded.

There were only three of them. He found the Bureau of Prison's report and opened it. It was almost twenty pages long and contained a lot of boilerplate because of the extensive records that are necessary in a federal institution due to lawsuits. He scanned it quickly until his eyes landed on the name Benjamin Charles Lavolet, a known associate of Victor James Radek. He had been serving a fifteen-year sentence for narcotics distribution and was paroled just a month before the first Pentad murder in Los Angeles. His last known address was 1414 Sistine Lane, apartment 2W, in Los Angeles. Vail located it on a map Web site and saw that it was about half a mile from the Spring Street house.

The factory on Keller Street was about a mile away. The building being refurbished on West Seventh was less than a ten-minute drive.

Vail pulled back into traffic. The sun was starting to set. The air smelled like rain and the temperature had dropped a couple of degrees. It would be a good time to set up on the apartment. Since the report didn't have a phone number for Lavolet, and since he could no longer call the FBI office to get one, Vail had only two options: The first was to try to get into the apartment, which, if Tye and Radek were there, could be disastrous. The other was to surveil it and see if any lights came on once it got dark.

The building had four units and two of them already had lights on when he got there. Benny's windows—assuming that 2W was the westernmost apartment on the second floor—showed no signs of life. He waited another half hour and still the unit remained dark.

Deciding to read the Bureau of Prisons report in full to see if there were any more associates of Radek in the area, Vail opened the laptop and turned it on. He took notes in case there were others who might have since moved to the L.A. area. But, as far as known addresses, Lavolet's was the only one. Vail was about to shut off the computer when suddenly it beeped. It was an incoming message—from Tye Delson.

It was a streaming video of her. But it couldn't be from her cell phone, because Radek had smashed it, plus there was no sound. Then he remembered her PDA. He had e-mailed some information to it for the search warrant at the steam laundry.

The angle of the image indicated that it was being taken by her, possibly from down at her side. It was shooting up at her face. A piece of duct tape was securely across her mouth, a second across her eyes. Somehow she had managed to pull up one corner, enough to have limited vision out of one eye. A trickle of blood from her nose had dried on her upper lip. The exposed eye was wide with fear, but Vail thought he detected something else—rage. If her condition wasn't disturbing enough, Vail could see a thin slice of her shoulder and chest. She appeared to be naked.

Then she pulled the device down behind her back as it flickered on and off indicating the battery was low. He saw the unmistakable double strand of a handcuff around one wrist, and then a chain with a padlock that hung from it and was attached by a second lock to a heavy radiator. On the floor was her purse, its contents scattered. Radek must not have known about her PDA, if he even knew what one was.

The camera moved to the window and showed the surrounding neighborhood. The image flickered again, this time the black screen lasting a second or two. An ornate two-story building seemed to be the target of her effort. It was distinctive and apparently the best clue she could offer as to her whereabouts. The screen went black, and Vail feared that the battery was finally dead. He waited a few interminable seconds but there was no more.

It started to rain. He turned on the wipers and let their rhythm hypnotize him for a moment. Then he closed his eyes tightly, trying to recall every detail of the building. It was more Victorian than anything else, but with some possible French influence. The architectural details were so elaborately overdesigned that he judged the structure to be at least a hundred years old. But how did you find a list of hundred-year-old buildings in Los Angeles, if he was even right about the age? Then suddenly it occurred to him that he had seen the building somewhere before, not from that angle, but from street level, maybe the day Bertok was killed. The windows were unusual, projecting out from the building face at least two feet and complex in their detail. They were bordered with stone pillars, the crowns of which were semicircles capped with triangles. He hadn't been to that many places in Los Angeles, so hopefully it was retrievable from wherever it was hiding in his memory.

Undoubtedly, someone with a better-educated eye than Vail would have been able to narrow down the architecture, someone who would have made a mental note the moment he first saw it and remembered its location. But Vail was the only one who had seen the video stream, and now that image was permanently gone. If he was right and the building was a hundred years old, it would most likely be around other old buildings. He thought about the house on Spring Street. One of the buildings next to it, not the scrap yard, but the one on the other side, had "Est. 1883" painted on a wall. That was certainly a century old, and the neighborhood had a mix of residential and commercial properties. He made a U-turn and sped off toward Spring Street.

Once he arrived at the house, Vail got out and scanned the neighborhood. He didn't see anything resembling the ornate two-story building. But the day he thought he had seen it, he and Kate had set up a block away. He drove to the spot, turned the car around, and pulled to the curb.

After getting out, he slowly turned in all directions. Then, in the distance, he spotted it. It was illuminated in the rain by a halo caused by the streetlights. He put the car in gear and sped toward it. When he got closer, he started driving cautiously, searching the surrounding buildings from which Tye's PDA could have sent the stream.

The rain was coming down harder now, making his recollection of the video even more difficult. When he got a little closer, he climbed out of the car, ignoring the downpour. There was only one building that it could have been shot from. It was a small three-story hotel, the kind that was popular at the turn of the twentieth century, a bar on the first floor and fewer than ten rooms on the second and third floors.

He could read the sign now—"The Lindbergh Hotel." There were four windows on each of the upper floors that were a possibility. Vail closed his eyes and tried to remember the angle of the video to figure out whether it was from the second or third floor, but then decided he couldn't chance being wrong.

A few doors down from the hotel, he pulled crookedly to the curb on the same side of the street and jumped out. No longer having a handgun, he went to the trunk and took out the shotgun. The rain was now a good thing, he decided; it had chased everyone indoors. He loaded the magazine with double-aught buck shells, filling one jacket pocket with deer slugs and the other with more double-aught. He held the weapon down at his side as inconspicuously as possible.

Immediately next door to the bar was the hotel's door. Vail tried it but it was locked with a thick metal plate, ensuring that even if he'd had a Halligan, it would have been difficult to open discreetly. That left going into the bar. A dangerous thing with a shotgun in hand.

The bar was small and dingy. Only four customers were inside, all of them sitting at the bar and looking comfortable. They had to be regulars. Vail knew that as long as he didn't interfere with their drinking, they wouldn't cause any problems. The bartender, an overweight but strong-looking man with greasy hair and acne scars, alerted and squared himself defensively once he saw Vail enter with the shotgun. Vail could read his streetwise eyes—he knew that Vail was some sort of cop and this was not a robbery. But for him, cops were usually as much trouble as criminals. Vail walked up to him. "You have four rooms facing the street." Vail took a wet mug shot out of his pocket and dropped it on the bar.

The bartender prided himself on not cooperating with the police, but something in Vail's eyes told him not to push it too far.

"Who are you?"

"You know who I am."

"I'm going to need to see a badge."

With his left hand, Vail held up the shotgun by the cocking grip and gave it a quick up-and-down jerk, jacking a round into the chamber convincingly. "Which room?"

"Three C. There's only two rented on that side; the other one's a Korean family on the second floor."

"The key." The bartender went to a drawer below the cash register and took out a ring of keys. He started to take one off when Vail said, "The master, the one that opens the door to the street." The bartender took a small ring from his pocket and pulled a key off of it.

Vail turned to go. "You'd better call the police."

"And tell them what?"

"There's been a murder."

Vail slid the key into the front door of the hotel, and it turned with a worn ease. He closed it slowly behind him to keep from making any noise and started up the stairs two at a time. The rain was still coming down hard and he hoped that it would muffle his movement up the stairs. The narrow hallway on the third floor didn't have any windows. A single low-wattage bulb cast the corridor in a dusty yellow light. Vail walked along the wall trying not to step on any squeaky floorboards, but there were too many of them. Hopefully they couldn't be heard inside the room.

When he got to 3C, he stood outside listening. When he didn't hear anything, he leaned his ear against the door and listened again. Still nothing. Standing to the side, he worked the master key into the lock slowly and started to turn it. A half-dozen shots exploded through the door.

From the way the window was positioned in the video, Vail knew Tye had to be in a different room. Without getting in front of the door, he extended the shotgun to arm's length and fired three rounds back through the door, slightly altering the direction of each. Then he heard the unmistakable sound of a body hitting the floor. He tried the key again, but something had hit the lock and jammed it, probably one of the bullets fired at him. Moving in front of the door, he jumped up and toward it, using his momentum and weight as he kicked at the lock. The door broke open but only a foot or so. Vail could see a man's motionless hand on the floor through the narrow opening, his body now blocking the door. Vail pushed in far enough to squeeze through. Victor Radek had taken one of the shotgun blasts in the chest, a black automatic still in his hand.

"Tye!" Vail yelled.

In response, he heard a cry. He went into the bedroom and found her still chained to the radiator, her PDA in her hand. When she saw him, tears from the eye that was not taped began streaming down her cheek. She was completely naked and curled up to hide herself as best she could. Vail ripped a sheet off the bed and wrapped her in it. As he started to take the tape off of her, they could hear sirens in the distance.

Vail checked the handcuffs. "Do you know where the key is?"

"I never saw one. But after he taped my mouth and eyes, he jingled a key ring in front of my face, and asked, 'Do you know what that sound is? It's the sound of freedom.' It's got to be on him."

"I'll be right back. You'll be all right—he's dead." She nodded, trying not to cry. He tucked the sheet around her a little more tightly to make sure it wouldn't come off. "I'll just be a second." In the other room, he rolled the body over and searched the pockets. Aside from a wad of hundred-dollar bills, the only thing Vail found was the key ring. It had six keys on it, none of which were for handcuffs.

Two LAPD officers burst into the room and pointed their guns at Vail. He told them he was FBI and was allowed to ease his credentials out slowly. Taking one of their handcuff keys, Vail went back in the bedroom and freed her, and then he helped her onto the bed. He collected her clothes from around the room. When he saw she was shaking, he sat down next to her, and she collapsed into his arms. She cried for a few minutes and then straightened up.

"I'm okay, I'm okay," she said.

"You know it's all right if you're not."

"It's just the relief that it's over, that's all. I'll be fine."

"Okay, but we're still going to the hospital to be sure."

She hesitated a moment. "We have to go—for legal reasons."

"Legal?"

"In case there's any question, either with L.A. or the FBI, about your having to shoot that animal."

"I don't understand," Vail said.

Slowly, as if each word brought new pain, she said, "We have to go to the hospital"—she looked down at her hands—"so they can do a rape kit."

Vail tightened his arms around her, and she began to sob uncontrollably.

THIRTY-THREE

FROM WHERE HE SAT IN THE EMERGENCY WAITING ROOM, VAIL watched Kate follow Kaulcrick through the door. The assistant director maintained his usual controlled facade, but not Kate. Her lips were drawn back into a flat line and her fists were clenched in anger. Vail stood up to meet them.

"How's Tye?" she asked.

"They're still examining her." He hesitated before adding, "They're going to have to do a rape kit."

Kate sank into the nearest chair, forgetting her anger. "How awful," she said. "How *awful*."

"Physically, she's a little banged up, but she's all right."

"Did she say how he got her?"

"I didn't ask her any questions. I have no idea how to help with this, so I didn't want her reliving anything she shouldn't be."

All Kate seemed to be able to say was "That's awful."

Kaulcrick could wait no longer. "And the three million dollars?"

In a tone that was neither defensive nor apologetic, Vail told them everything from the phone call warning of insider information, to delivering the money and surviving another of Radek's traps, to Tye's PDA video and the final shoot-out.

"Does she have any idea what he did with the money?" Kaulcrick asked.

"He tied her up and left her chained to the radiator in that hotel room and disappeared with it. She said he was gone for a couple of hours. She didn't see any sign of it after he got back."

"So you have no idea where it is."

"Maybe there's something back at the hotel room. I didn't get a chance to look around."

This time the assistant director didn't try to hide his disdain for Vail. "Now we've got to try to find that three million dollars *again*."

"Technically, you didn't find it the first time."

"*Technically*, you gave it away twice. Give me your credentials. You no longer represent this organization."

Kate said, "Don, don't you think we might need Steve's help looking for the money?"

Kaulcrick spun around, his anger rising. "Let me explain something to you and your—whatever he is—here. I've been letting this farce go on because at times it seemed to be moving the investigation forward, but without FBI credentials, without FBI equipment, without the systems we have in place and the official channels that we draw information through, your superagent wouldn't have been able to accomplish anything. It's this organization and its people that allowed him to achieve whatever success he's had. So, no, Kate, we don't need his help. We just need to work a little harder and we'll find the money on our own. Everyone is one hundred percent dead now, so nobody will be moving it around. It'll be much easier to come up with."

Vail handed him his credentials. "I hope you're right," he said. Kate looked at Vail, somewhat amazed. He was sincere. She couldn't believe that he wasn't insulted by what the assistant director had said.

But Kaulcrick assumed Vail's only response could be rancor. "I suppose that means you think you can find it without the FBI?" His face grew flush with lost control. "I'll tell you what"—his tone now lowered itself to a seething ridicule—"if you can find it, you can keep it. How's that, hotshot? Let's go, Kate."

"Give me a minute, will you, Don?"

"I guess this man hasn't done enough damage to your career. I'm waiting two minutes and then you can find your own way back. And I'm not talking about back to the office." He turned and stormed out of the room.

She stood up, her voice formal again. "Please tell Tye if she needs anything at all to call me. I assume you're all right." It sounded almost like an accusation.

"Kate, don't confuse what might have happened between us a couple of nights ago—or how I feel about you now—with the way I do things." He lowered his voice. "I wasn't going to call you on this because I knew, given any opportunity, I would probably kill him. I wouldn't expose anyone to that kind of trouble, least of all you."

"I don't know how many times I have to tell you to stop protecting me." Her voice calmed. "Maybe I should have simply told you to quit using it as an excuse. Now I understand why there are no faces in your apartment, or anywhere else in your life—you are incapable of trusting anyone. Not even me, who has stood by you to the point of getting shot and having my career left hanging by a thread. Only the bad guys deserved to be thrown through plate-glass windows. But that's all right. It's who you are. The good part is that you solve impossible problems. I appreciate everything you've done. Without you, we'd still be leaning back congratulating ourselves for hanging this on Stan Bertok. But unfortunately, the bad part makes it impossible for anyone to form an alliance with you on any level. So thanks for your help and, since I doubt I'll see you again, good-bye."

Vail watched her walk away. For the first time in a long time, he wanted to defend himself, to bring her back, but he knew most of what she was feeling was more right than wrong.

A half hour later, two men who had that detective's exhaustion about them walked in. "You Steve Vail?"

"I'm guessing you're homicide."

"We'd like to get a statement from you."

Vail knew that no matter how impure his intentions had been, the shooting was justifiable. "I can't leave, but if you don't mind doing it here, fire away."

WHEN THE DETECTIVES had finished they stood up, and each shook Vail's hand. It was a positive sign he could feel in their grip. They were sending the message that it had been a good shoot. One of them handed Vail his card. "We're going to need to take a statement from Miss Delson. Do you think she'd be up to it?"

"I understand that you have to interview her, and I understand that you have to ask her about the rape. But—"

"Don't worry, this isn't our first time."

Vail flashed an embarrassed smile. "Sorry."

The detectives made an inquiry at the nurses' station and were ushered through a door behind it.

Almost two hours later, a nurse came out and told Vail that Tye was ready to be discharged. When she walked out, Vail was surprised at her demeanor. She seemed relaxed and somewhat energized. He watched her closely, trying to see if it was an act, something he suspected tough women, having gone through what she had, tried to talk themselves into. She wasn't giving out any clues with her body language, but Vail knew that verbal clues could be more telling. "Feel like some breakfast?"

"What time is it?"

"Almost four thirty."

"A.M., right?"

Vail smiled gently. "Made that jump right from 'breakfast' to it being morning. Evidently your mind is working."

She gave a brief laugh, more courteous than amused. "I know you're concerned, but after some food and sleep, I think you'll be impressed how quickly I bounce back."

"Actually I'd be surprised if you didn't."

"That's very kind of you." She put her hand on his. "I haven't really thanked you for what you did."

"And now you have."

Her eyes had started to well up, but Vail's response made her smile. She sniffled away the tears and patted him on the hand. "Let's go find a truck stop and order the biggest, greasiest thing on the menu. I'm buying."

"That's the best offer I've had all day. Especially from a woman."

DURING BREAKFAST, Vail could see Tye's spirits gradually repairing themselves. By the end of the meal she was laughing with a seemingly reengaged sense of humor, maybe the best indicator of all. At one point, after a period of awkward silence, she became more serious. "Steve, there's only one thing I'm concerned about. Do you think Radek was the last of them?"

"I hope so. I'm out of ammunition." She gave another short, polite laugh, making him realize it was the wrong tack. "Sorry. As far as I can see, that's it." Vail smiled at her reassuringly. "Absolutely, I think he was the last of the Pentad."

This time it was Tye who read some doubt in his voice. "But you'd feel better if the three million had been sitting in his apartment."

"Well, the money is a consideration. If you don't know where it is, you don't know if someone's got it. But Radek had robbed eight armored cars; he knew how to hide bulk money. It could be off somewhere being laundered. The Bureau's searching his hotel room right now. Maybe the answer will be there."

Tye looked at him questioningly. "You said 'the Bureau is searching' instead of '*we're* searching.' What's going on?"

"I'm no longer with the FBI. I was just more or less fired. Who could have seen that coming?" Vail said, his smile relaxed, disarming. "I know what you're missing. Do you want me to get you some cigarettes?"

"No, no, that's all right. I think I'm going to try to quit." She patted him on the hand. "I'm okay. Really."

Vail nodded at her plate. "I'd ask you if you want anything else, but I think you've already eaten everything on the menu."

"While I'll never be able to thank you for what you did last night, I think I'm just as impressed with how kind you've been since . . . since you came and got me." She took a deep breath to demonstrate renewal and pushed her plate away. "Now, I'm ready to go home." Her words were meant to be filled with resolve but sounded tenuous, as if she were about to bungee jump off a bridge and wondered if the tether was the proper length.

A little later when Vail pulled into her driveway, she looked at the house solemnly. "Do you want me to come in?" he offered. "I could stay while you get some sleep."

"As tempting as that is, eventually it'll make it that much harder. No, this is it for you, Steve Vail. You're off duty. Go back to your life. It's time for me to climb back on the horse." She grabbed his hand and squeezed it, her eyes damp with emotion. "But I've got to warn you, the next time I get kidnapped, I've still got your number." She leaned over and kissed him on the cheek. "Thank you," she said, and got out.

AS SOON AS VAIL walked into the lobby of his hotel, two agents he recognized from the office came up and announced with forced authority, "The SAC wants to see you."

Vail laughed. "You do know that I no longer work for the FBI?"

"He still wants to see you," one of them said nervously.

"How long have you been waiting here?"

"A couple of hours."

"Then the SAC can wait a little longer. I'm going up to shower and change clothes. You can come up and make sure I don't *escape*, or you can wait in the bar."

The two agents looked at each other, not sure what to do. Vail turned to go. "While you two figure it out, I'll be in my room."

They hurried after him.

When they got to the FBI office, the agents took him directly to the SAC's office and waited inside the doorway like guards. Mark Hildebrand was sitting at a small conference table at one end of the room. Seated across from him were a couple of older agents who Vail assumed were supervisors. "Steve, have a seat," Hildebrand offered. Vail sat down. "Coffee?"

"Half a cup. I'm not going to be here that long."

One of the agents who had escorted him from the hotel filled a mug and brought it over. "We need to get a statement from you as to exactly what happened last night."

He took a sip. "Why?"

"Because this is an FBI investigation, and we don't know what happened."

"Normally I wouldn't interrupt a ruse as *clever* as this, but I've had very little sleep. So if I fast-forward this a bit you'll have to excuse me. Kaulcrick isn't here, so I'm supposed to assume that you no longer have any loyalty to him or interest in your own career? You're asking for my statement about what happened last night. That isn't what this is about. You don't have a clue where the money is." Vail searched the faces around the table. "No, there's something else. You think I found something last night, and I'm keeping it from you. That's it, isn't it?" He looked around the table again. One of the supervisors diverted his eyes, confirming Vail's suspicions.

"Steve, try to look at it from our side. We have to consider the possibility that you might have found something."

"Where are Kaulcrick and Kate?"

"Kate's in her office."

Vail waited a few seconds. "Since you're not saying where Kaulcrick is, I'll have to assume . . . he's searching my room, isn't he?"

Hildebrand's face reddened. "We have a warrant."

Vail roared with laughter. "When I was first an agent, I used to wonder if there was someone in a secret room watching everyone in the office who would feed management the answers to make sure that they got everything completely wrong. There had to be because how else could you guys get everything perfectly backward?" He looked around at the walls. "Come on, you can tell me, where are the cameras?"

"Would you be willing to take a polygraph to clear yourself?"

He smiled. "I'll be glad to take a polygraph. On one condition."

"Which is?"

"You take one first."

"Me? About what?"

"Kaulcrick wouldn't have waited for a warrant to search my room, especially if he knew I wasn't going to be there. You knew I was with Tye Delson at the hospital. Even though you did a quickie yesterday to lift my handgun, somebody had to go back to my room after the shooting for a little prewarrant reconnaissance. A little light lifting of the pillows to look for large chunks of money. Nothing that I'd notice. Just pass the box on that one question, Mark, and then you can hook me up."

"So you're saying no."

"Sounds like you're the one saying no."

"Would you mind waiting out in my secretary's office."

"Listen, if you want me to help look for the money, just ask. If not, I need a ride back to my hotel. Please call and ask them to have the courtesy of being out of there by the time I get back." Hildebrand hesitated for a few seconds, considering the advantage of joining forces with Vail, but knew that Kaulcrick was the surest route back to Washington. There was an old saying among managers: Contacts trump competence. The SAC nodded to the two agents at the door to take him back to the hotel. "Oh, two more things," Vail said. "First, I assume you'd like to know the identity of the body in the elevator."

"You know who that is?"

"A federal parolee named Benjamin Lavolet. He had an apartment on Sistine Lane."

"How do you know that?"

"Actually, Radek told me when he called with the ransom demand."

"Why would he tell you that?"

"He couldn't help himself. He was rubbing it in my face how smart he was. Also because, at the time, he knew I couldn't tell anyone. And he planned to kill me before I had the chance. Which brings me to the second thing, something he was even more proud of. Pendaran is innocent," Vail lied. "They set him up as a fall guy in case someone saw through their Bertok ruse. Go to Pendaran's lawyer and offer him an immediate walk if he passes the polygraph. I suspect you'll have better luck with him than you did with me."

Vail smiled enigmatically, almost as if to himself. He had bluffed them out of his taking a polygraph because he knew he couldn't have passed it regarding the whereabouts of the money.

EVERYONE WAS GONE from Vail's room when he got back. There really wasn't much they could disrupt. The bed linens had been removed and were piled on a chair. A copy of the search warrant lay in the middle of the mattress. He checked the return: nothing had been taken as evidence.

He pulled a sheet off the chair and arranged it across the bed. He considered sleeping for a couple of hours, but knew he wouldn't be able to. It was true what Kaulcrick had said, that he would have little success finding the money without the Bureau's resources, but he had something none of them did. There was a good chance that the answer to everything was in his pocket. He pulled out the ring of keys he had taken off Radek's body. "That's the sound of freedom," he had told Tye. Since the handcuff key was not among them, it had to be *his* freedom he was referring to—the money. And an assistant director of the FBI had told Vail that if he found it, he could keep it. Had he done three million dollars' worth of work for the FBI? Everything considered—he just may have.

One of the keys, cut on a manufacturer's blank, was for a car. There was only one place Radek's car could be.

AS VAIL PULLED UP to the Lindbergh Hotel, he let what had happened there the night before replay itself. All the little details that still didn't make sense kept forcing their way into his thoughts.

He still had the bartender's master key, which no one had thought to ask for. He let himself into the building and found the door to 3C sealed with plastic ribbon and an FBI document affixed to it warning that the premises were officially under the jurisdiction of the FBI and any entry would constitute a federal offense punishable by five years in prison and/or a twenty-five-thousand-dollar fine. He smiled. If he found the money, he decided he would FedEx the twenty-five thousand dollars to Kaulcrick in the original, recorded hundred-dollar notes. A South American postmark would be the crowning touch.

Vail peered through one of the shotgun holes in the door and then took out Radek's key ring and compared each to the manager's master. One of them appeared to be a match. He slid it in the lock and turned the cylinder partially before it seized up as it had the night before. He took a step back and kicked the door open.

A copy of the search warrant had been left on the couch in the small living room, listing everything that was taken. There were more than forty items. He quickly read them, looking for anything that might give a hint as to where Radek's car might be. "Miscellaneous documents" were listed without any specifics, and inexplicably the handcuff key hadn't been located. Maybe Radek never had one, which could mean only one thing: he was going to dump Tye's body still cuffed. Most of the items taken were clothing from the bedroom closet. No forensic reason existed to confiscate them, but experienced investigators had all sooner or later had a case where, staring at crime-scene photos after the fact, they wished that one small, seemingly insignificant item at the time had been collected. So they took almost everything, whether they could see its potential or not. After all, they knew that Radek wouldn't be demanding their return. The area rug that Radek had died on had been taken. His handgun, and even Vail's Bureau shotgun, had been tagged and removed.

The chain and handcuffs were listed, reminding Vail of their purpose. He went into the bedroom and stared at the radiator that Tye had been anchored to. Looking out the window, Vail recognized the downward angle to the building with the extended window casings. It was something he hadn't taken the time to do the night before, and it now gave him a sense of order. Then he quickly stepped back. Something had unknowingly caught his eye when he came into the room but was just now registering.

It was the radiator. He stepped back another couple of feet and examined its symmetry. Squatting down, he looked at it from a more direct angle. The small domed cap that housed the steam valve had been painted many times over the years. At the cylindrical valve's base, Vail could see a couple of brass threads. The cap had been put back on crookedly and twisted, cross-threading it.

Vail wrenched it off. When he saw what was inside, he collapsed onto the bed. His thoughts raced backward through the entire investigation, through every turn and dead end, ticking off every little inconsistency that, unknown to him, his mind had been collecting.

Everything now made sense.

As he walked back down the stairs, Vail checked his watch. It was almost noon and there was moderate foot traffic along the street. Because of the limited parking in the neighborhood, he had parked illegally directly in front of the hotel. He examined the car key on the ring he had taken from Radek's pocket. It was for a Chrysler product, the older type key without lock and trunk buttons.

Since the car had been used to transport a kidnap victim to the hotel, logically it wouldn't be parked far away. For the next half hour he searched the surrounding blocks. He found only one older Chrysler. As discreetly as possible he tried the key in the door lock but it didn't fit. A closer inspection of the key revealed that none of the plating had been worn away, indicating it was new. As deceptive as Radek had been, Vail wondered if he hadn't had another manufacturer's key duplicated onto a Chrysler blank. If so, it most likely would still have been for an older car.

He started back toward the hotel looking for any vehicle that the key might fit. At the end of the block was an overnight parking zone. As Vail approached it, he spotted an older Chevy sedan. On the windshield was a parking ticket suggesting it might have been parked there since the night before. To avoid suspicion, he stabbed the key into the lock as if he had done it countless times before. It turned in the lock. Pulling the ticket from under the windshield wiper, Vail got in. The interior had the odor of air freshener, the kind sprayed at a full-service car wash. It smelled the same as Radek's stolen Honda had, minus the gasoline odor.

He didn't think Radek would chance leaving three million dollars in the trunk of a car parked on the street, but stranger things had happened. As much as Vail wanted to look in the trunk, he knew that this was not the place. He was unarmed and had no idea who might be around. He put the key in the ignition and started the car. The glove compartment was empty. Between the two front seats was a deep console storage compartment. The only object it contained was a garage door opener. Feeling around inside, he found some kind of matting covering the bottom, but it was cut a little too large and bunched at the edges, suggesting the manufacturer had not put it there. He pulled it back and underneath was a California driver's license in the name of Terry A. Frost. The address listed was in Inglewood.

The man in the photo was Victor Radek.

THIRTY-FOUR

THE INGLEWOOD ADDRESS TURNED OUT TO BE A MODEST RANCH IN a neighborhood of similarly unpretentious homes. Other than the residence's grass being a little more brown than green, the lawn and the few shrubs edging it were recently and precisely trimmed. It had an attached one-car garage. After using the door opener, Vail drove into the uncluttered garage, pushing the button again to close it.

He got out and opened the trunk. Inside were two large suitcases that looked new. He opened one and found it was empty. He took it out and placed it on the floor. As soon as he hefted the second bag he knew it was also empty. The only other items in the trunk were the spare and a pair of jumper cables. "That would have been a little too easy, wouldn't it, Vic?" he said out loud. He took a closer look at the suitcases and estimated that they were large enough to carry the entire five million dollars. Vail tossed the bags back into the trunk and closed it.

Of the remaining four keys only one appeared to be a house key. It opened the door leading from the garage. The kitchen was clean and the sink free of dishes. There was a small living room and no dining room. The first bedroom was apparently where Radek slept. The bed was made and everything was put away. In the closet, the little clothing that he had was hung in an orderly row. The bathroom had a tub shower. Vail searched the medicine cabinet for multiple residents. There was only enough inside to indicate a single male occupant.

The other bedroom had been turned into an office. A secondhand metal desk sat beneath a small shaded window. The top right-hand drawer of the desk was locked. There were two keys on Radek's ring that were not house or car keys. The first one he tried opened the drawer. The only thing inside was a round plastic object that appeared to be an old distributor cap. It had been wiped down but engine grease and grime were still embedded in its recesses. He searched the rest of the drawers and, other than some cheap pens and a pad of paper, found nothing.

He turned on the desk light and held the plastic cap up against it, turning it slowly. It looked clunky, old clunky, made when things were built to last. Inside was a series of numbers stamped into it. He set it down on the desk and stared at it. Did it have any significance, or was it simply a new level of Radek's red herrings? After all, he had already used a key to mislead the FBI. Was he taking it one step further by adding some mundane object and locking it away as though it were an extortionist's Rosetta stone?

On the ring there were still two unidentified keys. One was cut on a generic blank and from its length and shape was most probably for a car. The other was short with a cylindrical hole in the head that fit over a pin in the center of a lock. If the long one was for a car, maybe it was the same vehicle that the distributor cap fit. There couldn't be any more than a million cars in the Greater Los Angeles area. That sounded like a typical piece of Radek misdirection, so why not? But why a distributor cap? The car key was certainly enough. Vail ordered himself to complete the search of the house before wasting any more time with pointless theories.

When he had driven up to the house, he noticed that the roof was so flat that any space between the roof and the first-floor ceiling would be too small to allow someone to crawl through. That left the basement. Back in the kitchen he found a door leading downstairs. He flipped on the light switch and walked down.

At one end was a furnace and hot water heater partitioned off. At the opposite end was a fairly elaborate collection of weight-lifting equipment: dumbbells, bars, plates, and a bench similar to the ones at the steam cleaners where Radek had stored the two million dollars. The walls were painted concrete, eliminating the possibility of false compartments. The ceiling was unfinished, exposing the joists supporting the first floor. Unlike the cleaners, there was nothing covering the concrete floor where the weights were sitting.

Returning to the bedroom, Vail picked up the distributor cap and again considered its possible significance. He also had an unidentified car key. At this point he had no choice but to assume that the two items were connected to the money. He went to the kitchen and called the FBI office, asking for Tom Demick.

"Steve, I was sorry to hear about what happened. Nobody around here can believe they let you go."

"Tom, I need one last favor."

"Just promise me it'll make Kaulcrick look like an idiot."

"I don't think you can improve on perfection," Vail said. "Can you get the radio room to run a Terry A. Frost for all vehicles?"

"Hold on." Vail heard him get up and go to another phone. Hopefully there would be more than the Chevrolet registered to Radek under his alias. If so, it might reveal the make and model of the car that the key and distributor cap fit. Demick came back on the line. "Just one car, Steve. A Chevy Caprice. Do you want the plate and VIN?"

"No, Tom, that's not the one I'm looking for. Thanks for the help. All your help."

"It's been a pleasure."

In the cabinet over the phone, Vail found the Yellow Pages and looked up auto parts stores. There were several, so he decided to take the book. The closest one was less than half a mile away. It was a national chain and the counterman was young. He looked at the distributor cap briefly before asking, "What kind of car is it for?"

"I was hoping you could tell me. There are some numbers stamped on the inside."

The door opened and another customer came in. "Sorry, I got no way to look them up on something that old," the employee said, and then to the man behind Vail asked, "Can I help you?"

The next store, another national chain, met with almost identical results. Vail scanned the Yellow Pages looking for a smaller store. He found one that was about a forty-five-minute drive away, which advertised "in business for four decades." When he walked in, the counterman, in his midsixties, was reading a newspaper. His greeting was an unhurried "hi."

Vail said, "Are you the owner?"

"For thirty-seven *glorious* years." "Glorious" was meant to be sarcastic, but Vail could see the pride in his eyes. He was already eyeing the cap in Vail's hand, so Vail placed it on the counter. The owner picked it up, holding it apprais-ingly as if it were a rare gemstone. "That's older than my store."

"Any idea what it belongs on?"

He looked at Vail curiously, now knowing he wasn't there to buy anything. "Usually people who come in here know what kind of car they drive."

Although he had no identification, Vail thought he'd try to invoke the magic three letters one last time. "This is part of an FBI investigation."

"Not the one that's been in the paper where they've been having those shootings?"

"Actually, yes."

"I've got to admit you look like an FBI agent, but I've had enough dealings with cops to know the first thing they do is show a badge. You didn't."

"I was fired today."

"Was that you in the shooting?"

"It was."

"Fired for what?" the owner asked in a way that told Vail if he answered the question correctly, they would be on the same side.

"Not letting management in on things they would screw up."

The owner laughed. "Now you know why I started my own business thirty-seven years ago. Bill Burton." He held out his hand. "Besides, business has been slow, so I'll do anything short of *extremely illegal* to keep from going nuts."

They shook hands. "Steve Vail. That's more or less how I got here."

Burton turned the cap upside down. "There's some numbers stamped inside. I can't read them." He handed it to Vail. "Can you make them out?" Vail read them and the owner wrote them down. "Come on in the back. I never throw anything away. I think I've got every parts catalog all the way back to the stagecoaches."

Once they reached the large storage room, Vail discovered that Burton hadn't been exaggerating. The shelves were organized but crammed full. Boxes were stacked along the walls almost to the ceiling. Burton stepped behind a six-foot tower of them and said, "The old catalogs from the fifties are back here. By the construction, that'd be my first guess when your car was manufactured." On the floor were piles of stained catalogs. He handed them out to Vail a dozen at a time until he had more than fifty of them. "This'll go a lot faster if you can give me a hand."

"Just show me what to look for."

For the next two hours, they pored over the catalogs, Vail occasionally asking for clarification. A couple of times customers came in and Burton stopped to wait on them.

Finally the owner said, "I've got it."

Vail stepped behind Burton, reading over his shoulder. "A 1957 Packard Clipper. That's the right number."

"Do you know what they look like?" the owner asked.

"I don't think so."

"Yeah, you're a little young. They were huge. You could

run one of today's cars into them and you'd total it, but that old Packard wouldn't even be dented. Come on, I'll show you what it looks like." Vail followed him into an even more cramped office. Burton typed on his computer and after a few seconds turned the monitor so Vail could see it. "There it is. The thing's a tank, isn't it?"

Vail studied the boxy vehicle with the heavy rolled chrome bumpers and could see how it would have been indestructible. "I need to find the one that distributor cap belongs to. Any ideas?"

"I suppose there are a few around belonging to collectors, but I haven't seen one in—I'll bet—thirty years. I don't know where you'd even get parts for one." Burton started to say something else, but Vail's focus had become distant, causing the owner to stop speaking.

Finally Vail said, "I think I do." He held out his hand to the owner. "Thanks to you, Bill."

THE HOUSE ON SPRING STREET where they'd found Bertok's body looked the same with the exception of the yellow crime-scene tape, which was a little more windblown and droopy because of the recent rain. A newly installed hasp and lock again secured the front entrance. The iron gate protecting it was also relocked. Vail pulled into the driveway and turned off the engine.

He grabbed the distributor cap, got out, and walked over to the fence that separated the house from the auto graveyard. Turning it in his hand almost as if it were a compass, he now understood its importance. He hadn't taken the time to consider why Salton was watching the house the day that Kate and Vail discovered the secret to Stan Bertok's "suicide," or why he would be driving around with the three million dollars in his trunk. It had nothing to do with the house. He, and possibly Radek with the two million in his car, was there to hide the money in the salvage yard. Then, having spotted Vail, they would know that their frame of the dead agent was going to blow up if they didn't do something about it.

Vail found the two fence boards that were not nailed at the bottom, pushed them to the side, and stepped through. He wound his way through row after row of cars, some of which had been crushed flat and stacked three high. A few of them he had to reconstruct mentally to decide whether they could be the boxy Packard. There must have been a couple hundred of them altogether. Finally, he found himself in a corner of the lot that was farthest from where he had entered the property. And there it was, sitting on the ground, its tires still inflated. Once pink and white, the steel body was now mostly pitted red-brown, but intact. He walked around to the driver's side and tried the last long key in the door lock. It turned easily. He got in and gave the interior a cursory search, finding nothing but some old registration papers in the glove box.

He reached back and unlocked the rear door, getting out. The hinge on the back door was rusty, and he had to use considerable force to pull it open. The rear seat came up easily, but there was nothing underneath it. That left the thing that he had been avoiding—the trunk. Remembering the "flamethrower," he slowly pushed the key into the trunk lock. Standing as far to the side as possible, he turned the key and suddenly felt his heart beat a couple of hard strokes when the lock snapped open. He held the lid down as he walked around the side of the car. When he was completely clear, he let it rise a couple of inches on its own. Nothing happened. He stepped a little closer and peered into the partially open trunk. It appeared to be empty. He raised the lid. All the way in the back of it was a new battery, which had a plastic carrying handle across the terminals.

Walking around to the front of the Packard, Vail searched under the hood with his hands until he found the release. Feeling around it, he tried to determine if there was anything connected that shouldn't be, not that he would be able to identify anything out of place in such an old vehicle. Slowly he pulled the release. The hood popped up an inch. As he had done with the trunk, he went around the side of the car. A strip of chrome molding was hanging off the side. He tore it free and, again keeping as far to the side as he could, pried the hood up. When it was raised a foot, he could see there was nothing out of the ordinary, except that the battery and distributor cap were missing.

He stepped back a couple of feet and examined the position of the Packard. It was surrounded by other wrecks. There wasn't enough room to drive it more than five feet forward, if that. So why had Radek disabled it by keeping the battery in the trunk and its distributor cap under lock and key at his home? Had the money been stored in the Packard's trunk at one time and moved to another location? But then why keep the part and key? He looked around to see if there were any other cars that might have become a newer hiding place. Finally he decided this was one of those problems that if you stared at them too long, you'd never find the solution. He had found the car. If there was more to it, maybe it would come to him when he stopped thinking about it.

When he got back in Radek's Chevrolet at the house, he took out the key ring and inspected the lone unidentified key again. It was definitely not a car key. Everything was starting to take a toll on him and he suddenly felt exhausted. He tried to remember when his last full night's sleep had been, but his mind wouldn't calculate anything more complicated than his most immediate perceptions. He leaned his head back and quickly fell asleep.

The 2 A.M. messenger came early, causing Vail's eyes to snap open. It was dark. He checked his watch to figure out how long he had been sleeping, but he had no idea when he had dozed off. Not remembering where he had put the key ring, he searched himself quickly. Then he realized it was in the ignition. He held up the last unidentified key and said, "Now I think I know where you go."

He went to the trunk and took out the two empty suitcases.

Turning on his flashlight, he made his way through the fence and back to the Packard. He shined the light under the car. The earth around three of its four tires looked flat and hard, but the left rear had the dirt pushed up around its base. Vail scraped it away with his hand. Underneath was a steel plate.

He took the battery out of the trunk and hooked it up to the terminals. Then he snapped on the distributor cap and attached the wires. He got in and turned the key in the ignition. It ground for a couple of seconds and then caught. He dropped it into gear and drove it forward until it hit the car five feet in front of it. After turning it off, he took the keys out of the ignition and went back to the steel plate, using his hand to clean the dirt off. Underneath was a two-foot square of steel with a keyhole in the middle. The metal had the color and rough-cut appearance of the steel plate that had almost crushed him in the factory and was the same as the box at the steam cleaners. The Packard's rear tire had rested right on top of the keyhole, so the car had to be moved before it could be accessed. He shined the light into the tiny opening and there was a pin in the middle of the lock. Vail fit the last key into the opening and turned it. He felt something release and lifted the lid. Inside, the compartment was crammed with neatly banded stacks of cash.

Kaulcrick's dismissive offer to let Vail keep the money if he could find it replayed itself hauntingly. He said to himself, "Well, Don, if you insist." He unzipped the suitcase lids and flipped them open. Then with a certain degree of sensual pleasure he dug both his hands into the thick, cool bundles of one-hundred-dollar bills.

THIRTY-FIVE

EVEN THOUGH THE SUN HADN'T FULLY RISEN, TYE DELSON DIDN'T switch on the light in her office as she entered. She went over to the window and raised it as far as she could. The air outside was warmer than in the room, and it felt good. She turned around, took a cigarette from her purse, and lit it. In the flaring light, she was startled to find Vail sitting against the back wall. "Steve, you scared me."

"Sorry," he said with intentional insincerity.

"What are you doing here?"

He stood up and carefully placed a handcuff key on the desk.

She calmly took a drag from her cigarette and studied him for a few seconds. His demeanor was somber yet composed, convincing her of the reason for his visit. A smirk tightened her features.

"I didn't really think I would fool you, not for long anyhow. I haven't slept since I set you up to kill Radek. I would apologize for that, but I'd be surprised if you felt bad about killing someone like him." She took another drag, and as she drew it in deeply, a small sob rattled down her throat, revealing she was not as calm as she was trying to appear. "How did you figure it out?"

"I didn't until I found the key hidden in the radiator. A dozen possibilities occurred to me how it got there, but only one of them made sense. Then when I ran all the little inconsistencies through my head, every one of them made perfect sense."

"Such as?"

"When Kate and I searched Bertok's apartment, we found those documents in the bathroom because of the finger smudges on the side of the vanity. I thought maybe the Evidence Recovery Team just wasn't very good, but since then I've worked with them and realized they wouldn't have missed that. Only a few people knew we were going in a second time, and of course you were one of them. You even delayed us from going in that night, citing not enough probable cause, giving yourself enough time to get in there and plant the evidence. At that point you had Bertok and his keys, so entry was no problem. Then the call to his phone that led us to being on hand for his *suicide*. That trail was just too textbook. Again, you were one of the few people who knew about the pen register. From the beginning there were indications of insider information. At first I thought it was the Pentad trying to give off that illusion. There were a dozen other things that didn't make sense until I found that key. You needed it because you had to be locked up when you sent me that video, but then had to get free to get Radek to try to kill me. And then lock yourself up again and hide the key while I was breaking down the door. You had to have it available if something went wrong like a fire starting or both of us lying there dead."

"It seems like you've figured out most of it. But have you asked yourself why I was involved?"

"There are usually only a few basic motives: money or love immediately come to mind."

"I certainly didn't love Radek, if that's what you're thinking. And the money is in that salvage yard next to where you found Bertok. Under an old car. If that were my motive, would I be telling you that now? In fact, I gave you a way to find it when you asked me where the handcuff key was and I directed you to Radek's key ring. It was to steer you to the money. You would have figured it out eventually. I even stashed Radek's phony driver's license in his car where you'd find it. It would have led you to everything. You didn't find it?"

"If it wasn't Radek or the money, what was it?"

"Has the name Michael Vashon come up in your investigation?"

Vail thought for a second. "Is that the inmate they suspected Salton of killing?"

"Salton, Radek, one of them. Michael and I were in love. I had just started with the United States attorney's office when he was sent to prison for insider trading. It was something he had been involved in briefly a couple of years before we met, and he had forgotten about it. He wasn't the main subject of the case but a good friend of his was, a guy named Danzinger. Because the trades had been made in Michael's name, he was the easiest one to charge. They offered him a deal if he'd give up Danzinger, but Michael was a loyal friend and went to prison instead. Don't get me wrong. Michael saw a way to make some easy money and he broke the law, but he was not a hardened criminal. He was sent to Marion for three years to see if the place wouldn't change his mind about talking. Unfortunately, it didn't."

"What was Radek and Salton's problem with him?"

She took another drag. "The prison pecking order being what it is, Radek and his crew immediately try to find out what they can get out of Michael. They just smack him around the first time and tell him they're going to lease him out to other inmates unless he can come up with a better idea. After Michael was involved in the insider-trading stuff, but before he got arrested, was a little more than two years. He was a genius with computers and had gone to work for a company called Investcomp. It was an online investment service and they were designing software for investors. I don't pretend to understand the technical aspects, but Michael was tasked with testing the finished product, actually to look for flaws in it. What it was supposed to do for the investors was when they brought up a stock on the monitor, it showed a chart of its progress. More important, it provided a green arrow indicating the time to buy and a red arrow when they should sell. Michael found a flaw by which the red arrows could be delayed for a couple of hours. He said it would have taken a major code change to correct it, and since it would have no effect on the software performance for the investors, he never told anyone. He just forgot about it until Radek threatened him. To save himself, he told Radek about the glitch and that if they delayed the red arrow by a couple of hours and then shorted the stock when it went down in response to the Investcomp customers selling off, they would make money."

"Let me guess. They needed someone on the outside to buy and sell the stocks, and Michael convinced you to do it."

"He had left a 'back door' in the Investcomp system, if you know what that is."

"A way to circumvent security."

"That's right. At first I refused to do it, because I was an assistant United States attorney. It was why we never told anyone about our relationship. But his situation in prison became more desperate by the day, so I gave in and we started shorting the stocks. Nothing big. A couple of thousand here and there. Enough to keep them off his back. He had less than a year to go for parole."

"Why did they kill him if he was their golden goose?"

"I don't know if Investcomp picked up on the delaying trend, or whether as a routine update of the software, they found the flaw or his back door. All of a sudden, Michael couldn't get in. When he told Radek, Michael said that he went nuts. That was the last time I talked to him."

"That's when he was killed," Vail said.

"Yes. Of course, I had no way of knowing since I wasn't listed anywhere in the prison records. A couple of days after our last conversation, the phone rings. It's Radek. He's vague, but he's talking to me like I'm his girlfriend, telling me he'll be out soon, and he's looking forward to seeing me. I'm freaked out, but I keep my cool and ask him to have Michael call me. The last thing he said to me was 'Oh, by the way, Michael was beaten to death today,' and hangs up. Just like that."

"So Radek gets out and has you as a ready-made accomplice for his extortion. One with the right connections. And you can't object because he'll implicate you in the Invest-comp scam."

"Exactly, but it wasn't quite that hands-off. The first I learn of his plan is when I wake up a couple of months later in the middle of the night, and he's standing in my bedroom. He introduces himself and proceeds to rape me. And I'm not talking about forcing me to have sex, I'm talking about how they do it in prison, starting with a beating and ending . . . well, I'll leave that to your imagination. Then he rolls over, lights a cigarette, and starts talking to me, again like I'm his girlfriend. That's when he starts laying out the extortion plan, and how I'm an important part of it. I must have looked incredulous, because he slapped me so hard I was almost knocked out. He never said anything about murdering people. But that was his MO. The plan presented never sounded that violent, until you were in the middle of it. "

"I assume he chose his murder victims by who was in the news and at war with the FBI."

"All but Arthur Bellington." Tye's eyes started to well up. "Then, I guess because he hadn't degraded me enough with the rapes, he tells me I have to pick the third victim. He said it was so I'd be as guilty as the rest of them, but it was really about finishing the destruction of any of my character that might have been left. So I told him he should kill Bellington. I knew he had represented Radek in those armored-car robberies. At first Radek protested, but I told him if he ever became a suspect in the extortion, it was a perfect defense for him. Why would he kill the man who had previously kept him from spending the rest of his life in prison? At that point I wanted Bellington dead for that very reason. Because of him, Radek was out of prison and was able to rape and murder at will."

"And you were the one who came up with Bertok's name for them?" Tears started running down her cheeks. She was shaking, unable to speak for a few seconds. "They needed an agent of questionable character; otherwise the Bureau would have known right away that he was not a thief and had been kidnapped. Then they would give the media the whole story of the extortion and murders in an effort to enlist the public's help in rescuing the agent. Radek would never have gotten another cent.

"I swear, Steve, he was just supposed to be kidnapped by masked gunmen and held until they had the entire five million. If I knew they were going to kill him, I would have come forward right then and taken the consequences. I know that sounds hypocritical because of the others being murdered, but as big a mess as Stan was, he didn't deserve to die."

"And you supplied Radek with Pendaran's undercover name so he could buy the extra Glock gun barrel."

"Like I showed you, it was in the computer."

"What about Dan West's murder? The tape of the conversation between him and his killer made him sound like an agent."

"That was Salton. We assumed the agent would be wearing a wire and wanted it to look like it was Stan. They worked out the dialogue ahead of time. I helped with that, too."

"What about Radek's car with the firebomb rigged in the trunk? How'd you know we'd find it?"

She gave a short, joyless laugh. "If it's any consolation, you were driving Radek nuts. He was naturally paranoid, but ever since you survived that tunnel drop, he was constantly in fear that you would somehow find him. It was his idea that I go to your hotel and seduce you. When that didn't happen, it got even worse. You killed Salton, and all that hate Radek had for the FBI was transferred to you. He knew he was the most traceable of the group because of his New Hampshire connection. So they rigged Radek's car and parked it in front of his house, figuring you'd be the one to find it. And because you had survived before, he decided that each trap they set should have something left behind to lure you to the next one. When you didn't fall for the car, he left clues to lead you to the building where they could kill you."

"What about the night you called me in Kate's room? That had to be Radek."

"He wanted me to lure you to my place again so he could kill you. When you didn't bite, he thought he could get you out at the movie ranch the next day. Then when he missed you there, we came up with faking my kidnapping as a way to get the three million dollars back."

"And that brings us to you having me kill Radek."

"If there's one thing I want you to believe, Steve, it's that I never wanted you to get hurt."

"I guess when Radek was firing through the door, I should have taken a little more time to realize how kind you were being to me," Vail said, his expression emotionless.

"After you and Kate—and the elevator—killed the others, it didn't take a great deal of insight to know that I was next. Although he never told me why, he had me start acting publicly like I was in love with you. I knew it was so when you disappeared with the three million, I would suddenly disappear and it would look like you and I took off together. And if you were found dead in that factory eventually with that other woman, they would have started looking for me. Any way you cut it, I was going to vanish. So I came up with a plan to kill him first. Do you know what GHB is?"

"Liquid Ecstasy."

"It does give you that euphoric buzz, but it also has a steroid-enhancing effect. You've seen the weights. He was always on it. But if you take a little too much, it can put you in a stupor; a lot too much and it'll put you in a coma. Two of the side effects are combativeness and paranoia, both of which were at their peak in him already. I drugged him into unconsciousness once, but I just didn't have it in me to kill him. So I figured out a way to have you do it. After he got the three million back, he took it to the auto graveyard to hide it. Then we started drinking to celebrate and, for the first time, had consensual sex. I wanted that so I could claim rape afterward, and prove it. I had put just enough GHB in his drink so he'd pass out. As soon as he nodded off, I staged the chained-to-the-radiator video and sent it to you. I was watching out the window and saw you coming up to the hotel with the shotgun. When I heard you on the stairs, I woke Radek up and told him you were at the door. I knew he would be disoriented and tip his hand too soon. His eyes went crazy, and when he saw the lock turning, he opened fire. I ran to the bedroom, taped my mouth and eyes, and chained myself to the radiator again. I didn't think that in a million years you'd come alone. I thought it would be a SWAT team. But I should have known better."

"How did you know I'd find you? The directions weren't exactly GPS."

"If you didn't come in a reasonable amount of time, I would have sent you another video or a short phone call, a little more detailed, or a text, something. That was always a problem—we never knew how much information to feed you. Too much would have made you suspicious, too little and you wouldn't find your way to where we were trying to direct you." She lit another cigarette off the stub of the one she was smoking. "You want to know what the most satisfying thing about causing his death was?"

There was a change in her; she now spoke mechanically, totally devoid of emotion. Confession in this case apparently wasn't good for the soul. Instead the recounting of her complicity was giving her some kind of awful realization, shutting off the defense of emotion.

"What was that?" Vail asked.

"Watching him go through the process of planning these terrible crimes. I had this perverted fascination about the way he went about it. You have to admit they were brilliant. I got caught up in the creativity of it all, occasionally making suggestions. Probably something like Stockholm syndrome. Whatever it was, he actually taught me how to commit unsolvable crimes—well, almost unsolvable. He handed me the tools to bring about his own death. He allowed me to finally get even."

"So with him dead and the money returned, no one would have known about you," Vail said.

"That was the plan. I was leaving the United States attorney's office and getting out of California, maybe the country. Originally when I announced it a couple of months ago, it was with the intention of getting as far away from Radek as possible. As of yesterday, it was to get away from myself, but that's never possible. Since Radek died, the fact that I'm the only responsible person still alive has been haunting me. The guilt has been increasing constantly. I can't sleep. That's why I'm here so early. I can't eat. I am tortured." She nodded at the wall where the morning light was finally shining on the framed quote from Martin Luther. " 'Each lie must have seven lies if it is to resemble the truth and adopt truth's aura,' " she read. "He certainly knew what he was talking about. Funny, isn't it? I put that up my first day as a warning against those who would lie to me, and I became its prisoner."

"Maybe it's time to take it down."

"Wouldn't it be nice if it were that easy?" she said. "I don't suppose there's any way you could let me turn myself in?" She lit a third cigarette off the one she had exhausted in four long drags.

"I thought you told me you were going to quit smoking." She sensed something humane in his switch to the trivial observation.

She gave him an exhausted smile. "This is the last one. I promise I'll quit . . . forever."

He searched her eyes. They had suddenly lost the jitteriness that he had seen in them since the day they met. Some resolution had settled in. Vail then realized what she meant.

To her surprise, Vail stood up and turned to go. "Did you forget? I'm no longer an FBI agent."

As he opened the door, she said, "It seems I'm always trying to thank you."

He couldn't look back as he shut the door.

When Vail got off the elevator in the lobby, he walked past the guard, who was speaking on the telephone in a panicked voice: "Send an ambulance to the federal building right away. Someone has fallen from a sixth-story window. Hurry."

THIRTY-SIX

AS KATE WALKED INTO THE FEDERAL BUILDING SHE COULD HEAR sirens in the distance. She took another sip of her coffee and headed for the elevators, distracted by thoughts of Vail. How was it possible to admire someone and dislike him so much at the same time? As far as him and her, it was probably better that nothing was going to happen. Irreconcilable differences, wasn't that what her mother had claimed in her divorce suit? "Give a man enough time, and he'll show you his hand," she had always said.

The doors started to close and Don Kaulcrick edged through them. They glanced at each other for a couple of uncomfortable seconds before she said, "Morning."

"Morning. I've got a couple of ideas I want to run past you. See if we can"—he looked at the other passengers and didn't recognize any of them as being from the FBI—"recover those units."

"My office is nice and quiet."

"Now a good time?"

She could see he wasn't trying to patch up their working relationship. She had heard this conciliatory tone before. In all likelihood, he had no ideas, at least not any he was confident in, and wanted her help. "None better."

As they walked through the office, there seemed to be a lightened mood even though both the agents and support staff knew that long days were ahead. Kate suspected that with everyone in the Pentad out of the picture, the hunt for the money would be considerably less stressful. Unlike chasing murderers, looking for money became less a priority with each passing day. Kate tried to push her key into the lock on her office door, but it wouldn't go in. "You didn't have me evicted last night, did you, Don?" She tried it again and then bent over to examine the lock. "There's something in it."

Kaulcrick looked and then scraped at it with a fingernail. "Someone's screwing with your lock. I'll call Demick."

Five minutes later Tom Demick was poking at the lock with a pick. "Looks like somebody superglued it."

"How do we get in then?"

"Let me go get some tools. The walls around the door are panels. I'll have to take them apart."

When he returned, Demick took a small crowbar to the sections of metal frame around the door and pried them away. Then, after lifting the fiber wall panels away, he used a hammer to collapse the metal-rib wall supports. Once he did that the door and its frame loosened and fell into the room. "Jesus Christ!" Demick said, looking into the office.

The others stepped up around him to see. On the floor was a three-foot-high replica of the Portsmouth Naval Prison, constructed completely of banded stacks of hundred-dollar bills. The rounded turrets had been fashioned from fanned-out bundles held in circular tubes with rubber bands, the notched turrets with folded single bills. Where supportive corners were necessary, the ends of the stacks were riffled into one another like half-shuffled playing cards. Kate noticed that the courses were bonded in a staggered fashion, like bricks. No one said anything, but instead walked slowly around the structure, being careful not to touch it. Finally Kaulcrick said, "Get someone from the accounting squad up here."

Four men came through the door and had the same reaction as everyone else, except for the older accountant, who was the one who had originally discovered the money missing. He walked around the structure analytically. "How much is supposed to be here?" he asked no one in particular.

"Three million," Kaulcrick said almost before the question was out of the accountant's mouth. "Give or take."

The accountant took another pass and said, "I'm going to guess it's closer to five million."

"That's not possible," Kaulcrick said.

"There's only one way to find out. We'll start counting it."

Demick said, "Hold on just a minute. I've got to get some pictures." Kate couldn't believe that Vail had recovered the money. And as anonymously as disrupting the bank robbery. Demick pulled out his cell phone and, circling the replica, started snapping photos.

Kate wondered why Vail had chosen to build the castlelike prison. Was it supposed to be a metaphor: stealing money gets you prison, or that money is a prison? Then she noticed on the parapet of the structure a one-dollar bill folded into the figure of a woman. She was wearing a floor-length dress; her arms were extended out to her sides gracefully, the left wrist turned upward. Now she wondered if Vail's message might be that it was she who was imprisoned by her career. Whatever it was, coupled with his dramatic absence, she was sure that he wouldn't be taking the director's offer of reinstatement.

Kaulcrick was watching the accountants intently, and when he realized that they were calculating beyond three million dollars, he said, "It can't be more than three million."

That's when Kate noticed that her computer was on. She never left it on. She moved the mouse and the screen lit up. There was a typed message. She read it out loud: " 'What's the difference between the ashes of two hundred bundles of hundred-dollar bills and the ashes of two hundred bundles of one-dollar bills?' "

The head accountant pondered the riddle and said, "So instead of two million dollars being burnt, it was just twenty thousand dollars."

Kate answered. "Of course. Radek knew we'd analyze the ashes but wouldn't be able to tell the difference between one-dollar bills and hundreds. Same weights of paper, same amount of ink. He just had the hundreds on top to fool us."

At the bottom of the page was a link for a dollar-bill origami Web site. She clicked onto it and a full-page photo came up entitled "The Faceless Woman." The image showed a dollar bill folded exactly like the one on the castle's parapet. Where the face would have been was one of the few blank spots on the bill.

Carefully she lifted the single folded bill from the castle and noticed that just a few touches of a pencil had produced a woman's delicate features. She knew it had to be her imagination, but she thought it resembled her. There was even a slight gray flick of color where her scar was.

AFTER

STEVE VAIL WAS WORKING ON A NEW SCULPTURE, SO HE IGNORED the knock at his apartment door. It was near dusk and the late-summer light was being extinguished by an impending storm coming off Lake Michigan. The wind had shifted to the northeast again and the temperature was dropping. There was another knock. He thought it unusual because it was not any more insistent in either volume or rhythm. He covered the figure and took a beer from the refrigerator. Before he got to the door, there was a third knock, this one also controlled. He decided it did not belong to a man.

He opened the door and Kate Bannon was standing there in a black dress. She smiled apprehensively. "Hi?"

"Hi."

"Don't worry, I'm not here as an employee of the FBI. Purely social."

He stepped out of the way. "Then you may enter and state your business."

"It's not business." She walked in and said, "Got another one of those?" She pointed at the bottle in his hand.

After retrieving a second beer, he handed it to her. "No glass?" she asked.

"If I don't like what you have to say, you can take it to go."

"Get a glass. I'll be sure to say something you like."

"I lose more glasses that way." He went to the cabinet and got her one.

"I assume you know about Tye Delson."

"I heard about it."

"Evidently she was smoking, lost her balance, and fell out her office window. I went to the service. It was pretty sad after all she went through."

"We probably don't know half of it."

Kate got that old feeling about Vail, that he knew something no one else did. "By the way, did you hear that we got the five million back?"

"No kidding."

She smiled. "Yeah, no kidding. Of course Kaulcrick tried to twist it around with the director. You know, his leadership and all."

"What makes you so sure he wasn't responsible?"

"Still can't stand to take any credit. I get it. I won't bring it up again," Kate said. "And in return for what you did, I won't thank you either."

"Thank you."

"Very funny. Also, Pendaran has been cleared. Well, cleared of being part of the Pentad."

"Did you finally get rid of him?"

Kate shook her head. "He's suing for false arrest. Looks like he'll be with us until he retires."

"Sounds about right."

"And the director has made a couple of requests. The first was of Assistant Director Kaulcrick. He explained to

Don how it was time to retire. He'll be gone after the first of the month. On behalf of the entire FBI, thank you. The second thing was he told me to get an answer from you this time. He really wants you to come work for us. Like he said before, anywhere you want. You can travel around the country picking and choosing cases."

"I thought you weren't here on behalf of the Bureau."

"I could have called you on the phone with the offer."

"Tell the director I appreciate it. But someone will be taking Kaulcrick's place."

"The job's been offered to me."

"And that's supposed to be an incentive for me?"

She laughed. "Don't worry, I'm turning it down. Way too far away from why I became an agent. Who knows, maybe we'd get to work together again."

"Kate, I wasn't really an employee this time, and I got fired in less than a week."

"That's right, less than a week, and you cleaned up the whole mess."

"I didn't do it by myself. I believe you got some nine-millimeter scars that prove my point," he said. "I like the work, but there was just too much to put up with. Thank the director for me, but I'm going to pass."

For the first time since entering the apartment, she looked around. "I see you got the walls painted. Are you working?"

"I've got a few jobs going. Enough to keep the lights on."

She looked over at his sculpting table. "Still finding time for that, too."

"Someone has to give dilettantes a bad name."

"Mind if I look?"

"I'd rather you didn't."

She noticed his eyes shift away from hers. She looked closer at the clay figure under the cloth. The bottom was not completely covered and looked like the upper hips of a human figure. Judging its height and the general shape of the covered portion, she could see that the figure had a head, and if it had a head, maybe it had a face. "Sorry," she said, and went over to the table, lifting the cloth. It was a nude woman's figure, finely detailed. It did have a face. It was Kate's, precisely captured, not with imagined perfection, but with a graceful accuracy. For the first time since the injury, she didn't mind the scar on her cheek. Somehow Vail had made it seem—a word he had once used to describe her—handsome, maybe even aristocratic. She turned back to him abruptly, her eyes starting to well. "I thought you couldn't do faces."

His expression became uncharacteristically warm. "I guess they were never that important before."

"Something tells me that's as close as I'm ever going to get you to a compromise." Kate set down her beer and gave him a quick, hard kiss. She then started unbuttoning her dress. "Well, bricklayer, let's see if you got the rest of it right."

If you enjoyed ***The Bricklayer***,
don't miss ***Agent X***,
the next Steve Vail thriller from Noah Boyd.
Available in hardcover February 2011
from William Morrow,
an Imprint of HarperCollins Publishers.

BEFORE

KATE BANNON THOUGHT SHE WAS HAVING A NIGHTMARE, BUT ACTUally she was dying.

Only her nagging self-awareness, even in this somnolent state, was forcing her to remember that she didn't have nightmares. The frightening images had always been there—people shooting at her, falling endlessly from towering buildings, running through thicker and thicker sand to escape something unknown—but her reaction to them had always been as an indifferent observer, curious and analytical. If the "danger" persisted, she would simply tell herself it was a dream and wake up. And that's what she had to do now, wake up and find out what was causing the chaotic images in her head.

She sat up and felt dizzy, the blood pounding in the top of her head. It hurt too much to be a dream. She felt nauseous and remembered driving home after the Thanksgiving Eve get-together at one of the local FBI watering holes with a large group of people from headquarters. She remembered having a glass of wine, and then a good-looking guy she didn't know brought her a small glass of—what did he say it was?—Drambuie. She had never tasted it before and took a mouthful. Finding it too bitter for her liking, she set it down and didn't touch it again. It must have been strong, because she soon started feeling woozy and decided to leave.

Throwing her legs over the side of the bed, she worked her feet into slippers and stood up. As soon as she was fully upright, she felt light-headed and had trouble balancing herself. With a hand on the wall, she started toward the kitchen. Walking left her short of breath. That couldn't be from alcohol. That's when she heard the low rumbling. She continued to the kitchen and saw that the garage door was opening. Now she could clearly hear her car running.

Without warning, her knees started to buckle, and she realized that she was not suffering from what she had drunk but from carbon monoxide poisoning. Carefully, she stepped down the three stairs into the garage, which was filled with the haze of exhaust fumes. The car door was locked, and she could see the keys in the ignition.

The garage's outside door was only a few feet away, and she lurched to it. Taking hold of the knob, she tried to turn it, but her grip failed her. She pushed on the door clumsily with her body weight but couldn't rotate the knob far enough to open it. Even using both hands, she couldn't get it to release. Next to the door, in a holder fastened to the wall, was a remote-control unit for the overhead door. She pressed the button, but nothing happened.

Beginning to panic now, she pressed it repeatedly, but still the door didn't rise. She tried to remember the last time she had changed the battery, but her mind refused to focus on anything requiring memory. All at once she crashed to the floor, knocking over her small gardening caddy and scattering tools in every direction.

She tried to get up but could only manage to roll over on her back. *Is this it?* she asked herself. After all she'd been through as an agent, this was how she was going to die? Then she saw a white light coming from the six-inch-square window in the door and wondered if it was what so many people who approached death had reported. She fell back and let her eyes slide shut. Even with her mouth closed, she could taste the thick fumes in her throat.

The actual source of the light was a small flashlight held by a man standing outside, dressed in black. When she collapsed, he turned it off and pulled the two wedges from under the door that had jammed it closed against her efforts. Then he went to the front door of the residence and removed two more. Calmly, he put his hands in his pockets and walked back to a waiting SUV.

Lying there felt pleasant, euphoric, but then it occurred to Kate that the light was gone. Shouldn't it be inside her head, too? She opened her eyes, and it was still gone. Did that mean the death sentence had been revoked, or at least delayed? Whatever it meant, she decided that she was going down swinging.

Next to her was a rake, its wooden handle thick and straight. Pushing up on all fours, she crawled to the rear of the car, dragging the rake behind her. The fumes were completely suffocating. She peeled off one of her slippers with its thin rubber sole and crammed it into the tailpipe. She was familiar enough with cars to know that the obstruction alone wouldn't stop the engine as the movies depicted but would eventually be blown out by mounting pressure. So she stuck the rake's handle into the tailpipe forcing the slipper even farther into the exhaust.

Then she maneuvered the wooden shaft, finally wedging the steel raking tines against one of the patterned groves in the overhead garage door, which was a foot and a half away. One of two things would happen now: Either the pressure would build up and kill the engine or the rake would blow a hole in the door and provide fresh air. One or the other could save her. Of course, it was more likely that the handle of the rake would simply snap. She reached up and held the rake in place before crumpling to the floor to wait.

Something with a sharp edge was underneath her. She realized it was a gardening trowel that had been knocked across the floor when she first fell. Inching closer to the garage door, she shoved it under the rubber cleat that sealed the entire length of the door and, using both hands, turned it up on edge to make a small triangular opening. Placing her mouth as close to it as possible, she breathed in the sweet, cold, late-autumn air.

Just before she passed out, her hand slipped off the rake and she thought she heard the car's engine sputter and die.

AFTER CLIMBING INTO the backseat of the SUV, the man in black nodded to the two men in the front that it was done.

The driver, in his early fifties, was tall and slender, his suit expensive and American. His hair was full and carefully cut. His face might have been described as elegant if it weren't for the splayed, crooked nose, which gave his appearance a vague warning of violence. He looked over at the man sitting next to him to see if he was satisfied.

The passenger reached over and turned off the radio-signal device that had jammed Kate's remote-control door opener, the limited markings on it written in Cyrillic. He, too, was tall, but powerfully built, and his age was difficult to estimate; he could have been in his fifties or in his sixties. His hands were thick and crisscrossed with dozens of thin white scars. His face was drawn and slightly exhausted, his eyes irreparably sad. Although his skin appeared a permanent gray, his lips were thick and an unusual shade of dark red. He looked back at the driver with eyes that never seemed to move from side to side. It was as if they were frozen in their sockets, making whomever he was talking to feel that turning away would be perceived as evasive, even when telling the truth. He searched the driver's face for any indication that they hadn't been successful and then leaned his head back on the headrest and closed his eyes. The SUV pulled away from the curb.

KATE BANNON OPENED her eyes and wondered if she was dreaming again. Bob Lasker, the director of the FBI, sat next to her hospital bed. Struggling to recall what had happened, she wasn't sure she really could. "Am I dreaming?" she asked loudly, almost as if trying to determine if she was actually awake. She went to scratch her nose but then realized that an oxygen tube was pinching her nostrils.

"This is real, Kate." The director smiled warmly. "You gave us a scare, though. But you're going to be all right."

"I remember being in the garage and not being able to get out."

"One of your neighbors was taking his dog for a late-night walk, and I guess in the cool air he smelled the exhaust from the opening you made. He dragged his owner closer, and then the guy broke in, dragged you out, and called 911. Any idea how you left your car on?"

She told him about being bought a drink and not feeling well, then waking up to find her car running and not being able to get out of the garage. "I can't imagine doing that. And then locking the car door with the keys in the ignition? Who locks a car that's in a locked garage?"

"And this guy who bought you the drink, you never saw him before."

"Not that I remember. I would have remembered him from headquarters. He was nice-looking."

"Maybe he was just someone at the bar and saw a pretty girl."

"Maybe," she said vaguely, her mind searching for other possibilities.

Lasker stared at her as though there were some question he wasn't asking.

"What?" she demanded.

"Kate, don't take this the wrong way, but have you been feeling okay lately?"

She gave a short laugh. "Wait a minute—are you asking me if I've been depressed?"

"Yes."

She thought for a moment. "You think I tried to kill myself?"

The question was asked with such self-assurance that Lasker couldn't help but say, "No, I don't."

"But others do?"

"A deputy assistant director almost dies, there are questions that have to be considered."

"Meaning what?"

"OPR is going to look into it. Very routine, very low-key."

"I didn't try to commit suicide."

"You know I can't call off procedure. I wouldn't for any other agent, and since everyone knows how much I think of you, I can't in this instance either." He smiled. "Please cooperate and try not to shoot any of them. As soon as you feel well enough to get out of here, you'll be returned to full duty while they conduct their investigation."

"This is ridiculous."

"I know it is. If it does get to be too much, come and see me." Lasker patted her on the arm. "For now, get well. Everything else will take care of itself."

She was staring down at her hands but finally looked at him. "I guess I should be thanking you instead of arguing."

"Just get better, Kate."

Soon after the director left the room, an agent whom Kate recognized as being from the Office of Professional Responsibility came in. "Hi, Kate. I'm Roger Daniels from OPR. How are you feeling?"

"Nonsuicidal."

He laughed. "I know this is a lot coming at you all at once. I can wait to take your statement."

Kate sat up and took a sip of water from a cup on the table next to her bed. "Don't be *too* offended, but the sooner we get started, the sooner I'll have OPR out of my life."

The agent chuckled. "Well, that carbon monoxide didn't damage your sense of humor."

"Who said I was trying to be funny? Roger, I'm sure you're a very capable agent, and maybe even a nice guy, but I did a stint at OPR, so please don't waste any of the artificial sweeteners on me. Just ask me your questions, and I'll give you my best answers."

"Fair enough, Kate." He opened his notebook. "Did you attempt suicide?" His tone was noticeably less friendly.

"I'm the one who stopped the car engine and wedged a trowel under the door to save myself. Does that sound like I was trying to commit suicide?"

"It's not uncommon during a suicide attempt for people to have a change of heart. They take pills and then call 911. Move the gun at the last moment and just wound themselves. It happens more frequently than you think."

"Yeah, well, I happen to like my life quite a bit."

"Don't take this the wrong way, but some people do it for attention."

"How could I possibly take that the wrong way?" she said, sounding more than a little sarcastic. She took a moment and then said, "If you knew me, you'd know I really don't care what people think. Why would I want to get their attention?"

"Not people—*person*," he said.

"Person? Who?"

The agent flipped back to another page in his notes. "Steve Vail?"

"Where did you get that?"

"Answers, Kate, remember?"

"Okay, what do you know about him? And me?"

"We know that he was fired as an agent more than five years ago. That the director brought him back to work on the Rubaco Pentad case in Los Angeles—with you—and that you guys have dated. Recently it ended abruptly."

"Sounds like you got a running start on this while I was still unconscious. Okay, I'll tell you about Vail on one condition—that you don't contact him."

"If you're forthcoming, there'll be no need to."

"One of the hardest things I've had to do in my life was tell him I didn't want him in it. If you've read the Pentad file, you know he was responsible for solving that case almost single-handedly. He would be an incredible agent, but he cannot conform to anything, and that includes a relationship with me. We've seen each other three times since L.A. The first time was— I hate to use the word, but it was pretty much perfect. The last two were absolutely awful. So I told him it would be best if we didn't see each other again. And that was a week ago. So no, I wasn't trying to get his attention."

"Trying to find out exactly who he was, I ran his name through some of our contacts at other agencies and got a hit with the State Department. Seems you and he are going to the Irish ambassador's reception on New Year's Eve."

"Boy, you have been busy. But you'd better check with them again. It should show that my escort is now Eamon Walsh."

"So you changed it."

"What's today?"

"Wednesday."

"I spoke with him Monday. He's with the Irish embassy and was the one who called me originally with the invitation. When I phoned him back to tell him Vail wasn't coming, he asked if I'd do him the honor. I didn't want to go alone, so I said yes. Maybe he hasn't gotten around to changing it officially yet. You can call him."

Daniels was making notes. "So it's definitely over between you and Vail. You told him not to come for New Year's Eve."

"Not in so many words, but I think 'We shouldn't see each other again' carries that assumption."

"That's helpful about Vail. It gives you one less reason to . . . you know."

"Off myself."

"Tell me what you remember about the night that this happened to you," Daniels said.

She repeated what she'd told the director about the stranger's buying her a drink that didn't settle well with her, then her coming home and going to bed. Then waking up and trying to get out of the garage.

He asked, "You said he told you it was Drambuie?"

"Yes."

"Hmm," Daniels said, more to himself than her.

"What?"

"I've had Drambuie, and it has a definite strong sweetness to it."

The OPR agent started making notes that she guessed were more than just about Kate's response. As she watched him, she remembered her time in OPR, how investigations were not about the incident but about the employee's involvement in it. They weren't criminal investigators, they were personnel investigators. As Daniels looked up from his pad ready to ask the next question, she knew that he was not going to get to the bottom of this. If anyone was going to find out what had happened, it would have to be her. "If that guy did put something in the drink, maybe he had some other intentions, and when he saw I drank only one sip of it, he got scared and took off."

"Your blood didn't show any kind of drug in it, but if you didn't drink much, maybe it dissipated before you got here."

"Are you going to try to track him down?" she asked, trying to judge just how far he was going to go with this.

"I'll have to see where everything takes me."

Right, she said to herself, becoming lost in thought. There was just something about a near-death experience that brought Vail to mind. And she couldn't decide whether that was a good thing or a bad thing. She knew that he would never just 'see where everything takes me.' A small smile creased her lips.

"What is it, Kate?"

"Oh, no, nothing. Did you need anything else?"

"That's enough for now." Daniels stood up. "Take care."

He closed the door, and after a moment her smile disappeared.

She was sure she was never going to see Vail again.

KATE BANNON OPENED her door. “What are you doing here?”

With mock surprise, Steve Vail’s head recoiled slightly at the level of protest in her voice. He stepped inside, setting down his suitcase and, for the briefest moment, allowed his eyes to trace the flawless symmetry of her face. “I’ve got the right day, don’t I? This is New Year’s Eve. Is it the wrong year?”

“After that last time, when I told you this wasn’t going to work, I assumed you understood that included tonight.”

He smiled crookedly. “Come on, Kate, it’s the twenty-first century. What woman wants to have to admit that she’s never been stalked? It’s become an accoutrement, like Italian shoes or one of those little purse-size dogs. ”

“We tried, Steve. Three times. And the last two, if you remember, were not pretty.”

“That means statistically we’re due.”

Kate shook her head slowly. She really couldn’t believe he was standing there. “You know as well as I do that we’re a disaster. We’re too different. Or too much alike. I don’t know. Every time we try to get close, we wind up driving each other crazy. You don’t know how much I wanted it to work, but it can’t.”

Vail looked at her dress. “I guess you were planning to go to whatever this was tonight without me. Why don’t we go together and see what happens? What’s the worst that can happen? So I ruin your career. That would probably be the best thing that could happen to us.”

“I have to go to this. It’s a command performance. And you know exactly what it is—an ambassador’s reception. Why else would you have a suit on? Even though the proper dress is a tuxedo. Which I'm going to guess was your way of letting all the *phonies* in the room know that you're a lowly bricklayer."

"A man has to seek amusement wherever he can."

"I'll never understand you. You could be whatever you want. You have advanced degrees. The director has offered you complete autonomy if you'll come back to the Bureau, but instead you choose physical labor just so you won't have to take orders. If that's who you are, fine, but you don't get to rub everyone else's face in it simply because they're not like you." She looked at him sternly. "It's called hypocrisy." She could see that her words had stung him, but she couldn't find anything inaccurate in what she'd said.

He reached up and traced the small L-shaped scar high on her cheekbone and then smiled gently. "You don't have to wonder anymore, Kate, whether we're too much alike. There was a time, and not very long ago, that you would have thought they were phonies, too," he said. "But you're right, I've been a phony myself. The only defense I can offer is that you make my compass go haywire reversed. The only reason I'm doing any of this is you."

He turned and opened the door. "Like you said, we gave it a shot," he said. "When it was right, it was like nothing I've ever experienced. That's why I had to try one last time."

"You can't just walk out like that. Not after everything we've been through."

"*This* is the best way to leave it. Then we won't have any lingering doubts."

"At least let me drive you to the airport. It's freezing out."

"I live in Chicago, remember? This isn't cold."

"I'll feel better about this if I can take you. It'll give us a chance to talk a little more. Right now I feel like we're supposed to hate each other."

"It'll be fine, Kate. I'll get a taxi."

"It's New Year's Eve—you'll never find one."

"You're probably right." He picked up his suitcase. "Okay, I'll take a ride, but only if we don't talk. I don't want to say anything that'll make this worse."

For the briefest moment, she considered telling him about the night before Thanksgiving and asking him what he thought about the guy in the bar. The day she got home from the hospital, she'd gone into her garage to change the battery in the remote for the overhead door. But it had worked fine. She thought that maybe she'd just pushed the wrong part of it in her semiconscious state. But three days ago she'd realized that it had been over a month and she hadn't heard anything from OPR. So she'd gone back into the garage and retraced the events from that night as best she could. That's when she realized that she couldn't have opened the inside door to her condominium if her keys were locked in the car.

Then she'd bought a bottle of Drambuie and tasted it. It had a honey-sweet taste to it, nothing like what she remembered from the bar.

The next day she'd checked with the Metropolitan Police, and they'd said they hadn't had any recent drug-facilitated rapes reported. Since she was sneaking around behind OPR's back, she didn't want to start asking questions of people who were at the bar and have it get back to Daniels. Vail, who saw these things on a different level,